ANDRE GONZALEZ

Wealth of Time

Diane,
Don't get lost in the
past!

First published by M4L Publishing 2019

First edition

ISBN: 978-1-7327762-3-4

Editing by Stephanie Cohen
Cover art by ebooklaunch.com

This book was professionally typeset on Reedsy.
Find out more at reedsy.com

To my mom, Julie, for always believing in this wild dream.

"Time slips away like grains of sand
never to return again."

-Robin Sharma

Contents

1

Chapter 1

One squeeze of the trigger and it's all over.

The pistol was cold on his tongue, like a metallic popsicle. It weighed upon his jaw, keeping it pried open as saliva pooled between his tongue and the small hole where the slug would come blasting out to end his life.

Pull it, you coward. Darkness is waiting just on the other side. No more pain, no more regret. Just darkness.

His hands didn't shake this time, nerves long gone after going through this same routine for the tenth time in just as many years. He already knew that this would play out with him removing the pistol, cursing the world, and passing out on the couch. The pills in his stomach swirled around the tide pool of whiskey, along for another ride.

Every September reminded Martin Briar of how much he hated his life. His once-normal life waited 22 years in the past. It was Labor Day of 2018 when Martin sat in his apartment with his pistol between his teeth. He had cried the first two years of attempting this, and knew that it was only a matter of time before the good graces of death would finally help him pull the trigger.

Minutes ago, he had smoked a cheap cigar while washing down a handful of colorful pills with a glass of whiskey. From the balcony of his rundown apartment, he had a view of the sunset with its blue mountains and orange glowing sky, but he took it for granted. Whiskey and tobacco came from the Earth, and that was the extent he cared for Mother Nature.

It was Monday the 3rd, and the upcoming Sunday would officially mark 22 years since his daughter's disappearance. The Imagine Dragons sang through his cell phone speakers from the balcony's chipped and rough handrail. He stood with his elbows on it, the only other neighboring object being an ashtray he never used.

Lela, his ex-wife from many moons ago, had gifted him the ashtray. The bottom of the tray was a yellow circle with black lettering that read: *World's Greatest Dad!*

He *had* been the world's greatest dad, too, at least according to Izzy. Izzy, formally named Isabel, had grown up to be quite the daddy's girl, always running to him when he arrived home from work and jumping into his embrace. She was only 12 years old when she had gone missing in 1996.

Kids have a way of distracting you from the fact that you are getting older with each passing day, and Izzy provided the same fountain of youth effect for Martin.

He was 32 when she disappeared. His entire twenties had gone by in a blur, thanks to Isabel. While his friends went out drinking and partying every weekend, Martin stayed home and watched shows like *Rugrats* and *Arthur*. He wouldn't have traded it for a single night out, loving every moment with his little family in their first home, a small ranch-style house just north of Denver in Larkwood.

2

Martin grew up in Larkwood, his parents having moved there well before he was born. His mother still lived in his childhood home, just two blocks away. While most people would flee the quiet town after such a tragedy like losing a child, Martin couldn't picture life anywhere else in the world. Larkwood was home and always would be. Going away wouldn't bring Isabel back. If she were ever to return, it would likely be to the last place she could remember.

Now at the age of 54, Martin didn't know if he'd even recognize his daughter. She would be 34 years old, a beautiful woman approaching the tail end of her prime. *Of course you'll know her face. You stare at it every day.* From the small picture he kept in his wallet, to the 8x10 on his nightstand, he would damn well know his own daughter if she showed up all of these years later.

Martin stood in front of a mirror in his living room, staring at his pathetic self. His body had swollen over the years. What was once an athletic, six-foot frame of muscle was now a round collection of fast food and booze. His brown hair was plastered across his forehead with sweat. He started to wheeze, feeling his heart rate increase by the second as he stared at himself. His pale skin was now a light shade of red.

"Isabel," he mumbled around the muzzle. Tears welled up in his eyes, but he fought their attempt to run down his face.

He ripped the pistol out of his mouth and threw it aside, falling into the soft couch waiting to catch him from behind.

Well, here we are again. You chickened out. Is the temptation really that hard to resist?

As he had done the previous nine times, Martin couldn't pull the trigger, knowing that his mother would have to clean up the mess and bury her son. His brother had moved across the country years ago, around the same time that Izzy went missing, and had remained mostly estranged to the family. His father had passed when they were younger, leaving Marilyn Briar all alone, should Martin end his shitty life.

Just wait until she passes away – then we can ride off into the darkness together.

His mom was in great shape and nowhere near death, so it would take a few more years to reach that point. Once she was gone, though, there would be no more roadblocks, no hesitations from entering the darkness and leaving his lifelong sorrow behind.

Tuesday awaited with a full day of work at the post office, as if he needed an additional reason to shoot himself. He took the job for the guarantee of having Sundays and holidays off. Days off were all he looked forward to anymore. The customers were needy and whiny.

So many goddamn entitled little shits! he thought at the end of each shift. The days felt longer than eight hours as the clock on the wall teased him all day. His coworkers lacked any sort of personality and seemed to hate life as much as he did. At least they had that much in common.

Martin had fallen into the trap of monotonously going through the daily grind. Leave for work at seven in the morning, slog through five hours of mind-numbingly boring tasks until lunchtime, eat a bland sandwich made half-assed while drunk the night before, slog through until four o'clock, go home to drink booze and eat microwaveable dinners, make the bland sandwich for the next day, and then go to sleep. *Work. Drink. Sleep. Repeat.*

Sometimes he fantasized about being adventurous, but he had no clue what he would do. The numbness that remained

4

in his chest since 1996 wasn't going anywhere and made everyday life difficult to enjoy. He'd tried going to sporting events, the shooting range, even a book club. They all had the same result in leaving him unsatisfied and longing for the next day, one day closer to death where he could forget all of his problems and either start over or enjoy the darkness. *Whatever the hell happens after this life can't be worse.*

The pistol was somewhere in the corner of the room as he started to doze off. He knew he wouldn't have the urge to use it again until next year. The intensity of sticking an instrument of death in his mouth was enough to last him a full three hundred and sixty-five days.

Work. Drink. Sleep. Repeat. Tomorrow is another day in the glorious life of Martin Briar.

2

Chapter 2

Martin had a nail jammed into the back of his head when his alarm buzzed obnoxiously at six the next morning. *God, I hate that fucking sound.* He downed his usual breakfast of two aspirin pills and a glass of water to remedy the situation.

He slid into his uniform of a dark blue shirt and gray slacks. *Larkwood Postal Services* and his name were stitched across the shirt on opposite sides. "Hi, I'm Martin. Where would you like me to send your lovely package today, Mr. Asshole?" he said into the mirror with a drunken giggle. He kept the lights dim, not wanting to see the streaks of white and gray clawing their way through his brown hair. A scruffy beard had started to sprout on his face. "Oh, you need it overnighted to Australia? Let me pull out my magic mail monkey and have it swim across the ocean for you today!" His head throbbed when he laughed, but he couldn't help himself.

Let's go live that dream today, since you couldn't complete your task last night. Martin winked at himself, the bags under his brown eyes remaining plump, having a slight regret at not pulling the trigger.

He maneuvered in the darkness to the kitchen to grab his lunchbox and left the apartment.

The outdoor air always helped eliminate the nausea that accompanied his daily hangover. To the east, the skyline glowed a magnificent purple and orange from the rising sun. Autumn had always been Martin's favorite season – that was, until his daughter went missing all those Septembers ago. Now autumn served as a reminder that life doesn't owe you an explanation. Bad shit happened to good people every day. Some rose, some crumpled. Martin liked to think he fell in the middle of the spectrum, functioning as a member of society, but having no interest in improving his life. *Just get me to the finish line already,* he often thought.

Hope kept him from pulling the trigger year after year. Hope that his daughter would return. Hope that his wife would come back and they could build a relationship for the twilight years of their lives. Hope that maybe one day, life would feel all right again. It couldn't always be this bad.

He and his mother had dinner together twice a week, each taking turns on choosing where to dine. His mother had always been a graceful soul, willing to open her heart to anyone in need. When she saw Martin struggle after Izzy's disappearance, and his resulting failed marriage, she convinced him to move into her basement until he could regain structure in his life.

Martin took joy in knowing his Tuesday evening would end with dinner with his mom. It was his turn to choose and he wanted nothing more than a juicy burger at the local joint, Roadhouse Diner. He might spend more time with his mother over the course of the week, with the anniversary of Izzy's disappearance looming on Sunday.

The morning dragged on as expected, but when lunch arrived he felt instant relief when he found the small break room deserted. The rusty microwave hummed in the corner while the stench of burnt popcorn filled the air.

Martin took the seat closest to the window with its breathtaking view of the parking lot for all of the mail trucks. He laid out his sandwich and chips before calling his mom.

"Hi, Marty," she greeted him warmly.

"Hey, Mom, how's it going today?"

"Oh, you know, just raked some leaves and made a pot of tea. Gonna be a long afternoon of soap operas."

"Of course, can't miss those. I just wanted to confirm that we're still good for tonight. I was thinking we could go to Roadhouse."

"Oh, perfect!" Her voice rose in excitement. "I just heard from Esther about a new antique shop that popped up a few blocks from the church. I don't remember hearing anything about it, but it's apparently open now. Do you mind if we stop by before dinner, since it's on the way?"

"I don't mind at all. I can pick you up at 5:30."

"Great, I'll be ready. See you then."

They hung up and Martin wondered what his mother's life was like. She spent her mornings in the yard, took a nap, and lazed the afternoons away on her recliner watching bad TV. Once a week she'd visit a thrift store or antique store with her friends in search of some rare find. Occasionally, she invited Martin to join her on these outings if her friends weren't able to go. He didn't mind keeping her company, but all these stores carried the same loads of useless shit and musty odors that reminded him of an attic.

Probably because all this shit is from someone's attic.

Regardless, he set his focus on the double cheeseburger with bacon awaiting him at the end of his day's journey.

3

Chapter 3

Martin's stomach growled as he pulled into his childhood driveway. He made it through another day, and thanks to the short week, tomorrow was already Wednesday.

His mother waited at the front door and stepped out of the light gray house as soon as he pulled up. Two patio chairs sat on the porch where Martin used to watch the sunset with his father as he spewed about baseball, the weather, and the mysteries of life. Many of his lessons came right from those two worn-down chairs, and Martin was glad his mother held on to them after making many renovations after his father's death. The front yard appeared leafless and immaculate. His father had always taken pride in a clean and green yard, and when he passed, his mother took the responsibilities in stride, claiming it made her feel close to her lost husband.

Martin watched his fragile mother wobble down the steps. She claimed to feel great despite her body starting to break down, and he had no reason to not take her word as she remained active, even as she was pushing 75. Her silver hair flowed graciously behind her as she cracked a warm smile in his direction. Underneath the wrinkles he could still see her youthful beauty. He remembered his mother being the most gorgeous woman he'd ever seen, and while time altered her outer appearance, he knew the woman from forty years ago was behind her gentle green eyes.

She pulled open the car door and plopped down in the passenger seat. "Marty! How are you?" she greeted him warmly, grinning ear-to-ear.

"I'm as good as can be," he said, forcing a matched enthusiasm.

This was the answer he reverted to whenever anyone asked him how he was doing, and it was true. He hated his life, but tried to make the best of the days while he counted down to his eventual death. That was the best he could offer the world.

"So what's this antique store we're going to?" Martin asked before his mother could dig into how he really felt on this dreadful week.

She clicked her seat belt and slouched back as Martin pulled back onto the road. "Oh, just a new store I heard about from Esther and Toni when we had lunch the other day. They told me it has an impressive collection of treasures. They walked out of there with a thousand dollars of stuff each."

A thousand dollars worth of shit, probably.

"I won't go spending all that," she continued. "I just like to look around. Maybe one day I'll see something that reminds me of my childhood or your father. Then I'll buy."

Martin nodded as she spoke, keeping his focus on the road. The church was only a five-minute drive, and this new store was supposedly a couple blocks from it.

"Well, I hope you find something you like, Mom. Don't keep us too late, though, I'm starving."

Smooth jazz poured out of the car speakers, his mom's favorite, and they hummed along until they pulled up to the store.

The building was a bland gray that blended in with the cloudy sky. Black, plain text lettered the front in a generic font: *WEALTH OF TIME.* Three panes of glass were centered below the lettering with the middle one serving as the only door.

"Has this building always been here?" Martin asked, unimpressed with the exterior.

His mother lowered her brow in thought. "I honestly don't know. In my sixty years living here, I can't say I've ever been in this part of the neighborhood."

They had passed the church and driven through a residential neighborhood for two blocks before spitting out into a random lot where the building stood.

"They certainly won't last long in this location. How is anyone supposed to find it?"

"We found it easily enough."

Martin wanted to tell his mom that wasn't the point, but let it slide as he sensed her growing excitement to get inside the store.

He parked, the lot empty with the exception of one other car, and stepped out to the brisk evening. The sun fought its way through the clouds before setting for the night, casting a hazy, orange glow.

A rusty sign hung next to the tall windows that read: *COME ON IN! WE'RE OPEN!*

Martin insisted this building had already existed, its exterior worn down from years of enduring the Colorado weather. A fresh coat of paint could make it look brand new.

He followed his mother as she climbed the three short steps and pulled open the door. A bell chimed as she crossed the threshold into the empty store.

The store stretched back into eternity. Martin craned his neck to see as far as possible and still couldn't find the back wall. The building hadn't looked this long from the outside, and his mind twisted in confusion. Obvious sections of furniture, music, kitchenware, china and ceramics, figurines, clocks, and jewelry separated the store.

Marilyn soaked in the inventory of old knick-knacks with wide eyes. "I've never seen a store so big. Not an antique store."

Her voice echoed, and she realized they were alone. "Anyone here?" she shouted.

A white head of hair popped up in the distance as an elderly man made his way down the never-ending aisle toward them. "Please come in!" His voice bounced off the walls. "Welcome."

He approached them and stuck out a bony hand with little white hairs curled around his knuckles. He smiled at Martin from his long, droopy face. The short white hair on his head matched that on his fingers. "Chris Speidel at your service, pleased to meet you fine folks." He shook their hands more aggressively than Martin anticipated. The old man's flesh felt cold as ice, as if he were holding a frozen drink for the last few minutes.

"I'm Martin Briar, and this is my mother, Marilyn." Martin spoke uneasily. He thought Chris's irises looked black at first glance, but realized they were dark brown after closer inspection.

"Glad to have you folks." He kissed Marilyn's hand when she offered it, causing redness to bloom in her cheeks. "What can I do for you kiddos today?"

"We were hoping to look around. I heard a new store was open in town, and I just love antique shops," Marilyn said as she held her kissed hand in front of her.

"Fair enough." Chris clapped his hands together. "Poke around. I have some great stuff you'll both enjoy. Do you like baseball, young man?" He turned to Martin.

"I haven't kept up much with it in recent years, but I used to be a big fan."

"Well, I have some very rare collectible cards. You can find them on a shelf near the dolls over there." Chris poked a skinny thumb in the direction of the wistful porcelain dolls that faced the front entrance.

"Thank you, I'll be sure to take a look."

"And you, young lady, is there anything in particular that you're looking for?" He offered what looked like a forced grin to Marilyn.

"Not really. If something grabs my eye then I'll take a closer look."

"With all due respect, madam, this is an antique shop. We are the keepers of time, the guardians of treasure, and the watchmen of memories. You should be looking for something to catch your *heart,* not your eye."

She blushed again, and Martin stood frozen in disbelief. *Is this how old people flirt?*

"But please have a look around. You can find me at the counter if you need any help at all." The old man winked at them and turned to head back to wherever he'd come from.

Martin locked eyes with his mother and they exchanged curious looks. "I suppose I'll go look at those baseball cards." Martin checked his watch. "Let's try to not be more than half an hour. I'm really hungry and have had that burger on my mind all day."

"Yes, of course." Her eyes remained locked on Chris as he disappeared into a row of shelves.

She stepped away from Martin, leaving him at the entrance as she walked to the china section and sifted through decades of old dishes.

Martin felt someone watching him and glanced around to see if any cameras were visible. Aside from the one pointing to the entrance, there were none that he could see, but the feeling wasn't a camera. He felt *eyes* on him. He shook the thought out of his mind and dragged his feet to the figurines section.

The shelves were lined with old collector's edition model cars, rare Barbie dolls and action figures, video games, and Pogs. Next to all of this rested a small wooden box with baseball cards lined up perfectly. He pulled the box off the shelf and cradled it in his arm like a football as he flipped through years of baseball lore.

Hank Aaron, Pete Rose, Cal Ripken, Ken Griffey Jr., Mickey Mantle. He paused on the Mantle card. *Isn't this card worth hundreds of thousands?* He pulled it out, examined its nearly mint condition. *Honus Wagner is the rare card, not Mantle.* He put the box back in its place and sighed as his stomach begged for food.

A quick glance around the store found his mother at the counter with Chris. She leaned in close to the store's owner, as if telling a secret, his snowy head nodding as she spoke. Martin shuffled his feet and cleared his throat as he approached. "We about ready for dinner, Mom?"

She turned and looked at her son with a stern face. "I may

have found something, Marty."

On the counter was a thick gold ring with a large emerald in its center. They had been inspecting it up close.

"This ring looks identical to one my grandmother used to wear. She handed it down to my mom, and after she passed, we've never been able to find it. Part of me wonders if it's still on her finger."

She picked it up and held it up to the light, tears welling in her eyes. "Chris says it's valued at $7,000 and that he'll sell it for $5,000. I just don't know. That's still a bit out of my range."

"Five thousand is a steal, trust me. If you find this anywhere else, you'd likely find a price tag of ten grand on it."

Marilyn pursed her lips and Martin could read the frustration boiling behind her eyes. She wanted that ring. "I'll have to think about it. Will you honor that price if I come back in a couple of days?"

"Of course," Chris said, sliding the ring back into its felt case and snapping it shut with a coy smile. "I'll keep it off the floor for a couple days. You come let me know." He patted the case before putting it in a cupboard underneath an old cash register.

"Well, thank you, Chris. I appreciate that. I think my son here is hungry, so we should be on our way."

"Indeed. Enjoy your dinner. I'll see you both around, and it was a pleasure meeting you this evening."

Chris extended his fragile hand and shook with both of them before they left.

* * *

At dinner, Martin gauged his mother's interest in the ring.

"I'm convinced it's my grandmother's ring," she said, shaking her head. "I don't know how on earth it would end up in that gentleman's collection, but I felt something when I touched it. I don't know how to explain it."

"What if I pitch in and help you buy it?" Martin offered.

"That's very nice of you, Marty, but you can save your money. I can afford it – it's just a matter of if I really *want* it. I didn't want to make an emotional purchase. I just need some time to think it over. If I'm still thinking about it in a few days, then I'll go back and pick it up."

They finished their burgers that night with countless stories of Martin's great-grandmother. He heard the pain in his mom's voice. Some scars never healed, and losing a grandparent never became easier. He could attest to that.

I'm going back tomorrow to buy that ring.

4

Chapter 4

Martin returned to Wealth of Time the following evening. The must filled his lungs again as he strode toward the checkout counter where Chris read a raggedy paperback. He looked up from behind the small reading glasses perched on his nose.

"Good evening, young man. I thought I'd see your mother before you. Was there a baseball card you liked?"

"Hello. No. Although, you have an impressive collection. My card collecting days are behind me. If anything, I may bring you some cards to see if you'd be interested."

"I see. What can I do for you this evening?"

"I want to buy that ring my mom was looking at."

Chris dropped his book on the counter top, revealing an H.P. Lovecraft novel, and retrieved the ring box as if he had been expecting Martin to come in.

"I was thinking about this ring and my encounter with your mother. I'd like to sell it you for $2,000. That's what I paid for it, and I don't mind breaking even on it. Your mother was entranced. I believe it really is the long lost family heirloom."

Martin's jaw dropped. "Two thousand? That's impossible."

Chris grinned. "I'd give it you for free, but this is a business. Let's call it even and you can take her a nice surprise."

"I don't know what to say...thank you."

Martin pulled out his wallet and slid his credit card across the counter with a wavering hand. *This has to be a fake ring. No way this guy takes $5,000 off the listed price. He felt guilty trying to hustle my mom, and is trying to make up for it. She won't know the difference, and she'll never find out about this. As far as she knows, it's her grandmother's lost ring.*

"Your mom said this was her grandmother's ring?" Chris asked in a curious voice.

"Yes. My great-grandmother promised to leave it for my mom when she was only a teenager. You don't remember where you got it from?"

Chris scrunched his face. "Can't say I do. So much product comes in, and it's usually in bunches. Especially the jewelry, you should see how much I have that's not on display in the store – there's no room for it all." Chris chuckled gleefully as he spoke. "That is an interesting story about the ring, though. A mystery. What a small world if this is the actual ring, but we'll never know."

Martin nodded. He remembered how his mom had a whole box of jewelry set aside to one day leave for Izzy, her first and only granddaughter.

Chris wrapped the ring box in gilded gift-wrap with a bow tied neatly on top before pushing it across the counter to Martin. "Say, young man, what's bothering you?"

Martin looked into Chris's eyes and sensed the old man picking apart his emotions. "Nothing. I'm fine."

"I see pain behind your eyes. You do a bad job of hiding it."

Martin hated the shrewdness of older people; his mother

was the same way. He looked down at the gift and fidgeted with it as he debated telling the old man what was on his mind. After a brief, awkward silence he decided to lay it all out there.

"This is a difficult week for me. This Sunday marks 22 years since I lost my daughter. Every day is a struggle, but this time of year is extra difficult."

"I'm sorry to hear that. May I ask what happened?" Chris leaned forward onto the counter and removed his reading glasses, his stale breath now oozing into Martin's nose.

"I don't know. That's the hardest part. My wife got into a fight with my daughter that night. And when we woke up she was gone. We assume she ran away, but have no idea where or why. Part of me thinks she's dead. I know she wouldn't go this long without speaking to us. But maybe she's living in some exotic country, starting a new life."

"That must be a horrific burden to carry."

"It is. Two decades without any closure is a long time, and it never gets easier."

Chris sat upright and crossed his arms, shaking his head. "You know, I've dealt with some traumatic loss myself. I suppose you could call it the inverse of your situation. I lost both my parents when I was only seven years old."

Martin studied Chris who looked down as he spoke, wondering how such an event would have affected his long life. The man had to be at least seventy. "I'm sorry, that must have turned your world upside down."

"It's funny. When you're a kid you can pretty much go with the flow. All your worries are about who's gonna pick you up from school and who's gonna make your dinner. I think I went through the next five years of my life numb. I bounced around foster homes and schools, and it never hit me until I reached high school. That's when you need guidance most in life, and I had no one to turn to. I spent many days after school crying in the bathroom. It was the only place I had privacy. At home, I had to share a bedroom with three other boys, and crying was frowned upon. Everyone had a sad story – therefore no one felt bad about your problems."

"That's not fair."

"Might not be fair," Chris said matter-of-factly. "But that's how it goes. All you can do is try to make it to the next day and hope for the best."

"I know how that goes. That's been the last twenty years of my life." Martin felt for Chris, relating to the old man's tragedy.

"Sounds like we have a lot in common," Chris said with a slow shake of the head. He leaned over the counter to see the main entrance. A young couple browsed the store toward the front, but appeared empty-handed. "Say, how'd you like to come into my back room and see some rare things I've collected?"

Martin returned a puzzled look, unsure what prompted the random invitation. "Are you sure you want to leave the store unattended?" Martin asked as he nodded his head toward the young couple.

"Ahh, they'll be fine. He brought her here to try and prove his false sophistication. I see couples like that all the time. Some guys go to great lengths to get some these days. Back in my day, just being charming was enough."

Chris winked and raised his bushy eyebrows suggestively. "We'll just be a quick minute. Come."

Chris turned to the door behind his counter and pushed it open. More of that ancient odor oozed out of the back room.

Martin muddled cautiously around the counter and followed Chris into the darkness. Chris led them to an old wooden desk that sat beneath a hanging light fixture, its yellow glow illuminating only the desk, leaving the surroundings in an eerie blackness.

"In this business, you tend to come across things you maybe shouldn't. I feel like I've had more of this random luck than anyone else. I assumed it's to make up for all my shitty luck as a child." Chris opened a drawer on the desk and retrieved a flashlight. He clicked it on and pointed it to the wall behind Martin where the door had closed behind him.

A five-foot wide framed painting hung on the wall. The image portrayed thirteen men on a sailboat in the middle of a nasty storm. One glowing face looked familiar to Martin.

"This painting is called *Christ in the Storm on the Lake of Galilee*," Chris said. "It was painted by Rembrandt in 1633. Today it's worth almost five million dollars. It's been missing since 1990 from a major heist in Boston."

He lowered the flashlight to a short table flushed against the wall. Baseball cards spread across every inch of it, and Martin saw one staring at him that sent chills down his spine. He reached for it with a trembling hand.

"Ahhh, so you know about the rare Honus Wagner card." Chris grinned as he watched Martin. "That card is worth three million. In fact, it's the rarest trading card in history."

Martin held the card unsteadily in his hand, studying every inch of its orange background, Wagner's pasty face and neatly parted brown hair, all the way down to the detailing on his gray uniform that read *Pittsburgh* in brown lettering.

"This is the holy grail of baseball cards. Aren't there only a hundred of these left in the world?" Martin kept examining the card and wanted to pinch himself.

"Fifty seven still exist. Only 200 were printed to begin with." Chris leaned back in his creaky chair.

"I don't understand," Martin said, not wanting to put the card down. "How do you have these? And why don't you sell them? You're sitting on seven million from these two items alone. You would never have to work another day!"

Chris shrugged. "I suppose I'm a busybody. It's always been hard for me to relax and lounge. Besides, money is no issue for me. I don't *need* $7 million."

The mystery of this old man kept growing stranger as Martin learned more about him. Martin glimpsed around the room like a child in awe, even though most of it was left in darkness.

"Well, if you ever need someone to loan these cool things out to, just let me know. I can be that guy." Martin tried to lighten the mood.

"That's a generous offer, but I'll keep these under wraps. I trust you won't make any mention of what you saw in here, either?"

Martin nodded. "Of course not."

"Good. I have an oath to keep the secrets of time."

"Is there a reason this room is so dark? You developing photos in the back?" Martin sensed a shift in the mood and tried to make the old man laugh. It didn't work, and all he wanted was to get the hell out of this dark closet.

"I build things in here. Like I said, I'm the keeper of time, and I need to make sure I can preserve all parts of history."

Martin nodded slowly, not sure how to respond.

"Would you like to see?" Chris asked, raising the pitch in his voice. He grinned. "You might have an interest in what I'm working on in here."

"Okay, sure," Martin said, now trying to hide the fear in his wavering voice.

"Come!" Chris said and stood with a youthful spring in his legs.

Martin watched as Chris disappeared into the darkness, footsteps fading away before coming to a halt. A fluorescent light flickered to life, revealing a tall black countertop covered with beakers, piles of a sand-like substance, and a microscope.

"You're a mad scientist on the side?"

Chris walked behind the counter and pulled open a drawer. "Something like that," he snickered.

His skeletal fingers rose from the drawer with a small red pill pinched between his index finger and thumb. He placed the pill gently on the counter as Martin watched with cautious eyes.

"Martin. I feel like I can trust you. Quite frankly, it doesn't matter if you trust me back, but I believe I can be of service to you." Chris spoke with sharp enunciation on every word. "I'm going to tell you something. You're probably not going to believe me. Again, that doesn't matter, because what I tell you is true."

Martin subconsciously took a step backwards as he noticed a slightly crazed look appear in the old man's eyes.

"You see this pill?" he asked, holding up a small white pill pinched between his bony fingers. "If you swallow this pill, you'll fall asleep within minutes. When you wake up, you'll be in March of 1996, right here in Larkwood, Colorado. You'll be your current self in the flesh. You'll appear for everyone else to see, including your past self."

Martin gazed at Chris and wasn't sure if he should laugh or run out the door. He looked out the corner of his eye and

24

noticed the door had disappeared. It was pure blackness where it had just been moments ago. His legs froze and a lump formed in his throat. *What the fuck?*

"Relax," Chris said calmly. "I know this is a lot to take in, but hear me out. You can go back to 1996 and find out what happened to your daughter."

Martin remained frozen, but regained his ability to speak. "That's crazy. You're obviously making your own drugs back here. You should—"

"Get some mental help?" Chris completed Martin's sentence.

Where the hell is the door?

"Now how would I know you would say that?" Chris spoke tauntingly, like a bully goading Martin on. "Perhaps, I took a peek into the future to see your reaction. Perhaps I already knew how you'd respond, and have an offer for you to give it a test run. Would you like to give it a try?"

"You're—"

"Crazy. Yes, yes, I know. And you're in denial. I have a pill that will take you back to this afternoon right when you got off work. I could've made you relive the work day, but that seemed a bit harsh." Chris checked his watch. "It's almost 7 P.M. If you take this pill, you'll return to four o'clock, just as you started your drive home. Like I mentioned, your current self returns to the past and is very much part of the world. You'll be here because when you fall back into the past, you'll awake where you took the pill. You can either wait around here until you arrive shortly after six to buy the ring, or you can take my car out back and meet yourself at home."

Martin gulped. His mind told him the old man was full of shit and it was time to leave. His gut, however, believed him, and his curiosity wanted to find out exactly what that pill could do.

After Martin remained silent, Chris said, "Tell me what you want to do. You can't leave without an answer, though. You can tell me no, and walk out that door and never see me again. You'll finish the rest of your life wondering what happened to your beautiful little girl. The unknowing will drive you mentally insane in your later years. I don't want to give away the spoiler, but it doesn't end well for you."

Chris strolled around the counter until he stood three feet in front of Martin, still frozen.

"Or." He paused a brief moment. "You can take a look and try to get the closure your soul desperately needs."

Martin felt a sense of control start to return, his nerves settling. "If you know everything, why don't you just tell me?" he demanded.

"I do know everything. I can see everything from the past, present, and future. Knowing things and *doing* things are different, though. I can easily go back to the time of the Holocaust, but to do something to prevent it – that's out of my realm. I'm the keeper of time, not the changer of history. I study time and study people, but I'm not here to ruin or fix lives. History follows its course and I'm simply along for the ride. Think of it like the cameraman filming the lion hunting zebras in the jungle. He's observing, not getting involved. It's important to know your role and stay in your lane."

Chris stood close enough where Martin could smell the stale odor radiating from the old man's mouth.

"What's your angle? Even if all of this were true, why would you do this? You don't even know me."

"I like helping people."

"If this is all true, then why didn't you go back in time and stop your parents' death?"

Chris grinned like a politician expecting a tough question.

"You have to understand that there are rules when going back. It's not a free-for-all. I did go back to my parents' accident. Multiple times, in fact. What they say is true: things happen for a reason."

Martin stayed quiet, processing everything Chris had said.

"Well?" Chris persisted.

"What are these rules?" Martin asked.

"We can go over the rules if you decide to go back to 1996. For now, I just want you to see for yourself. There's not much you can damage in two hours, just make sure you don't get spotted by your past self. That can throw your life into limbo."

Martin took a final look for the door, and it still wasn't there. He realized he'd been trapped, perhaps intimidated, into taking this pill. Agreeing to these shenanigans seemed to be the only way out now.

What if it's just a sleeping pill and he tries to kill me or kidnap me? What if he has another secret room where he keeps his prisoners?

Chris studied him with a grin as wide as the Cheshire cat's.

"What if I say no?"

The grin melted into a frown. "Well, you can say no and leave this room and store and return to your life. But just know, the curiosity and regret will drive you into a frenzy. It can take quite a while until you can forget about this discussion."

Martin still hadn't moved despite having the feeling return to his legs. *Your life has already turned to shit. Say he does kill you in your sleep, then you get what you really want deep down: an end to it all. But say he's not lying, and this somehow works.*

27

Then you'll have the answer to a question you've been asking for two decades. I'd call it a low risk, high reward decision.

Martin stared at Chris like a poker player, trying to see if he was bluffing or not. The old man smirked, as if he could hear Martin's thoughts out loud.

"Okay," Martin said confidently. "I'll try it."

The smirk widened again, reminding Martin of the villainous Joker from the *Batman* comics. "Fantastic!"

Chris hurried behind the counter and rummaged through his drawer until his fingers settled on a white pill. "This is the one! Follow me."

He dashed across the floor like a dancer and returned to his desk. He pulled out the squeaky chair and hung an arm out for Martin to take a seat.

"I don't have a bed in here or else I'd have you lay down. The chair will do just fine, though," Chris explained.

Martin stepped cautiously to the chair before sitting down, causing protesting creaks from the old wood. He plopped both arms on the armrests and watched Chris across the desk.

"Like I said, the rules are simple, at least for this quick journey: do not encounter your past self. Stay out of his sight, but feel free to hang around and observe."

"When will I wake up?" Martin asked.

"I'm going to give you two pills. One will take you back in time, and the other will bring you back here. Keep the return pill in your pocket. Anything on your body will go with you when you go back in time. When you're ready to come back, just take the pill. Regardless of how long you stay in the past, only ten minutes will have passed here in the current world. Just make sure you come back before 7 P.M."

Martin nodded, still wanting to talk himself out of such

nonsense, but it was too late. Chris placed the white pill on the desk. "This is to return. Put that in your pocket." Martin did as he was told. "And this is the one that will take you back to 4 P.M. Remember when you 'wake up' in the past, you'll be where your body currently occupies space, so you'll be in this room. I'll make sure the door's open."

Chris winked as he placed the new pill on the desk.

"You'll obviously see me when you go back. I'll know it's you. But as far as anyone else you interact with, they're going to assume you exist in the present time with them. Any questions?"

"Nope. Let's see what this is all about." Martin exuded a confident tone, but his heart pounded in anticipation to the point he could feel his fingertips throbbing against the wooden chair.

"Excellent. Feel free to roam around. You'll have two hours before your past self arrives to the store. Just stay out of your own way."

Martin picked up the pill and examined it under the hanging light. It was white and round, and felt no different than any other pill he'd ever taken. From his pinched fingers, he placed the pill in his mouth, letting it fill with saliva before swallowing. His heart pounded in his ears like distant drums.

Here goes nothing.

He closed his eyes and leaned his head back as he waited for what would come next.

5

Chapter 5

It only took a couple minutes for Martin to fall into a deep sleep. Blackness filled his mind temporarily while his body felt elevated by an invisible hand. His conscience remained alert as he waited anxiously in some sort of purgatory.

When the floating sensation stopped, his body jolted awake like it would after a nightmare. He sat in the same chair in the same dark room, only now the door he had longed for appeared, ajar with a stream of glowing light filling the darkness.

His body appeared intact as he studied his limbs and fingers. He stepped cautiously toward the door before pulling it all the way open. The bright lights from the store stung momentarily as his eyes adjusted. Once focused, he saw Chris sitting at the counter, reading his raggedy book. His frosty hair swirled in different directions as he kept his nose in the book, paying no attention to Martin.

"How do you feel?" Chris asked in an uninterested voice, startling Martin.

The old man didn't look up.

"Uh, fine, I guess. I don't feel any different. Should I?"

"Of course not. Nothing changes for you as long as you keep in mind the golden rule."

Chris flipped a page and continued his semi-ignoring of Martin. Martin looked around the store and saw the clock near the front entrance.

4:03. He could have just changed the clock. Doesn't make this real.

"If you're looking for proof," Chris said. "Then wait around two more minutes. An older lady will walk in and ask if I have any antique bookshelves. I'll point her in the right direction, she'll browse the two that I have, then she'll leave with a quick wave."

Martin didn't respond and walked around the store. He'd plan to see the old lady, but it still wouldn't prove anything. He could easily have paid some poor soul to come in and do exactly as asked.

Martin walked toward the entrance and looked outside where a car pulled in to the parking lot. The sun shone as bright as it did when Martin left the post office every day. *That's a nice touch, I wonder how the old man pulled off that illusion. The sun will be setting any minute now.*

The shiny sedan parked in the handicap parking space and a woman with a gray perm rose from the driver's seat and climbed the stairs, clinging to the handrail for support. She wore a large purse over her shoulder and moved with the fragility of someone with bad knees and hips.

She pulled open the store door and Martin froze where he stood, watching the woman with intense curiosity. She gave him a soft smile and walked past him to the counter where Chris had finally put his book down.

"Hello, ma'am, how can I help you today?" Chris said, sounding a bit scripted in Martin's opinion.

"Yes, I'm looking for an antique bookshelf. Do you happen to have any?" the old lady asked in a soft voice.

"I sure do. Have a couple right over there." Chris pointed in the direction, opposite Martin, and the woman wasted no time examining the bookshelves. Chris leaned over his counter and winked at Martin.

Okay, can still be a set up. This doesn't prove anything.

He struggled with his inner conscience, insisting this was all a well-planned sham, but believing deep down he would watch himself walk into the store in two hours. The thought made him nauseous.

Martin browsed a table of old, fine jewelry, but kept his eye on the woman. He could see her running fingers over the ancient wood, taking a mental picture of the shelves to imagine how they might look in her home. After a minute, she stepped away and headed for the exit. When she passed the counter she grinned and waved at Chris, who returned a grin.

"Thank you for stopping in," he said.

The bell chimed as the woman exited, and Chris gazed to Martin with a devilish smirk.

"I'm gonna go wander around outside. You said I can take your car?" Martin asked, not wanting to give Chris the satisfaction of acknowledging the events that just occurred.

"Yes, be my guest. Keys are in the glove box. It's the only car behind the store."

The smirk remained and Martin left the store with a newly found urgency. Surely it should have started cooling off by now, assuming it was still after seven, but the day remained hot.

You know this is really happening, he told himself. *Stop trying to resist. Go find whatever confirmation you need.*

He walked around the building and found a lone car parked, waiting for him. It was an old, blue Buick, much of the paint chipped away and giving way to brown rust.

"This guy sure lives a humble life for sitting on millions," Martin remarked before opening the driver's door. Despite its junky appearance, the interior was well kept, even smelling clean. He expected trash all over the floor, but there wasn't a single item in the car. He pulled open the glove box and found the key by itself.

The engine roared to life, stronger and in better shape then what Martin expected. The digital clock on the dashboard read *4:18*. "You pulled out all the stops. Great attention to detail."

Martin said these things to assure himself he wasn't going crazy, but the longer the sun didn't set, the more his doubt grew like a slowly inflating balloon. He drove out of the lot and left the Wealth of Time behind.

He drove in the direction of his apartment building, his mind racing out of control. The sun blinded him and he squinted as he weaved in and out of traffic.

What happens if I see myself? That would confirm this is either all real, or my friend at the store has been concocting some very powerful drugs.

It only took him five minutes to arrive to his apartment. He parked across the street from the main entrance and killed the engine. The clock read 4:24 as he drummed his fingers on the steering wheel, anxiously awaiting his past self's arrival.

He had stopped at the grocery store to stock up on more microwavable dinners and should arrive to the complex around 4:30. He faced the stop sign from which he should be turning,

33

and held his breath every time a car pulled up to it.

When five more minutes passed and he still didn't see himself, his doubt and anticipation grew in sync. "Any minute now," he murmured beneath his breath. Then he saw the glimmering light from the hood of a small blue car pull up to the stop sign. Martin's heart dropped to his knees as he shifted in his seat.

"Please turn right, please turn right," Martin begged.

The car's left turn signal flicked on and started to turn his way.

"Fuck, fuck, fuck!" The car approached and he had no doubt it was his old Chevy sedan. Martin slouched in his seat, his eyes barely seeing over the dashboard. The car passed and he saw himself clear as day: chubby, scruffy beard, cigarette pinched between his lips. The car turned into the complex and drove around to the back where he always parked.

Martin's heart hammered against his rib cage, his fingers pulsing against the steering wheel he had clenched without realizing.

"What do I do?" he asked the empty car. "Do I go back to the old man? Take this pill now? Where will I wake up? *When* will I wake up?"

He started the engine, still unsure what he was going to do, but knowing he wanted to get the hell away from his past self.

He sped off and pulled into the gas station three blocks down.

Martin panted for breath as he surveyed the area for anyone he might know. Once he decided the coast was clear, he popped the pill in his mouth and gulped it down dry. With adrenaline flowing through his veins, he wondered if the pill would still put him to sleep.

When two minutes passed without a weary feeling, Martin

panicked and reclined the driver's seat.

"Calm down. Relax. He told you this would work. You'll wake up from this bad trip. Drugs can't affect you forever."

He inhaled deeply. *There we go.* The world came in and out as his eyelids flickered in protest. It only took a few seconds before the world turned black and Martin returned to the floating sensation he had felt earlier.

6

Chapter 6

A sharp thud smacked Martin in the back as he jolted awake. He was back in the dark room inside Wealth of Time, his haggard breathing the only audible sound. The door was cracked open, letting in a lone beam of light. The light above him illuminated the desk, now clear of clutter.

"Have a nice visit?" Chris's voice carried from the corner where he kept his miniature laboratory. His slowly approaching footsteps shuffled along the ground as he returned to Martin's vision. The dim lighting revealed a sly grin that said *I told you so.* "Well?"

"That was very convincing," Martin said, trying to sound unimpressed.

"Oh, Martin, stop the act!" Chris giggled crazily as he spoke. "You're only lying to yourself at this point. There's nothing else I can do to prove to you that this is real."

"I believe it's real. I'm just refusing to accept it."

"Let's get out of this room. I sense it makes you anxious."
No shit.

Martin stood without hesitation and chased after the door

before it mysteriously closed again. He swung the door open with aggression, adrenaline still pulsing throughout.

The store remained the same, although the sun finally started to set, causing an orange splash of light across the floor. Martin spotted the clock near the entrance and it read 7:14. His heart sunk as every part of him gave in to the reality of what had just happened. He could barely hear Chris speaking to him as the pounding in his ears echoed.

"Now stop playing around and tell me your thoughts." Chris egged him on like a child daring a friend.

"Well, it definitely felt real. I saw myself . . . completely freaked me out."

Chris nodded attentively, smirking.

"So do you want to go back to 1996?" Chris asked.

"This all seems so crazy. What am I supposed to do in 1996, play detective? I don't know what I'm doing."

Chris nodded as if he understood, but Martin could see the thoughts swimming behind his eyes.

"Well, you could start planning now and go back to 1996 with a strict plan. Or you can just go back and follow your daughter. Like I said, it would be March when you arrive, so you'd have six months to get situated before she goes missing."

Martin nodded. "Will you give me a glimpse into 1996 like you did tonight? I just want to know it's real."

"This is all legitimate. And no, I can't give you a glimpse, that's not how this works."

"Then I want to know how this works. Everything. What's in those pills? What's in this for you? Who are you?"

Chris raised a hand to silence the flustered man.

"I'll tell you what you *need* to know. The rules. One rule

being that you can only do this once, and that's why I can't send you back for a peek into the past."

"But you just did!" Martin snapped.

"Yes, that was a three-hour time travel, has no effects. Going back twenty two years will certainly affect you."

"What do you mean affect me? What kind of drugs are in those pills?" Martin's voice rose to a near shout. He stood across the counter while Chris leaned back in his chair.

"These aren't drugs. The pills really do take you back in time, or forward, should you choose. But you don't seem like a guy who looks forward to the future. As for the effects, that leads to your other question of what I get out of this."

Chris stood up and leaned on the counter to look Martin straight in the eyes.

"This is serious business," he said. "I don't want any money from you. What I want in exchange is a part of you. During that brief moment when you feel like you're flying after taking the pill, you're in my domain. When you're in there, I can take from your soul as I please."

Martin narrowed his eyes on Chris, wanting to call a bluff, but remaining hesitant. "My soul?" he asked mockingly. "What are you? The Devil?"

Chris smirked. "I'm not the Devil. I'm the keeper of time, I've told you this already. Opportunities like this aren't free. All I ask for is a part of your soul."

"And what part of my soul will you be taking if I agree to this?" Martin played along. Every time the old man spoke, it seemed like a joke that was about to snowball out of control.

Chris pursed his lips and rubbed his head. "It may not seem like much to you, but I want to take your emotions."

Martin raised his eyebrows. "My emotions?"

"Yes. You'll keep your emotions when you go back to 1996. But when you return, you'll be emotionless. Apathetic. No more joy, no more anger. Just a wandering zombie."

"Bullshit," Martin said flatly. "You can't take my emotions, just like I can't move buildings with my mind. You're a goddamn liar! This prank is over."

Martin stormed away from the counter, stomping his feet toward the exit. Nighttime had finally arrived and darkness filled the void through the windows.

"Wait!" Chris shouted, and Martin stopped short of the exit. All he wanted was to leave this damn store behind and never come back, but that glimmer of opportunity proved too much to resist. "Come back and I'll tell you everything you need to know." Chris spoke as if making a hard statement instead of the pleading he was actually doing.

Guy must be desperate for my "emotions."

Martin returned to the counter in a slow dragging of steps. "Tell me everything, and I'll consider your offer tonight. I'll need to sleep on it."

"Sure, sure," Chris said. "For starters, I'm not kidding about the exchange for the emotional part of your soul. You'll still be a fully functioning person, normal for the most part. But you won't be able to care for others, laugh at jokes, or cry at movies. Think of it as that emotional numbness you felt when your daughter went missing. Only this time it won't be numb, just normal."

"How does this all work? Am I really going back in time, or is it all a hallucination?"

Chris nodded. "It's very real, my friend. I'm not going to get into the science of time, but what happens when you take the pill is a sort of transportation. When you arrive in 1996, you'll still be yourself as you are now. Also, anything you have on your body goes with you, so play that to your advantage. If you want to take money with you, keep it in your pocket. Your money today can go a lot further in 1996. Gas was only a $1.30 back then.

"If you have money, great! If not, use your resources to find easy ways to make money. There's really no restrictions on what you can do except for running into yourself."

"And what happens if I run into my past self?" Martin asked, wondering this the entire time.

"Well, think about it. You essentially have two souls when you go back in time. If they meet . . . let's just say it's disastrous for you. You can end up in serious trouble, or worse."

"Okay, I'll stay out of my own way. What about my family and friends, can I talk to them?"

"Sure. If you think they'll recognize you somehow, wear a disguise. I don't know how different you look today compared to back then, so use your best judgment."

"What happens if I lose my pill to come back to present day?"

"Then you stay and live the rest of your life out in that time frame. If you die in there, you'll die here as well. So please stay alive, and don't ever lose that pill."

"Can't you come find me if I lose it?"

"Sure, but that pill is a one-way ticket. Each pill I make is unique, so it's practically impossible for me to replicate them."

"What happens if I change something? What if I take my daughter and run away?"

Chris paused to consider the question.

"Well, changing an event in history will obviously alter the course of the future. You might come back to a completely different life if you change anything. I always recommend to not change anything too drastically. The results could be catastrophic."

"How do you know this?"

"Martin, you're not the first person who has gone back in time. There have been thousands before you and will be thousands after. Every person has their reasons for going back. I've seen some nasty consequences result from someone getting in over their head while in the past. The terrorist attacks on September 11th were a direct result of someone trying to tinker with the past. Your trip back in time is meant to be mostly observatory. Sure, you'll leave a footprint and can effect minor changes, but a decision like running off with your daughter can end in disaster. Just remember that things happen for a reason, as the old saying goes."

"Why me? Why did you pick me for this?"

"Simple: you have something I want, and you have something in the past that demands answers. I don't go around offering this opportunity to random people."

Martin wanted to ask what Chris did with the supposed souls he takes, but figured that would lead down a rabbit hole he had no business in venturing.

"I want to think things over tonight. Can I come back tomorrow?"

"Of course."

"And no matter how long I'm in the past, when I take the pill to return only ten minutes will have passed?"

"Correct."

"I'll be back same time tomorrow."

Chris smirked. "See you then."

Martin jogged out of the store and found his car waiting under the moonlight. He drove home thinking about his daughter and where she was in the world.

7

Chapter 7

When Martin arrived home he wasted no time emptying a bottle of whiskey into a tall glass. His mind paced in frantic circles as he debated his next move. A sliver of skepticism remained, and he considered pretending that the whole thing never happened.

But it did. I really went back in time and saw myself.

He lay down on his couch as the room started to spin, his body tingling from the alcohol, and debated his own sanity.

Is this the boiling point? Have I finally reached it?

He wondered if a person could know when they've gone crazy, or if it was something only visible from the outside. This all could have been a nervous breakdown in anticipation of the upcoming weekend. Izzy was always on his mind during this week more than any other time of year. Maybe he was dreaming and would wake up tomorrow to jump back into his normal routine of hating his life.

But he knew better.

You can't get drunk in your dreams, and I'm very drunk.

Martin tossed and turned for the next hour on his couch. He

usually had no issue passing out and snoring the night away, but his mind refused to shut down for the day. It demanded a decision on what would happen when the sun rose in the morning.

"Ten minutes," he whispered. "I could go in before work and still make it on time if all I lose is ten minutes."

He'd be spending at least six months in the past, depending on what he found. Six months in history to find out what happened to Izzy, all to come back to return to the post office like nothing had happened.

Every time he closed his eyes he saw Chris grinning, smirking, tempting him to go. *That guy is a demon,* Martin thought as he took one final swig to kill the last of the whiskey. *Ten minutes. No one will even know I was gone.*

He bolted upright and immediately regretted it as the blood and alcohol rushed to his head, causing the room to spin.

"I'm going," he declared. "I'm going. And if I die, then so be it."

Saying these words aloud provided him the confidence needed to take the gamble. He could either endure his life wondering what happened to Izzy, or he could take the chance to find out. How many people in his same situation would even debate the matter? It was a no-brainer and he couldn't believe it took him so long to arrive to the right decision. *I have to go. At this point, there's nothing for me to lose.*

Martin dragged himself into the kitchen to grab his laptop and a notepad. He rummaged through the cupboards for another bottle of whiskey, could only find vodka, and poured a glass of it mixed with orange juice before returning to the couch with all three items in hand.

The laptop wheezed to life and the screen's glow blasted

his face with bluish light. Martin needed to return to 1996 with a plan. First and foremost, he needed a way to make money, and he liked the idea of sports betting. Sporting results were all recorded and could be found with a quick search. Finding an underground bookie in Larkwood, Colorado, in 1996, shouldn't be too difficult. He'd had some friends who got involved with the gambling ring around that time, and he often remembered them saying that the bookies would set a spread on any wager offered, including politics.

Martin noted down all the significant sporting events that would occur between March and September of 1996, and was delighted to find the results for the summer Olympics in Atlanta. *Maybe I can afford to go.*

Should I use an alias? He debated the matter. An alias was only helpful if he planned to immerse himself in the community and chat with people around town. Since the younger version of himself already existed in 1996, an alias wouldn't do much—he needed to focus on dodging familiar faces. A disguise might be a better investment to not raise any suspicion. Besides, using a fake name would only cause confusion, and flying under the radar would be much easier to achieve.

After a half hour he had a handful of pages with every sports score listed neatly by the event's date. With his income settled for the past, he shifted his focus to his personal whereabouts and life events in 1996.

He was obviously in Larkwood, but what was he doing?

Was 1996 when I had that data entry job?

Of course it was. He took a month off of work after Izzy went missing. They were accommodating of his situation and worked with him throughout the process. Some days he simply couldn't make it through, and they sent him home with no complaints.

Synergetix. That was the company.

He had started there at the beginning of the year and would be well into his first year of employment by the time 2018 Martin arrived in 1996. He drove an old station wagon to work every day with his sack lunch packed every morning by his beautiful wife. Life was truly as good as it had ever been in the first half of 1996, and the nostalgia made him excited to go back to those times.

They would have been in the only house they lived in as a family, having moved in shortly after Izzy's birth. Lela was a part-timer at the local daycare center, working most weekdays from noon through six. Martin's data entry job provided a big pay increase and they enjoyed eating out every weekend as part of their new, luxurious lifestyle.

He would need somewhere to live in 1996, preferably close to his old house to keep an eye on things. All he really needed was to be around in September to keep a close eye as the eventual day of doom approached. March through August could virtually be spent doing whatever he wished. There was no need for investigative work during that time frame, as life had been rather normal. The night Izzy went missing was a night he had to work late and arrived home to everyone in bed.

This was a particular point of initial interest for the police. A missing girl and a father who had to work late the same night smelled awfully suspicious, but a couple of calls to Synergetix was all it took to clear his name.

September 9, 1996, he remembered. The day life went down the shitter and never recovered. Tears streamed down Martin's face and dripped silently to the floor. The feelings from that morning had never left him. With every minute that passed, every shout of "IZZY!", hope had slowly dissipated and gave way to fear, panic, and sickness.

"These things don't really happen to people," he had said to Lela when they returned home after an hour in the neighborhood. "Izzy wouldn't run away."

"She's gone!" Lela had screamed. "She's gone!"

That was all she had been able to say on that day 22 years ago. Even when the police arrived, she kept saying it, trying to assure herself that it was real.

The police had poked around the house and yard looking for any clues, coming up empty-handed. They technically had to wait another day before issuing an Amber Alert, but they had started the process and paperwork in preparation for the following day.

Martin and Lela spent the rest of the day driving around town, going to Izzy's friends' houses, her school, and the rec center. Those were the only places she ever went outside of the house. When the sun started to set and they accepted that they weren't going to find their daughter, Lela burst into heavy tears in the car as they pulled up to their house.

"Why, Martin? Why did she leave us?"

I don't know. But I'm going to find out.

8

Chapter 8

When the sun rose the next morning, Martin's head throbbed as he rubbed his swollen eyes. The stench of alcohol seeped out of his pores, causing him to gag. He had fallen asleep on the couch, the stinging sun blazing through the living room window. His notepad was splayed on the ground with his chicken scratch notes. The digital clock on the stove informed him it was almost seven. He had just over an hour until he needed to report to the post office. *Plenty of time to clean up and visit Chris for a trip back to the 90's. Hopefully hangovers can't travel back in time with me.*

When he stood, the room spun violently around him and he collapsed back into the couch. *Fuck, I'm still drunk.* Martin belched and felt the alcohol sloshing around in his stomach as he stood again, this time with a hand on the couch's arm for support. He staggered to the kitchen like a zombie to fill a glass of water and swallow a handful of ibuprofen. His brain felt like an over-inflated balloon trying to burst against his skull. *Worst hangover ever?* he wondered. He'd had plenty—more than he could count in the last twenty years—but couldn't remember the last time he felt he might actually croak.

After chugging the water, he dragged himself to the bathroom to relieve his throbbing bladder and stared in the mirror. His hair was frazzled in every direction, his eyes were bloodshot, and his face looked a different shade, slightly gray.

"Damn, Marty. You are hung the *fuck* over," he said to himself in an attempt for a laugh, but his body and brain ached too much to appreciate the humor. He spent the next ten minutes splashing water on his face, putting eye drops in, and swishing mouthwash until the taste of alcohol finally vanished. He stared at himself with a stern expression when he was done. "We're gonna do this. We're gonna save Izzy. No more booze until she's found alive."

The brief pep talk provided a slight boost of energy, but his head still pounded in protest as he gathered his papers and dressed for the upcoming trip, sure to wear jeans and a plain t-shirt to blend in for his 1996 arrival. He stuffed the cash he kept hidden in a coffee can into his wallet and left the apartment in a hurry.

The sunlight sent a shockwave of pain from his eyes all the way down his spine when he stepped outside. When he pulled his car out to the street, he looked around in every direction, searching for some past or future version of himself who might be watching. There was no one, and his paranoia settled down. Every time he saw a person on the road, he wondered if they were really from this current time, or if they traveled back from the next century to see what life was like in 2018.

It only took a few minutes to arrive at Wealth of Time. If ten minutes were all that would pass during his adventure, he'd be in great shape to make it to work on time.

He'd never asked Chris if he would be at the store at 7 A.M., but figured it didn't really matter. Chris probably *knew* when Martin would arrive and would be waiting patiently behind his counter with that devilish smirk.

The storefront glowed under the clear sky as he pulled into the empty parking lot. The building seemed to pull at Martin with a magnetic force. Chills ran throughout his body, but he assumed those were remnants from his massive hangover.

"This is all for you, Izzy." Martin parked his car in the front row and looked through the store windows. The lights were on, and he knew Chris was waiting.

The usual chime greeted him, and the silence from the room soothed his throbbing head. He could only hear the sound of his own breathing and heart pounding in his ears.

"Good morning, Martin!" Chris's voice carried from the back of the store. "Come on over!"

The voice was distant, and Martin knew the old man was waiting in the back room. He took weary steps toward the counter to find the blackness of the open door. Chris sat at the desk, below the hanging light. With that smirk.

"Looks like you had a rough night," Chris said.

Martin wasn't sure if Chris had somehow "visited" him the night before, or if he truly looked like shit. Probably both.

"I'm doing this. For my daughter. Whatever it takes." Martin spoke as confidently as he could.

"Do you have everything you need? Money? Resources for future income? A plan?"

"Yep." Martin had all of the above except for an actual plan. He'd have enough time to get a grasp for how this time travel ordeal worked, but the plan was simple: observe his house from a distance and follow Izzy.

"Perfect. Now, six months is a long time. You'll likely reach a point where you forget all about your current life and get caught up in the midst of being in the past. It'll feel normal. Don't forget to come back. I'll be around to remind you."

"Where can I find you when I'm there?" Martin asked.

"You won't be able to find me. I'll find you, don't worry."

Martin stared at him silently, not pleased with the answer, but realizing there was nothing he could do about it. "Fine," he said like a defeated child.

"You sure you're ready?" Chris asked.

"Yes. Are you trying to talk me out of this now?"

"Of course not. This is a big deal. You're sacrificing a lot, but it will be worth it. Once you make a deal with me, there's no going back."

"Sure. I understand the risks. I'll be emotionless when I get back. No big deal."

Not like I've had emotions the last two decades, anyway.

"All right then, let's get started, shall we?"

Chris stood and extended a hand to his vacant chair. "Have a seat."

Sweat dripped down Martin's arms as his heart raced. The world seemed to vanish as he focused on the chair. It hadn't been an entire day since he sat in that same chair and traveled back in time two hours. He would sit in that chair again for ten minutes while he went back to 1996 to get the answers he had longed for his entire life.

Martin stepped behind the counter and into the old man's office. Chris remained frozen with his arm extended while Martin made his way to the desk. He stepped aside as Martin sat down, and hobbled to the dark corner where he kept his stash of pills.

Chris moved in the darkness, rummaging through drawers

and talking to himself. Martin wondered how the hell the old man could know what he was grabbing, but decided probing him any further would only reveal truths he didn't really want to know.

"Shall we?" Chris asked as he emerged from the darkness with that fucking grin. Martin was ready to wipe the leer off the old man's face if he had to look at it any longer.

Martin waited in the chair, his trembling hands on the armrests, and watched as Chris placed two pills in front of him. This time they were light blue.

"Whenever you're ready," Chris said, the smirk gone.

Martin stared at the pills, grabbed one and slid it into his pocket. He wore jeans with deep pockets on purpose and would worry about stashing the pill securely when he arrived in the past.

"I'm arriving in March of 1996? In this same location?" he asked Chris, whose eyes had grown in excitement.

"Correct."

Martin thought back to this particular location, but his mind was too flustered to recall what the hell had been on this land.

It's time. Just go for it.

"See you in hell," Martin said to Chris and mimicked the grin he had grown so irritated of.

He popped the pill in his mouth and swallowed it in one motion.

No going back now.

"I'll see you in ten minutes!" Chris cried.

Ten minutes. 1996. Find Izzy. Don't encounter yourself.

He repeated these thoughts as he leaned back in the chair and felt all his worries melt away. The hangover faded, followed by his nerves settling. His eyes grew heavy as he fought the grip of sleep while bobbing his head. Then he slouched all the way back in the chair as darkness took control.

9

Chapter 9

Martin woke up in a deserted lot, lying flat on his back on a rough, dirt ground. His headache was gone, the alcohol absent from his breath, and overall he felt energetic and refreshed.

He hurried to his feet and regained his balance after the woozy sensation passed. Looking around, he wondered if he landed on a different planet. The dirt filled an entire open lot for the surrounding three blocks as far as he could see. A quiet neighborhood of one-level homes was to the south, separated from the lot by a stand of oak trees.

The sun beat down on him. It had to be at least 80 degrees as beads of sweat formed on his forehead. He felt nervous as he looked around and saw no signs of life.

"If this is 1996, the church will be in the same place," he reminded himself. He walked away from the neighborhood where the church would await three blocks to the north. Another neighborhood was at the north end of the lot where he could see actual homes, quiet and undisturbed in the warm day.

It has to be the middle of the day. He said I'd arrive in the same location, but not necessarily the same time.

Martin pulled his cell phone out and powered on the screen. Everything appeared to be properly functioning except for actual cell reception. And the time. He blinked his eyes and rubbed them to ensure he was seeing the time correctly as *00:00.*

"What the fuck?" he whispered, chills breaking out down his arms.

First matter of business is to confirm the date and time. Then I can plan from there.

A sliver of doubt remained within, but every instinct and voice of reason in Martin's mind assured him this was all real.

Even if this is a dream, or some sort of hallucination from the pills, I'm still here. At least, I think I'm here.

That was good enough for Martin and he walked to the north neighborhood, kicking up dust with each heavy step. A chain-link fence forced him to walk around the rows of houses instead of cutting through someone's backyard.

It took ten minutes to navigate around the neighborhood. The sun was straight above him and he figured the time was close to noon. When he passed the final house he saw civilization, and a wave of relief swept over him.

The dirt gave way to asphalt before changing to concrete on a sidewalk that ran along a paved road. The road stretched two blocks down and connected with a main road. "That should be 72nd, and the church should be one more block."

The church lot was surrounded by more trees, some bare, some green. *It's definitely March.* He paced faster toward the trees and crossed the street after another block. Cars zipped by on the main road ahead as he crossed into the trees, coming out the other side and seeing the building he was aiming for.

Martin skidded to an abrupt halt when he saw what re-mained of the church. The roof was collapsed and charred. Chunks of its once brick exterior lay scattered across the ground in messy piles of rubble. He could see inside the church where only the altar remained, also fried to a crisp.

"Holy shit," Martin said. "The fire of '96."

He thought back to this time when his mother had called him in a panic, sobbing uncontrollably into the phone.

"The church is gone!" she cried. "It's all gone!"

Martin didn't know how to respond at the time, and didn't know what to do in the present. The church would be repaired by December through tireless work from the parishioners and community. Izzy's memorial service was held there that month, two weeks after the reopening.

I forgot this happened.

All doubt vanished. His feet stood on ground from two decades earlier, and his lungs breathed air from a much simpler time in his life. There was no faking the burnt down church.

"It's 1996." He said this to make it *feel* real. His mind worked in overdrive to process the events of the last ten minutes, leaving him a bit lightheaded.

Snap out of it. What are you going to do now?

He reached into his pocket and brushed a finger over the pill, his return flight home. The idea of taking it crossed his mind. Why should a reckless alcoholic get the opportunity for time travel?

Without thinking about it, Martin started toward the church, feeling an urge to stand in the rubble. His mother had begged and pleaded for his help in rebuilding the church all those years ago, but between a packed work schedule and constant activities with Izzy, his free time was limited.

Martin stood at what used to be the church's main entrance and gawked at the collapsed doors. The smell of burnt wood oozed out of the piles of debris. The pews were buried underneath the roof. Stained-glass windows that once depicted each Station of the Cross lay shattered in ruins.

"Excuse me, sir, may I help you?" an older man's voice came from behind, causing Martin to jump and pivot around.

"Father Alfonso, you scared me," Martin said, not realizing his reflex reaction toward his former priest.

The old man squinted his eyes and put a hand over his brow to block the sun. "Martin Briar?"

Oh shit. Just run. Turn and run. Don't let him see you like this. How could I already fuck this up? I've only been in the past ten minutes and I'm about to blow my cover.

"Yes, Father, how are you? Long time since I've seen you." Martin forced every word out of his tense throat. *Play it cool, he may not notice anything different.*

"I'm doing just fine, aside from my church being a pile of ashes." The priest offered a soft grin. "How have you been? I haven't seen you around here in years. You look . . . different."

No shit. I'm 54 but you still think I'm 32.

"I've been good. Busy with the family and work."

"Too busy to give an hour to God each week?"

Martin looked to the dirt. *Fucking Catholic guilt.*

"I know I haven't been around, and I'm sorry. I rarely have a day off."

Father Alfonso spread a wide smile, revealing immaculate teeth. "I'm just kidding with you, lighten up, young man."

Young man? Have I not aged all this time?

Martin offered a shy grin, wanting to get as far away from

57

this situation as possible. "I really should be going. I just wanted to come see this damage for myself."

"It's a shame. I expect I'll see you around on some of the repair crews?"

"I'll do what I can. I know my mom'll be here for sure."

"Bless her. Well you take care of yourself. Hope to see you around."

The old priest extended a fragile hand, which Martin shook quickly.

"Great seeing you, Father."

Martin turned away and strolled toward 72nd Avenue without looking back.

I'll certainly never come back here. Especially with how much my mom will be here to volunteer.

Bulky cars zoomed by Martin as he reached the main road. He paused to catch his breath and wipe the sweat dripping down his face. Two more miles west and he'd find himself in his old neighborhood where the 1996 version of himself lived with a happy wife and daughter.

With $3,000 stuffed into his wallet, Martin remembered he still had plenty to get done. If he planned to be around for six months, he'd need a car. This walking business had already grown old after traveling an entire six blocks. He'd need an apartment, preferably close to his old house.

For now, he needed a place to stay and knew of only a couple hotels in the Larkwood area, one near his old house. He could stay a night there and plan for the rest of the week. They'd also be able to tell him the exact date and time.

"I guess I need to buy a watch, too," he said as he looked at his phone still reading as *00:00*. He had pulled it out to call for a car through one of his apps, but forgot he had no service. And there was no such thing as ride sharing apps in the 90's—it was still wrong to get in cars with strangers, believe it or not. Since Larkwood was a smaller town, there weren't exactly any random taxis patrolling the area.

Motherfucker, two miles of walking it is, then.

Martin inhaled deeply, letting the fresh air fill his tarred lungs. Two miles wouldn't be too bad, and he thought of how a car became his top priority as he walked to the nearest hotel.

10

Chapter 10

The Sunset Dream Motel welcomed Martin as he huffed and puffed, his face flushed as red as a fire truck. Cramps throbbed in his calves and thighs from the hour-long, two-mile walk across town. His smoker's lungs couldn't handle the merciless abuse of fresh air and exercise.

There were no hotels in Larkwood. Martin had gone his entire life without realizing it was a town of all motels. Being a main hub for truckers, the motel room provided an uncomfortable bed, dirty bathroom, and a TV with terrible reception. The odor of cigarette smoke clung to the walls of the entire building. A couple of diesels were parked along the back of the building of the otherwise deserted motel.

"If you're looking for some fun during your stay, call this number," the front desk clerk told Martin after checking him in. He slid a paper the size of a business card across the counter with a phone number written in scribbly letters. "Hundred dollars for two hours, you won't find a better deal around here."

The clerk spoke with a twang to complement his mullet

and handlebar mustache. The minty odor of chewing tobacco radiated from his breath.

"Thank you, I'll keep that in mind," Martin said.

"Glad to help. Name's Randy if ya need anything. I'll be here."

"Actually, Randy, can you tell me what the date is?"

"Today's March 18. You're not from around here, are you?"

"Thank you. And no, I'm not. Just passing through on a business trip."

"I see. Ya know, if you go about ten minutes south there's a hotel for business guys like you. If you want a more upscale place to stay."

"I'll be fine here. This is the perfect location."

"Suit yourself."

Randy pushed a key across the counter and wished Martin a good day.

Martin grabbed the key, left the office, and headed for his room six doors down. An old man sat passed out in a lawn chair in front of the room next to Martin's, cigarette still lit between his chubby fingers as smoke oozed into the air.

Martin's room welcomed him with the stench of cigarettes and bleach, causing an immediate migraine.

Maybe an apartment should be top priority.

He stared at his bed and wondered how many times a trucker brought his $50 per hour hooker for a night of romance at the Sunset Dream Motel. The number had to be higher than he wanted to know. Not wanting any disease to find its way into his bloodstream, Martin pulled the two extra pillows from the closet and laid them across the bed. It would be a long night sleeping on top of the pillows, but he considered it a minor inconvenience in the grand scheme of his journey.

He grabbed a pen and pad of paper from the nightstand and made a checklist for the rest of the week.

March 18, he thought. *Still don't know what day it is.*

He pulled out his cell phone and prayed the calendar application still worked. When he found it did, he scrolled for almost five minutes to 1996.

Today's Monday, March 18.

He scribbled this at the top of the notepad. The clock on the nightstand informed him it was also 11:37 A.M. He continued composing his checklist.

Apartment, car, watch, money, plan.

He circled the word *plan.*

What exactly am I gonna do for the next six months?

He debated continuing his 2018 lifestyle. Surely alcohol and tobacco were cheaper in 1996. More bang for his buck if he could get blacked out on twenty dollars.

Don't do it, he reminded himself. *You have a fresh start. No one here knows you. Except for your priest, apparently.*

The prospect of a job grew more appealing. He could make a little bit of money from work and gambling and take it all back to 2018.

I should have researched stocks. I still can. I'll know which ones hang around for the next two decades and have a pile of cash waiting when I return.

Martin wanted a quick nap. His mind felt like it had traveled on a twenty-hour flight across the world, but the sight of the bed with its stained sheets and comforter made him want to find an apartment instead.

He dropped the paper and pen and clicked on the TV. A fuzzy image came on, showing an old soap opera. The picture flickered constantly as Martin flipped through the channels in search of anything to watch that might distract his mind.

CNN came up and scrolled through the day's stock market prices, prompting him to grab his pen and write each price as fast as he could. Investing was a smarter choice than taking money from bookies. There would be no stockbrokers in Larkwood, so he'd need a car to get downtown.

With a short-term plan, Martin felt re-energized and ready to tackle his to-do list, leaving the motel in a hurry. The old man remained asleep and let out a hoarse belch between snores.

The sound of the highway behind the building roared with traffic, but the road in front remained deserted. His old house waited a short six blocks away, causing the temptation to swell as he debated taking a casual stroll down his old street.

Six months. Follow the checklist, he reminded himself.

From the motel, the nearest apartment complex should be two blocks north. It was the same building he lived in in 2018, and he vaguely remembered it opening in the mid-90's. With the leg cramps finally fading away, Martin started his journey north.

The sun didn't let up as the clock struck noon. Mid-March in Colorado meant there was still one more month of un-predictable weather that could swing an 80-degree day to a freezing blizzard the next day. It was the perfect day to sit on the balcony with a cigar and a glass of scotch. But Martin had no cigar or scotch, let alone a balcony. *Fuck this.*

Martin dragged himself the two blocks only to find an empty lot. "You're shitting me!" he shouted. Bushes and tumbleweed filled the landscape where his future residence would be built. "I could've sworn this was open by now." He rotated to check the rest of the area, seeing nothing but the houses in the neighborhood and no apartment building in sight. One more block north was the middle school where Izzy would be.

Martin's heart ached immediately at the thought. Here he was, one block away from his long-lost daughter, and all he wanted to do was barge into her classroom and hug her. Hug her and never let go. Take her from the school. Chris had cautioned against making drastic changes to the past. Surely kidnapping his daughter would change everything.

Stay patient. You'll see her soon enough.

Tears welled in his eyes. Just seeing her in person would be enough to call this a successful trip. One last hug and kiss on her forehead that he could hang on to for the rest of his life would suffice.

Go back to the motel. It's day one and you're already risking your cover. Finish your plan, then worry about seeing Izzy.

Martin swiveled around on his heel and dragged his feet in defeat back to the motel. His thighs protested the additional walking, but his mind stayed too consumed to notice. He closed his eyes while he trudged along the sidewalk, picturing Izzy with her round, green eyes, brace-filled smile, and childish giggle that echoed in his heart and mind.

The walk back to the motel felt shorter, thanks to his racing thoughts. He entered the lobby where Randy sat behind the front desk, a cigarette pursed between his lips as he watched *Seinfeld* on a small, portable television.

"What can I do ya for?" he asked, not looking away from the TV.

"I think I'm going to be in town much longer than I planned. Do you know where the nearest apartments are?"

Randy plucked the cigarette out of his mouth and turned his

attention to Martin with a scrunched face.

"Couple miles east of here. Off 84th by the flea market."

"Perfect, thank you. Are you able to call me a cab by chance to take me there?"

"Yessir."

Randy snapped the phone off its cradle and turned the wheel on the rotary. Martin patted the cell phone in his pocket, thankful for how far technology had advanced through the new century.

While Randy ordered the taxi, Martin perused the lobby that he had ignored earlier. Pictures of diesel trucks decorated the wood-panel walls, fake plants stood in each corner of the room, and a table with magazines about guns and trucks was tucked along the back wall next to a raggedy water cooler. The ashtray on the table overflowed.

"Cab's here," Randy said, having already returned to his TV with the cigarette back between his crusty lips.

"Thank you, sir!" Martin replied as he crossed the lobby, excited to travel by vehicle.

The yellow cab waited outside the main entrance, smoke puttering from the exhaust pipe. The paint was chipped in scattered areas and the driver side taillight appeared busted in by a baseball bat.

Martin opened the door and plopped down behind the driver. A bald, black man greeted him. "Hey, mon. Where to?"

A small Jamaican flag hung from the rear-view mirror, just above his ID card that identified him as Clinton Green.

"Hello, I'm heading to the apartment complex by the flea market. I'm not sure of the name, but it's right off 84th."

"Got it," Clinton responded in a thick Jamaican accent. "Five minutes."

"Do you know the name?"

"Larkwood Suites."

"Thank you."

Martin looked out the window during the drive. He'd never realized how clean the town had become over time. Seeing it in the 90's again reminded him that it hadn't always been the safest of places to live. Broken-down cars were parked in front of run down houses. Graffiti decorated abandoned warehouses that blended into the city's skyline. A group of teenagers huddled in the warehouse's parking lot, smoking cigarettes while passing a brown bag around the circle.

Ahhh, Larkwood. You've changed, but you're still the same.

Seeing the city's transformation over the course of his life showed Martin that even the worst of situations could one day sprout a better future. In 2018, the same area had an outdoor strip mall with a restaurant, nail salon, and liquor store.

Driving through town felt like a trip through the history books. They passed the block where his mom lived, and he craned his neck for a view of her house. It stood with its beige exterior, not having changed one bit over the years. Seeing the house caused gooseflesh to break out across his arms. The trip started to feel more like a fucked-up vacation mixed with a sickening nostalgia.

What would happen if I visited my mom? What could that mean for my future self?

Martin knew he needed to suppress these thoughts before they snowballed out of control. Temptation to push the boundaries would surely keep pounding on the door.

"We here, mon." Clinton stared at Martin in the rear view. "Six dollars, please."

Fuck. All my money's in a single wad.

Martin didn't want to pull out a bundle of three thousand dollars in front of the cab driver. He was new in town and didn't need any locals murmuring about the new guy with all the cash. With a balled fist, he stuffed his hand into his pocket and wriggled his fingers to work out a lone bill from the wad, hoping it was bigger than a single.

Alexander Hamilton stared at him when he pulled his hand out and Martin handed the ten-dollar bill over without hesitation. "Have a good day, mon." Clinton watched Martin leave the cab with a quick head nod in return.

The cab drove off and Martin faced Larkwood Suites, an apartment complex he had a hard time remembering from any point in his life. It was tucked behind a neighborhood, away from the main roads. He had never ventured to this part of town and made a mental note to come back to this spot in 2018 to see if the building still stood.

The complex stood three stories tall with a brick exterior. Each window had an air conditioner visible from the outside, and many of them buzzed as they worked on the hot March day. The entrance had double doors that Martin pulled open, letting out a gush of cool air that felt marvelous on his sweating neck.

A wall of mailboxes, each marked with unit numbers, greeted him before passing through another set of doors into the main lobby. A vending machine hummed while its light flickered next to an open office door where Martin peered into in search of help.

A middle-age man sat behind a cluttered desk, his attention focused on the boxy computer monitor that took up nearly all of the space on his desk. The screen glowed on his face to highlight his thick, black mustache and wavy hair. A couple of crumbs clung to life on the bottom edge of his facial hair.

Martin cleared his throat to get the man's attention.

"Oh, hello there. Is there something I can help you with?" The man's voice came out deeper than expected, and when he stood, Martin noticed bulging muscles stretching his polo shirt to its limits when he stuck out a hand to shake. "Vincent Mack. You're not from this complex, are you?"

"No, sir. I was actually hoping to see if you had any open units for rent."

"That I do. What's your name?"

"Martin Briar. I just got into town a few days ago and need somewhere to live. Been staying at the Sunset Dream Motel."

"Yikes. Are you a trucker?"

"No. I'm a writer. Just traveling around the country looking for new material." The lie came out naturally, and Martin decided to make this his story going forward.

"I didn't think so. You don't exactly look like the kinda guy who'd stay at the Sunset. Is it just yourself?"

"Yes."

"I have a studio unit that just opened up – I was actually putting together a flyer for it right now. 450 a month, includes water and electric."

450! Martin fought off a gasp. He had over six months' worth of rent, at that price, in his pocket. He could stay and not worry about a job.

"That should work fine," Martin said in his best expression-less voice.

"Awesome. I'll print out the contract for you to review. Will you have first and last month's rent?"

Buddy, I have all the rent.

"Yes."

"My man. Gimme ten minutes and I'll get you that contract.

Bring it all back tomorrow and you got yourself a place to live."

"Thanks, Vincent, I appreciate you working with me on such short notice."

"Call me Vinny. And it's no problem."

Martin waited in the lobby while listening to the printer whoosh back and forth. This landlord didn't ask for any credit information, identification, or references. Life was simple in the 90's, and Martin celebrated by buying a 25-cent Coke from the vending machine.

11

Chapter 11

Vinny never asked for any of the standard background information that was common in 2018. Martin returned the following morning after a rough night of sleep at the motel. His neighbor apparently paid for a deluxe service from Randy's business card as screaming and moaning carried through the walls until 3 A.M.

Martin expected to live in a closet based on the tiny amount of rent due for his studio, but was surprised to find a spacious room when he entered. He walked into a full kitchen with his living room/bedroom combination behind the island counter, and a bathroom and closet in the far corner. The studio was roughly the size of his 2018 unit, and also had a balcony where he could continue his nightly traditions. A lemony scent filled the air, so Martin cracked open the window above his air conditioning unit to freshen the space.

The empty studio stared back at him, the white walls bare and demanding decorations. He'd need furniture. Sleeping on the floor for six months wouldn't suffice. A couch, bed, and some barstools were all he really needed. He could eat like a king every night if he wanted to go out and about. Downtown Denver was only a ten-minute drive in the 90's, before the constant rush hour that began after 2010.

Finding a car was his next objective now that he had shelter away from the hooker-loving truckers. As much as he wanted a flashy car, he knew he needed to blend in with his surroundings. Larkwood didn't exactly have BMWs rolling down the street.

Every time Martin had a thought pop into his mind he pulled out his phone to open Google, only to find it useless and disconnected. The Internet wasn't in homes at this point in time, and Martin realized he'd have to go to the library should he need to use a computer.

How did we function before the Internet? The thought of driving to the library to search for the nearest car dealership, then printing the directions to get there, seemed like an ancient practice.

The Yellow Pages! Vinny would have a copy in his office for the tenants to use.

Martin left his apartment and flew down the one flight of stairs to the lobby, where Vinny's office door stood open.

"Martin! There's not something wrong with the place, is there?" Vinny asked.

"No, not at all. I was actually looking for The Yellow Pages. Do you have one?"

"Of course."

Vinny swiveled in his chair and rummaged through a pile of papers on the desk behind him. He pulled out a thick yellow book heavy enough to knock a senior citizen unconscious and dropped it on the desk with a hard thud. "Here you go."

Martin flipped through the pages in the "C" section and

appreciated the simpler times of life. If you truly wanted a piece of information, you had to go get it.

He arrived to a section labeled "Cars" and found a list of a couple dozen dealerships, mostly in Denver.

"Are there any car dealers you know of in Larkwood?" he asked Vinny.

"Yes. They might not be listed in there. Good buddy of mine runs a dealership on Quebec Street called Caracas. Tell him I sent you and he'll take good care of you."

Martin used the phone in the lobby to call a cab and only waited five minutes for its arrival, and another five to arrive to the dealership.

The dealership was a small building, no bigger than a fast food restaurant, with at least 100 cars surrounding it in the lot. A few clunkers were visible, but the front line showed some promise.

A scrawny man wasted no time meeting Martin on the lot when the cab departed.

"Hello there. Anything I can help you with today?" he asked in a squeaky voice and slight Latin accent. Martin studied the man's slicked back hair and the cheap jewelry adorning his wrists and neck.

"I'm in the market for a new car. Just need something reliable to get around town, nothing special." Martin watched the man's brown eyes bulge in excitement at the hot lead that just walked on to the lot.

"Yes, sir. My name's Antonio. Anything you need. Do you have a preference for American or foreign?"

"I don't. Just looking for the best deal."

"Of course. Come."

Martin followed Antonio, who darted around the corner of

the building, and braced himself for the attempted screwing he was about to take from the car salesman. They passed a row of American makes, and headed deeper into European and Asian models.

Antonio, dressed in a cheap suit, stopped in front of an early 90's BMW. "This is one of the finest cars we have."

Martin studied the car and loved it, but a BMW was out of the question.

"I'll give you a great deal, yeah?" Antonio pressured as Martin remained silent. Antonio glanced at the information sheet on the driver's window. "Only 30,000 miles. Its price is $15,000, but I'll do ten for you. Yeah?"

Antonio nodded at the end of each sentence, finally receiving a smile back from Martin.

"I'm looking for something a bit more subtle. I wanna blend in, not be turning heads at every red light. I have $2,000 cash in my pocket. What can you give me for that?"

"Ahhh, yes, of course. I have just the thing." Antonio's skinny fingers clasped together as he led them away from the BMW and toward the back of the lot. He stopped in front of an old Buick and stretched a hand out to present it to Martin.

"1988. 120,000 miles."

"How much?"

"Two thousand."

"Bullshit." Martin stepped up to the information sheet and saw the price clearly listed at $1,600. "That's not what it says here. You trying to pull a fast one on me?"

Martin turned and walked away, not making it five steps before Antonio pleaded.

"Please, please. Sorry, sir. I made a mistake. I thought this was priced different."

Martin turned back to Antonio and saw the immediate regret on his face. He never planned on leaving; he had nowhere to go. Besides, he could negotiate an even better price now that he caught the salesman red-handed.

"So you'll give it to me for $1,000 then?" Martin asked.

Antonio looked to the sky as he made mental calculations. "I can do $1,200."

"Perfect." Martin played him like a fool.

"I'll draw up the paperwork." Antonio returned to the office building with his tail between his legs.

* * *

An hour later Martin pulled out of the dealership in his "new" Buick Regal, black paint chipped and fading, and bubbles about to burst from the poor tint job on all the windows. Now he felt like he fit into the Larkwood scene and knew no one would pay him any attention.

With wheels underneath, Martin felt ready to explore this 1996 version of the world more freely. He could even plan a road trip and visit the rest of the country. Perhaps a trip to the Olympics would be a reality after all.

He drove through town with the windows down, letting the air flow and ruffle his hair. The air conditioning was broken, so he had no other choice. He passed the pile of ashes that was once his church and sped through the intersection.

It's time. I just want to drive by.

It only took three minutes before he pulled into his former neighborhood. Cars lined the sidewalks as always; the residents never quite seemed to grasp the concept of a driveway.

The trees that normally shaded the block in the summer stood tall and leafless, and this allowed Martin to see his home the moment he turned on to Cherry Street. He coasted at a steady five miles per hour as he passed all of the familiar houses that were once his neighbors.

The nostalgia overflowed as he felt the effects of living in a different dimension.

There it is. The hairs on his arms stood at attention as he stopped the car across the street from his old house. The ranch home stood out with its light green siding and forest green trim. The lawn was still yellow but had clearly been aerated in preparation for the upcoming spring season.

The clock on the radio read 12:33, so he knew no one would be home, and pulled into the empty driveway. A squirrel stared at him from the front porch and darted away when he stepped out of the car. The house radiated its many memories as he walked around to the backyard to get out of sight from any nosy neighbors.

More yellowed grass stretched twenty yards to the back fence where thick bushes blocked the view of the neighbor's yard. A cement patio ran along the house with a basketball hoop at the far end. Martin had liked to come home from a long day and shoot around to release the tension, sometimes playing into the darkness if he arrived late from an overtime shift. He envisioned the younger version of himself, dribbling, shooting, and shouting as he worked to perfect his skills on the court.

A breeze swirled around and rattled the house's screen door, loose on its hinges, a small project that took him months to fix. He remembered how Lela curled into a ball beside him in bed the first night the door made constant banging sounds. She giggled when Martin inspected and returned with the cause of the noise. They had made their own banging sounds in the bed that night once the initial fear had worn off.

Martin walked up the two short steps to the door and pushed it closed, keeping his hand on its cool, metal surface. He wanted nothing more than to walk through that door and see his old home, smell its familiar scent, and bask in its charm.

The time will come. It's day two. Go home and plan out what you're going to do for the next six months.

A gust of wind whistled overhead, rocking the power lines and blowing his hair over his eyes. The screen door would have surely slammed against the house had he not been holding it. *Just one of the small things I'm preventing here in the past.*

Martin smirked joyfully before kissing the door and returning to his car. Tears welled in his eyes as he pulled out of the driveway to return to his "new" home.

12

Chapter 12

Martin spent the next three days planning the rest of his time in 1996. He only left the apartment to get food, basic furniture like a bed and couch, and more clothes to last him a couple weeks between loads of laundry. His cash supply had dwindled after the car purchase and rent, so the first task on his list was to establish some sort of income. He planned to place a couple of small bets with a local bookie and had a hunch Vinny could point him in the right direction. With his winnings, he'd reinvest into bigger bets with a more established bookie downtown. He calculated his cost of living to be $1,000 per month, including extra cash for entertainment. He loved movies and 1996 was a huge year with the releases of *Scream, Twister, Independence Day, and Mission Impossible.* Spending the summer in a movie theater sounded all right in his book. Unfortunately, alcohol wasn't allowed in theaters like it was in 2018, but he would manage.

I haven't had a real urge to drink since arriving. Martin figured he had simply been too distracted to go out of his way to the liquor store. Perhaps travelling through Chris's fucked-up time vortex killed his inner alcoholic. *Or maybe you just have hope again,* he thought. The drinking hadn't really begun until the reality sunk in that Izzy was never coming back.

Whenever he returned to life in 2018, he wanted things to be different. *No more binge drinking. Drink responsibly and stop before the world turns black.* What better time than the past to work on yourself? He also wanted to follow through with investing. He could arrive back in 2018 with a broker account loaded with millions, and tell the post office to go fuck themselves.

Until then, Martin's first matter of business on March 24 was to win money. It just so happened one of the many bets he had written down was taking place this evening. He went to see Vinny in his office.

Vinny was sipping a glass of scotch when Martin entered. His office hours on Sunday ran from nine to noon, and it was already eleven.

"Martin. Happy Sunday, my friend," Vinny said with a wide grin. Martin noticed the screen saver of bubbles bouncing around the computer monitor. "What can I do for ya today?"

"Good morning, Vinny. I was hoping to place a bet on a basketball game tonight, and wondered if you might know where I could do that."

"Ahhh, you're a betting man? What did you have in mind?"

"I have a hunch Toronto is gonna upset Chicago tonight."

Vinny gulped down the scotch and burst out in laughter. "That's a fool's bet!"

It was a fool's bet. Chicago sported a 60-7 record and was about to make NBA history as the best team ever. Toronto had only won 17 games compared to 49 losses. There was no reason for Chicago to lose this particular game other than an act of God, but Martin had it noted for a reason, knowing it would have a huge payout for betting on Toronto.

"I know it sounds crazy. I just think the Bulls are gonna go in there too laid-back. Toronto will be ready and surprise them."

"If you say so. Go see a buddy of mine, Delmar Graff, down at The Devil. You know where it is?"

"I sure do." The Devil still existed in 2018 and was the same old dive bar it had always been.

"Ask the bartender for Delmar. Tell him Vinny sent you."

"Got it, thanks."

"I'll pour you a glass after you lose this bet. I almost feel bad for ya."

"And I'll buy you a new bottle with all of my winnings."

Vinny threw his head back and howled as Martin left him to finish his scotch in peace. He could still hear his landlord laughing through the walls when he arrived to his car, and couldn't help but chuckle. Vinny must have thought Martin was a lunatic, but when he arrived tomorrow with a brand new bottle of scotch, he'd have a new friend for the next six months.

The drive to The Devil took a quick five minutes west from the complex, and Martin arrived to find it hadn't really changed in its two decades of existence. The pub was a small wooden building with neon lights in the windows advertising different beers. A white sign ran the length of the entrance with red letters that read *THE DEVIL*, a pitchfork on each end of the name.

Martin approached the front door, music booming behind its walls, and pulled it open to let the sound pour outside for a brief moment. It was Sunday morning, a few minutes before noon, and six men already sat around the bar with their beer mugs filled and their cigarettes burning. A smoky haze filled the bar and mixed with the stench of alcohol.

The bar was oval-shaped. In the center of the pub, a young black man worked his way around to serve each customer. No one paid any attention to Martin and sipped their beers as if they didn't notice a man from 2018 stroll into their haven. TVs surrounded the room, each showing various spring training baseball games from Florida that were underway. The bartender made brief eye contact with Martin before returning to pour a beer.

Martin sat at the end of the bar, his back facing the entrance.

Two older men sat to his left and carried on a conversation about the upcoming election between Bill Clinton and Bob Dole.

The bartender strolled over, staring Martin directly in the eyes.

"Good morning, sir. What can I get for you?" the young man asked. He was clearly college-age, likely working this job to pay his way through school.

Martin's mouth watered at the thought of a drink, but wanted to stay disciplined as long as he could. Deep down he knew he'd eventually give in, but for now he felt sharp and healthy, and intended to keep it that way.

"I'll just have a Coke. I actually came to meet with Delmar. Is he in?"

The bartender hesitated, confused as to why someone would come in to a bar at noon to order a soda, and then poured the Coke without any questions.

"Mr. Graff is in. I can have him come out to meet you." The young man avoided eye contact as he pushed the plastic cup across the bar.

"I'd appreciate that."

The bartender left without another word.

Martin pulled in his soda, suds bubbling over the edge, and took a long sip through the straw.

"Damn, this could use some Jack in it."

Keep your eye on the prize, his inner angel reminded. *You're here for a serious reason, not to get drunk.*

Martin watched the bartender cross to the other end of the bar and pick up a phone off its cradle, bobbing his head as he spoke. After hanging up, he returned to another customer and topped off a beer.

Martin sat back and watched baseball for the next ten minutes, wondering what to expect of this bookie he would soon meet.

* * *

A man dressed in dark jeans and a gray blazer strode from the back corner of the bar and approached the bartender. The two spoke, the bartender looked over his shoulder and nodded in Martin's direction, and the man waved him over.

Martin did a quick double take before hopping off his stool and walking around the bar. The two old men shouted at each other, one in clear favor of Clinton, the other adamant that Dole needed to bring America back to its roots.

"Delmar Graff at your service," the well-dressed man said, sticking a pudgy hand out. He was heavier up close than he had looked across the room.

"Mr. Graff, I'm Martin Briar. Vinny from the Larkwood Suites sent me here to meet you."

"Vinny!" Delmar barked in a scruffy voice. "I love that guy. Great businessman. So what can I help you with?"

"I was hoping to place a bet," Martin said in a lowered voice, despite the booming music, and wishing he had used an alias to meet with this obvious mobster.

"Let's go back to my office so we can actually hear each other," Delmar said as he put a hand on Martin's shoulder. Martin noticed a ring on each thick finger, gleaming through the indoor smog. Delmar turned and started toward a door that had a frosted glass window with *OFFICE* centered in neat lettering.

Delmar held the door open as Martin entered the office where a behemoth of a man in an all-black suit stood in the far corner watching a baseball game. He wore sunglasses above a perfectly groomed goatee, and had his hands crossed in front of him, gold rings on every finger. The man didn't budge as the two entered.

"Please, have a seat." Delmar crossed behind a desk in the crammed room. Martin thought it might have been a custodial closet at one point that had been redone as a fully functioning office space. The desk was cleared except for a stack of papers on its edge and a thick notebook in the middle with dozens of sticky notes protruding from its tattered edges. Martin shot uncomfortable glances toward the silent man in the corner. "Don't mind Hammer over there. He's my trusted adviser and personal banker."

Hammer? This guy is definitely a mobster. Martin's senses heightened at the thought and he wondered if this was a mistake.

"I do some bookmaking here. What did you have in mind?" Delmar asked, shifting the focus back to business.

"I was hoping to bet on the Toronto Raptors tonight."

Delmar nodded and flipped open the notebook on his desk, running a finger down multiple pages until he found what he wanted.

"I have Toronto as a 14 point underdog, I'll give you even odds on that."

Martin nodded as the bookie stared at him. There was no laughing like Vinny had done; this was serious business for all parties involved.

"I was actually hoping to bet on them straight up, no spread."

This caused a slight eyebrow raise from Delmar, but he remained composed otherwise. A straight bet meant that the Raptors would have to win the game outright and Martin would forfeit the 14-point cushion originally offered.

A fool's bet.

"How much were you wanting to bet?" Delmar asked as his finger paused on a different line in his notebook.

"Three hundred dollars."

Delmar looked at Hammer and nodded for him to come over.

Hammer took three steps sideways and craned his neck to see what his boss was pointing at. He took a moment, stood up straight, then nodded before returning to his corner.

"15 to 1 odds on that bet," Delmar said flatly.

Martin did quick math. *$4500. That'll cover some groceries.*

"Deal."

Delmar stuck his hand out and the men shook to solidify their wager.

"Tell me something," Delmar said in a softer voice. "You

know something I don't? MJ not playing tonight?"

"No, sir. Just a hunch. The Bulls haven't lost to a bad team all year. It's bound to happen sooner or later."

"You better be right. If I find out Jordan or Pippen don't play tonight, I'll kill you."

Martin's heart froze. He had no fucking clue who played or didn't play in this game, but so help him God, Michael Jordan better suit up tonight.

Delmar watched as Martin's face turned pale. "I'm bustin' your balls, guy. Calm down!" The bookie threw his head back and cackled. Delmar walked around the desk and threw an arm around Martin's tense shoulders. "You hang out here and watch the game tonight, I'll cover your tab. Least I can do since you'll be giving me free money." He laughed again before opening the door, letting the music return in all its glory.

The tension somewhat left Martin and he managed a grin as he stood. "Very good one, Mr. Graff. You had me going there for a minute."

"Go see Teddy at the bar. Tell him to put whatever you want on my tab."

Delmar smacked him on the back again as Martin walked out. The door closed behind him and he could only wonder what the bookie and his "banker" were saying about his crazy bet.

Of course I get an open bar when I'm not drinking. Maybe I'll just have one.

13

Chapter 13

Two drinks in, Martin started to feel the room spin. Did traveling through time reset his alcohol tolerance?

Stop right now, dammit, he demanded of himself. *Stop before this entire day gets out of control.*

Martin stopped after the two drinks and returned to sipping Cokes. It was ten past one when he swallowed the last remnants of whiskey. He had nothing to do for the remainder of his Sunday and decided to spend the day at the bar while he waited for his payday at the end of the night.

Teddy, the young bartender, kept his soda topped off and small talk to a minimum.

Martin didn't mind as he sat by himself all afternoon, enjoying the spring training game on the big screen between the Colorado Rockies and Seattle Mariners.

Smoke continued to fill the bar, prompting Martin to take a brief stroll outside for fresh air. The day ended up warm, low 70's and sunny, a perfect day to be drunk on the balcony.

"What am I doing?" Martin asked himself as he leaned on the building. He wondered if getting mixed up with a bookie was worth it. Delmar had joked about trouble if Jordan didn't play in the game, but was he really joking? Would he find himself behind the bar tonight with his kneecaps busted?

He desperately wanted another drink to settle his nerves. If Jordan didn't play, maybe then he'd get blackout drunk to numb his body for any potential beating that might come.

As the sun descended toward the mountains, Martin returned to the bustle inside the bar where the smoke, music, and loud chatter battered around his head. The afternoon baseball games were ending, and there was one more hour until tip off for the basketball game at five.

The lull between games gave Martin the opportunity to order a greasy burger with hopes of it settling his stomach. Placing this bet was the first big change he made in the past, and not knowing how it could affect the rest of his time in 1996 kept him on constant edge.

You shouldn't have come here. You could have gotten a job anywhere. For fuck's sake, you're from the future. Go invent Google or something no one's heard of yet!

His inner wise man was right. The world was his oyster with the knowledge he brought from the future, yet here he was fighting off alcohol in a hole-in-the-wall bar owned by a not-so-subtle mobster.

After a few minutes of sulking in his regret, Martin watched as the main TV above the bar switched to the Bulls and Raptors game, Delmar and Hammer walking out of the office in sync. The mobster pulled out the stool beside Martin and plopped down, placing his ring covered fingers on the bar top.

"Thought I'd join you for the tipoff," Delmar said with a smirk. Martin's faced turned pale immediately. "Don't worry, I'm not gonna sit here and watch the whole game with you.

I'll come back toward the end if it's a close one."

"Sounds good to me," Martin said nervously.

Damn, I could really use a drink. His armpits soaked with perspiration as the pregame show concluded and the final commercial break came on before the start of the game. Michael Jordan came on to the screen, pushing an advertisement for Gatorade, and Martin's heart drummed as he waited to see Jordan come on for the actual game.

The commercials ended and the screen showed a bird's eye view of downtown Toronto where the game was taking place. The music continued to boom through the speakers, and Martin remembered how much he hated watching sports in a bar where he couldn't hear the game.

A young, dark woman came on the screen, speaking into a microphone while the players warmed up on the court behind her. The players cleared the court and headed toward their respective benches in anticipation of the tipoff.

Just show me Michael already. How have you not showed him yet?

The fact that they hadn't even shown a glimpse of the most famous athlete on the planet made him wonder if he was actually sitting out the game.

Finally, Michael Jordan stepped on to the court, adjusting his red shorts as he slapped hands with his opponents.

Thank Christ. Martin felt all the tension leave his body as he slouched in the barstool. Scottie Pippen also walked onto the hardwood and Martin knew the universe wasn't quite ready to fuck him over.

"You know you don't have a chance in this bet," Delmar leaned over.

Martin, feeling loose and relaxed, responded, "Just you

watch. Bulls are on the end of a long road trip. They want to get to the playoffs already. It's the perfect combination for Toronto to come out and steal a win."

Martin had no idea if any of this was true, but played the year to his advantage. Delmar couldn't log on to Google to confirm the Bulls schedule and would have to take his word.

"We'll see. Here we go." Delmar chuckled then leaned back and crossed his hands behind his head.

Martin's pulse pounded in his head and he wondered why he was still nervous. The starting lineup was healthy for the Bulls, eliminating any suspicion from his off-the-wall bet. He knew the outcome, so why the rush of adrenaline?

The thrill of gambling had its same attraction even when the result was set in stone. Having the bookie rub elbows with you during the game added extra spice as well.

The Bulls started the game on a 14-2 run, and Martin could see Delmar nodding his head out of the corner of his eye.

"Well, at least you tried," the mobster said, taking a sip from a glass of beer. "I'll be back later," Delmar said and returned to his office, Hammer following behind like an obedient puppy.

"C'mon, Raptors," Martin said under his breath and finished the glass of Coke in front of him.

The crowd in the bar shifted from the day drinkers to a somewhat younger crowd coming in for pre-dinner drinks. Many sat around the outer tables, with a young couple getting cozy on the opposite side of the bar where Martin watched them out of the corner of his eye. The woman wore a tight, glittery dress that revealed every curve on her slender body.

Her date, a buff man in jeans and a dress shirt, leaned over and whispered in her ear. She giggled as she brushed a lazy hand on his back. The man kept his face hidden, but Martin could sense him staring across the bar in his direction.

Martin returned his attention to the game and was pleased to see the Raptors tighten the contest to a six-point deficit after the sloppy start. On the next commercial break, he watched as the couple had their tongues in each other's mouths for a few seconds before they stood and exited the bar, the young man keeping a steady eye on Martin as they crossed the room, sending chills down his back.

"Excuse me!" Martin shouted to the bartender as soon as the couple was gone. "I need a shot of Jameson, please."

The bartender nodded and brought the whiskey over within a minute.

He said I would lose my emotions, not my mind. Goddammit, Chris, what are you doing to me?

Martin leaned back in his bar stool and tried to focus on the game, eyes staring at the basketball game, but not watching. Somewhere in Toronto the Raptors led the Bulls by one point at halftime, but all Martin could think about was Chris.

14

Chapter 14

Three shots later Martin cut himself off. He basked in the pleasure of knowing Delmar was nervous. Toward the end of halftime, Hammer approached Martin at the bar and proposed an offer from his boss.

"We'll pay you out on half your odds right now," the gargantuan man said.

That's not a bad offer, Martin thought, but he knew the outcome of the game. At the moment, he would win $4500 should the Raptors hold on to their lead. Hammer's proposal was to pay $2250 right now and call the bet off. Martin had never heard of such a proposal in sports betting, but supposed bookies were constantly wheeling and dealing to stay in the black. *He's sweating back there. He thought the Bulls would already be winning by 30, which they should be.*

Martin stared down this first crossroads since arriving in 1996 and considered his cash flow, his kneecaps, and his overall future. Hammer breathed heavily beside him as every scenario ran through his mind.

"Well, do we have a deal?" Hammer insisted.

"I'll pass. It's tempting, believe me, but I wanna see the game through the end."

"Whatever you say, pal – it's your money lost," Hammer said in a final attempt to pressure Martin. The lackey wheezed as he turned and left. It likely made no difference to Hammer what Martin did; he still got paid the same.

The game resumed and people started to trickle out for dinner, leaving Martin alone at the bar. The alcohol finally numbed his mind, and his confidence burst through the roof. "Let's go Raptors!" he barked as they extended their lead over the Bulls to six points. The music that had boomed all day now felt like background noise as all of his attention focused on the game. Even with no volume, Martin felt like he was there, hearing the squeaks of sneakers on the court, the players shouting, and the roar of the crowd. He grew so entranced and didn't realize he was the only person in the entire bar once the third quarter ended.

The game tightened, and the Bulls took a four-point lead into the final quarter, prompting Delmar to come out of his cave.

The music cut to silence, leaving only the sound of the buzzing neon lights decorating the bar.

"Well, here we go," Delmar said calmly, approaching Martin at the bar with his hands clasped together. "Fourth quarter time. We all know this is when Jordan puts the nail in the coffin."

The game broadcast blared through the speakers, bringing with it the steady hum of a sold out arena on the TV.

"The Raptors are very much in this game going into the final period. I'll tell you, no one here saw this coming tonight," the color commentator said as the game returned from the commercial break.

Martin sensed that Delmar was genuinely enjoying this bet and poked back.

"Jordan's tired, tonight's not the night. Just wait and see."

Delmar clapped Martin on the back and kept his hand gripped tightly on Martin's shoulder. *All those fucking rings.*

The mobster released his grip and sat in the stool next to Martin. "Mind if I finish the game here with you? I'll help wipe up your tears when it's over." He chuckled hoarsely. Hammer wasn't in sight, possibly staying in the room to prepare the crow bar that would bash Martin's knees into tiny shards.

The final twelve minutes dragged, practically staying frozen in the moment. Martin watched every single second tick off the game clock and approach zero. The contest continued its back-and-forth, the teams trading buckets. At one point Delmar ordered a round of shots for the two of them when the Bulls pulled ahead by eight with six minutes left.

"You're done!" he shouted over the speakers. "It was close, but it's over!"

Clearly someone has never watched basketball. It only takes 90 seconds to score ten points.

"Eight points in six minutes, you're getting cocky now," Martin said calmly.

On queue, the Raptors roared back, leaving the game tied with 30 seconds remaining. The Bulls had the ball and prepared to inbound. Martin watched Delmar out of the corner of his eye. The mobster fell silent, rocking in his barstool as the game had become a virtual coin toss.

Even though he knew Toronto would win the game, Martin still sat on the edge of his seat because he didn't know *how* they would win.

The Bulls threw in the ball to Michael Jordan. He made a quick spin move and darted toward the rim, elevating an outstretched arm towards the basket. Doug Christie, a long-time role player in the league, came from behind and swatted the ball out of Jordan's hand. Jordan then fouled the Raptors' center, who had rebounded the ball, out of frustration.

"Holy fucking shit," Delmar muttered.

The Raptors made one free throw to take a one-point lead, but the Bulls had one more chance and sprinted down the court. The Raptors fell out of position and left Steve Kerr, a three-point shooting specialist, wide open as the clock winded down to three seconds. Jordan passed the ball to Kerr and the stadium held its collective breath as he lifted for the deep shot.

The ball hung in the air forever, and actually looked in line to go in by Martin's judgment. It came down and hit the back of the rim, bouncing out and falling to the ground as the stadium erupted in chaos.

"The Raptors win! The Raptors win!" the commentator screamed as the players jumped around like they had just won a championship.

Delmar slammed a fist down on the bar, causing the empty shot glasses to hop and rattle.

"You have got to be shitting me," Delmar said, and gestured to his bartender to cut the volume. Seconds later, the empty bar fell silent. "Well, congrats. I'm shocked at what I just watched."

That makes one of us.

Delmar stood from his stool and stuck out a hand to Martin. "I hope you'll give me a chance to win this back."

Like I'm ever showing my face here again.

"Of course. Next time I have a crazy hunch, I'll be sure to

let you know." Martin winked at the mobster, his confidence soaring along with his alcohol levels. Delmar had ordered two more rounds of shots, and Martin now felt a familiar numbness in his lips and fingertips.

"Give me a few minutes to get your cash together," Delmar said before trudging away to his office. The heavy man seemed more disappointed than angry, and Martin suspected his knees would stay intact, at least for the time being.

The bar stayed silent as Martin watched the muted post game report where fans in Toronto danced outside the stadium. The win over the Bulls would serve as their best memory of an otherwise failure of a season.

Delmar returned moments later, a wad of cash wrapped in a white band. "Here you are. $4500 to spend on all sorts of fun things." He didn't stick the cash out toward Martin, instead holding it close to his body.

Martin stuck out an open hand, and Delmar forced himself to hand over the money. "Thank you for taking my bet. I'm new around here, so I'll definitely be back."

Not!

"I appreciate that," Delmar said softly, still a sliver of defeat lying beneath his attempted stern tone. "Don't go spending this all in one place."

"Of course not, I'll see you around." Martin stuffed the money into his back pocket and shuffled his feet backwards. Delmar held his ground and watched as the chubby man from the future inched toward the exit. The silence in the bar was deafening after a long day of constant noise.

Delmar didn't break his stare with Martin until he leaned into the exit door and a gush of fresh air blew through the doorway. In the dark lot, Martin ran to his car with a hand on

94

his back pocket to keep the money from spilling out. Crickets chirped in the silent and abandoned parking lot. The lights from inside the bar provided a soft glow, but no actual visibility to its surroundings. He felt eyes watching him, but had no idea where they were hiding in the night.

Get in your car and get the hell out of here.

Martin reached the car and fumbled in his pockets for the cool metal of his keys. He unlocked the door and turned on the ignition in a swift motion. Toni Braxton came on the radio as Martin sped out of the parking lot to the main road. He drummed his fingers on the steering wheel and kept checking his rear-view mirror for anyone who might be following.

15

Chapter 15

The next morning brought a pounding headache, but a wad of cash lay on Martin's nightstand, and he knew he was set for the next few months. He had driven to his apartment with a constant eye on the rear view, but no headlights followed after leaving the bar the night before.

"What now?" he asked his apartment. With money in hand and nothing but free time ahead, Martin decided it was time to finally track down his daughter. Before doing so, he'd need to find a liquor store as he owed a bottle to his landlord.

He dressed quickly, knowing a day of fun awaited with more booze. And Izzy. Thinking of her, knowing he would see her, caused a tense heartache that wouldn't go away. So many years had passed where all he wanted was to kiss his daughter on the forehead and smell her sweet, innocent scent before bedtime. *I'm gonna save you, Izzy, if it's the last thing I do.*

Once he was dressed and swallowed a few sips of mouthwash, Martin headed back to his car to drive to the local liquor store. The store was a few blocks past The Devil, which he drove by with regret. The money was nice, but his inner guilt reminded him that he had won his small fortune by cheating the system. What would Delmar do if he knew the truth? He'd either kill him or hire him to set absurd lines for future games, assuming he believed it.

Speculation did no good in a stressful time, and he reminded himself to focus on the task at hand.

He pulled in to the liquor store parking lot, seeing only one other car at its opening time of ten in the morning. A homeless man sat on the ground, leaning against the store, snoring. Martin parked and closed the door quietly to not wake the passed out drunk. *We've all been there, brother.*

Neon lights hung in every window, but none had been turned on yet. The sign on the door had been flipped to say, "We're open, come in!"

The hobo tipped over and grunted, licking his dry lips in a sticky sound that made Martin queasy. Martin pushed the door open and walked in to a chime from above.

A young Asian man stood behind the counter and watched Martin cautiously as he strolled in for what would surely be the first of many visits.

"Hello," Martin greeted from across the floor as he searched for the scotch section.

The clerk nodded in response, maintaining an awkward amount of eye contact toward Martin.

"I'm looking for a high-end scotch for a friend. Do you have anything special?"

"Yes. Back there." The clerk spoke urgently and nodded toward the back corner of the store where a rack of bottles stood next to fridges full of beer.

"Thank you." Martin pivoted and walked to the back, sensing the man's eyes on him the entire way. A radio blared with a morning talk show, filling the store with background noise. When he arrived to the rack of scotch, Martin was surprised to find such a wide selection for a hole-in-the-wall liquor store in Larkwood. Not many in town had the resources to buy expensive bottles of booze, but there were four different options priced over $100 for him to choose from.

Vinny would've been pleased with any free bottle, but Martin wanted to make a stronger gesture than a friendly wager. He wanted his landlord to know he was a man of his word, and that he took care of his friends. Vinny's reaction to receiving such a fine bottle would also show Martin everything he needed to know about the man.

Martin settled on a bottle of Johnnie Walker Blue Label, a newer blend, for the time, from the iconic distiller. He held the bottle in two hands, admiring its perfection, and knowing he could never afford such a bottle in 2018. *You better pour me a glass, Vinny.*

He turned to return to the cashier and froze, his heart leaping up his throat.

The Asian man stood five feet away from him with a rifle pointed directly at his face. Martin saw the blackness in the barrel, death taunting him with its black eye.

"Whoa, man, I don't want any trouble," Martin said, trying to sound calm beneath his panicked surface.

"Who are you? What do you want from me?" the clerk asked, his lips trembling nervously.

Martin gulped, wondering what the hell he did to make this man think he needed to pull a rifle on him.

"Look, I think you have me mistaken for someone else. All I want is this bottle." Martin stuck the bottle in front of him, but the clerk kept the gun aimed at his face.

"Bullshit! Who sent you?"

"No one sent me. I live down the street. I'm new in town."

"That's exactly what a Road Runner would say."

Road Runner? What the fuck?

"Okay, can you please put the gun down? I have no idea what you're talking about."

The man refused, and Martin's heart tried to burst out of his chest. The adrenaline heightened his every sense as he caught the light reflecting off the man's shiny black hair, heard the buzzing of the lights above, and could smell the overall fear present in the room. The man's eye appeared magnified through the scope he looked through.

"Tell me what year you came from and what your business is here," the man demanded.

"Uh." The question smacked Martin with shock and confusion. "I'm sorry, what did you just ask?"

"You heard me just fine," the clerk barked, not budging his shotgun.

"How do you know?" Martin uttered in a soft whisper.

"Stop playing with me and tell me who sent you!" the clerk screamed, his hair ruffling as his body convulsed in rage.

"An old man named Chris sent me here. I'm from the year 2018." Martin decided to stop asking questions and cooperate with the crazed gunman.

The clerk lowered the shotgun from Martin's face, but kept it pointed to his chest. The rage behind the man's eyes softened as he cocked an eyebrow. "And *why* are you here? In this year? In this city?"

Martin hadn't realized his hands were raised in defense, so he lowered them to his sides. "I've always lived in this city, born and raised. My daughter went missing in 1996...was never found. I'm here to figure out what happened."

The clerk lowered the shotgun more as it now pointed to Martin's knees. "Prove that Chris sent you."

"How do I do that?"

"Tell me the name of his store."

"Wealth of Time," Martin said with complete confidence.

"How did he send you here?"

"With a pill."

"What's the painting hanging on the wall in his back office?"

Martin closed his eyes and imagined the painting. "I don't remember what he called it, but it was a sailboat in a storm with Jesus Christ."

The response satisfied the man and he lowered his gun all the way to the floor, loosening his tense shoulders in the process. "Okay, I believe you. What's your name?"

"Martin," he said, his heart rate dropping back to normal.

"How did you meet Chris?" the clerk asked, still sure to keep his distance.

"At his store. My mom loves antique shops and dragged me in there."

"How did you know to come find me here?"

Martin threw his hands in the air. "I don't know what you're talking about. I don't know who you are. I honestly came in here to buy this bottle. Can you please tell me what's going on?"

"Did Chris not tell you?"

"Tell me what? That there are people who know I'm from the future? No, he didn't."

Martin's earlier fear had now morphed into anger.

"Okay, okay. Come with me to the front. I don't want someone to walk in and see us like this."

The clerk turned and shuffled his feet back to the cashier's counter. Martin saw the homeless man still outside, falling deeper into sleep as the morning grew warmer. The clerk returned his shotgun underneath the counter and slapped his hands on top, leaning in to Martin who studied the miniature bottles that stretched the length of the front wall.

"Where to start?" the clerk said under his breath.

"You can tell me your name," Martin said.

"Ahh, yes, of course. My name is Calvin Yoshiki. I'm a political historian from the year 2076 and am here studying the re-election and impeachment process of President Clinton for references that we need in the future."

"2076? But that year hasn't happened yet. It's only 2018."

Calvin raised an eyebrow to Martin and rubbed his chin aggressively. "Chris really didn't tell you much on how any of this works, did he?"

"Apparently not. I don't know anything about 2076, or Road Runners, or why you know I'm not from here."

"Okay, okay. I can explain." Calvin repositioned himself to face the door while he spoke. "Time is always happening; we just live in our current times based on birth. Just because it's 2018 where you come from, doesn't mean 2076 isn't happening somewhere else. Every era in history and the future rests in its own dimension. Chris provides us the means to jump across these dimensions for our work."

"Okay, I understand the time travel portion, just didn't understand going to the future was an option."

"Yes, of course. You can go anywhere, but you must have a reason. He doesn't send you for vacation. You need a purpose."

"So who are the Road Runners, and why do you want to

shoot them?"

"The Road Runners are evil bastards. They stole the potions from Chris and have been jumping through time trying to take over the world in every era of time. They will kill anyone who travels through time and doesn't join them on their mission."

"Why wouldn't Chris warn me of these people? How do you know who they are?"

"Look at me." Calvin stepped back and held his arms out.

"I don't see anything. You look like a normal guy to me."

And he did. Calvin was a twig of a man who would likely be toast against these Road Runners if not for his shotgun. Martin shrugged his shoulders.

"Look carefully. Stare at my arms."

Martin adjusted his focus, zeroing on the skinny arms that trembled slightly. A subtle, golden haze glowed from the man's skin.

Calvin saw the confusion fall over Martin's face and smiled. "You see it, yeah?"

"I think so. Are you glowing?"

"Yes! Exactly! Once you travel through time, your body emits the smallest amount of light. Something happens in the process that causes this, but everyone has it."

"You make it sound like there are a lot of people who travel through time."

"There are thousands of us. That's how I knew you were from another time."

Martin thought his eyes might be playing tricks on him; the glow wasn't visible unless he really focused on it. He held his own arm out and studied the same glow emitting from his skin.

"It's so hard to see," he said to himself.

"Yes, but in time you'll know how to look for it more easily."

"So what made you think I was one of these Road Runners?"

"Well, word is there are a couple in town. They usually like the finer things in life; they're very rich. So when you asked for an expensive bottle, I assumed you were one."

"Makes sense, but I can't be the only person to travel back in time and spend money. I might be poor in 2018, but with inflation, I'm rich now. I'm sure you're loaded with money, seeing how far from the future you've come."

"On the contrary, that's part of why I'm here. The year 2076 is ugly, my friend. We're on the verge of a dictatorship, and the economy is collapsing. We're studying the impeachment process, which is why I'm here."

"A dictatorship? In the United States? Impossible."

Calvin chuckled. "That's exactly what we all thought, but here we are, fighting for our democracy one day at a time. But we can have that conversation another time."

Martin nodded, not sure what to think. Fortunately, he'd be long gone by the year 2076.

"That'll be $126.98, please," Calvin said, placing the scotch in a brown paper bag. "You come find me if you need anything. We don't typically mingle, best to not be grouped together in case the Road Runners show up, but we do help each other. Don't be afraid to introduce yourself when you see another one of us."

"How do I know who the Road Runners are?"

"Oh, you'll know when you come across one," Calvin said and shot Martin a wink.

Well, that does me no good.

"It was great meeting you, Calvin. I honestly had no idea there were other people doing this."

"Pleasure's all mine. Best of luck finding your daughter. Come back any time if you need more booze, I'll give you a deal."

Martin had never heard more beautiful words spoken.

16

Chapter 16

With pieces of the puzzle finally falling in to place—granted, he hadn't been aware there was more to the puzzle—Martin returned to his apartment with a sense of accomplishment. Calvin had just taken him through Time Travel 101, and he now felt ready to take on whatever the past would throw his way.

Despite the information he had just learned, Martin felt relaxed, like he belonged in his current situation. He considered buying a gun to protect himself from the Road Runners, wondering if they would even bother a desperate father out on his own agenda. Martin felt relief knowing he was not alone in his time traveling adventure. Even if he never saw Calvin again, just knowing there were others out there made him feel less lonely on this journey.

He arrived to his complex and walked straight into Vinny's office where the landlord peered over a stack of documents. Martin kept the bottle hidden behind his back as he stepped into the office.

"Hey, Vinny."

Vinny looked up with droopy, tired eyes that quickly brightened up at the sight of his new tenant. "Mr. Martin! Quite the game last night. I saw the highlights. You were right, I can't believe it!"

"I know my basketball." Martin grinned and pulled the bottle out, dropping it on Vinny's desk. The landlord stared at it, and his eyes exploded once he realized the type of scotch. He grabbed it like a frantic child getting a new toy.

"Are you shitting me?" he whispered. "Where did you find this?"

"I have some connections," Martin said with a smirk.

"I've only ever heard of this scotch. It's like the fucking unicorn of scotches, but here it is on my desk! Holy shit!"

Vinny placed the bottle back on the desk and pushed it across to Martin.

"It's for you," Martin explained, realizing Vinny thought he was just showing off.

Vinny looked at the bottle, then to Martin with his giddy grin. "Get the fuck outta here," he said, revealing his inner Jersey accent that had remained hidden thus far. "Are you shitting me?"

"Not at all. I told you I'd get you a new bottle with my winnings. So there you go."

"And this is the bottle you decided to buy?" Vinny's eyes bulged.

"I won really big, what can I say?"

"Well get on over here and let's have a drink," Vinny said, standing to fetch a couple of glasses from his back cabinet.

"It's not even eleven yet, are you sure? I can come back later."

"I don't give a shit about the time when there's cause for

106

celebration. Have a seat."

Martin obliged and sat down while Vinny popped the bottle open and filled two short glasses with the expensive liquor. Vinny pushed a glass toward Martin.

"Cheers," the landlord said while holding his glass in the air. "To the Bulls shitting the bed. God bless it."

The two men talked, Vinny suddenly interested in learning everything he could about his new tenant. Martin told of his faux life as a fiction writer traveling the country in search for new inspiration. He lied about having no wife, no family, no history, really. Vinny never asked about any past books he might have written, keeping the conversation fairly high level. Half an hour later, they both had finished their glass of scotch when Vinny offered to refill it.

"I'll have to pass on round two. This has me ready for a nap, I don't know about you."

"Guess you can't hold your liquor at this high altitude." Vinny chuckled as he slapped his desk. "Suit yourself, but know you're welcome any time for a drink."

"I appreciate that," Martin said and extended a hand to shake.

"You let me know if you ever need anything at all. You seem like a good guy, so just let me know."

Martin nodded before walking out of the office. Because of one ludicrous bet he now had a friend and a half in Vinny and Calvin, not to mention the knowledge gained about how this time travel business actually worked. He returned to his room and collapsed on to his bed, falling into an instant sleep with a wide grin slapped across his face.

* * *

Over the next six hours, Martin enjoyed the deepest sleep of his stay in 1996. When he woke, his mind felt clear and energetic, ready to tackle his next task.

"Dammit!" he barked when he checked his watch, realizing he had slept the whole day away. He had planned to see Izzy today, ideally after school during her walk home, but it would have to wait another day now. She would be at home already, doing her homework while Lela cooked dinner.

I can still drive by, maybe catch a random glimpse.

Martin needed no further convincing as he grabbed his keys and ran out the door. He drummed his fingers on the steering wheel as he mentally planned his route. The house was a mile west of The Devil, so he pulled out and drove in the same direction for the third trip in a row, admiring the fiery orange sky above the deep blue mountains as the sun began its evening descent.

Heavy traffic appeared on the road for the first time since he'd been in town. Everyone was on their way home after a long Monday's work, and Martin enjoyed the fact he wouldn't have to work one single day while he poked around in the past. Somewhere in 2018 his body lay asleep, an entire minute having passed, while he continued his search for his daughter. One day this would all end and he'd wake up to go back to the post office for another miserable day at work.

Until then, he needed a taste of his own past and turned onto his old block, pulling over immediately at the corner where he could see his home eight houses down. Two cars were parked in the driveway, both his and his wife's.

"We're all home together," he said to himself, a wave of emotions running through his body. He imagined the inside of the house: Lela cooking, Izzy at the table with books and notepads splayed all over, and himself at the sink washing dishes. That was the routine as long as Martin worked a day shift. That would change later in the summer when he moved to the graveyard shift.

He pulled the car back onto the street and coasted toward his old home, its light green exterior sending ripples of memories. The grass appeared freshly cut, likely for the first time that spring.

He pulled up directly in front of the house and gazed at it when the front door swung open suddenly, and he saw himself.

The man who he had once been, athletic build and chiseled jaw, locked eyes with the familiar looking face in the car. Martin floored the accelerator, tires screeching in the quiet neighborhood, and zoomed out of sight. A sharp pain struck the back of his head like someone had stabbed him with a chef's knife. The world spun around him as he approached the end of the block, nearly clipping a few cars parked along the sidewalks. He slammed on the brakes once out of sight and panted heavily as if he had just run a mile.

"What the fuck?!" he gasped, fighting for breath. His lungs felt like someone was squeezing them.

"I told you not to see yourself!" Chris's voice echoed in his mind, except it didn't feel like a memory, it felt like he was actually speaking in his head. "You'll survive this encounter, but be careful!"

The invisible hands released their grip from his lungs, and the imaginary knife pulled out of his head. Martin grabbed his chest and rubbed his skull simultaneously. "What the fuck?"

he whispered.

This must be the price for seeing your past self.

Martin shook his head, unable to shake the intensity of what his body had just gone through. "Okay. So that's no bluff. Don't even look at my past self, got it."

He pulled back onto the road. Izzy would have to wait another day. He wouldn't approach her and would remain invisible with the many cars parked on the street. All he needed was to see her, to remember her presence. He could close his eyes any moment and see her face, hear her giggle, and smell her sweet scent. Feeling her presence, her soul, however, was not so straightforward. He couldn't picture the way she used to walk or the way her head bobbed when she spoke. These were the finer details that had faded as time passed.

Martin now knew exactly where the line was drawn in terms of interaction with his past self. He imagined the consequences would have been less severe had his young, handsome self not locked eyes with his uglier future version.

He drove back in the direction of his apartment, pulling into a restaurant parking lot. Dinner sounded like a good way to take his mind off things, perhaps a margarita, too. The Mexican restaurant, La Casa del Rey, had the lovely smells of grilled chicken and fresh tortillas oozing from its clay exterior. The sign in the front read "Bienvenidos, We're Open!"

His stomach growled at the thought of chips and salsa. The parking lot appeared packed for the dinner rush.

Martin killed the engine and strolled into the restaurant's lobby, ready to eat. A mariachi band played in the main dining room, their horns and guitars filling the air. A young boy who couldn't be older than twelve manned the host stand and greeted Martin with a warm smile.

"Good evening, sir," he said in a voice that cracked with the earliest signs of puberty. "Are you dining in tonight?"

"Yes, I am."

"I can get you a table, or you can find a spot at the bar if you'd like to not wait."

Now you're talking my language, kid.

"I'll try my luck at the bar. Thank you very much."

"Of course, just go through the dining room behind me and you'll see the bar on your left. Enjoy your dinner."

Martin nodded at the boy and followed the music into the dining room. Waiters ran frantically, serving the full tables, as dinner patrons carried on their conversations and enjoyed the ambiance. A waiter passed by Martin with a tray of sizzling fajitas, and he decided he would have that for dinner.

The bar had two vacant stools, front and center, facing a TV that hung above. Martin pushed his way through the crowd to claim his rightful spot. A young Mexican man tended the bar and wiped down the area in front of Martin as he sat.

"Good evening, sir," the bartender said, slipping a menu on the bar. "My name's Gio and I'll be taking care of you. Anything I can get you started to drink?"

"Yes, please. I'll have a glass of water and a margarita on the rocks."

See, you can be responsible, ordering the water. Your 2018 self would claim there was enough water in the ice cubes.

"House margarita?"

"Yeah, that'll be fine, thank you."

A waitress approached from behind Martin, reaching an arm over his shoulder with a loaded basket of tortilla chips followed by a bowl of salsa. He wasted no time diving in as he watched Gio create his margarita. The bar was also crowded, the empty

111

seat next to Martin the only open spot, but Gio appeared to have everything under control as he moved quickly and with purpose from one customer to the next.

Martin received his drinks, ordered his fajitas, and leaned back to relax and watch the sports highlights running on the TV. The music and chatter had finally drowned into background noise when someone tapped Martin on the shoulder.

"Excuse me, is this seat taken?" a blond woman asked, pointing to the open stool.

"It's all yours," he replied, sitting up and shifting over to allow the woman room to squeeze into the tight fit between stools.

Once she situated in her seat, Martin glanced from the corner of his eye and admired the slender, smooth legs coming out of her skirt, and followed them all the way up to her porcelain face. Her hair draped over her face as she read the menu, blocking his awkward gawk. She wore a tight blouse that revealed the slightest of pudge on her belly. He studied her hands and noticed they lacked the softness of youth.

She sat back and pulled her hair behind her ears as she turned to Martin. "Are you here alone?" she asked in a gentle voice.

"I am," Martin responded in his best calm voice. Blood started to rush to an area he hadn't felt in years as she looked at him with big hazel eyes.

"Yeah, me too. Was a long day at work. Just wanted to come have a drink to unwind."

"I hear that. What do you do?"

"I teach eighth grade history. I love the kids, but goddamn, at their age it's constant teenage drama. My head hurts, especially on a Monday after a quiet weekend." She spoke with a smile that revealed perfect teeth beneath her red lipstick.

History? Check her skin for the glow.

Now that he was skeptical of everyone he met, he focused on her skin in search of the golden glow. No glow, just silky flesh he had a sudden urge to run his fingers over.

"That's very cool, I'm sure it's fulfilling."

"It has its ups and downs for sure, but I enjoy it."

"What was your name?"

"I'm so sorry. It's Sonya," she said as she stuck out a hand for a formal introduction. "Or Ms. Griffiths, if you ask my students." She chuckled at herself and Martin grinned.

"I'm Martin Briar."

"Briar? I thought you looked familiar. Does your daughter go to my school?"

Holy fucking shit. Still think that alias was a bad idea?

"Uhhh... I don't have a daughter. You must be mistaking me for someone else." Sweat formed around Martin's head as he felt the heat in the room suddenly rise. The combination of tequila, sexual arousal, and nearly being caught by the random woman at the bar proved too extreme.

"Oh," she said, brows furrowing as she looked down at the bar. "I must be mistaking you. I'm pretty sure there is a Briar girl at my school, but I'm sure anyone could have that name."

Martin gulped his water in relief. Sonya had damn near caught him in a complicated web of lies, but she fortunately blew it off.

"So what is it you do?"

Your lie won't work here. This isn't going to be a brief conversation.

"I work at the post office."

"How cool! The one here in town."

113

"No, actually in Denver, but I live here."

"Ah, I see. That's too bad, I'm at the post office at least once a week. Would be nice to see a friendly face for once."

"We're not all bad," Martin said, leaning in with a tipsy grin. The tequila started to kick in and ballooned his confidence. "So, is there a reason you're out alone? Or do you just insist on the quiet time?"

"My teacher friends don't really like going out. Well, at least on a Monday. It's not exactly quiet here, just feels good to be around normal functioning adults every once in a while."

"Do you have any family here?" Martin asked, really wanting to know if she had a significant other.

"My parents are down in the Springs, but that's it. I'm a lone child. Got a couple cousins out in California, but that's really it."

The sizzle of fajitas arrived to disrupt their conversation after Martin had forgotten he had ordered them. Steam filled the air in front of him as the sizzle slowly died down.

"That smells *so* good!" Sonya said, not having removed her eyes from his plate. "Makes me feel like I missed out since I ordered a boring enchilada."

"You can have a bite of mine." Martin shot her a soft grin.

"You don't need to do that. I'm gonna be going soon – I ordered mine to go. Didn't think I'd meet such great company tonight or I would've planned to stay." She chugged the rest of the mojito she had ordered and slammed the glass down on the bar. "Do you have a phone number?"

Martin's heart raced, realizing he didn't have any way to be contacted. "I actually haven't set one up yet. Just moved in a week ago and still have a lot to take care of."

"Oh, I see." Sonya paused and studied her fingers as an

awkward silence hung between the two. "Well, how about this. Let's meet here next week. Same time, same place."

"Deal," Martin said quickly.

A waitress brought Sonya a white box with the enchilada inside.

"Great, it's a date. I'll see you next Monday, and next time I'm getting those fajitas."

Martin grinned. "Fajita date it is!"

She giggled as she stood from the stool and rubbed a hand along his back. "Have a good night, Martin." She disappeared into the crowded dining room and he watched her blond head bob toward the exit.

He returned to his dinner with a dumb smirk stuck on his face.

Did I just get hit on by someone way out of my league?

Her body language showed interest, and she did ask for his number. Meeting someone romantically had never occurred to Martin as a possibility when he prepared for his trip back in time. What could be better for a six-month stretch with nothing to do?

17

Chapter 17

The rest of the week proceeded with anxious anticipation. Martin couldn't remove Sonya from his mind for one second. The purpose of this trip was not to fall in love. While Sonya provided a great mental distraction, he needed to regroup and focus on his mission.

After the close call at his old house, he needed to plan for what should happen, what could happen, and the worst-case scenario, should Izzy see and approach him.

Staying in his car was critical. If she saw him, he would drive off again and hope to God his head wouldn't explode. Even though Chris had told him to not encounter his past self, he didn't want to chance bumping into anyone he might know. Chris apparently liked to leave out important details, so Martin would take caution with every action moving forward.

By Friday, Martin felt his plan was as close to perfection as possible. Every conceivable situation was addressed, scribbled down sloppily in a small notepad. He remembered seeing Calvin at the liquor store with a stuffed notebook and supposed everyone who bounced around time had to keep some sort of log and rules to keep their matters in line. Now he had his.

He kept his apartment free of booze, wanting to create his plans with a clear and focused mind. The temptation for a glass of whiskey always crept up, especially at night when he lay on his couch to watch TV, but anything that might compromise his mission could go and fuck itself.

After lunch he took a brief nap, setting his alarm for 2 P.M. When he woke, he slipped into his shoes and was out the door without a second thought. It was time to see Izzy.

* * *

School let out some time around three by his memory, so he wanted plenty of time to find a good hiding spot while he waited for the final bell to ring. He drove to Larkwood Middle School, a mere three blocks from his old house.

Martin arrived in a couple minutes, the brick school standing tall just as he remembered. Being the only middle school in town, he assumed Sonya was also inside the building.

Two school buses lined up in front of the school, meaning the final bell was indeed close to ringing. Martin found a spot under a tree across the street. He made a U-turn to face the direction where his daughter would walk, and slipped on a fedora and sunglasses.

He brought the latest edition of *Sports Illustrated Magazine* with Dennis Rodman on the cover, posing the question if he was the best rebounder ever. The pages flipped between his fingers, but his eyes remained glued to the school; he couldn't take a chance in missing Izzy walk out.

The clock on his dashboard read 2:32, and Martin put the magazine down to enjoy the beautiful day by rolling down his window for fresh air. This would also allow him to hear the bell ring.

He waited as cars passed and parents walked by. The air felt still, and Martin couldn't help but wonder if the past was somehow preparing for his secret encounter with his daughter. As the neighborhood fell eerily silent, the bell rang, echoing around the schoolyard and surrounding houses.

About twenty seconds passed before the school's front doors swung open and students poured out of the floodgates.

"Holy shit," Martin whispered to himself. Within a minute there were at least fifty students scattered around the entrance, some lining up for the bus, others walking back to the parking lot to meet their parents, and the rest walking off the schoolyard to cross the street where he waited.

He felt like a detective as he slouched in his seat, allowing only his eyes to see out of his rolled down window. Izzy would be one of the smaller girls to cross the street, having always been behind the curve in terms of size. When she was twelve she could have passed as nine by looking at her, but once she opened her mouth and let her wit and intelligence flow out, one might think she was actually sixteen.

Little boys and girls crossed the street, adamantly looking both ways before doing so. Giggles and screams bounced around as Martin narrowed his focus on the main crosswalk. It was half a block ahead of him, a clear view. When Izzy entered the crosswalk, he'd pull onto the road and drive behind her as she walked the three blocks home, following like a secret guardian.

Countless little people crossed the street as the crowd on

the school's front lawn slowly died down.

"Where are you, Izzy?"

Both buses pulled away, and Martin's heart stopped mid-beat as his hands started to tremble. There she stood, backpack slung over her shoulders, hands crossed over a thick textbook in front of her chest, as beautiful as he remembered with her sandy hair tied in a ponytail that bobbed with each movement she made. She hugged another girl and started toward the crosswalk.

Martin wiped away the tears that streamed from his eyes. "Izzy," he mustered, a bowling ball lodged in his throat. Seeing her proved way more intense than anticipated; Martin couldn't stop his hands from shaking. His lips quivered as he could no longer hold back his emotions. The slow welling of tears burst into a flowing river down his face.

Twenty-two years.

He thought he'd never see her again, but there she was, crossing the street. Martin turned on the car through blurred vision. He slouched as the engine fired up, hoping it hadn't drawn any attention to himself, but Izzy crossed the street, oblivious that her father from the future had his eyes locked on her.

He pulled onto the street, coasted one block, and turned right to follow her, remaining roughly five houses behind her as she strolled through the neighborhood, ponytail swinging from left to right with each step.

Martin physically couldn't take his eyes off her. What was she thinking about on her walk home? Did she know her life would change in just a few months? Did she know her parents would never stop searching for her, even when the police had given up hope? Did she know just how much she was loved and adored?

He desperately wanted to run her down, squeeze her, kiss her face, and never let go. The past and future be damned, he wanted to hold his daughter right now. But the reminder from his prior encounter with himself kept him gun-shy from making any other moves.

Aside from the fact that he was looking at his daughter, the walk home was uneventful. She moved at a steady pace with her head down, not stopping to greet the dogs that ran up to her at the fences she passed, not looking at the cars that passed by. She'd always had that tunnel vision, an intense focus on the task at hand, and apparently walking home from school was treated no differently.

The walk took an entire five minutes as he watched her turn into the front yard and climb the porch steps to the door. He stopped before the car would be visible to his old house, not wanting to chance anything after such a beautiful moment of stalking. A wall of bushes that separated his house from his neighbor's provided the cover he needed. He could see her through the bushes, rummaging through her backpack for the house key.

No one's home.

The temptation to knock on the door swelled even more, but it was only day one.

"You're not here to kidnap your daughter. Father Time probably wouldn't like that too much." Martin had to constantly remind himself that he was only here to learn what happened. *And intervene when the time comes.*

She entered the front door and closed it behind her, leaving Martin to ponder what she was doing inside as he drove away, knowing himself and Lela would come down the block within the next hour.

18

Chapter 18

Martin spent his weekend unable to focus on anything, not that anything required serious attention to begin with. After finally seeing Izzy and knowing she was okay, he couldn't bear the thought of waiting in anticipation of her future disappearance. *There has to be a way to both prevent it and keep the time travel gods happy.*

He had already tested the boundaries, though by accident, in regards to encountering his past self. Now, he needed to know exactly how far he could get away with changing an event, ideally a drastic one, that didn't involve his past self or family. Larkwood wasn't exactly an eventful city, but Denver would surely have some tragedy he could try to prevent or alter. Martin pulled out his cell phone, praying by some miracle that it would work so he could research 1996, but it continued with a red X where his service bars should have been.

He thought back to all the tragedies he could remember from the 90's. The ones he remembered would have already happened by 1996. Then, as if someone had flipped on a light switch and slapped him across the face, he remembered what he had so closely followed in the final year of the decade: the Columbine High School shooting.

The shooting wouldn't occur until April of 1999, but the two shooters, who were seniors at the time of the shooting, would have been wrapping up their freshman year in the spring of 1996.

"Eric Harris and Dylan Klebold," Martin said to himself, sitting down on the couch. He had saved every newspaper article about the massacre in the months following it, wondering what could have turned two high school boys into such monsters. He remembered they had constructed bombs in their parents' garages while gradually building up an arsenal for the shooting. "Can I actually stop this from happening?"

There was no denying the effects the massacre had on society, seemingly kicking off what would become a normal part of American culture with bullied young men lashing out against innocent people.

I can get to these boys years before they may have even thought about shooting their classmates.

The thought sent chills up his spine. Who was he to try and stop what would be the deadliest school shooting for years to come? Would the past allow him to even contact these boys? He had no idea where to begin such a task. Should he talk to them, try to preach love and change their hearts? Should he just walk up to them in their garage one day after school and shoot them on the spot? That would certainly be the biggest attempted change to history, or the future, depending how you looked at it.

The chills gave way to twisting knots in his gut. Doubt shuffled its way into his mind. "I can't actually stop Columbine from happening."

Having skipped out on drinks all week, he poured a glass of whiskey to help settle his nerves. *Maybe this is my fate. To save Izzy and save all those innocent kids.*

He refilled his glass and chugged the booze to lull himself into a long Saturday nap. All he really wanted was someone to bounce these ideas off, but he'd have to keep them buried in his mind until he saw Chris again. *Come and find me, old man.*

* * *

Martin jumped out of bed on Monday morning. He had spent the rest of the weekend keeping his mind distracted with alcohol and fighting the urge to drive by his old house and see what his once happy family was doing. He also soaked in his responsibility as the man to stop a travesty across town, three years away. The fact that the event was so far out is what ultimately convinced him to move forward with it. He wouldn't be around in 1999 to see what eventually happened. When he returned to life in 2018, he could look up Columbine High School and see there was no tragedy that had ever occurred. He'd be the city's biggest hero without anyone knowing why. Living with a fulfilling secret like that seemed like a much needed addition to his dismal life in 2018. Chris could take his emotions and shove them up his ass. Martin would know he had done the right thing, and emotions wouldn't matter at that point.

Martin dressed quickly and left for the library. The library was one block from the church and he saw its pile of ashes dwindle as construction crews filled the lot. His mom was probably there helping, but he managed to push the thought of her out of mind.

He hadn't been to the library since he was a child, but it all looked the same from his memory: plain brown siding, dirty windows, and not an open spot in the tiny parking lot. He parked on the street and walked a block to the main entrance that welcomed him with the musty smell of old books.

The entrance opened to a wide, open floor, shelves of books to the right, tables in the middle, and three computers to the left where two elderly people occupied the machines. In front of the bookshelves stood a tall desk where a heavyset woman sat behind a computer screen, her eyes peering around behind pointed glasses. She smacked her red lips as she watched Martin approach her desk.

"Good morning," he said. "Do I need a library card to use the computers?"

"Yep," she replied in a snotty voice.

"Can I get one?"

"Yep. You got an ID?"

Martin paused. He did have an ID. From 2018. "What do you need an ID for?"

"Need to verify your address."

Martin pulled out his wallet and held it open to the snarky librarian, keeping his thumb over the important dates on his driver's license, but allowing her to see his address, which was still in Larkwood.

"Thank you," she said flatly. "Give me five minutes and I'll have your new card ready. Feel free to grab the open computer. If you need to print anything, it'll be five cents per sheet."

"Thank you kindly," Martin said in the gentlest voice he could muster, hoping he could make this miserable woman's day a little better.

He crossed the library and sat down at the open computer. The elderly couple paid him no attention and continued clicking around on their screens. Martin opened the browser and punched Google into the web address. After thirty seconds of loading, the screen came back with an error message: THAT DOMAIN DOES NOT EXIST.

Oh, shit. Do I buy that domain? What could come of that?

The thought left his mind quickly, as he needed to gather all the information available for Columbine High School. He went to MapQuest instead, the main source for finding where to go at the time. The results came back and let him know that the school was 31 miles away, a 40-minute drive, and included turn-by-turn directions on how to get there. Martin printed these directions. There was no satellite imagery available, no way to view the school from the street. The technology of the future was something he had taken for granted as he realized his capability to research the school was limited.

He switched the browser to Yahoo, the new search engine that everyone was talking about since they could find any bit of information. *If you all only knew how obsolete Yahoo will become.*

Martin typed the school's name into the search bar and waited another minute for the results to come back. The elderly couple had left Martin alone to wait impatiently for the slow computer to work its magic.

The search returned exactly what he wanted: Columbine's official website. He clicked on it and found nothing but disappointment. The site had the school's name in big letters across the top banner, and *HOME OF THE REBELS!* Beneath. *That's it?* There was no menu, no pictures, nothing.

Jesus Christ. Martin had to remind himself that people were literally in the learning stages of building websites and using the Internet in general. The school's IT person, if such a position existed, likely threw together the most basic HTML knowledge he could find off Yahoo.

With zero information, aside from the directions, Martin called it quits, accepting defeat to the lost cause that was mid-90's Internet. He grabbed his directions from the printer next to the computers, dropped 15 cents into the change box, and visited his favorite librarian to pick up his card.

"Done already?" she asked, sliding over the card.

"Yeah, just needed to print some directions."

"Fine then, we'll see you next time."

"I look forward to it." Martin winked at her, yet she remained cold and stone-faced. *One day I will get you to smile.*

Martin left the library to return home and set an actual plan in stone. He also had a date later that night to prepare for.

* * *

Martin stopped to buy a telephone on his way home and would need to call the phone company to activate his line and get his new number. By his memory, phone numbers were still only seven digits, as there hadn't been a need for area codes quite yet. The nostalgia seemed to snowball a little more with each passing day as something always reminded him how simple and silly life used to be.

When he arrived home, Martin pulled out the notebooks he had also purchased at the store and flipped one open to its first, fresh page.

COLUMBINE, he wrote across the top and underlined with a jagged line. He wrote down everything he could remember off the top of his head:

-*April 20, 1999*
  -*Eric Harris and Dylan Klebold*
  -*Pipe bombs and handguns*
  -*Started in the cafeteria*
  -*Ended in the library*
  -*Both had parents who weren't around*
  -*Both were bullied throughout high school*

That was all he could piece together for the time being. With these few facts in front of him, he decided he had a few options as how to approach his heroic act. Would the right move be to try and stop the bullying? Help the kids feel more involved with their peers?

He'd have plenty of time to solidify his game plan. Later in the week he'd drive down to the school to see if he could even locate the two boys. It would likely require multiple visits to find them, then follow them, and learn their routine. They may have not even been friends yet during their freshman year, so he might have to follow them separately to see exactly what they did after school.

Martin closed his notebook and stuffed his papers neatly inside. He'd had enough of playing detective for the day, and began to prepare for his date with Sonya.

19

Chapter 19

The ambiance at La Casa del Rey was the exact same as last week. The mariachi band sang the same songs (they all sounded the same to Martin), the chatter echoed around in a way that made his head ring, and Gio poured drinks at the bar.

Martin shuffled through the crowded dining room to find a spot at the bar when he saw Sonya already sitting there with two full margaritas in front of her. Her back was to him, and he took the chance to admire her beauty. He was glad to have dressed nicely for the occasion, seeing as she wore a sparkly black dress that cut off mid-thigh to show off the legs that had driven him wild when they first met. Her hair curled down to her bare back, and Martin caught the scent of perfume as he approached her.

"I hope one of those is for me," he said.

She turned in her stool with a wide grin that showed her perfect teeth and gentle eyes. "It sure is. I was thinking we have a drink and get out of here. I know somewhere that's not so chaotic where we can actually converse without yelling."

"Works for me."

Sonya handed him his drink and he remained standing beside her, as no other seat was open at the bar. They talked about their weekends, Sonya having used hers to grade papers and catch up on sleep.

The small talk faded along with the margaritas. They both devoured a basket of chips and salsa before Martin waited for Sonya to suggest the next move.

"Let's go," she finally said after listening to one more song from the mariachi. She jumped off of the barstool and grabbed Martin's hand, pulling him through the crowded room toward the exit. The smells of food mixed with her trailing scent of fruity perfume.

Sonya didn't slow down as she barreled through the door, taking them back outside where the evening started to cool off.

"I like it here, don't get me wrong, but I thought we'd make this a more formal date," she said, continuing to walk to the parking lot. "I can drive."

Martin followed his spontaneous date to her car, a newer Toyota sedan with a bumper sticker that read: *IF YOU CAN READ THIS, THANK A TEACHER!*

"Sweet ride," he said casually as he closed the passenger door. "So, where are we going on this mystery date?"

"There's a restaurant right outside of Denver that one of my student's parents owns. He has a standing discount for any faculty from the school, and I like to take advantage from time to time."

"I see. I can drive us if you wanted to drop your car off at home."

"It's fine. I insist."

She giggled again, an innocent, charming sound that now

combined with her scent in a mixture that made Martin's head spin, and his heart tingle.

Don't fall in love. That's not what you came here for. You're here for Izzy and nothing else.

"Martin?" she asked, interrupting his thoughts.

"Sorry, I zoned out for a minute."

"I asked if you like steak?"

"Yes, absolutely."

"Okay, good. Because we're going to a fancy steakhouse. Just wanted to make sure."

She popped in a cassette tape and they listened to a young Celine Dion during the rest of the drive across town.

* * *

They pulled up curbside to a valet parking attendant who greeted them with a warm smile. Martin grabbed her hand and led them toward the golden double doors that led to the stone building called Lavender.

Shrubbery decorated the outside of the building, purple neon lights running along the ground on the walkway into the entrance. Soft jazz greeted them as they stepped in to the lobby, where the host welcomed them from behind a tall stand.

"Welcome to Lavender," he said in his most formal voice to match his three-piece suit. "Do you have a reservation this evening?"

"Yes, sir," Sonya said. "It should be under Sonya Griffiths."

The man peered down a list with a keen eye and pursed lips

until he found the name. "Perfect. Give us one minute to prepare your table, Ms. Griffiths."

"Cool-looking place," Martin observed as he looked around at the dim lighting and upscale art covering the walls.

"Yeah, don't think I'd ever be able to eat here if it wasn't for the discount. Ray takes such good care of us teachers."

"This way, folks," the host said, now holding two menus as he stepped out from behind his stand. He led them through the main dining room and to a back private room where a lone table awaited them, candles flickering in the center, two glasses filled with red wine in front of each seat.

The host pulled out a chair for Sonya and shuffled around the table to do the same for Martin, who thanked the man.

"Your server will be with you folks in just a minute. Have a pleasant dinner." He bowed out of the room hastily.

"So what's good here?" Martin asked.

"Everything," Sonya said. "I usually get a steak, but I've heard the seafood is great, too, if that's your thing. I'm not a fan of seafood in general."

"Neither am I."

"Well, then, no sushi dates for us!"

Martin chuckled and opened his menu, falling deep into the many options to choose from, and noting the hefty price tag with each item.

"Good evening, folks," a voice came from behind Martin, whose back faced the door. It sounded older and a bit too familiar for his liking. He looked up to Sonya and saw a wide grin on her face as she watched the approaching waiter. "How is the wine?"

The waiter stood at the side of the table, looking down at them from his dark eyes, his frosty hair standing out in the dim room. The man locked eyes with Martin, making him feel somewhat possessed.

"My name is Chris, and I'll be taking care of you folks tonight. Have we had a chance to look at the menu?"

"The wine is delicious, and I don't think we've decided on dinner yet," Sonya said.

"Very well," Chris said, turning to Martin. "Any questions, sir?"

Martin gazed up like the waiter was a planet in the night sky. His throat clenched as no words came out when he opened his mouth to speak.

Chris laughed. "Very well, sir. I know our menu can be a bit overwhelming. I'll come back in a couple minutes to check on you." The old man left the room as Martin's jaw hung open.

"What's wrong with you?" Sonya asked in a stern tone. "Are you okay?"

"I'm fine," he mustered. "I just . . . need a minute. Let me use the restroom and splash some water on my face. This room is hot, don't you think?"

"Okay?" Sonya's face scrunched into confusion.

Martin excused himself, stepped out of the private room, and followed a long hallway to the restrooms. He pushed open the swinging door and found Chris standing at the sink, hands under the faucet, an evil smirk on his face in the mirror.

"Martin, my friend! I knew you'd come find me here." Chris's voice returned to the more laid-back, eccentric version of itself that he had known.

"What are you doing here?" Martin asked.

"Take it easy. I'm here because you asked me to come. Did you not?"

Martin thought back to the other day when he had wished

for Chris in his thoughts, but couldn't recall saying anything out loud.

"You don't have to say it out loud. I can hear your thoughts, my friend."

The statement sent a new wave of chills through Martin's body as he felt his arm hairs standing stiffly underneath his sleeves.

Martin studied the bathroom stalls, looking for feet beneath the doors.

"Don't worry, we're alone. You should get back to your date. You look to be doing just fine." Chris grinned as he turned off the faucet, and splashed his wet fingers into the sink.

"I asked for you for a reason. Why did you leave out so much information?"

"You talked to Calvin, yes? He's a good guy. I send all of you through time on a level playing field. I only inform you of the cardinal sin to not break." Chris smirked, staring into Martin's soul. "There are lots of little things to know, more than I could ever cover. It's best to learn as you go."

"So I'm supposed to just live each day like normal and hope some crazy Road Runner doesn't snipe me from a rooftop?"

Chris laughed. "You should worry about the Road Runners, but they're not as intense as Calvin might have you think. Yes, they have an evil agenda, but they don't just attack for no reason."

"How do you know all this? Do you have some master security cameras that you watch in your tiny room and get off to watching me struggle?"

Chris threw his head back and howled, his white hair dancing. "Of course not. I'm the keeper of time, I can jump around to wherever and whenever. If I wanted, I can know what you're going to do before you do."

Martin stood in silence and looked down to his feet.

"Look, I'm here to help if you need. I can't help you on your actual mission, but I'm here if you need to talk. For now, just go back to your date – she's starting to worry. Try to relax, everything will be fine. Enjoy the 90's. What a time to be alive!"

"I swear to God, if anything happens to me, I'll kill you."

"I'm sure you will," Chris mocked with a wink. "Now, I have a table to wait, I suggest we get back out there."

Chris shuffled past Martin, leaving him alone to stare in the mirror and wonder what the fuck he had gotten into.

"Be normal. Breathe. You have a beautiful date, go enjoy the night," he said to himself before stepping out.

He walked back down the long hall and returned to the private dining room where Sonya waited with a now empty glass of wine. A basket of bread had been placed in the middle and she started to apply butter to a slice.

"I'm so sorry. Can we just start over right now?"

"Sure," she said. "Is everything okay?"

"Yes. I've got so much going on, my mind has been in the clouds. I haven't been able to focus and give you all my attention, so I do apologize for that."

"No worries. Let's move on. I'm ready for dinner."

"Me too. I think I'm just gonna order the prime rib, something nice and heavy."

"That's what I was gonna get! I already ordered sides, so those should be out soon."

They dined and drank wine for the next two hours, falling into deep conversations about past relationships, family, and hopes for the future. Trust developed easily between the two as they swapped stories, a new waiter dropping in from time to time. Martin's mind tried to wonder where Chris had gone, but he maintained his focus on the beautiful woman across the table.

"Let's get out of here. Wanna have one more drink back at my place?" Sonya asked after they paid the check.

"I'd love to," Martin said, his heart fluttering at the thought. *Maybe I'll save Izzy and just stay in 1996 after all.*

20

Chapter 20

Martin hadn't made love to a woman in nearly ten years, settling for quiet evenings with bottles of whiskey and his reliable hands. He rarely sought women after finalizing the divorce with Lela, and had only had a fling with a low-rate stripper over a drunken weekend in Las Vegas. She was a classy lady who offered to share her cocaine before she took her clothes off in the one-star motel off the strip.

Sonya was a drastic improvement. There was no cocaine, just a glass of wine before she stepped out of the bathroom wearing lacy, black lingerie with a seductive smile. She led him into her bedroom where they spent the rest of the night together.

In the three weeks following, they had done this same routine at least five times a week, sometimes at his apartment, unable to keep their hands off each other. For Martin, it was more than sex; he felt a tingle in his soul that had fallen dormant. While he couldn't bring himself to call it love, he knew that's what it was. Falling in love could devastate his plans to save Izzy. If Sonya was present in his life every day, then how would he explain what he was up to without blowing his cover? Would Sonya even care? Or believe him?

She still had school every day, but summer break was fast approaching. As far as she knew, he had to drive downtown every day for work. He'd have to start spending the days outside of the house, and Columbine High School would be a good place to start.

So, the answer is yes, Martin. You can have a relationship and accomplish what you set out to do.

As the final week of April began, Martin felt ready to jump in to his half-hearted plan. He wanted more information before driving all the way to Littleton, but it was simply unavailable thanks to the technological restrictions of the time. He really wished he could jump back to 2018, even for ten minutes, to gather needed information, but he'd have to approach this like a true detective.

On Monday, April 22, Martin jumped in his car with the printed directions to Columbine. His first task was to locate the two young boys who were still three years away from shooting their classmates. *Find them and follow them.*

Once he had an idea of their routines, he'd then decide what action to take in trying to stop them. Aside from stopping the massacre, Martin hoped to learn the boundaries of changing history. Because of this, he stopped at the liquor store first to have a brief chat with an old friend.

When he entered, Calvin greeted him with a warm smile. "Martin, how are you?"

"I'm doing good, how have you been, Calvin?"

"Very good, thank you. You need more of your fancy scotch?"

Martin laughed. "Not today. I actually ran into Chris, and

he told me to come see you if I had any questions."

"Chris was here?"

"Well, not here, but a restaurant downtown. He said you're a great guy to come to with any questions, that you know a lot about how this all works."

"Yes. We need to keep these conversations quick, though."

"Understood. I really have one question today."

Calvin looked around the store to confirm they were alone. Apparently no one ever visited him in the mornings. "Okay, go ahead."

"I want to know about making changes to the past. Can it be done? How big of a change can you make?"

"I've never made big changes personally. But I do know of people who have attempted." Calvin spoke in a lowered, serious tone, keeping his eyes glued to the door where anyone could walk through.

"Attempted?"

"Yes, attempted. It's practically impossible to change a major historical event. The bigger the impact an event had on society, the more resistance you'll run into. I know a guy who traveled to 2001 to try and prevent the terror attacks of 9/11. His truck exploded the night of September 10 while he was driving to dinner, never to be seen again."

"Holy shit."

"Holy shit is right. However, saving your daughter shouldn't have too much resistance, as it wasn't something that directly impacted society as a whole. There will be some challenges, don't count it out, but I doubt it will be anything life-threatening."

"I've been toying around with the idea of stopping the Columbine shooting."

"Columbine? Can you refresh me what that was?"

"Major school shooting in 1999. The two shooters are currently freshmen at the high school."

"I see. Where I'm from—er, *when* I'm from—a lot has been removed from the history books. Censorship has skyrocketed under the administration. That's why many of us have traveled back in time to rewrite history books for our safekeeping. It's like an underground Wikipedia we're trying to build."

"Oh, so you still have Wikipedia in the future?"

"Sure, but it's all censored. I guarantee you there's no trace of Columbine High School if I were to look it up. Anything negative toward the Second Amendment gets automatically censored."

"Damn, glad I'll be dead long before then."

"Yeah, it sure is an interesting time. To answer your question, though, I'd say you'll have to be the judge as to how big of an effect this shooting had on society. I'm not familiar with it myself."

"At the time, it was the deadliest school shooting ever. President Clinton flew out here to deliver a speech. Personally, I consider it the shooting that sparked the hundreds that followed afterwards."

"Hundreds of shootings? I remember when I was younger, maybe around 2020 or so there were a few shootings, but they slowly started to fade. Then again, they could still be happening, we just never hear about them."

"I'm not gonna lie, I'm pretty intrigued to visit your future, just to see what the world is like."

"It's not pretty, believe me."

"What do you think I should do?" Martin asked, tossing his hands in the air.

"Why do you wanna do this? I thought you were here for your daughter. Seems silly to me to risk her life for anything else."

"I have a lot of time to kill between now and September. My daughter is in her routine; nothing changes between now and then."

"So you're bored and wanna change the world?"

"Not bored, I've just never had the opportunity to do good for the world. I've lived in a black hole since Izzy went missing and have run on autopilot for the last two decades of my life. But, here, I feel so *alive.* So alert and sharp. It would be a waste to sit around and watch baseball all summer."

Calvin nodded, a closed fist over his mouth. "It sounds to me like your mind is already made up. Just make sure you're careful, the past has a way of knowing what you're thinking, and will push back. I don't wanna hear about your car exploding while on a drive. I'd say if the president flew out here, then we're talking about a very big deal."

Martin nodded. "I'm just gonna follow these kids around and see what kind of opportunity there is."

"No harm in that. Just be ready for resistance. When you feel it, it's time to let off. You should probably get going now. We've been talking way too long. Try to stay away from here for at least another month if you can."

The way Calvin spoke made Martin wonder if someone was watching them. Surely Chris was, but there was no reason to fear the old man.

"Understood, thanks for your help again." Martin stuck out a hand to shake with Calvin. He left the liquor store behind and would never return, if he could help it.

21

Chapter 21

Martin arrived at Columbine High School forty minutes later. The directions took him on a couple of wrong turns, stranding him in the middle of an unfamiliar neighborhood. He had to resort to an old practice that had since gone out of style in the mid-twenty-first century: going into a gas station to ask for directions.

The attendant pointed him in the right direction and he pulled into the school parking lot two minutes later. He sat in the parking lot, facing the school's main entrance. The entrance was a wall of blue glass that reminded him of a shallow beach. Beige stone walls made up the rest of the school's exterior. Nostalgia filled Martin's tiny car as he stared at the building where hell would break loose and change the landscape of America for many years to come.

Maybe I shouldn't be here.

He sensed the magnitude of his side project and a natural doubt crept in.

"Don't be a chickenshit – you're here, just go look around. It's 1996, you can probably walk into the school and no one will pay you any attention."

Schools didn't have a reason for high security measures yet. The doors would be unlocked, there would be no security guard on duty, and there might not even be a sign-in sheet.

"Hi, I'm here to meet Eric Harris and Dylan Klebold so I can save your life," Martin said to the imaginary secretary.

He stepped out of the car and took a deep breath of fresh air. The grass on the front lawn was already a deep shade of green where a handful of students sat cross-legged with textbooks in their laps and composition books on the side. The school had to have housed at least 2,000 students based on its sheer massiveness.

We're not in Larkwood anymore, he thought, remembering his high school was lucky to even have patches of grass to sit on for mid-morning studying.

Martin glanced at his watch to see lunchtime would be right around the corner. He walked to up a young girl on the lawn, and she looked up at him from behind big glasses and flashed a smile full of braces.

"Hello," Martin said. "I just had a quick question."

"Good morning, sir," she replied warmly. "Are you looking for someone?"

"No. I'm actually just wondering about your school. My family has moved to town and I'm out and about today checking out the different campuses."

The girl stood up, brushed grass off her jeans, and stuck out a skinny arm to shake his hand. "Welcome to town. My name's Amy. I'm a junior here."

"Nice to meet you, Amy." Her overwhelming kindness caught him off-guard. "My name is Martin."

"What kind of questions did you have?"

"How big is your class?"

"I think we have a little over 400 students in my class."

"Are the classes separated? Like are freshman in one section of the school? Seniors in another?"

"For the most part. Classes are in different parts of the school, but our lockers are all separated by class, so everyone stays within their class for the most part during the day."

"I see. Do you know if the school offers any tours?"

"I think so. You should be able to go into the office and they can help you with that."

"Thank you, I think I'll do that. You've been very helpful, Amy."

"You're welcome."

The school's bell rang out across the lawn at noon, prompting everyone to return inside the building. Martin waited back until it appeared everyone had gone inside, and then he followed.

He stood in front of the school, watching dozens of students cross paths through the glass, and wondered if Eric and Dylan were in the mix. The thought sent chills up his back that he didn't notice.

Once the halls had cleared of traffic, Martin strolled to the building's double doors and pulled. The door didn't budge, shuddering in place as he kept pulling on it. His heart raced as he wondered if this was the past already pushing back at him. Schools didn't lock their front doors until *after* the shooting that changed the world.

The entryway was wide with three sets of double doors, so he shuffled down to another and pulled the door open with no resistance. He giggled at himself for panicking so quickly at one door being locked out of the six.

The hallway in front of him led straight back 100 feet before splitting into two separate directions. The walls were lined with blue lockers and a banner hung from the hallway's entry that read: *HOME OF THE REBELS!*

The main office was directly to Martin's right. He started toward the office when a cold hand tickled his back. He turned around to find no one. The hairs on his arms stood stiffly as he decided it was all in his head.

The secretary inside the office watched him through the doorway, and waved him to enter. "Hello, sir, is there something I can help you with?" she asked. The nameplate on her desk identified her as Ms. Helms, an older woman pushing sixty with curly gray hair and a bright smile that shined through her early wrinkles.

"Yes, ma'am, I was actually wondering if you do tours of the school?"

"We sure do. Is your child here?"

"Actually, he's not. My family is moving from out of state. My wife and son are still back at home while I get things started here, so it'll just be me for the tour."

Nice reaction, Marty. Looks like you do have a knack for this detective life.

"I see. If you want to have a seat I can find someone to show you around the school in a few minutes."

"Sounds good, thank you."

Martin sat in the row of chairs that ran along the office's wall. He could see into the empty hallway toward the exit that had played with his mind a couple minutes earlier.

The office walls were lined with portraits of the school's past principals. The photos all led to the back wall where an enlarged portrait of President Bill Clinton hung beside an American flag. A handful of offices were below these pictures, including the principal's office. The clock on the wall approached noon, ticking away in the silent office among the soft hum of computers.

Martin waited, not sure what to do. Normally, he'd pull out his phone and check his emails and social media accounts, but that was no longer an option in his current situation, so he fidgeted with his fingers and tried to erase the fact that some sort of force had brushed its coldness on his body when he entered the site of a future massacre.

"Excuse me, sir?" a voice interrupted his thoughts. A young woman stood in front of him who looked like she was maybe a day removed from college. "You're looking to tour the school?"

"I am, yes."

"Great! My name is Jessica, and I've been a teaching assistant here at the school all year. I'll be showing you around and I can answer any questions you might have."

"Terrific. My name is Martin Briar."

"I understand your son won't be able to make it in for a tour."

"Correct. He's still back home with my wife finishing up the packing."

"I see. Where are you all coming from?" Jessica asked in her cheery voice.

"California. I got a new job opportunity I couldn't pass up here."

"Very cool. Well, welcome to Colorado and welcome to Columbine High School, we love to add to our growing community."

"Thank you. I've been very impressed with the town so far."

"Perfect, well follow me."

Martin followed her back into the main hallway where she stood with her hands clasped under her tiny bosom.

"So, this is the main entrance as you probably figured out. All of the administration is in the office should you ever need to meet with any one. Our school is two levels with the majority of the classrooms on the upper level. Down this hallway are most of the freshman lockers. Will your son be a freshman in the fall?"

"Yes," Martin lied.

"Terrific. So this is most likely where his locker will be, somewhere in this long hallway. If not, he'll be around the corner closer to the cafeteria, which we'll go take a look at now."

They walked down the freshman hallway, Martin knowing behind two of the locker doors was the property belonging to Eric and Dylan. He remembered they had both kept disturbing journals and couldn't help but wonder if those journals were already in the school building today.

Martin recognized the cafeteria when they reached the end of the hallway. White circular tables with blue chairs spread across the entirety of the room, dozens of students filling the room to eat. The view from the cafeteria faced the massive Rocky Mountains in the distance, and overlooked the soccer field where hundreds would flee when word broke of a shooting in the school.

He closed his eyes and remembered the images of the cafeteria he had seen on the news. Backpacks, books, and jackets were all left behind on the ground while abandoned food trays and drinks stayed on the tables, as if never touched. Two propane tanks had been placed around the cafeteria with hopes of blowing up that entire section of the school. Over 400 students were in the cafeteria at the time, but the bombs never detonated. Had those bombs gone off, the school would have surely been demolished and no longer exist in the future.

"Mr. Briar?"

He had gone so far off the deep end in his mind that Jessica's voice had droned into a cluster of noise in the cafeteria.

"Sorry, what did you say?"

"I asked if you had any questions so far."

"Oh, sorry. I do not, thank you."

"Great. If you'll follow me through the cafeteria, I can show you the few classrooms we have on the first floor."

She led them through the cafeteria where Martin couldn't help but stare out the window to the open soccer field. *If only you knew.*

Jessica guided them through a side door on the other end of the cafeteria, and when the door shut behind them, they stood in a short hallway in complete silence.

"Is that a soundproof door?" he asked.

"It is. Since we have lunch hours from 11 to 2, we don't want any of the noise to carry into this hall." More blue lockers lined the wall as they walked down and passed numerous classrooms in session. "These classrooms are home to our business and foreign language departments. So basically, any math class is over here, and then we offer Spanish, French, German, and Latin."

Martin looked around, hoping to see a glance of young Eric or Dylan somewhere. With the school's size, it would be a long shot tracking them down so easily.

Jessica kept strolling through the halls, and Martin followed as she pushed open a small door that led them back to the lobby at the main entrance. "Let's go upstairs."

Martin hadn't noticed the stairwell when he first entered, but it was directly to the right of the doorway and twisted upward to the second floor landing. Two long hallways stretched in opposite directions.

"Up here are the rest of the lockers. As you can see, the space spans all the way to the back of the school. The rest of the classrooms are up here, too. Language arts, science, the art studio, and the music room are all on this floor along with the library."

The library. He needed to see it—that's where all the drama occurred just before the boys turned their guns on themselves and called it a day.

"Let's go check out the east hall first and we can finish in the library," Jessica said, starting in that direction.

A knot twisted in Martin's stomach. He didn't know why he was so nervous. The library was a regular high school library. It hadn't seen any tragedy and it would be filled with students studying like any other day. He started to sweat and wiped it quickly off his forehead before Jessica could notice.

They walked down the hall toward the band room in what felt like slow motion. Martin suddenly felt lost in his mind, as if walking down a dark hallway by himself. He watched his body walk down the long hallway, having a true out-of-body experience.

Am I dying? Martin felt like he should be panicking, his heart should be pulsing, adrenaline should flood his body, but nothing happened. Everything felt numb. Jessica kept talking, probably creeped out by the strange father and wanting to end the tour as soon as possible. Her voice echoed in his mind, how it might sound when you could somewhat overhear a conversation through walls in a hotel room.

A sound filled his vacant head, reminding him of slithering snakes. "Get out," a voice whispered. "Get out. Get out."

As if shoved in the back, Martin returned to himself, feeling control over his body. He studied his hands as if he'd never seen them before.

"I'm sorry, Jessica. I'm feeling a bit off. I think I should leave."

"Oh. Are you sure? We're almost done."

"How much longer?"

"We can skip the classrooms and I can show you the library and gym before we wrap up."

Don't go to that library.

"Okay, I think I can manage." The temptation to see the library proved too strong for Martin, even in the midst of whatever was happening in his head.

Just go look, nothing bad will happen from looking at the library.

He wondered if a place could be haunted before a tragedy occurred, because walking through the halls of this storied school certainly felt like it.

"Can we just do the library and call it a day? Seen one gym, seen them all." He offered a forced chuckle, feeling normal again, but terrified of what had just happened to his senses.

"Oh, sure thing." She led them back down the hall, no longer speaking, and walking a bit faster than she had earlier in the tour.

Martin could see the library at the end of the hall, a set of wooden double doors leading into the infamous room where the two shooters killed most of their victims and themselves.

There was no further sense of an out-of-body experience

as they approached the library.

"Here we are," Jessica said, the perkiness fading from her voice, as she pulled open the double doors.

They stepped in. And nothing happened.

He wasn't sure what he thought would happen, but life carried on as normal in the quiet library. Students huddled around the few computers available, while others claimed their territory at the many tables scattered about the room between the dozens of bookshelves.

"Anything in particular you wanted to see in the library?" Jessica asked, more relaxed.

"Nothing in particular. I'm just a believer that you can judge a lot about a school by its library, and I must say it's impressive."

"Well, thank you, Mr. Briar."

Martin peeked at his watch, wanting it to appear that he had somewhere else to be. "I really should get going, though. I've got some errands to run this afternoon, but I really appreciate you taking the time to show me around."

Jessica smiled, looking comfortable again. "It was my pleasure. I hope your family decides to join our community here."

Martin shook the girl's hand before they parted ways. He informed her he would find his way out of the school no problem, then deliberately took the longer route that passed through the freshman hallway.

22

Chapter 22

Martin thought of the high school as a historical landmark even though nothing had yet happened within its walls, aside from adolescent drama and education. He took a final pass through the freshman hallway in hopes of bumping into one of the boys, but the swarm of students when the lunch bell rang made it impossible.

The past flexed its muscles by toying with his mind. He still couldn't shake off the feeling that he had nearly fainted or died—he wasn't sure exactly what it was—and felt a stressful tension lingering in his chest.

Martin returned to his car and grabbed his notebook. He noted the resistance the past had pushed on him, comparing the sensation to possibly a stroke or heart attack. He mentioned the cold presence that lingered in the entryway and cafeteria. The past gave him no choice but to acknowledge its authority. Everything Calvin had told him was true, and he would need to tread carefully going forward. Maybe it was a good thing he didn't see one of the boys today.

Martin threw his notebook aside and inhaled deeply, his

stomach gurgling anxiously.

This is bigger than you. You're messing with the wrong history. Go home and don't ever come back.

His subconscious had provided sound advice since he arrived in 1996, but he ignored it, believing there had to be a way to stop the shooting without getting himself killed.

After a ten-minute debate on what to do next, Martin fired up his engine and drove home. It had been at least a decade—in 2018's standards—since the Denver highways were clear of traffic in the middle of the day, and he enjoyed every second of driving 70 miles per hour on I-25. He powered on the radio and let the youthful sounds of the Spice Girls distract his mind. Izzy had loved the Spice Girls, and he remembered her dancing around the house with a hairbrush in hand as her imaginary microphone, singing her lungs out to every one of their hits.

"I can go back every day and try to find them on their way home. Can't go in to the school again, I'll become too suspicious."

This would require heavy detective work, but he had nothing better to do with his time. He'd like to follow Izzy home a few times a week to see her, but would have to treat that action with kid gloves to avoid being caught by her or an observant resident in the neighborhood.

The day had taken an emotional toll on Martin—it wasn't every day one encountered a supernatural force while traveling back in time. When he arrived back to his apartment, he snuck by Vinny's office, and went up to his unit for a glass of whiskey and to take a nap. Sonya would be over later for a dinner date, and he'd need his energy if she wanted another piece of Martin Briar for dessert.

* * *

Martin prepared dinner that night. They had been going out too often and wanted to save money, so they agreed to alternate cooking dinner at home throughout the week, and would eat out on the weekends.

Sonya arrived promptly at six as Martin put the finishing touches on the taco bar he had set up on the kitchen counter. She walked in to a margarita that lit up her face.

"It smells delicious!" she said, sitting on his couch with her drink and taking a deep inhale.

"Why, thank you. You *look* delicious," Martin crooned as he kissed the top of her head. Sonya never stopped showing off her toned legs, and he never stopped looking.

They caught up on each other's days, Martin lying about another long day at the post office, keeping the haunted high school in the back of his mind. He had gotten into the habit of telling these lies so much that he started to believe them. Every time the topic of work came up, he remembered, somewhere in 2018, he was asleep in Chris's office, waiting to be woken up to go in to work. The thought gave him the empty feeling you have on the final day of a long vacation.

With the table set, they sat down for dinner, Martin diving immediately into the juicy tacos he had spent the last hour preparing. After a couple of bites, he noticed Sonya poking around at her food, not having taken a bite yet. She maintained a smile, but Martin could see through it.

"Something wrong?" he asked.

She looked at him, her hazel eyes sparkling with natural beauty, a secret swimming behind them.

"Nothing is wrong. I've just got something on my mind is all."

Martin nodded, took a bite, and stared right back into her soul in an effort to hide how nervous he suddenly became. She remained silent and sipped the margarita.

"Are you gonna tell me or make me guess?"

She smiled, and it assured him that whatever was bothering her had nothing to do with him, at least in a negative sense.

"I suppose I have to tell you, or it's gonna eat at me for the next week." She paused, took another sip, and poked at the tacos again. "I want to tell you something, but I'm just afraid of how you'll react."

"You can tell me anything," he responded quickly and confidently.

"Okay, here it goes. I know we've only been seeing each other for a few weeks, but I feel like there's something between us."

Martin nodded and couldn't help but grin. Things were going very well. He'd never thought his first relationship in twenty years could feel so natural.

"At our age, I feel like it's okay to move quicker than normal. We're about halfway through life, probably more, so no point in taking things slow."

She paused for another sip, and Martin noticed the slightest tremble from her hand.

"I guess what I'm getting at . . . I wanted to ask you what you think about moving in together."

She grabbed her glass in sync with the words leaving her mouth and took a long swig as she watched Martin.

He sat back in his chair, one arm crossed, his free hand on his chin.

"Wow," he said, shocked.

"I knew it. It was too aggressive of me. Pretend I never said anything. Crazy thoughts, I know."

"Wait, wait, wait," Martin cut in. "I haven't even said anything. It *is* a fast move, but I agree with you. At this point in life we should both know what we want. We don't have to wait it out five years to be sure."

His eyebrows dropped in thought, scrunching his face into a shape that made him look closer to seventy years old.

"You know," Martin continued. "I haven't been able to get you out of my mind. I think about you when I wake up. I think about you when I go to sleep. Getting through a shitty workday has become so much easier knowing I get to see you at the end of it."

Sonya blushed, her entire face pink, as she took a giddy sip of margarita.

"So is that a yes?" she asked.

"I want to say yes, but have you thought about where would we live? Your place? My place? A whole new place?"

"I was thinking my place. My mortgage is low and I have plenty of space."

Martin nodded. "Okay. I just signed my lease, though, and I'm not sure I can get out of it."

"Aren't you friends with the landlord?"

"I wouldn't call us friends, but we get along just fine."

"It won't hurt to just ask him. Let him know the situation and he might be understanding."

"I can do that. I doubt he'll let me out of the lease for free, but maybe he'll work with me."

Sonya clapped her hands like a giggly teenage cheerleader. "I'm so excited. I was so scared you'd freak out and tell me to leave."

"Why would I do that?"

"I don't know. Some men are afraid of commitment, so I didn't know how you'd take it."

"Well, I'm certainly not afraid of commitment; I've been married before. It just didn't work out. I have feelings for you I can't deny. If anything, I'm relieved to know you feel the same way."

Sonya smirked and shot Martin an intense stare, suggesting that they get in bed right away.

"Well, since we're on the same page then, what do you say we put away these dishes and have some fun?" she asked him, refusing to break her gaze.

He pursed his lips and nodded as if in deep thought. "I suppose we could do that." He spoke in a serious tone, but couldn't keep the grin off his face, prompting a seductive giggle from his girlfriend.

They did the dishes as quickly as they had ever done. Sonya pulled him onto his bed and cut the lights. As they made love, a thought kept tugging at Martin, leaving him unable to focus.

If I live with Sonya, how am I supposed to pull off any of my plan without letting her know what this is all about? Is she the distraction sent by the past to hold me back?

These thoughts would keep him up late into the night as she snored softly on his chest. He ran gentle, steady fingers over her head while she slept, wondering if she was even real.

23

Chapter 23

After a brief internal debate of calling the move off, Martin decided to move forward with it. He *wanted* to move in with Sonya, that he never doubted, but his concern grew in regards to his actual purpose for being in 1996. He couldn't afford to compromise saving Izzy, so he would plan a fake work trip out of town during that dreaded week in September. He'd book a hotel nearby, preferably anywhere besides the Sunset Dream Motel, and keep an eye on all activity surrounding his old house. If he had to sleep in his car at the end of the block for the entire week, then so be it. He was here to keep his daughter safe and alive.

The Columbine mission could also continue. Martin wasn't expected home until six o'clock, leaving him plenty of time to scope the area surrounding the high school, follow the boys for a bit, and drive back across town for his now permanent dinner date with Sonya.

The conversation with Vinny had gone much easier than expected. His landlord gave zero pushback when asked if Martin could break his contract and move out as soon as possible.

"You're good people, Martin. For anyone else, I'd say no. Just promise to come see me from time to time."

"I can do that," Martin replied, wondering why things were falling into place without any resistance.

The two caught up for a few more minutes over a glass of scotch before Martin returned to his apartment to tell Sonya the news. By May first, Martin could officially move out with nothing further owed to Vinny, and they could begin a life together.

Despite it being a cause for celebration, Martin lost a few nights of sleep after cementing his decision. Somewhere down the road he would be faced with the crossroads of either telling Sonya the truth or vanishing from her life without a word. Both options terrified him.

Telling her the truth could open numerous possibilities. She might believe him and wish him a good rest of his life in 2018. She could become enraged that he had knowingly dragged her along for six months after admitting they were both at no point in life to waste time on meaningless relationships. Or, and most likely, she would think him crazy for discussing anything like time travel and kick him to the curb.

These possibilities continued to pick away at his mind as they had since the decision was made three days earlier. While the unknowing bothered Martin, he needed to keep a clear mind to continue his work at Columbine. He also jotted new rules for himself in his spiral notebook regarding the project. If anything felt off about the situation, he vowed to turn around and leave. He'd already had close calls with that sense of vertigo that came with fucking with the past. He'd found the red line and couldn't afford to cross it so soon; if there were a time to do so, it would come in September when saving Izzy.

His racing thoughts kept him occupied during the entire drive to Columbine. The final bell would ring in twenty minutes, at 3:30, and all he wanted was to locate at least one of the boys to follow, and learn their daily after school routine.

He assumed they would exit from the main entrance, so he waited in the same parking lot he had parked during his first trip. Space was tight as many cars awaited their students, but he was able to squeeze into a spot that faced the doors. Then the fun part of waiting began.

Stakeouts weren't everything they made them out to be in movies. Martin grew bored within fifteen minutes of sitting in his car, staring at the same building, watching the kids who all looked the same pour out as they carried on their conversations and laughed with each other.

High school really is the easiest time of life. These kids have no idea what's waiting for them outside of these walls.

He watched some older kids walk out, wearing their blue and white letterman jackets, and felt silly for having always longed for one in high school. Those kids had always seemed so cool, but looking back on it, they were just assholes like everyone else.

Thirty minutes passed without any sight of Eric or Dylan. This part of the process was painful, and Martin didn't want to waste any more time. The boredom allowed him time to think of different ways to locate the boys, and he settled on a rather obvious solution that he should have thought of in the first place: the White Pages.

The White Pages was a directory of people, the past's version of Google searching someone's name to find their phone number and address. Before privacy had become such a major pain point in the new century, one could easily look up someone's name and know exactly where they lived and what number to call them on.

Pay phones! Martin had a grand revelation by remembering there should be phone books that hung at each pay phone around town. He left the school behind, no longer concerned with the crapshoot chance of finding the boys within the mob of students, and returned to the gas station around the corner, where he had stopped for directions the first time.

Most gas stations in 1996 had a payphone outside, and this location was no different. The pay phone stood in its hefty, silver box, a white book at least five inches thick dangling beneath from a chain. A suited man stood at the pay phone, talking with his hand over the mouthpiece, and looking around suspiciously. He briefly locked eyes with Martin before hanging up and returning to his white BMW and skidding out of the parking lot.

When the coast appeared clear, Martin strode to the pay phone and lifted the dangling phone book, flipping to the middle.

There will be too many Harrises listed. Klebold will be my best bet.

He flipped to the K section, running a finger down the page until he found what he needed: Thomas and Susan Klebold, the only Klebolds on the page.

"There you are." Martin pulled out his notepad and jotted the address; the phone rang out in a screaming, piercing chime.

Martin gazed around, seeing if someone nearby was expecting a call. No one was in sight, so he picked up the phone.

161

"Hello?"

"You'll never get away with this," a raspy voice said, sending chills down Martin's spine.

"Who is this?" he demanded.

The phone clicked, filling his ear with the dial tone.

What the fuck?

Martin hung up and returned to his car, staring at the payphone through his windshield, wanting it to ring again.

"You'll never get away with this," he whispered to himself. He racked his mind for a familiarity in the voice, but could find nothing. Chris was never one to cower behind a disguise. *Could it be a Road Runner?*

Martin lacked the knowledge to know exactly how the Road Runners operated, but if anyone was trying to prevent the changing of a major historical event, they seemed the likely candidates.

He stepped back out of the car and went inside the gas station.

"Hello," the clerk welcomed him.

"Hi. I'm looking for maps of Denver, do you have any?"

"Yes, sir, in the magazine section." The clerk pointed to the row against the front window.

"Perfect, thank you." Martin hurried to the row, reminiscing over the old days of browsing the wide selection of magazines, books, and newspapers in the corner stores. Those times were long gone in 2018. At the end of the row was a rack of atlases and maps. Martin grabbed the one marked as Denver Metro Area, flipped through it to make sure Littleton was included, and took it to the counter.

"Is there somewhere in particular you're looking to find?" the clerk asked as he rung him up on the register.

"No, I'm just new to the area and seem to get lost every day."

"Fair enough. This map should get you around town just fine."

"Thank you," Martin said, grabbing his map and change before bolting out of the door. He'd normally contribute to meaningless chitchat, but he had pressing matters to tend, and apparently someone trying to stop him.

When he returned to his car, he thought, *Is this all worth it? I could get myself killed trying to stop these kids, and that's not what I'm here for.*

"It may not be what I came here to do, but I owe it to the world to at least try," he said out loud, backing out of the gas station and pulling onto the main road.

24

Chapter 24

The drive to the Klebold residence took longer than expected; they lived eight miles away from the high school, roughly the same distance it would take him to get from Larkwood to downtown Denver.

He followed the map carefully, turn by turn, as the quiet residential neighborhoods gave way to multi-level homes, before turning into open fields in the foothills of the Rocky Mountains. At first, Martin thought he had taken a wrong turn as he zigzagged through a stretch of green hills and thick trees, but when he finally saw Cougar Road appear on a street sign, his heart beat a little faster.

This is it.

He turned onto Cougar Road, immediately feeling out of place in his junker of a car. All of the homes on Cougar Road were hidden behind tall stands of trees, somewhere at the end of a private driveway that started from the main road and ended in the woods, out of sight. Each driveway had a black mailbox at the front with the street numbers in white lettering.

The homes were spaced hundreds of yards apart, providing

plenty of privacy from neighbors. Martin drove another mile just to pass five different properties.

He came around a blind curve that opened up to more trees and the towering red rocks that were a staple in Colorado. He passed a small red barn when he saw the mailbox reading 8370, and pulled to the side of the road, directly across the barn that stood on the Klebold property.

Martin killed the engine and stepped out onto the dirt that served as an unofficial sidewalk along the road. Cicadas buzzed from the surrounding trees, echoing everywhere. He looked around, seeing nothing but green trees and more slanted red rock formations before stepping toward the Klebold driveway, to find it curved into more trees and vanished from sight.

Do I really want to go up this driveway? If someone's home or arrives home while I'm walking up, there's very few explanations as to why I'm here, in the middle of nowhere.

"I didn't come here for nothing," he said and started up the dirt driveway. *If anyone asks, I can say I got lost and my car broke down.*

The driveway twisted a quarter mile uphill, causing Martin to huff and puff, as he still hadn't been in any shape for the smallest of hikes. "At least it's all shaded," he remarked.

When he reached the top a few minutes later, his jaw dropped at the massive white house. The driveway turned back into pavement that spiraled into a roundabout in front of the garage. Behind the garage stood the house with gigantic windows that he could see through into the kitchen and dining room. A swimming pool and hot tub were to the side, behind an open space with a basketball hoop where young Dylan likely played.

"Holy shit." Martin had forgotten just how wealthy the Klebold family had been. Plenty of comfortable families lived in Littleton, but this private area of the city was clearly where the high rollers lived. He couldn't even see the entirety of the house from where he stood, but knew there was plenty of room for the boys to hide their stash of firearms that would accumulate in a couple of years.

This has to be where they filmed those tapes of them shooting their guns in the woods, he thought, admiring the surrounding foothills. Taking in the scenery, Martin quickly understood the ease the two boys would have had in keeping their plans a secret. Even if they chose to not hide their arsenal in the house, there would be plenty of spots around the property to keep everything under wraps. With no visible neighbors, they could have taken their time at their homemade shooting range, firing rounds that would surely be heard down the road, but no one would be able to pinpoint the exact location.

Martin stepped toward the house, planting his foot in a pool of mud six inches deep. "Motherfucker!" he barked, kicking his foot to shake it off.

One of the garage doors, about fifty feet in front of him, started to slide open, prompting Martin to pivot and dive into the trees. The garage's motor hummed softly as Martin positioned himself behind a tree stump to ensure he wasn't visible. He watched as a silver Mercedes backed out, circled the roundabout, and disappeared down the driveway, leaving a trail of dust in its tracks. A woman, presumably Dylan's mother, drove the car alone, but he couldn't make out any features aside from shoulder-length hair and a pearl necklace.

He saw no other cars inside the garage, leaving him alone at the Klebold residence. Martin tiptoed back to the driveway, the mud hardening on the skin around his ankle. Sensing his time was limited, he jogged to the main windows that overlooked the home's kitchen.

Everything appeared as pristine as he'd expected: polished marble countertops, wooden cupboards, and shiny black appliances—a standard luxury kitchen for the mid-90's. He put his face up to the glass for a better look, but could only see into the living room where a boxy big-screen TV faced a couch, and a gray cat stared back curiously before returning to its afternoon bathing session.

It's time to go. You've been here too long, Martin warned himself. He wanted to go around the house and see the rest of the property, but going any further would be too risky. *You have what you need for today. You know where the kid lives, and can follow him to and from school until you figure out what the hell you're gonna do.*

Martin surrendered and jogged back toward the driveway, skidding on his heels to keep from rolling down the hill like a boulder. As he left, he could feel the house pulling at him with a magnetic force, daring him to come back and have a look around.

"Just get out of here," he wheezed to himself, finally seeing the main road. "Go home."

Martin reached the bottom of the driveway and sighed in relief at the sight of his rust bucket waiting for him. Not a soul was present as he crossed the abandoned road. He sped off, eyes unable to look away from the house in the rear-view mirror until he rounded a corner and left it out of sight.

25

Chapter 25

Martin took the rest of the week off, wanting nothing more than to sit around and drink himself into tranquility. The Klebold house had a pull on him that didn't lift until he lay down on his couch, surrounded by a handful of moving boxes, that he felt at peace with the events of the prior two days.

He was set to move in two weeks, leaving him that much time to set a solid plan before Sonya would be around during all of his free time.

"This is never going to work," he said, pacing around his apartment. It was now Saturday afternoon, and he had spent the last hour reading over the notes he had taken on Columbine, trying to figure out what exactly to do next, and how the knowledge of the Klebold residence could be used.

First thing I need to do is meet the boys. I need to see how mentally stable they are as freshmen. It's four years until the massacre, so they may be completely normal and happy.

He briefly considered seeking employment at the school to be closer to them, but then he remembered that intense, death-like feeling he had experienced in the building.

I'll follow them until I learn their routine, then I'll approach them casually, ideally in public if possible.

The last thing he needed was to be the crazy fat guy who stalked teenage boys around a wealthy town. That would punch a quick ticket to the police station for questioning.

The police. I could tell the police what the boys plan to do. Leave an anonymous tip.

Martin scratched his head and rubbed his eyes in frustration. "It's too early. They haven't even considered getting a gun yet."

What about a private note to the school's principal? I could tell them the exact date of the shooting so they can be prepared.

"Still too early. Can be taken as an empty threat. Why would an educator in one of the best school districts in the state believe a secret note about an event that would happen three years later?"

Martin sensed his inner voice wanting him to drop the plan altogether, and deep down he knew the risk was too big to guarantee his own safety.

He sat on the couch and dropped his face into open palms. *You're here for Izzy. Not for Columbine. Izzy. Just forget about Columbine. Move in with your girlfriend, make love every night, and save Izzy in September. You don't owe the world a damn thing.*

"You're right."

The world could move on as planned. Even if he managed to prevent Columbine, there would just be another school shooting to take its place as the spark that changed the country.

"I still need to know my limits. I can't have any surprises in September when it comes time to save Izzy."

Martin poured himself a glass of whiskey and drank until he fell asleep.

* * *

The nap was the deepest Martin had slept in a few days. When he woke three hours later, he felt rejuvenated and ready to take on the world again. He decided he wouldn't completely put off the Columbine project, but rather have it on the back burner. There was only a month until summer break anyway, so he might as well wait until school started again in August to track down the boys. The longer he waited, the closer they would be to their turning point that eventually pushed them over the edge. He could plan a couple of trips to the Klebold residence just to see if the boys might be around; he could even wander around the property from the backside, in hopes of finding their hideout in the woods.

He still had a persona to maintain. Sonya would expect to see him off in the mornings and return home around the same time as her. They could cook dinner together, watch TV, take showers, and fall asleep in each other's arms. The more normal he could make life in 1996 feel, the easier his mind could stay distracted from Columbine and focused on Izzy.

He'd spend the days at the library or wandering around downtown. Denver wouldn't be nearly as busy as it had become in 2018, and he could eat lunch in peace at the 16th Street Mall and watch the businessmen pass by with their hectic lives.

Sonya had given Martin a key to her house and told him

to start moving things in whenever he felt ready. With three boxes ready to go, he loaded them into his car and headed to his home of the next five months.

"What the fuck am I going to tell Sonya in September?" he asked his empty car. He couldn't up and leave her with no word. Even in the past, he couldn't afford the kind of karma that would come with pulling the rug out from someone who actually loved him.

Why does she have to exist in 1996? Why couldn't I find her in 2018?

Sonya would be in her late 60's when he returned to 2018, over fifteen years older than him. Could two souls still love each other after going through time travel?

"I could bring her back. Anything on my body when I take the pill comes with me. I can have Izzy in one arm, Sonya in the other, and we'll all live happily ever after."

Or maybe she'll continue to fall deeper in love with you over the summer and she'll want to follow you into the future. Just take it one day at a time.

Martin smirked as he pulled into Sonya's empty driveway. It was a small ranch-style home with an unfinished basement, the perfect place to maintain a low-key lifestyle as he awaited the day he would save his daughter.

"Or maybe I save Izzy and stay."

No, Martin, that would be selfish. Rescue Izzy and return to the future. See where life will have taken you with her around. Don't forget how much you loved your life before she disappeared.

That much was true. He'd had a steady high-paying job where Lela didn't have to work. Izzy came home every night excited to see her parents and tell them about her day. Lela loved him just as much Sonya did now. Life had been perfect, and that's all he really wanted.

26

Chapter 26

On the first day of May, Martin stood in his apartment door-way, staring at the empty space. The sunlight filled the room much brighter than he recalled, as the studio no longer had a trace of his existence. The car was packed with the final few boxes, and all Martin had left to do was drop his key off with Vinny.

Vinny gave Martin a sad smile when he arrived in his office.

"You're out of here for good?" Vinny asked, disappointment in his voice.

"Afraid so. Thank you so much for everything these last couple of months, and for letting me leave like this."

Vinny put up a hand. "No need. You were a good resident, and a good guy. You're welcome here any time. But you go enjoy that girlfriend of yours, seems like a keeper."

"Thanks, Vinny. I'll stop by and see you, maybe we can grab dinner sometime."

"I'd love that." Vinny stood and shook Martin's hand, but they both knew the dinner invite was nothing more than a polite pleasantry. "I'll see you around, Martin."

Martin left the complex and looked up the brick building, appreciative of the stable home it had provided him when everything had felt uncertain upon his arrival.

He drove away, the next chapter of life waiting at Sonya's house, and had never felt so excited about the future. When he pulled into Sonya's driveway five minutes later, he felt at home for the first time in years. Sure, he had his apartment in 2018, but that had housed nothing but cheap booze and cheaper frozen dinners.

With Sonya he had a home: a clean house, home-cooked meals, decorations. And with him moving in, they now had a life together.

Despite all of the budding positivity, that nagging voice in the back of his mind kept reminding him that September wasn't that far away, and he'd be forced to make a difficult decision regarding Sonya.

Next month, you'll be halfway through this trip.

Six weeks had passed since he arrived at the empty lot and wandered by the burned down church. All it took was six weeks to build a life and fall in love. "The past is dangerous," he said as he stepped out of his car.

It was a Wednesday afternoon and Sonya was at school, leaving Martin the day to unpack and settle in to his new home. Birds sung in the pine trees that stood in the front lawn, stretching its shade over the driveway.

The perfectly groomed front yard had freshly cut grass and vibrant flowers that decorated the walkway to the front door. The porch was covered by the tree's shade where two rocking chairs sat around a table big enough to hold a couple cups of coffee. Martin had never seen a neighbor in the surrounding homes in his many visits to Sonya's house, yet today he spied an older couple across the street working in their garden. They waved, and he returned the gesture with a warm smile.

Martin went inside before unloading any of the boxes, wanting a glass of water to kick start the busy afternoon ahead. When he walked into the kitchen, he found a note on the counter.

Hey mister,

I'm so happy we're taking this next step in our relationship. I want to go have dinner where we first met to celebrate, then we can bring the party home.

Sonya

Martin folded the note and slipped it into his pocket with a grin on his face.

See, everything is going to be fine. You won't have any time to think about Columbine. Just need to figure out what to do during the days.

He could take some pretend time off from work to truly get settled in to the new house, maybe even tend to the garden and yard work.

How believable would it be if I "retired" from the post office right now?

Martin pondered this as he aimlessly unloaded the car and dropped the boxes into Sonya's guest room. Instead of fighting over closet space, he would use the guest room to store his clothes and any belongings. Over his six weeks in town, he hadn't accumulated much outside of some kitchenware and essential toiletries.

Once he unloaded the car, he lay down on the living room couch to do one thing he had missed dearly: watch TV. He flipped through the channels, not coming across much beside *Days of Our Lives*, *The Young and the Restless*, and a plethora of infomercials for guaranteed workout results and power washers, and eventually settled on reruns of *The Adventures of Batman and Robin.*

The afternoon dragged through two episodes when a knock came from the front door, startling Martin. He flailed as he rolled off the couch to rush to the door. He could make out the figure of a man through the blinds and figured it to be the neighbor across the street.

Martin pulled open the door, creaking at the hinges.

"Martin Briar! Hello, good sir," Chris said with a devilish smirk. "May I come in?"

Martin's eyes dashed around the neighborhood, again seeing no one else. "Hi?" The hairs on his back prickled in fear.

"You don't look excited to see me," Chris said with a cackle.

"Why are you here?"

"Why am I here? Why are *you* here?"

"I live here now."

"Shacking up with the locals, I see. Not a bad strategy, only five minutes away from your daughter's school."

"What do you want, Chris?"

"Relax, you shouldn't be so snippy. I'm here to let you know I won't be around for the rest of your stay here in 1996. I have a matter to tend to: a civil war is breaking out in Africa in the year 2182."

"Okay, but what does that have to do with me?"

"Nothing, just thought you should know since you're new to this. There's going to be a day where you need me, but just know I won't be around. I'll see you back in 2018."

"What do you mean I'll need you?"

Chris grinned. "Just be careful with everything you do. Until then, take it easy, my friend."

Chris patted Martin on the shoulder before turning away and walking out of his life for the rest of his journey in the past.

His gooseflesh spread from his back to his arms and legs. The more he saw Chris, the less he trusted him.

The old man walked down the driveway and turned down the sidewalk.

Martin returned to his couch, arms trembling from a mixture of rage and fear.

"You can't throw me into the past with one rule, and then drop little hints like this. This is bullshit!"

Martin rummaged through Sonya's liquor cabinet, finding nothing but vodka and cheap tequila. He went into the guest room to find his bottle of whiskey, packed away in a box, and poured a glass to settle his nerves.

27

Chapter 27

Martin lied to Sonya about taking the rest of the week off from work. Thursday and Friday he unpacked all six of his boxes, setting things up where he wanted in the bathroom and kitchen, and filling the guest room closet with the clothes he had gathered since arriving in 1996.

They made passionate love during their first four nights living together. On Sunday, Martin examined himself in the mirror after stepping out of the shower and noticed he had lost weight. The reduced alcohol and constant exercise between the sheets did a miracle for his gut.

When Martin stepped out of the bathroom he found Sonya on the couch, folding a basket of laundry.

"I was gonna wash your uniforms for the week, but didn't see them anywhere. Are they packed still?" she asked him with a gentle smile.

Shit, he thought. He had never been one to cover all of his bases, and changing eras didn't fix that.

"We actually have a changing room down at the post office. They do our laundry for us."

"Wow. The *post office* does that?"

"Not many do," he continued. "But the ones in bigger cities will. The downtown post office is the place to be."

Martin's voice sounded fake to himself, but he kept a careful watch on Sonya, who apparently thought nothing of it.

"I see. That's pretty cool." Her hands kept folding while her eyes remained fixated on the VHS of *Romeo + Juliet* playing on the TV. If young Leonardo DiCaprio put her in the mood, then so be it. "I've been thinking," she continued. "With summer break coming up, maybe you can take some time off and we go on a trip?"

"I thought you teach summer school?" Martin asked.

"I do teach summer school, but it's only through the third week of June," she said, still not breaking her stare from young Leonardo. "We could plan for a trip in July."

"All right, did you have somewhere in mind?"

"I've always wanted to go to D.C. Have you ever been?"

Martin rarely went on trips for leisure, mostly passing by new cities on work trips where he spent ninety percent of his time in a hotel. His mom and dad took him on a trip to Disneyland when he was twelve, and he went to Cancun for a friend's bachelor party before he married Lela. Those were the only trips he'd ever gone on for fun; he and Lela never had the budget to take Izzy anywhere out-of-state.

"I've never been. How long would you wanna go for?"

"I was thinking maybe ten days, if you can get that much time off. Give us time to see the city and maybe spend some time in Baltimore, too."

"I should be able the make that work. I've accrued so much time off and never use it," he lied.

Sonya clapped giddily as she jumped from the couch, squealing as she ran to Martin. "I'm so excited! I'll call a travel agent and get everything arranged for us."

"Perfect. Our first trip together – I look forward to it."

Sonya kissed him, her lips moist as he tasted the bitterness of her lip balm.

"I love you," she said, wrapping her arms around his waist.

Martin grinned at her, looking into her eyes, knowing what all lay ahead. *I can't keep lying to you,* he thought.

"I love you, too," he said, and kissed her forehead.

* * *

As their relationship continued to evolve, they learned more about each other's past. Sonya could talk for hours, while Martin could only offer a few lines at a time to keep the conversation going. He decided to stick to his actual life history, finding no point in making things more difficult in his web of lies. When she asked him about his past marriage, he told her it was a matter he didn't like to discuss.

"Some things are best left in the past where they belong," he said. "It was a very dark time of life for me. I hope you can understand."

"I've had some nasty relationships myself, and I'll tell you all about them. I hope you'll confide in me one day." She always stroked a steady hand through his hair when they talked in bed.

"I do trust you. It's just one of those things I've pushed so far back in my mind, it's like it never happened. And I'd like to keep it that way."

"Alright. If you change your mind, I'm here and would love to listen."

Sonya lay her head on his bare chest, rising with each breath. "I just feel like I know you from somewhere," she said. "Do you ever feel that way?"

It's because you've probably seen my younger self passing around the school.

"I feel like I've known you forever. Hard to believe it's only been a few weeks."

"I know. They say time flies when you're having fun. I guess it's true."

They lay in bed that night listening to the gentle rustle of leaves outside as a soft breeze blew through the cracked open bedroom window. Sonya curled up into a ball beside Martin, an arm resting peacefully across his chest. She always fell asleep before him, he being the night owl, leaving his mind to ponder life.

Is this relationship even real? My reality is in 2018 where I'm out cold at a crazy old man's desk, probably from some fucked-up drug he gave me. Sonya might not even exist in my reality, but only in this dimension.

Martin had plenty of late nights thinking, but this was the first time he had stared at the beautiful sleeping woman and wondered what exactly her purpose was. The fact that she only existed in 1996, when he would have been in his thirties, suggested that her purpose was not to be the love of his life, but rather something else.

So, then – who are you?

Martin wanted desperately to travel back to the future to learn more about Sonya. A quick search online could pull up her information. She might even be on social media where he could see what she was up to in her older years; she would be seventy, assuming she hadn't passed away.

Would she remember me if I left her and visited her again in the future?

Martin supposed a visit to Calvin was in line, but didn't want to keep pestering his friend, or possible foe, from the future.

What if you can't save Izzy? His mind continued to wander, settling on a topic he had never considered. What if everything happened so fast that he couldn't react in time? *Would Chris actually set me up to fail?*

The thought made Martin question his own purpose. So many nights he had wanted to put his pistol in his mouth and pull the trigger. There would be no more sorrow, no more pain, no more lack of direction in his shitty, whiskey-chugging life. But every time he sat down to really consider it, his inner voice of reason whispered for him to wait, promising it would all be better one day.

It's still possible that Izzy is not why you were sent back in time. He could have baited you with her, but what if your real objective is to stop that shooting?

Martin closed his eyes and pictured all of those innocent, young faces they had shown on the news on April 20, 1999. He remembered wondering what he would do if he had to see Izzy's face on the news after such a tragedy.

"I would hunt down the shooters and make sure they never breathed again," he whispered in the silent bedroom. "And that's what I'm gonna do."

The faces of Eric Harris and Dylan Klebold spun around his head as he dozed to sleep.

I'm not letting you get away with it.

28

Chapter 28

A couple weeks passed, but the thought of confronting Eric and Dylan continued to throb in Martin's mind like a tumor.

You're doing this for Izzy. If you can stop this attack, you can certainly stop her disappearance.

He would wait for school to let out for summer break, and then stalk Dylan by hiding in the woods behind his mansion. If he could get Dylan alone, he'd tell him if he ever saw him talking to Eric Harris again, he would come back and slit his throat.

One thing Martin had learned over time, thanks to the several mass shootings every year, was that a lot of the shooters were nothing more than chickenshits. They might be frightening when they had time to plan their attacks on unsuspecting people, but they were no better equipped to handle a random confrontation than a child.

The plan surely wasn't a guarantee, but it would certainly throw a wrench into Dylan's life. Threatening a mass murderer three years before an attack would have to alter the track of history.

Maybe it would all backfire and the Columbine shooting would end up worse than it had originally. Maybe Dylan would kill himself before making the decision to harm his classmates. Martin had no choice but to at least try and hope for the best. Taking no action would lead to the same result, but making a move, even a small one, could change everything.

Sonya continued to work every day, leaving Martin at home to lounge around the house and get lost in his chaotic thoughts. Eric and Dylan remained front and center, with Izzy on the back burner. He had followed her home from school a couple more times. She giggled with friends and held her books between her skinny arms just like always. Her life was normal.

Martin had gone to the library to find Columbine High School's phone number and called them to find out when the last day of school was. May 23rd, and he marked it on his mental calendar. It was currently May 16th, leaving him another week until school would let out and Dylan had a whole summer to lounge around his castle. All the students in his class would have a summer full of fun at the swimming pools, day camps, and baseball parks, unaware their lives would be forever changed or ended just before their graduation in 1999.

I have to save them.

Martin no longer felt nervous when thinking about confronting the tall, scrawny high school student. He felt rejuvenated, like fate was on his side.

Every morning Martin got dressed along with Sonya, but he had the advantage of her needing to leave first, due at school at 7:30, while he didn't need to report to the "post office" until 9:00. Sonya didn't leave school until five in the afternoon, the same time Martin supposedly got off work. However, with his drive much further than Sonya's, he would cruise around, arriving home around 5:30 when expected. Often times Sonya stayed late and he'd still get home before her.

On this particular Friday, Martin headed to the liquor store, wanting to see Calvin, but to also buy a new bottle of whiskey. The weekend was upon him, after all. He pulled his car into the parking lot, noticing two other cars in the usually vacant lot. It was later than when he normally stopped by, almost noon, and he didn't think much of the extra visitors, only dreading that he might not get the chance to speak with Calvin.

As he stepped out and approached the entrance he noticed the neon lights were off. When he reached the door, he saw that none of the interior lights were turned on, either. Only the natural sunlight illuminated the store, seeping through the windows on the sunny day. Martin's heart skipped a beat as something immediately felt off. Even though he had only met with Calvin twice, he gathered that he was a man of habit and would never forget to turn on the lights.

Martin put his face to the door, tugging on the handle as it refused to budge. In front of the checkout counter, four men stood in a semicircle with their backs to Martin. As they wavered side to side, Martin caught a glimpse of Calvin tied to a chair with duct tape over his mouth and blood streaming from his forehead to chin.

Martin froze, unsure if he should distract the men or run and call for help. He mustered the strength to get out of sight and darted away from the door, peering through a side window instead. From here Martin would stay out of sight, obstructed behind a row of beer boxes, but he still had a clear view of Calvin.

They appeared to be in a discussion, the men bobbing their heads as they spoke, Calvin's eyes following their speech back and forth like a tennis match.

Are these the Road Runners? Martin wondered, now realizing this was not a robbery of any sort. Thieves made plans to get in and out as quickly as possible, not discuss dinner plans in front of the store's owner.

Each man wore a long gray pea coat, strange for a day expecting 85 degrees and sunshine. They had the collars flipped up to cover their faces, showing nothing but the tops of their heads, which all had identical black hair slicked to one side.

One of the men tossed his hands in the air before reaching inside his coat, and retrieved a black pistol. The two men beside him threw their hands up in protest, one even grabbing the gunman on his arm to plead with him. Calvin's eyes bulged in terror, his body trembling in fear.

The man appeared to have been talked off the ledge, lowering the pistol. There was a momentary pause where time felt frozen before the man whipped the pistol to Calvin's forehead and pulled the trigger, splattering blood droplets in every direction. Muffled through the glass, Martin heard the men shouting at each other. One shoved the gunman in the chest and sent the pistol in the air. Martin couldn't look away, trembling from the window and now fearing for his own life.

What the fuck?

The men remained in a circle, no one having moved and continuing their conversation above the dead liquor store owner, head split open and brains spilling out. Calvin's face had disappeared under a coat of blood.

The men all nodded in unison before turning toward the door. Martin used the adrenaline pumping in his system and dove around the corner, completely out of sight from the pea-coated terrorists. He heard the faint chime of the bell as the door swung open and one deep voice say, "Get it done with. Now!"

Three car doors opened and closed in near unison. Martin squatted, waiting for the fourth and final door to slam. When no sounds came after a few seconds, he tiptoed to the corner of the building and peeked a curious eye around to see what was going on.

Two men sat in the car furthest from Martin, on the far side of the entrance, while one man sat in the car next to it. They all had their eyes glued to the fourth man emptying a five gallon container of gasoline across the store's entryway.

"Hurry up, let's get out of here!" the man behind the wheel shouted through a rolled down window.

The gasoline man pulled a box of matches from his coat, and struck the tip to light a flame. He held the match to the box until the whole thing caught fire, and tossed it on the door. He dashed for the car, falling into the passenger seat as he tossed the gasoline container over his shoulder to the back seat.

"Let's go! Let's go!" the driver barked to the other car as they both fired up their engines and skidded out of the parking lot, leaving a trail of smoke from the burnt rubber.

Martin came out of hiding, gawking at the small flame that had already grown the height of his knee. The flame crackled violently, growing by the second, and spreading further across the building's façade. He pulled at the front door, wanting to save Calvin's corpse, but the handle was already scorched to the touch.

"God dammit!" Martin squealed, flailing his hand in the air. Realizing he couldn't save Calvin or the store, he jumped back into his car and burnt his own rubber. He kept his eyes on the store as he drove further, watching the flame grow in his rear-view mirror, knowing it would eventually swallow the entire building.

What the fuck is going on?

For the first time since Martin had traveled back in time, he felt genuinely terrified. If those men—who he assumed to be Road Runners—could murder a man and burn a building so quickly, what could they do to him? Calvin had been more prepared than he would ever be, watching every person that entered his store like a vulture ready to pounce.

I guess Chris was right: I need to be very careful.

29

Chapter 29

Martin watched the news every hour, sick to his stomach at the images of the roaring flames that devoured the liquor store. The firefighters arrived too late, showering flames that had grown too wide to contain. By the time the flames died down, the building was nothing but a pile of ashes. The news didn't report a body found in the rubble, and he could only assume Calvin had been completely cremated in the fire.

"That was my liquor store," Martin told Sonya. "I spoke with the owner numerous times; he was a good guy."

"I hope he was able to get out safely," she said.

"Yeah, me too." Martin could see Calvin in his mind, his brains spilling out of his skull from the gunshot wound. "I'm sure he did."

As more days passed, Martin managed to push the tragedy further back in his mind. Knowing what Calvin was working on, and seeing his end result made him wonder if those men were sent to prevent him from taking his knowledge back to the future, or if they were some figment of the past pushing back to make sure nothing changed in Calvin's future.

The whole ordeal made Martin want to hide in his house until September. He even took his pill out of its hiding spot from the small zipper in his suitcase. He could swallow the pill and go back to normal, work at the post office, and go home afterwards to drink until he passed out, forgetting about the past and not worry about being hunted and killed. Life wouldn't be any different if he called it quits right now and returned to 2018. Izzy would still be missing and the Columbine shooting would have still happened. The world was just fine without his interference.

You have to see this through. Going back now would just mean you've wasted two months of your life.

"Ten minutes. That's all this is costing me."

You don't actually believe that old man, do you? You're probably dead and trapped in some fucked-up purgatory.

"As slimy as he is, he's never actually lied about anything."

It happened much sooner than he had expected, but Martin wanted to see Chris immediately. He wanted to ask him how death worked: if he died in the past, what happened to his body in 2018? Who were those men? Why did they want Calvin?

Martin could only try to figure these things out on his own. Without Calvin or Chris, he was left to accept his questions would never be answered.

Just be cautious everywhere you go. You drove up to that liquor store without a care in the world. There could have been a gunman in the cars next to you when you pulled in, waiting to kill you. You've got to do better.

Every future move would be carefully planned. He needed a gun for protection, and would keep it on him whenever he left to fuck with the past. The past seemed to leave people alone so long as they stuck to a routine. Calvin must have been closing in on something, or else those men would have never showed up.

You can still stop Columbine, just take it slow and be ready for anything. The lives you save will thank you later. And so will Izzy.

* * *

Sonya had two more weeks of summer school. Once she was home for the summer, he'd have to leave the house every day and kill time while she thought he was at work.

For now, he sat in his car, fighting off nerves, remaining confident in his mission. He pulled out of his driveway, not knowing what could happen as he started his trip across town to Littleton. His plan was simple: park a half mile down the long road, out of sight from the Klebold house, and walk to the property in search of a workable path to the woods behind the home. Then wait.

It could be a day wasted, possibly a few days, but he had to stakeout and see if Dylan ever wandered into the woods, or at least step outside. If Dylan stayed inside all day, Martin would be left to peer through the windows from a distance.

During the drive he listened to the sports radio station where the two hosts discussed the upcoming summer Olympics, eagerly awaiting to see how the Dream Team would follow up their prior gold medal in basketball. Martin smirked, knowing the team would win again without any issues. The talk shifted to the Colorado Rockies down season a year after making the playoffs when Martin pulled into the discreet neighborhood. He twisted down Cougar Road and pulled off, driving no more than ten miles per hour to quietly approach the familiar red barn.

He squeezed the car into the tight space of dirt between the pavement and a ditch, and killed the engine, surprised he wasn't shitting his pants, considering how close he was to touching the past.

The day was already warming up and would be scorching by noon. Martin hadn't planned how long he would hide out in the woods, but with one water bottle, knew he wouldn't last too long.

Don't be such a pussy. You drove all this way. A little warm weather will not send you home.

With his reassurance, he stepped out of the car and took crunching steps toward the long driveway, roughly a quarter mile away.

A man in a Porsche drove by, but didn't look in Martin's direction. "Coast is clear," he said, not seeing another car in sight, and broke into a slight jog, slowing as he approached the driveway.

Everything appeared the same as his last visit, only this time he knew the future mass murderer had to be inside. High school kids rarely woke up before nine on summer break.

Martin hid in the trees, darting from spot to spot like a fox as he made his way closer to the house. When he reached the top of the driveway he worked his way around the left side of the house, seeing the swimming pool as he passed.

If Martin could know for certain he was alone with Dylan, he would approach him carefully. Surely the boy wouldn't do anything to him, but this wasn't exactly a neighborhood where a random stranger could get lost and need to ask for directions.

Martin worked toward the back of the house, which revealed nothing of significance: a couple of frosted windows suggested bathrooms, and another window was blinded shut. *It could be his bedroom. Back of the house, why not?*

The trees grew thicker behind the house, so much that Martin had to peer between multiple stumps for a clear view. He checked his watch to find the time as 8:15, and sat on the ground, sticks crunching beneath his heavy body. He thought back to when he was in high school and tried to remember what he did during summer break.

He'd wake up around nine, lie in bed for another half hour, then eventually make his way to the kitchen for breakfast. After that he'd lie on the couch and watch TV until lunchtime, which at that point he'd finally get dressed for the day. With a sandwich made, he'd go back to the couch where a crater formed from his ass, and sat there until the news came on, meaning his parents would be home shortly, prompting him to finally make his bed and pick up his room.

The good old days.

Hopefully Dylan was a bit more active and would go for an afternoon swim or hike. Martin heard gravel crunching from the other side of the house and his heart started to rattle his rib cage.

What the fuck?

Someone was pulling up to the house and Martin sprinted through the trees to get a view of the front door and garage. Adrenaline flushed his system when he saw a cop car parked in the roundabout, and he positioned himself behind a thick tree stump that hid his whole body.

A police officer stepped out of the squad car, taking a quick look around, before strutting up to the front door. He pounded on it with a hard fist, surely waking up anyone who might have still been asleep. The officer stood with his arms crossed as he waited.

The door swung inward and Martin saw the face that sent chills down his spine.

He'd only ever seen Dylan on the news, but knew him right away from his tall and lanky frame, long sandy hair, pale skin, and big nose. A face that would be etched forever in the history books. Martin hadn't expected anyone else to answer, but seeing the boy for the first time threw his mind into a whirlwind. Dylan wore a striped bathrobe, and his hair was frazzled wildly in every direction.

Rise and shine, he thought, now trying to focus his hearing on the conversation between Dylan and the officer. Martin was too far to hear anything, but could see the officer pointing toward the main road, where Dylan looked and nodded his head in acknowledgement.

Did that asshole in the Porsche call the cops on me?

He could imagine the conversation: the officer telling young Dylan to stay on the lookout for a suspicious man in the neighborhood, to not answer the door for anyone he didn't know, and to call the police if he saw anything out of the ordinary. Only in an uppity neighborhood like this would the police arrive ten minutes after a "poor" man was seen walking around.

Maybe I just wanted to go on a hike today. Is that illegal now?

The officer handed Dylan what looked like a business card before returning to his squad car. The shiny Ford Crown Victoria circled the roundabout and disappeared down the driveway, crunching gravel on its way out.

Martin remained frozen in the trees and watched Dylan close

the door. "You're home alone," he whispered, knowing a parent would have answered the door under normal circumstances. His mind raced with possibilities and anticipation, yet his inner voice kept him in line.

Leave. The kid is probably on high alert. What else would the police have come to the house to discuss? The past is already pushing back, don't take any more chances.

Martin could feel the house pulling him, daring him to ring the doorbell and see what would happen. His cover had already been somewhat blown for the day, however, but a trip back tomorrow would have to suffice. He now had the knowledge that Dylan was indeed still asleep as of 8:30 by the looks of his dazed and groggy face when he opened the door. He could plan to come back closer to nine to start his stakeout in the woods, and hopefully go unnoticed by any passing vehicles.

As much as the decision pained him, Martin dashed through the trees back to the driveway. Once out of sight from the house, he stepped onto the gravel and walked at a brisk pace downhill. Panting for air by the time he reached the bottom, he looked around carefully in both directions to make sure there were no other cars, especially a police car.

Damn this day, he thought. *I had him right where I wanted: home alone. But now the whole town is on high alert because some rich asshole saw me walking on the road on his way to work.*

The past could go fuck itself, as far as Martin was concerned, and he continued to let his mind rage as he started on the quarter mile hike back to his car. *Hopefully they didn't tow me already.*

The sun beat down on him unforgivably, creating sweat beads around his neck that dripped down his back. He kept his head down as he walked, watching his shadow move with each step as gracefully as a dance partner. Birds sung tunes from high in the surrounding trees, and Martin caught a whiff of manure mixed in the freshness of the outdoors.

Only Colorado has city life and farm life within a mile of each other, he thought in an attempt to take his mind off the botched morning. When he rounded the corner of Cougar Road he felt instant relief at seeing his car parked exactly where he had left it, and started whistling now that he could relax, knowing he could get home without a visit to the car impound.

See, the past doesn't have to ruin everything. It just wasn't the right timing. Come back tomorrow, it'll happen when it's meant to be.

He strolled to his beaten up car, wondering if he should have purchased a luxury vehicle to fit in better in Littleton. But, that was all in hindsight now, and he'd have to make do with what he had.

He slapped the hood of the car, creating a hard thud that echoed and vibrated throughout the rest of the steel frame. "Ol' reliable," he cackled before pulling open the door, feeling an immediate heat wave escape like he had opened an oven door instead. The temperature had to have risen at least fifteen more degrees during his quick ninety minutes away from the car. Maybe it was best he had to call off his plans for the day. The last thing he needed was to be passed out on the side of the road from dehydration. Ten Porsches, Mercedes, and BMWs would pass him before someone decided to help, then he'd have to explain to the Littleton police why he was stranded in the middle of an upper class neighborhood in his junk car.

Sorry, officer, I was looking for Arvada and took a wrong turn. And that's why I'm half an hour away from the nearest middle class town.

Surely that excuse would hold up – it was the 90's, after all, and no one had handheld gadgets yet that could direct them from point A to point B as efficiently as possible.

How did we ever survive? he wondered as he stared at the printed out directions on the passenger seat.

After a minute of letting the heat escape the car, he sat down behind the wheel and fired up the engine. He waited, the gentle vibrations of the engine relaxing his body as he sipped the final remnants from his water bottle.

I should find a pool. A pool and a frozen drink would go perfect right about now.

The clock on the dashboard read 9:53, leaving him plenty of time to get drunk and still sober up before arriving home after five. Saliva pooled in his mouth at the thought of a piña colada. He'd have to find a library first to see where might even offer booze in the middle of a weekday.

Maybe we can plan a trip to Vegas. I could get my drinks by the pool, and bet big money at the sportsbook without worrying about a bookie wanting to cut my dick off.

Martin's mind drifted into the fantasy that was Las Vegas as he put the car into gear. "Viva Las Vegas!" he shouted with a mad laugh.

Last time he left the Klebold residence the route took him another ten minutes away from the highway, so today he turned onto the road to make a U-turn to save time.

Martin didn't see the speeding semi-truck until it was too late. The truck boomed its intimidating horn as the tires screeched, smoke filling the air like a wildfire. Martin looked out the passenger side window to the sight of dormant headlights and a chrome grill with *Freightliner* inscribed across the top. For a moment, he wondered what would happen if he died in the past, then the truck slammed into his car, sending him tumbling like a boulder down the road as the windows shattered and the metal caved in.

After an eternity of rolling in the car, it came to a halt. Martin looked out his window and saw the asphalt from the road. The car was on its side. Drops of blood had splattered everywhere in the car, and he could feel the liquid oozing from his forehead. He tried to move his hands, move his legs, but nothing would respond.

Oh dear God, please no. Don't let this be happening.

His consciousness faded in and out, and all he could see in his mind was a laughing Chris. "I told you to be careful. You wanted to tango with the past, and this is what you get."

That old, evil smirk stayed in the front of his thoughts until blackness draped over, leaving Martin in a free falling sensation as the rest of the world turned dark.

30

Chapter 30

Sonya arrived home at 5:30 like most evenings, kicking off her shoes and changing into sweatpants to lounge around the house. Martin would be home in a few minutes, and she thought she just might have a drink with him. She had a rough day at school where two of her students broke into a fight in the middle of a lecture. Apparently, young Christopher stole a Gameboy from little Tyler, and Tyler didn't take it too well. Ah, summer school, where half the students genuinely need help and the other half are there to be kept off the streets. Sonya had caught a flying fist to her breast as she tried to break up the fight, and while it didn't hurt, it still put a funk on the rest of her day.

Once in her loungewear, she plopped down on the couch and cracked open a new romance book called *The Notebook.* Her and some of the other teachers at school participated in a book club where they read one new release each month, usually a steamy romance to escape the daily grind of the booger-flicking and hormonal preteens.

She dove into the book, getting lost in the other world for

a good half hour before realizing Martin still hadn't arrived. *Where could he be?* she wondered as she put in her bookmark and tossed the novel on the coffee table.

She crossed the room to the window overlooking the front yard and pulled back the shades to see if he was in the driveway or maybe coming down the street. He had always been prompt in coming home, but it was now 6:04, and he had never been home past six without giving her notice.

The post office would have been closed already, too, so she couldn't call to make sure he was okay. He had talked about buying a pager, but hadn't got around to picking one up yet; that would have been handy in a moment like this and she'd be sure to remind him of that.

Maybe he stopped at the bar for a drink. We could have both had a rough day, we're usually in sync that way.

She gave up on looking through the window and went to the kitchen to start dinner. She didn't have much energy and boiled water for spaghetti, her go-to meal when she didn't really want to cook. While the noodles cooked, she returned to her evening read, standing over the stove to stir the pasta every couple minutes. Surely Martin wouldn't be any later than seven, when they typically sat down for dinner.

The meal was ready by 6:26, and still no Martin, so she put some garlic bread in the oven to kill more time. Her lazy meal was turning into multiple courses now, and she grew more worried with each passing minute he didn't arrive.

What are you doing, Martin? This isn't funny.

"He's just at a bar having a few drinks I'm sure. Maybe he went out with some friends after work."

But he had never mentioned any friends from work, let alone any coworkers in general. As far as she knew, he went in to work every day without speaking a word to anyone. His daily recap of the work day typically consisted of "Same shit, different day, how was yours?" He never complained about his boss or coworkers, or even the job itself. Sonya scratched her head, debating what to do.

She could drive around to some of the local bars he liked to frequent, but if he had gone out downtown that would be a waste of time. The only friend he had ever mentioned was his old landlord. Maybe she would drive around just to see if his car was parked at any of the bars.

Just give him until seven before you do anything. Do you really want to appear so clingy and paranoid?

No, she certainly didn't want to do that and would wait at the kitchen table until seven before making any decisions. There could have been a long line at the gas station, or maybe he got a flat tire. Maybe he stopped to buy her flowers and dessert for later. There were hundreds of possibilities and not all of them had to involve him being at a bar.

What if he was in a car accident? She had kept this thought in the back of her mind as long as she could, but could no longer contain it. Martin had shown he was chaotic behind the wheel, but getting in an accident during rush hour would be difficult as the traffic coming north on I-25 was a sitting parking lot for the entirety of the drive.

The oven dinged and she jolted out of her chair. She forgot about the bread and pulled it out immediately. The clock on the oven read 6:39 and she tried to keep her mind distracted. She could no longer wait and poured a glass of vodka, mixing in soda, and taking an aggressive sip.

Just as she had done this, headlights poured through the living room window and brought instant relief. "Thank God," she whispered, and pulled out two plates from the cupboard. *See, you were just overreacting. Everything's fine and now he's home to have dinner and hear about your shitty day.*

She started to set the table when a booming knock came from the front door. *Did he lose his house key?* She crossed the room and froze when she saw a bulky policeman standing on the other side of the door. Even though a curtain hung over the door's window, she could tell by the man's build and hat, and the crackling of a radio.

Oh, my God. No.

She pulled open the door, it creaking and groaning, dreading what waited on the other side.

The officer stood wide, broad shouldered, with his arms crossed. His name badge read *Rawlings,* and she could see the bad news swimming behind his brown eyes and stone face.

"Good evening, ma'am," he said, tipping his hat. His voice came out hoarse and he had to clear his throat. "Are you Sonya Griffiths?"

She wanted to tell him no, close the door, and crawl into her bed to pretend none of this was happening. *He can't be dead. He just can't.* A bulge formed in her throat that she had to force down before responding.

"Yes, I am. Is everything okay?"

No, Sonya, everything is not okay. Martin is over 90 minutes late and there's a state trooper standing at your front door.

"I understand Martin Briar lives here with you, is that correct?"

Hearing the officer speak Martin's name sent an instant rush of blood into her belly. *Oh, no, this is bad.*

"Well, ma'am, I have some unfortunate news. Mr. Briar is currently in a coma in Littleton Adventist Hospital. He was in a nasty car accident involving a semi truck."

Her hands shot to her mouth as relief and panic both settled. Relief from knowing he wasn't dead, panic about the coma. Her hands started to tremble, and the officer noticed.

"From what we've been told, he'll make it out. The doctors aren't considering the coma to be life-threatening. There's also no timetable for when they expect him to come to, so it might be best for you to go to the hospital and speak with them yourself."

"You said he's in Littleton? What was he doing all the way out there?" she asked, running through any possibilities in her mind, but coming up with nothing.

"We were hoping you might know. We recovered his MapQuest directions in the car and found his starting point as his old apartment. We went there and spoke with the landlord who informed us that Martin had moved in with you not too long ago. Does the last name Klebold mean anything to you?"

"Klebold?" She paused and rummaged through her mind's filing cabinets of random knowledge. "It's not ringing a bell for me, sorry."

"That's strange, we reached out to their family and they don't know who he is, either. Hopefully he'll be able to tell us more when he wakes up. Do you know your way to the hospital in Littleton?"

"Yes, I should be able to find it. Will they let me visit him now, or do I have to wait until the morning?"

"You're good to go there now. Here's my card, let me know if you think of anything later on that might help."

Sonya took the card and forced a fake smile to the officer who tipped his hat, wished her a good evening, and left. She closed the door and thought deeply of any connection Martin might have had in Littleton, still unable to come up with anything. She'd have to go there first to speak with the doctors, make sure he was okay, and then try to get to the bottom of what he was doing in Littleton after work.

She rushed back to the kitchen, threw the pasta in a container before grabbing her keys and purse, and headed out.

It was now 7:15, the sun descending behind the mountains as Sonya drove, wondering what Martin was hiding from her.

31

Chapter 31

Sonya had never been to Littleton. The drive felt like an eternity, the thought of Martin lying comatose weighing down on her. After forty minutes on the road, she finally pulled up to Littleton Adventist Hospital.

The hospital stood four stories tall, its fluorescent lights glowing in the night sky. Within those walls was a man she loved. Anxiety had gnawed at her during the drive; she wanted to make sure he was okay, but at the same time wanted to shake him awake and demand answers.

Just go in there and make sure he's okay, because that's all that matters right now.

With her courage finally built up, she stepped out of the car and walked toward the main entrance on a mission.

"Good evening," Sonya said, approaching a young nurse at the front desk. "I'm looking for Martin Briar. I believe he was admitted here today."

The nurse's eyebrows perched up. "Yes, Mrs. Briar, he's in our care. If you can have a seat for a moment, I'll have another nurse take you to his room."

Mrs. Briar, Sonya thought, not wanting to correct the nurse. *It does have a nice ring.*

The hospital was rather quiet, one family gathered in the main lobby where two kids ran circles around their seated mother and father. Sonya strode toward a seat and plopped herself down. A couple of vending machines hummed, and somewhere in the distance a radio talk show chattered softly.

Mrs. Briar, she thought again. She had ruled out marriage after she turned 45, believing at that point it was well too late to begin a family, so why bother with the formalities of signing a government document to seal a romantic relationship?

The mere thought of a wedding still sent a flutter to her chest, just as it had when she was 23 and madly in love with her college sweetheart. She had the dress, wedding colors, and songs all picked out in her head and knew exactly how her big day would play out to the finest details. That was until a year later when she walked in to her boyfriend's apartment to find him in the shower with another man. The shock had never really left, and she wasn't sure if she was more surprised that he was gay, or that he had cheated on her.

This incident had sparked a chain of trust issues that would haunt her in every following relationship. She could never fully submit her soul to another man, the sounds of her ex-soulmate moaning in the shower as the other man groped his crotch forever ringing in her head.

"At least this happened now instead of after you two got married." That's what all the women in her life, from her friends to her grandmother, told her following the tragedy, as if they could relate.

Being cheated on was one thing. Living a lie was a whole new ballgame, and reality sunk in that five years of her life were wasted, a feeling that ate her alive from the inside. There was no lesson to be learned from the relationship; everything had become moot the second she learned her fiancé was living a double life.

Now she sat in the hospital, almost twice her age since that tragedy, wondering if this was the same thing playing out before her eyes. Surely Martin would have a reason to be in Littleton; he didn't exactly take random cruises around the state. But could she believe his reason if it didn't sound truthful?

They had mentioned the Klebold family, but she had never heard of them. Did he meet a rich housewife at the post office who took a liking to him?

"Excuse me, ma'am," a nurse shouted from the door next to the reception desk. She was an older black woman, staring at Sonya with bulging brown eyes. "Follow me, ma'am."

The nurse pushed the door open as Sonya approached, allowing her to pass through to the main hallway that stretched to dozens of patient rooms.

"We're gonna take the elevator to the third floor. We have Mr. Briar stabilized, but the doctor will want a word with you."

"Is he still. . ."

"Yes, he's still comatose. The doctor will give you all of the details on his condition. Just to clarify, you're his only living relative, correct?"

There had clearly been some miscommunication between the Littleton police and the hospital as they all tried to piece together who exactly was Martin Briar.

"He has no living relatives that I know of. I'm his girlfriend; we live together in Larkwood."

Sonya thought she heard the nurse snicker at the mention of

Larkwood, but brushed it off as the elevator doors spread apart in front of them. She followed and watched as she pushed the button for the third floor.

"No family at all?" the nurse asked. "That poor man. At least he has you to look out for him."

The nurse had to say no more to kick Sonya's mind back into panic mode. What kind of person had *zero* family? Martin had to be hiding something. Things weren't adding up, and every revealed detail led to more questions that she'd have to wait to ask until he woke up.

"He's right this way, ma'am," the nurse said as she led them out of the elevator and down another hallway. The third floor was even more deserted than the first, many of the lights dimmed and providing an eerie glow over the Intensive Care Unit.

The nurse stopped in front of door 317, poked her head in, and held out an open arm to guide Sonya into the room.

"Have a seat and the doctor will be with you in just a minute. You can even talk to Mr. Briar if you wish. They say people in comas will sometimes respond to a familiar voice. I'll leave you to it."

The nurse vanished as Sonya entered the room, lit by a lone lamp standing on the table next to Martin's bed. She hardly recognized him with the tubes running in and out of his body. A clear oxygen mask covered his face while other wires ran from his forehead to a nearby machine charting what she assumed was his brain activity; it was practically a flat line. An IV ran into his arm for hydration, and more wires appeared from his chest area to a heart monitor machine, beeping softly with each pulse.

Sonya remained frozen in the doorway and could tell, from

a distance, that Martin's skin had turned a tint of yellow, making him appear as if he had aged another decade overnight.

When she mustered the courage to get closer, she approached her lover with trembling hands over her mouth, standing directly over him and looking into his closed eyes, wondering what he was doing lost in his own mind. His hair splayed out wildly beneath his head and she noticed more gray and white hairs than before.

"Oh, Martin," she whispered, running a hand along his arm. His index finger twitched when she touched him, causing her to recoil.

"That's perfectly normal," a squeaky voice said from behind. She turned to see an older man in a white lab coat. "Good evening, I'm Dr. Benjamin Lincoln."

The doctor stood short with a slight hunch in his back. He smiled warmly at Sonya as he stuck a hand out, short white hairs on his fingers that matched the curls on his head.

"Hello, Dr. Lincoln. My name is Sonya; I'm Martin's girlfriend."

"Pleased to meet you." Dr. Lincoln pulled out a pair of glasses from his coat pocket and slid them over his crooked nose. He turned in a swift motion to grab a file on the table next to the heart rate monitor. "Now, would you like to speak in here or in my office?"

Sonya turned back to Martin, seemingly gasping for every puff of air. "I'd like to stay in here if that's okay."

"Absolutely. Let's have a seat on the other side of Mr. Briar." Dr. Lincoln shuffled across the foot of the bed to the two chairs tucked in the corner beside the window overlooking the hospital's parking lot. Sonya followed and took her seat next to the doctor, who had already flipped open his folder

209

and rummaged through a stack of papers. The anticipation had reached its peak and she couldn't stand to wait.

"Just tell me the news, doctor. I've been losing my mind the whole way over here."

He looked at Sonya with heavy blue eyes, but that smile never left his face. "Let me start by saying you're boyfriend here is very lucky. Did the police give you any details of what happened?"

"No, not really."

"Mr. Briar was in his car, in the middle of the road, I believe making a U-turn, when a diesel truck came flying around the corner and collided with him. The truck struck his car along the passenger side, which is good, and sent his car rolling three times over itself."

Dr. Lincoln paused and grabbed a tissue box for Sonya when he noticed the tears streaming down her cheeks.

"How exactly is this *lucky*?" she asked through her sobs.

"Well, if his car had been turned the other way, the impact would have hit him directly, and we wouldn't be having this conversation. It appears his head came into contact with the driver's side window as we found shards of glass in his skull and hair. If it had been anything else, say the steering wheel or the actual door, again, we wouldn't be having this conversation. His head broke the window and the impact was enough to put him into a coma."

"How serious is the coma?"

"Comas are always serious, but it appears this one is not fatal. I'd guess a week maximum until Mr. Briar wakes up. We've tried different therapies to get a response from his brain, with some success. I'd say Mr. Briar is very much alert within his coma, whatever that might mean, we're not exactly sure."

"How can you know when he'll wake up?"

"It's not an exact science, nor is the technology to say for certain. All we can do is make an educated guess by comparing his brain's responsiveness to cases in the past. The way his mind is trending makes me think this is very much a short term coma."

"How will he be when he wakes up? Will he remember anything?"

"That we don't know. A majority of comatose patients will have struggles with short-term memory, often forgetting the event that may have put them in to the coma in the first place. But, every case is different, so it's a matter of waiting and seeing when the time comes."

Sonya shook her head, trying to absorb the information along with the intensity of the situation.

"Are there any other questions you might have?" Dr. Lincoln asked.

"What am I supposed to do while he's in the coma? Can I stay here with him?"

"There's honestly no need for that. I can say confidently that he will be fine. He suffered no damage to other organs, and it's just a matter of waiting. There's no chance for him to have any sort of relapse into a dangerous zone. He's stable and functioning as best as we could hope for. You can come visit whenever you wish, but know that we will call you as soon as he wakes up."

"Please do. I don't care if it's two in the morning."

"Of course, ma'am," he said with a grin. "If you have nothing else for me, I'll leave you alone with Mr. Briar. Talk to him. Touch him. It sparks responsiveness in the mind, and that's all we're looking for."

Dr. Lincoln patted Sonya on the shoulder before leaving her alone with Martin.

She turned back to him, a lifeless collection of tubing and wires, and could no longer hold back the floodgates swelling behind her eyes.

"Oh, Martin, please don't forget who I am," she cried, tears dripping onto his limp arm. "I love you and can't lose you. I can't do this again."

She would stay beside him for another thirty minutes before the tears cleared up and she was able to drive home.

32

Chapter 32

Martin knew he was in a dream, but could sense it wasn't an ordinary one. He felt awake within himself, like wandering through an endless fog of emptiness.

The scenery in this dream constantly changed. One moment he was walking through an empty town with cobblestone roads and ancient buildings lining the sidewalks. Then he'd free fall and land in a new place. Sometimes it was another deserted city, other times an empty room. This cycle continued for what felt an eternity, changing locations every few hours.

He currently stood in a dark, empty room, where a long bulb flickered on the ceiling, providing light no brighter than a single candle. Silence filled his head, piercing his mind as he could only hear the sound of his breathing.

"Hello?" he asked the room, his voice echoing into unknown depths. He couldn't make out any nearby walls as he paced around, his hands splayed in front of him in search of anything to make contact with.

He held his breath to better hear what he thought were voices whispering in the distance, but found it to be his voice still echoing faintly, as if traveling down a tunnel.

Martin had wandered at least thirty steps away from the flickering light, but the room felt no less dark than where he had stood previously.

The ground rumbled and he immediately knew a change of scenery was underway. He sat on the ground, having learned his lessons from the first two instances when he collapsed, out of balance and flailing. Since then, he sat every time the ground rumbled and waited for his arrival at the next unknown destination.

The ground became light, a floating sensation as he pictured himself flying on a magic carpet like Aladdin. If he could see the walls around him, he'd see them passing by in a blur, like riding a train and staring out the window. He wasn't sure if he was teleporting, falling, or flying, and he didn't care to find out.

Just sit down and enjoy the ride.

The rumbling of the ground beneath his ass settled into a soft vibration before halting completely upon his arrival.

The darkness of the prior room gave way to bright lights. When the gravity returned to normal, Martin stood on weary legs to explore his newest location: an empty library.

Shelves of books stretched as far as he could see. The librarian's desk stood thirty feet to his left, abandoned, a lone computer monitor turned on to a black screen with a digital clock bouncing around as a screensaver.

The silence didn't feel as thick in the library, not ringing in Martin's head. He looked up to see a second floor with more bookshelves and tables overlooking the first floor. The library felt familiar, but he couldn't quite piece it together.

He'd had that problem when he first arrived in this dream,

struggling to remember the most basic things. A voice within told him he wasn't in a dream, that maybe he had died. And while he knew he wasn't in a regular dream, he couldn't muster the mind power to piece together what had actually happened. All he could do was explore the ever changing places around him.

Martin moved his legs that felt like bricks, dragging them closer toward the computer, the sensation like walking through two feet of mud as he forced his legs to move every inch forward.

"Pssssst!" a voice whispered from behind, sending an instant chill down Martin's spine. "Hey, mister."

The voice sounded adolescent, and Martin pivoted around to face it.

Two pale boys stood ten feet away. *How did they get there?* The library had rows of books in every direction, no exit in sight. The boys stood side-by-side, each holding a gun in hand.

The boy on the left had a long face, pointy noise, and short, spiked brown hair. A smirk revealed a charming countenance to go along with his light green eyes. The boy on the right was taller by at least six inches and had his flowing, sandy hair brushed back to reveal his green eyes. Both wore matching black trench coats that covered them from neck to ankle.

Eric Harris and Dylan Klebold. This is all a dream. They're not really standing in front of you.

Martin reminded himself of this fact as he looked from Eric's pump-action shotgun to Dylan's semiautomatic TEC-9.

"We *are* standing in front of you, dipshit!" Eric barked in a shrill voice.

Dylan smirked, nodding in gratitude. Both boys cradled

their guns like babies in their arms, striking Martin as an odd pose. Martin accepted that anything was possible in his dreamscape, now knowing the future mass murderers could hear his thoughts.

"What can I do for you boys?" he asked, ignoring his trembling legs. An instinct told him this moment was critical to what he was doing, but he couldn't remember *what* exactly he was doing before arriving in the never-ending dream.

"You can mind your own fucking business," Dylan snarled, now raising his pistol in the air. "Long live the Trench Coat Mafia!" He pumped the pistol upward.

Eric howled at the ceiling like a rabid wolf. "Don't come near the school. Don't try and stop us. You'll pay if you do. I'll slit your throat and piss in your blood."

"Long live the Trench Coat Mafia!" Dylan shouted again, almost robotically.

Both boys studied Martin with hungry grins on their face, like a pair of lions about to pounce on a zebra. As if a light switched on in his mind, Martin remembered everything he had been working on before falling into this dream. The boys and the library had felt familiar because they *were* familiar. He had just stood in this very library within the last few weeks, and remembered his plans to try and stop the boys from slaughtering their schoolmates. Now, he wondered if this was a subconscious ploy to talk him out of it. The past seemed ruthless in preserving its history, and getting to someone through their dreams didn't seem too drastic for Father Time.

"Eric. Dylan," Martin said authoritatively, looking from boy to boy. "Let's talk this out. Why do you want to do this?"

Martin drew on his bomb threat training from years at the post office. If a bomb threat ever came in to the post office, either via phone or an in-person threat, they were instructed to ask the suspect "why are you doing this?" as the first question. In ninety-nine percent of bomb threat cases, the suspect was always equipped to answer "where is the bomb?" or "how much time until it goes off?" with a pre-scripted response already in mind. Asking the perpetrator their reasoning for their actions was the last thing on their mind, and he hoped to catch the boys off guard in the same way.

Eric smirked, turning to Dylan, who kept his own drunken grin fixed on Martin. "You know why we do this," Eric said calmly. "You saw it all over the news. Nobody at that goddamn school cares about us. They tease us. They think we're different, but we're the only ones truly grabbing life by the balls."

"Long live the Trench Coat Mafia!" Dylan shouted again, and Martin thought he saw saliva leaking from the corner of the boy's mouth.

"Dylan," Martin said. "Can you even say anything else?"

Dylan snickered, keeping a steady eye on the old man in front of him.

"You know, you're absolutely right," Martin continued. "I did watch all of the news reports, and read all the articles when they came out. It was a truly fascinating story. The first of its kind. If we only knew then the rest of the shootings that would follow your lead."

Eric threw his head back, cackling uncontrollably. "Yes! Yes! Yes! It's been a treat watching the others carry on our work. There's been so many, and there will be many more. They all will be taken care of by the Trench Coat Mafia."

Martin remembered the Trench Coat Mafia as nothing more

than a group name for the less popular kids at Columbine. In the videos Eric and Dylan had filmed of their target practice in the woods, they made multiple references to the Trench Coat Mafia, and wore the same trench coats they had on during the massacre.

He remembered when those disturbing videos had leaked. They aired on the late night news, not wanting to risk any children coming across the footage in the old days before the internet made everything accessible. In the video, they had made multiple references to not only the Trench Coat Mafia, but also to the Nazi party, and Adolf Hitler. They worshiped Hitler, hailing his name numerous times in the video and in their notebooks that surfaced further down the road.

"I understand that life can be hard, especially in high school," Martin said, deciding to do what he could while he had both boys' attention.

"Save it, old man," Eric snapped. "We don't give a shit what you say. Everything is going to happen as planned."

"Yeah," Dylan finally said another word. "Tell someone who gives a fuck."

The boys chuckled at each other like they had shared an inside joke.

"You know, Dylan, Eric is only bringing you along because he's too scared to do this on his own. He doesn't actually care about you."

"Shut up!" Eric screamed, cocking his shotgun and raising it to Martin's face. "Shut the fuck up!"

"But it came out on the news, Eric. All the stories said you were a big loner. No friends. How sad. But you came up with this sick idea and brainwashed the only person who would give you the time of day. Dylan was a happy kid before he started spending time with you. Why bring him down?"

"Shut up, old man. I swear to God!" Eric shouted. Dylan stood by his side, jaw hanging open in surprise as he watched the exchange.

"God? You don't believe in God, remember?" Martin responded calmly. "You shot a girl after she admitted believing in God."

"That did feel good. That Bible-thumping bitch," Eric said proudly, still aiming the shotgun at Martin.

"Was this all worth it? Killing each other after leaving such a mess behind. Too chickenshit to face the consequences?"

"You're just like the rest of them," Eric said. "You need a lesson in how to be nice to people. You walk around here with your rules and ethics, thinking you're better than everyone else."

"Do you know how stupid you sound saying you killed people because they weren't nice?" Martin asked.

"Go to hell, and stay away from our school."

Eric squeezed the trigger and the shotgun let out a booming sound, echoing across the empty library. The slug caught Martin square in the chest, spreading a burning sensation throughout his lungs.

Eric and Dylan both giggled as Martin collapsed in slow motion to the ground, hand clasped over the hole where the warmth of blood started to ooze.

"We told you to stay away," Dylan said, stepping up to Martin with his pistol aimed between his eyes. Martin had never stared down the barrel of a gun before, but seeing the small black hole of death created a strange sense of comfort as he knew what would come next.

I'm in a dream. I'm not really going to die. If he shoots me, I'll wake up. That's how this works. Martin reassured himself as a sliver of doubt crept in.

"No one remembers you two. Ten years down the road, after your shooting, your names are long gone and forgotten. I hope it's all worth it." Martin spoke with a forced smirk, *wanting* Dylan to pull the trigger so he could leave this endless nightmare.

"Long live the Trench Coat Mafia!" Dylan shouted, and shot Martin in the head.

Chapter 33

Martin jolted awake, glued to the bed beneath him by sweat, and looked slowly around the room to the sight of beeping monitors and dozens of wires and tubes running in and out of his body. He held up his hands to find an IV running into one and a pulse monitor clipped to his index finger on the other. Breathing felt as fresh as he had ever experienced, and he realized an oxygen mask was strapped around his head and clasped down over half of his face.

A chalkboard hung on the wall across the foot of his bed with his last name written in big, round lettering. It also showed his main doctor to be Dr. Lincoln and a list of the three nurses who likely took care of him.

Why am I in the hospital? He patted around his body, feeling for any sort of pain or missing limb. *Did I get attacked trying to save Izzy?* He squeezed his eyes shut and tried to gather his thoughts on what he had been doing, but all he could see was Eric and Dylan, laughing, taunting, and shooting him while they sung praises to the Trench Coat Mafia.

An older man dressed in a white lab coat strode into the

room after a quick courtesy rap on the door.

"Mr. Briar," he said as he approached Martin's bedside. "Welcome back. I'm Dr. Lincoln, and I've been looking after you the past week."

Martin stared at him dumbfounded, and the doctor recognized this immediately.

"Mr. Briar, you've been in a coma for the last six days. You've been coming in and out of sleep for the last twelve hours, so we've been expecting you to wake up soon for good."

Coma? What the fuck?

"Do you remember what you were doing before you arrived here?" the doctor asked in a sympathetic voice.

Martin opened his mouth to speak, but felt his throat tighten with mucus. If he'd really been knocked out the last six days, his body likely wasn't functioning correctly.

He cleared his throat twice, lifted the oxygen mask off his face, and mustered out, "Water."

"Yes, of course."

The doctor spun around and filled a cup from the sink in the room's bathroom, returning with a wide grin. "This should do good for you. We'll get you some bottled water in a bit."

Martin grabbed the cup in a weak, shaky hand, and used all of his concentration to guide it to his mouth. When he took the first sip, he felt an instant clearing and soothing in his throat as the cool liquid went down.

"Much better. Thank you," Martin said. He curiously looked around the room more. "Where am I?"

"You're in Littleton, Colorado."

"Littleton?" Martin asked. "I'm not from Littleton."

"We know that. We were hoping you might remember what you were doing out here, so far from home or work?"

Martin closed his eyes and took a deep inhale, testing his lungs' capabilities without the oxygen mask. The last thing he could remember was having dinner with Sonya. But how long ago was that? Clearly something happened to put him in a coma. Why wasn't the doctor telling him?

"I'm sorry. I can't remember anything."

"What's the last thing you remember?" the doctor asked, now scribbling on a clipboard.

"I remember having dinner with my girlfriend. Is she okay?"

"Do you remember her name, Martin?" the doctor said, seemingly ignoring his statement about his last activity.

"Yes. Sonya."

The doctor nodded his head and continued writing notes. "Very good. I need to gauge your memory skills. It helps us know how badly the coma has affected your brain."

"Shouldn't all of these machines tell you that?" he asked, pointing a finger to one of the many wires taped to his forehead.

"Those tell us how your brain is doing physically. You suffered a concussion, but otherwise your brain is in good shape. You were very lucky."

Lucky enough to not know why the hell I'm in Littleton in a hospital bed?

"This will be a process, Mr. Briar. Just know that. There will be some basic things you probably can't remember off the top of your head. Things like names of people and places. That's common, and they will come back in good time. I want to make sure you're not suffering beyond that. Do you know where you live?"

"Larkwood. Born and raised."

"Good. Do you remember your mother's name?"

He opened his mouth, but paused before speaking. He had wanted to respond as a reflex. He could picture his mother, could describe her to the finest detail, but her name was coming up short in his mind.

"Don't worry. Perfectly normal. Do you know what year it is?"

Martin certainly hadn't forgotten that he had traveled back in time.

"1996."

Dr. Lincoln raised his eyebrows, apparently not expecting a correct answer.

"Do you know who the current president is?" the doctor asked.

"Bill Clinton," Martin said confidently, his voice finally feeling back its normal self.

"Very good. I'd say by these early tests that you've suffered mild memory loss. You're still very much aware of the current happenings. Head trauma has some bizarre effects on the mind."

"Are you going to tell me what happened?"

"Yes. You were struck by a semi-truck."

"A semi? Where?"

Martin racked his mind, the memory refusing to come to the forefront.

"You were found in front of the Klebold residence in their private neighborhood," the doctor said, studious eyes on his patient.

The name Klebold must have been the trigger word as Martin's mind released a floodgate of memories. He could remember exactly what he was doing. He had just finished snooping around the Klebold house and saw Dylan answer the door for the police officer.

"Does that ring any bells?"

Martin stayed in his mind, tracking the events that had happened chronologically. After the cop left, he fled the scene, knowing the officer's visit had to do something with his rust bucket of a car being spotted on the side of the road in the glamorous neighborhood.

He scrunched his brow in thought. "I'm afraid I'm not remembering. You said the Klebold house?"

"Correct."

Martin tossed up his hands, feeling a slight tug from the tubes in them. "Sorry. That name doesn't sound familiar at all."

Martin made sure to stare the doctor in his eyes, not wanting any chance of him catching on to his lie.

"Don't stress. It will eventually come back to you. The police may still want to speak with you to get a statement on the accident. I believe the truck driver is in jail; semis are forbidden to drive through that neighborhood."

And they probably never do, until the past decides to push me out of the way.

Martin now understood what Chris had meant. Changing a historical event, whether for better or worse, wouldn't be straightforward. Columbine would have to proceed as history had planned, and the thought burned Martin inside. He'd come this far only to find himself in the hospital from a coma, and having nightmares about the two howling lunatics who would one day carry out their destiny.

Eric and Dylan win. I can't push any further than I already have. Anything more will get me killed. I need to recover and get ready

225

for Izzy in September.

"I'm gonna let you relax for a bit. I'll have a nurse stop in later to get some of these tubes taken out, and I'll discuss the next steps with you at that time," Dr. Lincoln said. "Is there anything I can get for you right now?"

"I want to see Sonya."

"We're going to call her right now. Anything else?"

"No, doctor, thank you. I'm just going to try and think back to what happened."

"Don't push yourself. Your mind has undergone some drastic things in the last week. Try to clear your thoughts, I promise you'll recover just fine."

Dr. Lincoln offered a kind smile before leaving Martin alone.

Martin couldn't keep his mind clear as the doctor instructed. That had always been a tall task, but now with a week's worth of time unaccounted for, his mind worked overtime as he debated what to do when he got out of the hospital. One thought, however, tugged at him.

How the hell am I going to explain this to Sonya?

34

Chapter 34

Six days after Martin had been admitted to the hospital, Sonya's phone rang and rang, echoing its piercing chime throughout the house. She had managed to crawl to the couch and place herself under a blanket for a drunken nap. Alcohol had seemed the only viable option to shake her mind of the disturbing news she had encountered after a week of being alone in her house, a constant knot of anxiety twisting in her gut at the thought of Martin lying comatose 20 miles away.

She had called Larkwood Middle School the day after Martin's accident to inform them she wouldn't be coming in for a few days, and planned to visit Martin every day until he woke up.

After making a quick breakfast of toast with jelly, she pulled her Yellow Pages telephone book from the hallway closet and flipped to the D section. Her finger ran up and down the pages until she found the listing for the Denver Post Office.

She dialed the number on her rotary phone and slid the receiver between her head and shoulder as it rang back in her ear. She had never known what exactly Martin did at the post office and hoped whoever answered the phone would recognize his name.

"Denver Post Office," a man's short voice crackled.

"Yes, hello, I was hoping you might be able to help. I'm trying to get in touch with Martin Briar's manager. Martin's been in an accident and I wanted to let you know."

"Sorry, ma'am, we don't have anyone employed by that name," the voice responded, softer after learning of the accident.

"I think that's a mistake. Martin Briar is his name, if you didn't hear me correctly."

She waited for a reaction from the other end, but nothing came except silence.

"Hello?" she asked.

"One second, ma'am, let me check our most recent directory. One moment."

The silence remained thick in her ear, the lone sound of flipping paper making its way to her phone. After a minute, the voice returned.

"Yes, ma'am. As I suspected, we don't have any employee by that name in our records."

"I don't understand."

"I'm not sure, either. I've worked here for 27 years now and I've never heard that name."

"And this is the Denver Post Office? The one downtown?"

"Yes, ma'am."

A twisting feeling surfaced in her gut.

"Okay, I'm sorry for taking your time today. Thank you for your help." Sonya felt robotic as she spoke, and replaced the phone on its hook like a dazed zombie.

Relax. There's an explanation. There has to be. Maybe you

misunderstood all along where he said he worked.

She clenched her eyes shut and thought back to the rare time Martin actually discussed work. She wasn't mistaken; he had definitely mentioned working downtown, sometimes going to the 16th Street Mall for his lunch break.

Maybe he lied to you. Here's another guy living a double life. He's secretly rich, has a 30-year-old housewife in Littleton, but gets off to having an affair with a poor teacher from Larkwood.

"No!" she barked to her empty kitchen, pounding fists down on the table, rattling the silverware. "This isn't happening again!"

Joke's on you for thinking you could actually have a real relationship. Just admit it, Sonya, you're gonna die alone. Men just can't commit themselves to you. You turned a man gay, in case you forgot.

Sonya returned her Yellow Pages to the closet, exchanging the massive book for the White Pages, the equally large book containing local residents' phone numbers and addresses.

Her hands refused to steady as she browsed for Briar, but her finger nearly stuck to his name when she found it.

Briar, Martin and Lela. 7762 Cherry St. Larkwood, CO 80022.

"Lela Briar?" Sonya said out loud, the name sounding oddly familiar. "Lela Briar."

She scratched her head angrily as she tried to place a face to the name.

"You son of a bitch!"

She knew the name Lela Briar from school. One of her student's parents.

"Isabelle Briar's parents. Motherfucker!"

Sonya jumped up from the table, blood boiling throughout her body.

He lied to you. You said he looked familiar. Even told him you had a student with that last name. And he lied to your face. He's not having an affair across town; he's having it right here under your nose.

"Fuck!" she screamed, slamming a fist down on the kitchen counter. Her body trembled as her fists clenched.

You should have known better than to try and fall in love. These things have a way of working themselves out. You're the mistress. How does that make you feel?

Sonya's legs surrendered and she slid slowly down to the kitchen floor, just below the sink.

"I'm the other woman," she said to herself, needing it to feel real.

They had mistakenly called her *Mrs. Briar* at the hospital, and she had liked it. Now, the idea made her queasy.

She didn't want to act out irrationally to the news, rather wanting to flip the script on Martin and put him on the hot seat.

Six days of living with this burden had pushed her to her mental limit when she finally dragged herself to the liquor cabinet. Though the constant nausea had subsided, her arms and hands still shook at the thought of being the other woman. She couldn't help but think about Martin as she opened the cabinet and saw three bottles of his whiskey, grabbing one and drinking straight from the bottle.

This led her to the couch where she had fallen into a dream where she was trapped in the bathroom from twenty years ago, the room steaming as two men giggled with each other in the shower. She screamed, but the giggling grew louder, the steam thicker and hotter. The sound of the running water was steady, and she tried to focus on that, wanting to break free of the nightmare.

A dim ringing sound poured out of the showerhead, and it too grew louder with each passing second, eventually causing the bathroom to vanish as her eyes snapped open and she returned to her living room, head throbbing in protest.

It took her a moment to process that the phone was ringing, but when she did, she jumped and tumbled across the room to take the phone off the cradle.

"Hello?" she managed groggily.

"Yes, hi, is this Sonya?" the familiar voice asked.

"Yes. Who this is?"

"Sonya, this is Dr. Lincoln down at Littleton Adventist Hospital. I have some good news."

Martin.

Naps had a way of erasing memories, at least temporarily. She of course remembered her panic attack in the kitchen, the cursing of his name, but the sting of her rage seemed to have vanished for the moment.

"Mr. Briar is awake."

"Oh, thank god."

"Yes, it's surprisingly quick progress he's making."

"So what can I do? Should I come down there?"

"I wouldn't worry quite yet. I'd say to relax the rest of the night and plan to come by in the morning. We'll be running some tests to better gauge where he is mentally."

Sonya glanced at the clock ticking on the wall and found it was already a quarter past midnight. She would be up late unless she popped some sleeping pills. Her head still pounded violently, her brain shrinking into itself from the excessive alcohol.

"Thank you, Doctor. Is there anything I can bring Martin

231

from home? Maybe something to help him in his recovery?"

Maybe his wife? His daughter? His other life?

"I think just yourself will be fine. This has been a mild coma, so I'd expect things to go smoothly from here on out."

"Great, I can plan on that. Thank you again, and I'll see you in the morning."

"Have a great night."

The phone clicked off and Sonya replaced the receiver on its cradle, a smirk forming on her face.

How did the police not find any relation back to his actual family? Sounds a bit lazy for detective work.

Regardless of the blunders they may have made, Sonya knew what she wanted to do: trap Martin in his lie. She would play dumb, go along with everything, even bring Martin home and help him recover. She'd pay close attention to what he said, looking for any glaring loopholes that might slip his stealth.

Then, when the time seemed right, she'd pounce the truth on him and revel in seeing the shock on his face once he realized he'd been caught.

I'll be the one with the last laugh this time.

35

Chapter 35

Sonya hadn't felt such a conflict of emotions since the tragic shower situation. She wanted to barge into Martin's hospital room, throw things, curse him out, and make him feel like the snake that he was. But that voice in the back of her mind, the one that lived in the land of naivety, insisted there had to be an explanation. After all, they had gone a good two-month stretch where they spent every free moment together. Even for an affair, that seemed a bit too much to balance for a double life.

She also wanted to confront him on the post office claiming to have never heard of him, but decided to wait until the hospital released him. It would be better to challenge him at home, not in a public place where any nurse or doctor could interrupt them mid-conversation.

For now, she would only concern herself with his well-being. A lot depended on how the doctors said he was recovering, too. Dr. Lincoln had assured her it was a mild coma, one Martin should be able to recover completely from, but sometimes doctors were wrong. How could they know for sure until he woke up and they started running tests?

Sonya pulled in to the hospital's parking lot and shook her mind free of all the poisonous thoughts trying to form within.

"You're here for Martin. Everything else will take care of itself when the time's right," she said to herself.

The parking lot had changed, this her first time visiting in the morning. Hundreds of cars filled the lot, the sun glaring off the sea of metal. She squeezed through the rows of vehicles on her way to the hospital's main entrance where she took her first right to the elevators at the end of the hall and called for the third floor.

Will he even remember me? A hard enough rattle to his brain could have completely wiped her from his memory. It wouldn't be the most absurd thing to happen to her love life.

"Just shut up and go in there," she whispered to herself, walking down the third floor hallway on unsteady legs.

She reached his closed door and took a deep breath before pushing it open.

Martin lay where he had when she last visited, only this time his eyes were open and he turned his head to meet her stare. She hesitated, having an immediate thought that he didn't recognize her, but he cracked a gentle smile that revealed he was okay.

"Sonya," he said, extending a hand out. She stepped into the room and glided to his bedside, throwing herself onto him as tears flowed. Her body convulsed beneath his arms and he started rubbing her back for a soothing effect that felt perfect.

"I didn't know where you were that night," she said, muffled into his arms. "I was so scared."

"I'm gonna be okay," he said, continuing to rub her back that had finally calmed down. "The doctors have had nothing but good things to say about my recovery."

"Where is Dr. Lincoln?" she asked, wanting to hear for herself.

"I don't know. He left after doing tests. There are some things I can't remember. Especially the accident."

"How do you not remember the accident?" she asked, sure to keep her voice calm. She stood up, staring into his eyes as he scratched his head.

Martin tossed his hands in the air. "I don't know. The doctor described the accident to me, but none of it sounds familiar. I don't even know what I was doing in Littleton. The whole day is like it's deleted from my brain."

"You don't know why you were in Littleton?" she snapped. Through all the shit she had going on in her mind, that was the one question she wanted to pin on him, and he came out and beat her to the punch, providing no information about his time in the rich suburb. She wanted to call him a liar, but refrained, keeping her emotions in check.

And you thought there was an explanation. Your explanation was flushed down the coma toilet where all good explanations go.

"How are you feeling?" she asked, changing the subject before she spilled all she knew. "Did nothing else get injured in the crash?"

He shook his head. "My ribs are a little sore, but the doctor said there's no damage, just some bruising."

"Did they say when you can go home?"

"He said I can likely go home tonight, pending some tests."

As if he heard them talking, Dr. Lincoln entered the room with a rapid knock on the door.

"Sonya," he said. "Glad to see you here. Martin was asking for you right away when he woke." The old doctor shuffled to

Sonya's side and read the monitor next to the bed. "How are you feeling, Mr. Briar?"

"Much better. That food really helped."

"Perfect," the doctor said, and turned to Sonya. "We gave him his first solid meal since he's been in here. Eggs and toast – glad to see it's sitting well."

"Can you fill me in, Dr. Lincoln?"

"Of course. My apologies. Martin is doing better than we could have hoped. He's going to struggle a lot with his short term memory for the next couple months, so it's best for you to remain patient with him. He's going to forget basic things like where he put his car keys, or maybe what drawer utensils go in your kitchen. Nothing major or life threatening, but those little lapses in memory can be frustrating for you as his partner."

She nodded, feeling sympathy for the first time since arriving.

"Aside from that, there may be instances of long term memory showing some trouble, but nothing I suspect will last too long."

"And when will he be going home?" Sonya asked.

"Today. While comas are serious by nature, there's not really much else we can provide here at the hospital. As long as we feel a coma patient is coherent and can function normally, we'll release them. The best treatment is rest and relaxation, and you can do that at home just fine. The final tests will be for Martin to walk around and use the restroom on his own. Once he shows he can do that, he's free to go."

"And there's no treatment of any kind I need to worry about at home?" Sonya asked.

"Just keep the environment relaxed. I'd say for the first

couple weeks, be there with Martin to assist with daily tasks. Do things like yardwork, cooking, and cleaning together. Really anything that distracts the mind is good for recovery."

This all sounded manageable for Sonya, but a realization also grew within like a slow burning flame: she would have to wait some time before confronting Martin with the truth. Not out of a courtesy for his recovering brain, but as a strategic move. Anything she threw his way in the coming weeks could be deflected by using his coma as an excuse. *Oh, you don't remember lying about your job at the post office? Or that you have a family across town? How convenient for you and your damaged mind.*

She'd have to wait the couple of months as instructed by the doctor until Martin showed signs of a full recovery. There would be an eventual point in time where the coma seemed a distant memory, and that's when she would unleash her arsenal of truth bombs. For now, and for the sake of her sanity, her main focus needed to be on Martin's recovery so she could one day get the answers she desired. She'd have to carry on as normal, knowing a showdown would eventually come along with the next turning point of her life.

Just go drop him at his wife's house when you leave from here. Tell him you know everything and leave him to continue his life as it was before meeting you. Imagine the look on his face then.

The idea sounded like the ultimate way to end a relationship, a last laugh kind of situation. But, she wanted the satisfaction of catching him, wanted the deer in headlights look as he watched his world crumble all around him.

"Well, what do you say, Martin? Wanna go for a walk around the halls?" Sonya asked, patting him on the legs. "Let's get you back home."

"We'll need a nurse for that, for an official evaluation, but you are more than welcome to join Mr. Briar on his walk when he feels ready."

"I'm ready, doc. I just wanna go home."

Martin sat up in his bed and swung his legs over the edge. All of the tubes from the last week had been removed earlier, after he woke. His body was again independent after a week of machines feeding him and shitting for him. His feet hit the ground with a heavy thud as he swayed to catch his balance.

"Easy, Mr. Briar," Dr. Lincoln said, putting a hand on Martin's shoulders. "Your body has been idle for a week, so you can't just jump off the bed and make a run for the exit. Let me call that nurse for you and she'll assist you through the halls."

Sonya had paid a visit to the library and researched treating comas. The nurses would have rotated his body over the week, changing the side he laid on to help prevent blood clots, among many other possible side effects. Standing so suddenly would have made the blood rush to his head, causing him to topple the way he had.

So, you're really gonna go through with this? Sonya's inner voice chimed in.

"C'mon, babe, let's take it slow and get out of here. The nurse will be here any minute."

Her mind was set on trapping Martin in his lies.

238

36

Chapter 36

The drive home was silent. A gentle rainfall had started, leaving the only sound as the drops hitting the windshield and the wipers screeching across to clear the view. Martin lay in the passenger seat, reclined, with a small stack of hospital papers on his stomach.

Sonya didn't speak, and Martin was fine with that. He needed to sort out his story and be able to cover his tracks; she would certainly have questions.

There's only one way out of this, he thought. *You have to tell her the truth. There's not a lie that can hide this anymore. No one has a clue what you were doing or why you were at the Klebold house. Just tell her.*

Martin toyed with the idea of spilling his deepest secret. Even a free thinker would need some convincing of time travel being true. This could go one of two drastic ways. She would either run for the hills and call the asylum on Martin, or take a leap of faith and believe him, being practically forced to join him on his adventure. No possible outcome existed where their life together could continue as normal. *Have fun at work today, I'm gonna go stop the 9/11 attacks this morning. Be home for dinner.*

He accepted the ultimatum that awaited, and wanted to rip the bandage off and get it over with. Was now the right time to bring up the matter? She had also gone through a lot in the past week, an emotional roller coaster surrounded by the unknowing. Was today, the most joyous day of the last week, really the best time to spring such news on her?

You can either tell her, or keep it a secret. Just know that if you wait long enough, she'll be the one asking the questions. Don't let her control where this conversation goes. This is all for Izzy – she'll understand once you explain.

Martin considered this. They may have not been dating long, but Martin knew Sonya well enough to anticipate the sea of questions floating behind her silent façade. She was curious about most things, and the topic of why he was in Littleton would surely be on the top of her list.

He would tell her when they arrived home; he didn't want her emotional while driving. Martin recognized the scenery outside of his window, knew they were back in Larkwood, but couldn't remember where or what her house looked like. It was like a blank spot on his internal map of the city, a Bermuda triangle of sorts when he tried to imagine the house's location. It terrified Martin that he couldn't remember where they lived. He could picture the apartment building and Vinny, his old house where Izzy would one day go missing from, but not his current residence.

Martin reached over the center panel and rubbed Sonya's arm, her soft skin gliding beneath his fingertips. "I love you," he said, prompting a flustered look of delight from the driver's seat.

She grinned at him, and he could see the pain and fear hiding behind her eyes. "I love you, too." She grabbed his hand and raised it to her lips for a quick kiss.

"How far are we?"

Her grin turned into a flat line. "We're about three minutes away. Do you not remember your hometown at all?"

"No, I do. It's just your house I can't remember. I remember my old apartment, the liquor store, our favorite restaurants. I just can't picture where the house is."

Sonya nodded, but remained quiet. She probably had no idea what to say to him. The doctor had spoken with Martin in private, letting him know that those close to him might appear to struggle with his recovery more than himself. The forgetfulness could wear down those who loved him. They could grow sick of having to repeat themselves and explain things a dozen times. But Martin believed Sonya to be a good-hearted person, even in the darkest times.

The car turned into a neighborhood and pulled into a driveway. Everything *felt* familiar, but Martin still couldn't piece it all together in his mind. It felt as if someone had dumped a 5,000 piece puzzle on the floor and left him no picture for guidance.

You're on your own. Sonya will try to help, but she's not lost in your head with you. She can't truly help without knowing what's going on. It's like calling for directions, but you don't where you are to begin with.

"Home sweet home," Sonya said, killing the engine. "Can I make you a soup?"

"That sounds delicious. The hospital food was nothing to write home about. And I only had one meal the whole time."

"Sounds lovely. Go lie down on the couch and I'll get

something together. It's a perfect day to cuddle up and watch movies. How does that sound?"

"As long as you're there, it sounds heavenly."

Martin loved her, and should have known better than to get involved romantically with anyone while traveling to the past. Romance has a way of complicating even the simplest of plans. It didn't matter if she was sent to him as a gift from the past. The past would have to try a lot harder to keep him from his daughter come September.

Martin still hadn't regained his natural sense of time and checked the dashboard clock to find it was twenty minutes until five. The day had passed in a blur once Sonya arrived at the hospital, and he hadn't noticed, entranced by the chance to spend a day with her.

"Where's my car?" Martin asked. "Was it destroyed?"

Sonya nodded her head. "Your car was practically flattened. They found pieces of it 200 yards away from the accident."

She spoke in a wavering voice before collapsing into a new round of tears and heavy, painful sobs. "It's a miracle you're still alive. You should be dead."

Sonya threw herself across the center console and into Martin's arms that opened naturally for her. The sweet smell of her hair wasn't present as usual, and he figured that she had skipped a few showers while he lay in the hospital, his mind drifting to another dimension.

"I'm here."

"I love you," she said, giving him a half-hearted squeeze thanks to her awkward angle. "Can we please go inside?"

"Yes," Martin said, and he felt this was as good a transition as any. "Let's go sit down on the couch and talk. There's something I need to tell you."

Sonya recoiled and sat up stiffly in the driver's seat. "What do you mean?"

"I mean we need to have a talk."

"Those words are never good." She stared at him sternly, daring him to tell her bad news after the week she had just endured.

"It's not what you think. But it is about us and our future. Let's just go inside."

Sonya wasted no more time bickering in the car and swung her door open. Martin followed suit, only a bit slower. Sonya was already opening the house door when Martin closed the car door and shuffled around to meet her. He watched as she moved with a hell-bent purpose into the house, throwing her purse and keys on the table and nearly running to the living room. She reminded Martin of a kid being told it was finally time to open the presents at their birthday party, only he didn't sense the same kind of excitement.

Martin walked at his new, slow pace. Although it was temporary, it still frustrated him that his legs couldn't keep up with how fast his mind wanted them to move. And to think it wasn't even a direct result of the coma, but rather from lying in bed for an entire week.

He joined Sonya on the couch, her legs bouncing uncontrollably as she had her hands crossed in front of her face as if in prayer. Her eyes stared to the ground and ignored him when he sat down beside her.

She jumped up from the couch and paced around the coffee table. "I'm not letting you do this," she said, an obvious hint of anger hiding behind her words.

"Let me do what?"

"Spill your guts and confess. No, sir. You must have hit your head pretty hard if you think I'm gonna let you sit there and be all saintly for making your confession before I caught you."

"Confession?" Martin said, more to himself. "Sonya, I'm not sure what you're talking about."

"Good, then let me explain for you." The boiling rage could no longer hide and was in full force with every motion she made. "I know everything. I know your lies, your secret life. Everything."

Martin's crippled mind raced in hundreds of directions, unable to make any sense of her words. The only way she could know that he had travelled through time would be if she had also travelled in time and knew what to look for. He examined her skin for the golden glow, but did not see anything.

"Tell me what you know, because you've lost me," Martin said calmly, hoping the composure would rub off on Sonya.

"Sure, Martin, if that's your real name," she said, sarcasm clinging to every word. "Let's see. For starters, I know you don't work at the post office. I called them to let them know about your accident. They said they've never heard of you, had no record of your employment. That's lie number one. I know you're married. How's Lela doing? That's lie number two. And I know that you and Lela have a daughter named Izzy. Because she goes to my school! What a shame that a sweet girl like that is stuck with a lying piece of shit father like you."

Martin sat stunned, eyes bulging at Sonya in a way that probably made him look guilty. He supposed if he hadn't just come out of a coma, she would likely be throwing things at him as she ranted.

Well, here it is, he thought. This *is the past pushing back.* This *is the past using Sonya to throw you off. You better explain yourself quickly before this woman goes in the kitchen for a knife to stab your fat, useless gut.*

Martin could sense the anger seeping from Sonya's pores, but remained calm himself as he knew she had it all mistaken.

"Are you going to say anything, liar?" she snarled. "Or can liars not speak when they've been caught?"

Martin shook his head and hoped for the best.

"I can actually explain all of this. But, I need you to sit down and really listen. This isn't at all what you think."

"Save it, Martin. What were you doing in Littleton? Fucking your rich housewife? Does she give you money when you're a good boy?"

The question caused a giggle to form in Martin's throat that he choked down.

"Sonya," he said, keeping a high level of composure. "I can explain."

She crossed her arms and cocked her head like a pissed off teenager. "Well, then start talking."

Martin patted the open space on the couch next to him, but Sonya didn't flinch and kept staring at him with hateful eyes.

"Okay, then," he said. "This is all going to sound crazy. Because it is. But it's all true, I need you to trust me, and you can ask me for any proof that you need."

He paused to stand with Sonya, not wanting to talk up to her the whole time.

"I'm not from here. I suppose that's the best way to put it. I'm from Larkwood, but I came here from the year 2018."

Martin paused again to read Sonya's expression that remained hot, but he could see the dials turning behind those hateful eyes.

"You're absolutely right about Lela and Izzy. In 1996, they are my wife and daughter. In September Izzy will go missing and never be found again. That's why I'm here: to stop that from happening. Her disappearance led to the collapse of my marriage. If you go to my family's house right now, you'll probably see me, Lela, and Izzy all there together. And I'll still be here. It's been made clear that I can't interact with my past self."

Martin noticed Sonya's arms loosen, but remained crossed.

"I've been here since March, tracking Izzy, and finding ways to kill time until the big day in September. I didn't plan to meet someone and fall in love. But, here we are. I'm not sure what I'm supposed to do about our relationship. I don't know what will happen when I go back. You could even come with me, I suppose, if you wanted."

Martin paused once more and let his words settle. Sonya's face morphed from anger to confusion as she scrunched her eyebrows.

"Martin, I think we need to get you back to the doctor. I think you hallucinated during your coma." She spoke with the slightest hint of fear in her voice.

"I wish I could take you to the future for a quick look to see for yourself, but that's not how it works."

"Well, I can't exactly ask you questions about the future, either – how would I ever know if you're telling the truth?"

Martin noticed her hands shaking, still likely flowing with the adrenaline of her outburst moments ago, but her voice had almost returned to normal, and that put him at ease.

She wants to believe me.

"Okay. I do have some minor things you could use as proof. I have a notebook of sporting outcomes that I use to bet and make money while I'm here. I can show you the outcomes, down to the exact score, and you can see for yourself."

"So you really don't work for the post office?"

"Well, I do in 2018. That's why I used it as a cover-up. It's easy for me to explain because I actually do work in a post office."

Sonya finally uncrossed her arms and let them fall to her sides. "I don't believe this. Time travel isn't real, and you know it."

Martin reached his arms out for her, expecting her to avoid them, but she didn't resist and let him squeeze her as if never wanting to be let go.

"I know this sounds impossible. I thought so, too. Sometimes I still wonder if this man in 2018 just drugged me and I'm on a hell of a trip. But it's been too long. No days have been skipped, and everything I know will happen *has* happened."

Sonya was silent, her heavy breathing the only sound filling the quiet house. She gently pushed her way out of his embrace and took a step back. "I think I need some time by myself to process this. I'm not asking you to leave or anything. I *want* to believe you, but I can't right now. It's too absurd to even consider. I want to see the proof you have, but part of me doesn't really want to - that would make it real."

"I understand. I damn near drank myself to death when I found out this was real. It's a lot to process, and only gets stranger the more you learn. So, what do you want me to do?"

"It doesn't matter. You need to rest and relax like the doctor said. I'm gonna go out, try to clear my mind if that's even possible at this point. I'll bring you some dinner later – just try to get better."

Martin wondered if she still thought this was a result of his head injury. It made sense for her to think that; he had never shown any signs of such chaotic thoughts before the accident, so it was a convenient enough of an excuse to use if she wanted to stay in denial.

"Okay, take your time. Don't be too late – I'd love to explain everything I know and answer any questions you have."

Martin stayed calm, wanting to show Sonya that he was perfectly fine and not delirious like she assumed.

Sonya nodded and turned for the kitchen where she swiped her keys off the table. She opened the front door, looked back at Martin with terrified eyes, and closed it behind her on the way out.

Martin returned to his spot on the couch, hearing the car outside turn on seconds later.

She'll come around, don't worry. Just give her some time.

Martin lay down, intent of falling asleep for a quick snooze, but knowing his racing thoughts would never allow it.

37

Chapter 37

Martin fell into a light sleep after all. He could only stare at the ceiling for so long before the fatigue kicked in. He slept for an hour and a half before Sonya's car pulled into the driveway. He sat up on the couch, neck sore from sleeping awkwardly. The clock read 7:38 P.M.

His stomach growled when Sonya swung the front door open, a bag of Taco Bell in hand, the smell of questionable ground beef slowly filling the house.

"Hey," she said flatly. "I brought us dinner."

"Thank you. How was it? Where did you go?"

She looked down and drew circles in the carpet with her toe. "I went to a park. There's one just outside of downtown that overlooks a lake and the mountains. It's somewhere I've always gone when I needed to sort things out."

Martin stood, expecting her to say more, but she didn't.

"What did you decide?"

She looked back down to her imaginary artwork and spoke just above a whisper. "I think I believe you."

Knowing he wasn't getting kicked to the asylum, Martin

crossed the living room to her. He grabbed the bag of food, placed it on the counter, and grabbed her hands, one in each of his. Her head stayed down, but he could hear a soft sniffle.

"Sonya," he said. "Tell me what you're feeling."

She raised her head and had tears welled up in her eyes, bringing out her true hazel color, glistening majestically. He felt her staring into his soul and could feel her trying to enter it, as if she could lunge into his being.

"I love you, Martin. And I believe you."

He raised his thumbs gently to her face and wiped the tears out of her eyes.

"Thank you. I love you, too. More than I've ever loved any other woman."

"Before I went to the park, I went to your house. Well, your old house, I guess." Sonya spoke with uncertainty.

Martin felt an immediate pit fall through his stomach. If she went to his old house and interacted with his past self, she may have thrown a wrench into everything. If his past self met her, how would that affect him going forward? Martin still had a novel's worth of questions he wanted to ask Chris, but knew the old man was long gone.

"I only drove by, but I saw you mowing the lawn. It was clearly you, but younger. I wanted to stop and say something, but something inside me told me I shouldn't."

"That's good. I don't know what would've happened if you did."

"After I saw you, I felt like I had been knocked in the head. I felt dizzy and sick. It was like I was back in college and learned that the Vietnam War was a big hoax. It was just a sick feeling to learn something that you'd never guess in 100 years to be true."

"I know what you mean." Martin didn't understand the Vietnam reference, he was barely born when that all happened, but he could relate to the sensation of realizing that time travel was real and not something made up in the movies.

"So, I went to the park and tried to make sense of it all. I think I've come to accept it, but I still can't wrap my mind around it. I don't know how it's possible."

Just go for it. This might be your best shot.

"You can come back with me to the future. See for yourself," he said, caution clinging to each word. He watched Sonya for a reaction, but none came. She only nodded her head in a slow motion.

"I thought you might ask me that," she said. "I just don't know. Don't get me wrong, I'd love to go just for the experience."

She paused for an eternity, her head bobbing in thought.

"But at the same time it's terrifying. I don't know what the future's like. What if I'm not cut out for a world of flying cars and advanced technology?"

Martin chuckled. "There aren't flying cars. There are cars that can drive themselves, but nothing that flies yet."

"I just don't know, Martin. I feel like there's a thousand questions I need answered before I can even consider such a thing."

"I understand, I went through the same thing. Fortunately, I was given a sort of test run."

"So how does it work?" Sonya asked, her tone shifting to a curious one. "Is there a secret door you walk through and fall into another year?"

Martin sensed her list of a thousand questions was about to come. When dealing with this topic, he knew one question always led to another.

"No. It's actually a pill you swallow. Although, you wouldn't have to. There's only one pill left."

"Then how would I-"

"I would hold you. Anything that's attached to me will travel with me through time. I can show you my cell phone."

"Cell phone?"

"By 2018 just about everyone carries a portable phone with them. Mine doesn't work here in the past, so I can't show you all that it can do, but I have it."

Martin turned and hurried to the guest room where his belongings were. "I'll be right back."

A minute later he returned with a small rectangular piece of plastic clenched in his hand. Its shiny surface reflected the above lights as he held it out like an offering for Sonya.

She stared in curiosity, but hesitated touching it, like it was an alien species that had landed in her backyard.

"That thing's a phone?" she asked after a few minutes of studying it with only her eyes. "How? Where do you talk? Where do you listen?"

Martin grinned, her questions reminding him of his mother's reaction when they had bought her first cell phone some time in 2010. For a good two years she had called him at least once a week from her landline saying, "Marty, I don't know how to use this damn gizmo."

Martin held the phone at Sonya's eye level, on its side. "You speak into here and listen from here." His finger glided from the bottom of the phone to the top, pointing at small holes she had to squint to see.

"And that works? There's barely anything there."

"It works just fine. These phones also do more than make

phone calls. You can send text messages if you don't feel like talking, play games, search the internet, update your calendar. All kinds of things."

"You're telling me you can walk around with the internet in your back pocket in 2018?"

The thought would have never occurred to someone in 1996, as the internet was barely accessible at the library.

"Oh, yeah. It happens even sooner than that. A little after 2000 is when everyone started getting cell phones. The internet part came a little later, but didn't take too long before everyone had it. Do you want to hold it?"

"Okay." Sonya finally reached out and grabbed the futuristic portal of knowledge from Martin's hand. She studied it, turning it as she held it up the light. "I just don't get how this little thing can do all that?"

"A cell phone is only the start. You should see the technology in the future – it only becomes more advanced every year."

"Don't get me wrong, this is cool, but it's not enough to convince me to go. What's the world like?"

Martin looked at Sonya, who still hadn't taken her eyes off the cell phone.

"Sonya. I need you to trust me when I tell you the world is fine. I'll be there with you every step of the way. I want you to come with me. Not just so you can see the future, but so we can continue our life together."

"What happens to my life here?"

Martin opened his mouth to speak, but snapped it shut when he realized he didn't actually know. The rules that applied to him for traveling to the past might not work for her since she wasn't taking the pill. He didn't know if her body would fall asleep for ten minutes and patiently await her return that might never come.

"I honestly don't know. For me, I'm asleep in 2018, and whenever I go back, only ten minutes will have passed. I'll actually need to go quit my job when I wake up."

Martin decided he didn't want to slog through life any more, regardless of what would end up happening with Izzy and Sonya. He felt a new sense of purpose in life and found he actually enjoyed being sober more than the constant state of drunkenness he had grown accustomed to.

"Why would you quit?" Sonya asked, pure curiosity in her voice.

Martin smirked. "Do you think traveling through time is something you can just do and go back to your normal life after it's all done? Pretend it never happened? My life will never be the same, and I think that's for the best. Don't worry, I'm going to make sure I have plenty of money ready to pick up when I arrive back."

The shock and worry that had physically consumed Sonya gave way to anticipation. Martin could see the dials turning in her head, digesting everything he said. He knew she would agree to visit, but not necessarily stay. A history teacher would never be able to resist a chance to see the future, no matter how absurd it might sound.

She pursed her lips and stared into Martin's soul.

"I'll go with you under one condition . . . and some other questions." Sonya spoke and her eyes seemed to follow the words out of her mouth, wondering if she could reach out and take them back.

"Of course. What's the condition?"

"You need to tell me what you were doing in Littleton. Did it have something to do with the future?"

Martin had witnessed a carousel of Sonya's emotions over the last few hours, and now saw one he hadn't yet seen: hope. Hope that whatever he responded with would be to her liking. Hope that whatever was in Littleton was part of some futuristic project she wouldn't understand. Martin offered a soft smile before delivering the good news.

"Yes, it did have to do with the future, but I clearly ran into problems. Do you know Columbine High School out in Littleton?"

She nodded. "I've heard of it, yeah. Huge school, virtually unlimited budget. What does a high school have to do with anything?"

Martin cleared his throat, knowing he needed to explain what would happen without scaring her out of joining him in 2018.

"In 1999, two seniors at the high school are going to take guns and homemade bombs to school and kill more than a dozen kids and teachers, and injure many more."

Sonya's mouth hung open and she slapped a hand to it.

"I figured since I'm already here in the past, I'd see if I can do anything to stop that from happening. You see, by 2018, America will have more mass shootings than any other countries combined. And it all started with the attacks at Columbine."

Martin watched as fear washed away the look of hope in Sonya's eyes. He remembered a time where shootings were still shocking to hear about, and he envied Sonya for still living in that era.

"Two students bring guns to school and shoot everyone?" Sonya asked. "I can't even imagine. What would I do if that happened in my classroom? I'm just a teacher."

"Exactly. It turns in to such a hot topic in the future that it literally polarizes everyone against each other and nothing gets resolved."

"Martin," she said, her brow furrowed in seriousness. "You have to stop it. You have to go back. I can help you."

Martin crossed his arms and nodded in appreciation. "That's nice of you, but I can't let you get involved. And I shouldn't stay involved, either. You see, one thing about traveling to the past is anything I try to change may resist. The day of the accident I was at one of the shooter's homes. I think I was close to having an encounter with him, and the past sent that semi-truck to stop me."

"There has to be something you can do, even without getting physically involved. What if you called the police? Or wrote a letter?"

"I thought about that. A letter would probably just get lost in the mail. And a phone call would never be taken seriously. If I called the Littleton police to report a crime that's going to happen in three years, they'll probably come and lock me up instead."

"I'll do it," Sonya demanded. "You can't tell me otherwise."

"Sonya—"

"Nope. I'm doing it. I'll take the chance and hand deliver a letter to the school's principal. If you want to help, you can watch out for me to make sure nothing happens."

Martin wanted to protest but recognized the determination on Sonya's face. Her mind was made up and there would be no talking her out of it. He could only hope she would forget about all of this and avoid a potentially deadly decision.

"Okay, we can discuss it more. I really need to explain more how the past will fight back."

"I don't care. Sometimes you have to do what's right, no matter what."

"Is this worth dying over? Because that could happen."

Sonya's look of determination gave an inch to doubt. She wanted to stay strong, but the notion of death may have planted the fear he hoped might change her mind.

"I'll think about it."

"Okay. Let's discuss it later. Is there anything else you had questions about?" Martin asked, pleading her to change the subject.

"Yeah. What's the date of this shooting?"

38

Chapter 38

Sonya wouldn't let it go, and after three days of constant nagging, Martin surrendered and agreed to let her deliver a letter to the school. She had even drafted a copy of the letter that she would take to the principal.

Sonya kept Martin company, watching many movies to pass the days while he remained a quasi-vegetable. He became fatigued easily, and one hour of each day, she helped him move around the house, refresh his memory on where things went, and if he was up to it, go for a relaxing walk around the neighborhood.

If there was one thing Martin remembered, it was why he fell in love with Sonya. She tended to him with a motherly touch he hadn't felt since he was a child. His heart still skipped madly every time she pressed her lips onto his.

She's the one, he thought. *I had to travel back in time to find the person I'm meant to love.*

She loved him so much, apparently, that she wanted to put her life on the line to carry out *his* goal of stopping the Columbine shootings. It had obviously struck a personal chord with her being a lifelong educator, but she might have obsessed a bit too much over the matter, bringing up the topic at every chance.

"We need to sit down and make a plan, and get this note delivered next week," Sonya said. "I already found out that their summer school is open one more week before they close down until the fall. You're going to be too consumed with saving Izzy by the time the next school year starts, so this needs to happen within the next seven days."

Sonya had practically hijacked the mission, telling Martin how things would play out. If he didn't like it, then she would just go on her own and enter the unknown battlefield without protection.

"Okay, Monday morning. Let's get it out of the way," Martin agreed reluctantly.

Monday morning had been the original date for their flight departure to their romantic getaway, but the doctor said it would be best if they wait another month or two as Martin needed to remain as stress free as possible.

Sonya was able to get most of their money back, and obliged to cancel the trip. She would, after all, be taking a different trip in September. One for the ages, you could say.

They spent a couple hours on Saturday crafting the final draft of the letter. It didn't say much, but Sonya was a perfectionist. It read:

Dear Sir,

I've come across some disturbing information that needs to be brought to your attention. Two of your students, Eric Harris and Dylan Klebold, are currently plotting a violent attack that will take place at Columbine High School. Their current plan to carry out this attack is April 20, 1999, when they will be in their final semester of high school.

Please do with this information as you wish, but know this is not an empty threat. You must consider this note with care to save future lives.

God bless,
  A concerned citizen

Martin would have never been able to phrase such delicate information in the manner she had. Five simple sentences handwritten on a piece of notepad paper would stop one of the most horrific terrorist attacks in modern history, assuming they could deliver it without any problems.

There will be problems, Martin thought. *You weren't even doing anything when the truck hit you. And you think this time will be any easier?*

The thought wrung Martin's stomach like a rag. He had to be ready for anything, and also had to prepare Sonya to be ready. She didn't understand how aggressive the past would be, and he didn't want her to find out the hard way.

The plan they made was simple. She would drive, and Martin would ride shotgun to keep an eye on the road for the unexpected. She would enter the school with Martin following close behind, waiting outside to avoid being noticed again inside the school.

"And that's all we can plan for," he said, sipping a cup of tea. "As far as the unknown, I have no idea what'll happen. There could be another car accident, maybe the car will catch on fire. I just don't know. We have to be ready for anything, and you

260

have to be ready to move at my command. If I say jump out of the car, you better swing that door open and jump like your life depends on it."

Sonya nodded silently, and Martin thought the severity of the task had finally settled in. She didn't do well with the unknown, but had committed too deep to back out now.

"Martin?" she asked, the slightest tremble escaping from her lips. "Do you think I might die?"

Remember, you don't know how the rules will apply to her. She's not the one traveling through time.

"Not likely," he said. "I think I'm still going to be the one at highest risk. When Monday comes, we need to move quickly and efficiently. We should plan to go during the peak of the morning rush hour. The slower we drive, the less likely for something to go wrong."

Sonya nodded. "Monday morning. I don't know if I'll be able to sleep between now and then."

"Of course you will – just try to keep your mind clear. You don't even know these kids or the severity of their attacks."

"That doesn't matter. I've agreed to do this, both as a sign of faith that I believe you, and to help keep the world a good place."

Sonya lay down on the couch and curled up beside Martin. He rubbed her up and down along her back while they both fell into a deep sleep.

* * *

They spent the rest of the weekend much how they had spent

the entire week, dragging themselves around the house, not wanting to do much but stay rested for their eventful Monday morning. On Sunday, Martin decided to give grilling a shot once the sun started its descent and left them with a picture-perfect evening. He sipped a glass of neat whiskey while tending to two sizzling steaks. He couldn't remember what the different ways to cook steak were called, but knew they needed to have the slightest shade of pink in the middle to be considered finished and still juicy.

Sonya approached Martin from behind and placed her own glass of whiskey on the grill's side table. She slung her arms around Martin's waist and rocked back and forth with him as they stared out to the backyard. The grass had grown scraggly, but not too tall yet. Martin had always mowed on Sunday nights, but had taken the last two weeks off from that chore. Perhaps in another week he'd feel more up to managing machinery that could cut a limb off if used improperly.

"I love you," Sonya said from behind him, sounding almost hypnotized.

He put down the tongs and turned to her. "I love you, too."

"No, really. I've been thinking all weekend now. How could any of this have happened? How does life lead us where it does? This can't be some miraculous accident. The fact that you were sent here from 2018 and met me...it just can't be dumb luck."

Martin grinned and kissed her on the forehead. "I've thought the same thing since I arrived. I thought I was coming here for a sole purpose, but it turned out being three purposes: Izzy, Columbine, and you."

Sonya returned a grin as she looked into his eyes.

"I've tried to make sense of all of it," he said. "But all

I can come up with is that it's some sort of fate—a cross-dimensional fate, at that. I've debated so long on when to tell you, knowing I would have to at some point. It means the world to me that you're going to join me."

He kissed her again, this time on the lips, and she returned the favor with a brief flash of deep passion.

"I'm terrified, you know," she said. "I'm terrified of tomorrow, I'm terrified of 2018, I'm terrified of the future in general. You don't know what happens beyond 2018. Unlike now, you could tell me everything that happens between now and then."

"I'm still here. You can ask me anything."

"I'd rather read the history books when I get to the future, and then I'll ask questions. The only thing I want to know is if we see a woman president by 2018."

Martin smirked. "Almost. Clinton's wife – Hilary – she loses in the 2016 election."

"Really?" Sonya's eyes bulged. "Lost to who?"

"That's a long story. Probably better for another day."

"So there *is* some hope for the future."

"Things aren't as bad as they might sound. Sure there's more violence in the future, but I've never felt in danger. I honestly think the violence is mostly the same, there's just more coverage of it with the internet and social media."

Sonya nodded silently, and Martin figured she had no idea what social media even meant.

"How will we know if what we're doing tomorrow will have worked?" she asked.

Martin took a sip and flipped the steaks, their sizzle slowly quieting as they came closer to completion.

"Well, we won't be here to find out for ourselves. We'll have

263

to look it up when we get back to 2018. We can do a quick search on Columbine High School and see what shows up."

"It's that simple, huh?"

"It really is. You can find out literally anything you want to know. Not all the answers may be real, but you'll eventual learn how sort out what's fake or not."

"That needs to be the first thing we look up when he get back. Is the library close to your house?"

"We don't need to go to the library. Remember, it's all on my phone."

"Duh, right! How could I forget your portable encyclopedia? My apologies."

She grinned as she locked eyes with Martin, and he felt something he hadn't in the last two weeks: lust.

They hadn't lost their connection, but he was unable to perform physically grueling tasks. Now, he felt a familiar tingle in his crotch and an urge to kiss every inch of her body. If dinner went well, maybe he'd see what she thought about dessert in the bedroom.

39

Chapter 39

Monday morning, just before the sun poked above the horizon, Martin's nightmare of Eric and Dylan had recurred. Only this time there was no conversation, just the two boys laughing like rabid hyenas as they both lined up their firearms and shot Martin square in the chest. It was a quick dream, the kind you think back and realize had lasted only five seconds, but had felt like an eternity. The layers of evil that waited beneath their howling laughter sent chills down his spine both in dreamland and in his 1996 bed.

Sonya tossed and turned all night, likely facing demons of her own. He knew she had finally recognized that she had gone in too deep with this commitment, but would never admit it.

She had rolled out of bed shortly after 5 A.M., and Martin heard her rummaging around the kitchen, debated if he should join her, then rolled back to his side to try and steal another hour of sleep.

Their plan was to leave the house at eight, meaning they would hit the rush hour traffic toward downtown by 8:15 to have a slow trek the rest of the way to Littleton. There was a brief disagreement about the strategy to catch the rush hour. Sonya believed that more cars on the road increased the likelihood of something going wrong, while Martin argued something *would* go wrong regardless, so it would be best to drive as slow as possible. I-25 in the morning, between eight and nine was typically stop-and-go all the way to downtown. If something were to go wrong on the highway, they'd have plenty of time to react.

Martin ended up fidgeting for the next hour in bed, hearing the clatter of pots and pans from the kitchen, and the sizzle of what was either bacon or sausage cooking. Apparently Sonya was ready to get the day started.

The boys' laughter kept ringing out in his mind much like how the piercing blare of a fire alarm might echo even after it turned off. He forced the thoughts of the future day where all those innocent students were flashed across the screen to celebrate their lives that had ended too soon. He remembered all of the tears that were shed at the graduation ceremony a few weeks later, an event broadcasted by the local news stations.

Doing this replenished Martin's sense of purpose, and he finally jumped out of bed at six, ready to tackle the unknown challenges that lied ahead.

He dragged himself to the kitchen where Sonya stood over the stove, eggs cooking in a skillet, bacon *and* sausage in another, and the sweet smell of fresh bread oozing from the oven.

"Good morning, Chef Sonya," he said with as much comedic tone he could muster so early in the morning.

She jumped, startled, and turned to Martin with a nervous grin. "I couldn't really sleep, so figured we'd have a feast before setting out for the day."

Martin admired the gluttonous spread of food. "I'd say I'm sorry, but I'm not. This looks fantastic."

"Thank you," Sonya said quietly, her innocent smirk returning. "How did you sleep?"

"Not much better. Was hard to fall into a good, deep sleep."

He refused to tell her about the dream; she didn't need anything else to worry about.

"I know what you mean. When this is all done, I just wanna come back here and take a long nap."

"That sounds perfect," he said, hoping deep down that they would, in fact, make it back home. He still had a hunch that things would play out differently by having Sonya do the dirty work, but he couldn't gamble his caution away, either.

"Breakfast is ready," Sonya said, turning the dials off on the stove. "Would you like some vodka in your orange juice this morning?"

"More than you know."

Martin helped her set the table and serve the food. They sat down and enjoyed the meal with minimal conversation, the weight of their mission hanging heavily above their heads.

* * *

When they finished eating, they sat at the table staring at each other. Neither of them wanted to make the move to stand up because that would mean it was time to get the day officially started. If Sonya asked to stay home and watch movies all day, forget the simple task of delivering a letter to a high school almost an hour away, Martin would happily agree.

His entire body tensed up and his teeth chattered from time to time throughout breakfast.

This has got to be the most nervous I've ever been, he thought, unable to think of another time where he had felt more sick with anticipation. The thought of death kept jumping into his mind, hard to shake. *No one's dying today, stop worrying.*

The words sounded fake within his own head, and he stood up from the table, anxious to get the trip over with. "Let's head out," he said, mustering a confident voice. "Traffic will be starting to back up soon and we want to make sure we catch it."

Sonya nodded, and stood slowly, keeping her head down to her empty plate. Martin could only assume she felt the same way he did. He debated a final attempt of trying to talk her out of it, but knew she would never give in so late in the game.

"Let's go then," she said softly, passing the dishes to the sink and walking to the front door. "I'm driving, you're keeping watch. That hasn't changed."

They had known that was the plan, but it sounded to Martin that she spoke those words for her own comfort, needing to feel in control of something.

"Let's get this done. Then we can go have a big lunch later to celebrate." He offered a smile, but she didn't return it, grabbing her keys off the rack on the wall, and swinging the front door open.

Martin followed her outside to a perfect morning. Golden rays splashed across the front lawn, while dew from the prior night glistened in its glory. Birds chirped from the trees while Martin took a deep inhale of the pure, fresh morning air. His senses had seemed to strengthen since the coma, but it wasn't all the time. At times he could hear the slightest whisper, or smell a neighbor's cooking from down the block, while at other times food tasted bland, no matter how much seasoning he dumped on it. Today was a perfect day, and he wanted to enjoy every passing second of it.

Sonya was already in the car and had turned on the engine, giving it a minute to warm up. Martin broke out of his trance and joined her. *At what point does the past realize we're trying to change it?*

He had expected some sort of resistance to start the day, but was pleased to find nothing had happened yet.

"Are we ready?" Sonya asked, putting a shaky hand on the gear.

Martin noticed and grabbed it, squeezing it. "If you need a minute, just say so."

Sonya exhaled heavily. "I think I'm okay. I don't even know why I'm nervous. I think I just have your car accident in the back of my mind."

"That's why we're driving slow and being cautious. I wasn't ready last time. I had absolutely no awareness of my surroundings. Stay alert and everything will be fine."

She nodded her head rapidly and pulled the car onto the street. "I trust you. Let's go save some lives."

She drove quickly through the neighborhood, the freeway just minutes away.

40

Chapter 40

Sonya's knuckles turned white from her death-like grip on the steering wheel. Martin considered telling her to loosen up, but decided to let her cope with the stress as she saw fit. He had bigger issues to worry about, anyway.

The tension heightened whenever a car passed them by on the freeway. They were still a few minutes from where the traffic would logjam, so other drivers zoomed by them at 70 miles per hour compared to their leisurely 50.

Sonya drove in the far right lane and kept an eye glued on her driver's side mirror when a new car approached. Martin leaned over the center console each time for a clear look into the mirror, and studied the car, tracking its trajectory to make sure it wasn't headed for their back bumper.

When the car passed, his focus would then shift to the car's tires, watching them for any sudden movement that might cause the car to swerve into their lane.

These fifteen minutes of action felt like two hours of constant paranoia, and when they reached the outskirts of downtown, they both felt at ease at the sight of a sea of red brake lights. Cars honked and music blared as they joined the gathering of drivers on their way to start the work week.

Denver looked so young, Martin observed. There were less buildings than in 2018, less surroundings where the city would eventually grow, and Martin felt a tugging in his soul that he dismissed as nostalgia.

I'm downtown right now, he thought, recalling that he would've already been at work. He had worked on the 16th Street Mall as an underground parking garage attendant, and he needed to be there at four in the morning to welcome the early starters.

It's funny how irrelevant a job seems when you look back to it after many years had passed. Martin remembered busting his ass to receive a measly 50 dollar bonus each month.

Young and dumb, he thought. *And here you are. Back in the same year doing a mission that will probably get you and your lady killed. Why couldn't you have just gone to the beach with her like she wanted?*

He glanced over and saw Sonya's grip hadn't yet loosened on the steering wheel, but she otherwise appeared to have her emotions in check as she drove with a relaxed expression.

"Here we are," she said as the car came to a near stop to join the unofficial parade making its way through the city.

"All right," Martin said. "Let's keep our eyes open and alert. There could still be something that happens out of the blue."

Sonya nodded and let the car inch forward every few seconds.

Martin kept his stare out the windshield, observing every surrounding car and possible obstacle that could fall in their way. There was a pickup truck ten cars ahead with a refrigerator and various junk overflowing the cargo bed; he half expected something to spill out and block the road. To their left, a young mother in a rusty Chevy brushed makeup on her face in her rear-view mirror while a one-year-old baby screamed hysterically in the backseat.

With his bearings and surroundings covered, Martin leaned back in his seat and kept his vision wide, waiting for what the world would throw their way.

Five minutes passed with no activity, only moving one mile, and Martin wondered why it had moved slower than normal. He found his answer after another five minutes passed when they drove by the scene of a nasty accident.

The front half of an SUV was smashed flat like a soda can. The vehicle was flipped onto its roof in the middle of a pool of shattered glass and freckles of blood splayed across the road. The accident appeared near the end of its clean up phase, as there wasn't another car in sight. Police cars blocked off the shoulder and left lane, directing traffic into the right two lanes and creating a bottleneck of vehicles.

"Oh my God! Oh my God! Oh my God!" Sonya screamed and hyperventilated, squirming behind the wheel. "Martin, is this a sign?"

"No, it's not a sign. It's just an accident," he said, trying to lie to himself as well. *No shit, it's a sign. It's either a sign of what will happen or a warning of what* could *happen.* Martin didn't care for the particulars of the matter and his heart rate spiked. "It's okay. Just slow down a little, we're still doing great on time."

Sonya fell silent and kept her eyes glued to the cars ahead of her. She wouldn't break that stare if he told her Elvis Presley was in the back seat.

"Just keep going steady, nothing to worry about here,"

Martin said in his best soothing voice. The words must have bounced off her ears as she made no acknowledgement.

They continued in silence, and on high alert, through downtown.

* * *

When they reached the end of the traffic jam, and the road opened up to higher driving speeds, they both let out a long exhale. The sight of the pulverized car had created a palpable tension that neither of them wanted to discuss.

"We made it through that portion of the trip unscathed," Martin said cheerily. He had expected something to happen during the traffic jam – they were sitting ducks, after all. But nothing happened, and that fact made Martin even more uneasy. The unpredictability of the past drove him near insanity.

"What now?" Sonya asked.

"Now, we're only ten minutes away if we drive at full speed. I'll let you decide how you're feeling if you'd like to do that or not."

"I'll go exactly the speed limit," she said sternly, never breaking her concentration from the road. "Just tell me when to exit because I don't remember. My brain can't really focus right now on anything else besides driving this car."

"That's fine, that's all you need to worry about. We're almost there." Martin wanted to put a hand on her leg, but felt the radiating tension from her and decided to not distract her.

She accelerated the car to a steady 55 miles per hour, and they headed toward the Littleton exit, eight miles away.

* * *

Littleton had much less traffic clogging its roads when they arrived. The town was primarily residential and still growing into the bustling suburb Martin knew it as in 2018. Sonya drove steadily through the city, never going above the speed limit, keeping a constant eye on the rear-view mirror.

"I think we're gonna make it without any issues," Sonya said in a tone Martin couldn't tell was scared or happy. "Does that seem right to you?"

"It ain't over 'til it's over," Martin replied, using a quote his father had often told him, borrowed from some baseball player from his era.

"What's that supposed to mean?" Sonya questioned, focus unaffected.

"It means to not get excited until we actually arrive. I'm glad we made it this far, but there's still five more minutes to the school."

"Right," she said.

She continued to guide them through Littleton with Martin's directions. When they finally turned onto the block where the school became visible, Martin noticed Sonya jolt in her seat.

"There it is! There it is!" she cried, like a little kid driving by a favorite amusement park.

Her sudden movement sent a wave of terror through Martin, and he giggled to release the tension.

"Where do I go? Where should I park?" He could hear the anticipation in her voice.

"Settle down, you need to stay focused. Go around the school and you'll see the main entrance. It has a parking lot right next to it."

"Sorry, I'm just super nervous right now. I can't even feel my legs. That feeling started in my stomach and spread."

"It's okay to be nervous. Nerves keep you alert."

Martin found himself calmer than he expected as Sonya drove the car around the school's massive campus, passing by the football, baseball, and soccer fields kept in pristine condition.

"This school clearly has money to spend," Sonya commented. "I wonder what the teachers get paid down here."

"Not enough to be killed," Martin said flatly, wanting to bring her back to reality. Her daydreams would sometimes take her on a tangent, and right now was not the time for such small talk.

Sonya pulled the car into its final destination where only two other cars filled the lot.

Perfect, Martin thought. *Less chance of someone remembering Sonya.*

Martin still felt a tingling doubt in his mind, dreading how this would all play out. Would the past make sure the letter got accidentally bumped into the trash can, hence explaining why they had encountered no resistance? Would the principal read the letter and dismiss it as a silly prank? This was, after all, in a time before school shootings were a part of everyday life. There wasn't any stock in such a wild threat. Would the school take the threat seriously and notify the authorities? What would the authorities do with a threat still three years

275

away?

Probably laugh their asses off and toss the letter.

There were too many external factors for Martin's liking, but he had no choice. Getting too close to Dylan nearly cost him his life, and he'd have to finish this mission from the sidelines, cheering on his courageous girlfriend.

Sonya found a spot she liked and parked the car so it faced the school's main entrance. She killed the engine and rested her head on the steering wheel, taking deep breaths.

Martin reached a hand over and rubbed it down her back. "It's going to be okay. We've come this far. This is the easy part now."

Sonya nodded, her hair jiggling and hanging over her buried face. "Let's get it over with."

She looked up to him with terror-filled eyes, the color having rushed from her face. "I love you," Martin said. "Remember the plan for inside the school?"

"Yes. Walk in, go into the office, and tell them I have a letter for the principal. And make sure I see them deliver it to his desk."

"Perfect. Quick and easy."

Sonya nodded. "Letter?"

Martin pulled it out of the glove compartment and slid it into her trembling hand.

"Okay. Here goes nothing," Sonya said, and pushed open her door.

Martin watched as she walked confidently up to the school, not a shred of hesitation in her steps. She paused a moment when she reached the entrance, as if studying the door, then pulled it open and vanished inside.

* * *

The next two minutes felt like an eternity. The whole process should've taken maybe thirty seconds, in reality, but Martin gave her some cushion for any external factors. Maybe the receptionist wasn't at the desk. Maybe the principal was there and had struck up small talk with Sonya. Maybe Eric and Dylan were waiting with their guns and attacked everyone in the office.

Martin doubted the latter, but anything was possible, he supposed. The clock read as 9:27 when Sonya had stepped out of the car. If she wasn't back by 9:32, he would go inside and see what the hold up was.

He sat on the edge of his seat, leaning forward on the dashboard and never taking his eyes off the school's front doors. When he saw the door swing open it would signal success, or at least verify that nothing had gone fatally wrong. The clock crawled, teasing him: 9:29.

Martin drummed the dashboard with nervous fingers. *It's a simple letter drop off. Should be done by now.*

9:30.

Relax, knowing Sonya, she's probably exploring the school now, in shock of what a deep budget can do. If anything, she's probably asking for a transfer to teach here. Our next stop will be looking around the neighborhood for homes for sale. Maybe we can be neighbors with the Klebolds.

Martin shook his head. Sonya would be the one to strike up a conversation with the principal and probe about possible employment. She certainly had the charm and good looks to garner a middle-aged man's attention. Maybe she was already signing the contract to start teaching in the fall.

He chuckled under his breath and pushed open the car door.

9:31.

One more minute, and you're going in. Yessir, you can take that to the bank. Go in there ready to lay a smack down on anyone trying to hold Sonya host-

The door swung open and Sonya reappeared from its shadows, walking at the same pace she had entered. She kept her head down and gradually increased her pace as she got closer to the car. When she was thirty feet away she was practically jogging.

"Let's go! Let's go!" she squealed excitedly. "I did it! It's done!"

She dropped into the driver's seat, rocking the car, and fired up the engine with one fluid motion. "It was so easy!" She panted for breath, likely from the release of tension that had built up over the last hour.

"What took so long?" Martin asked.

"Nothing. There was no one there in the office. It was super quiet. I waited a couple minutes to see if anyone was going to show up, and when they didn't I went back to the principal's office—his door was open—and left the letter on his desk. Front and center where he won't miss it."

"That's perfect!" Martin cried, still hesitant to get too excited, knowing the past wouldn't let this slip by so easily.

"I know. It was like the perfect storm of events. Perfect timing for everything. I'm so excited!"

Sonya drove like normal again, throwing caution to the wind as she zigzagged through town in search of the freeway. "I can't believe how easy that whole trip was. It's like the past *wanted* us to deliver that letter."

"Right. Seems like it was the first easy thing the past has let me do."

"Let *me* do," she corrected him.

"Of course."

Martin and Sonya, two vigilantes traveling through time and saving the world one catastrophe at a time. I'm the brains, she's the muscle.

It would make for a silly movie, but maybe it could be their reality. He'd need to wait to find out to see if all this trouble was worth it. They wouldn't know until 1999 to see if the shooting had occurred or not, and still, it would actually be 2018 when he got the chance to look it up.

Martin leaned back in his seat, a sense of ease settling for the first time in many days. He gazed out the window, thinking of the next ten weeks ahead until his attempt to save his daughter.

41

Chapter 41

Martin and Sonya spent the next two weeks trying to return to normalcy. With her off for the summer, and Martin's secret out of the bag, they spent every waking moment together. Martin had a follow-up appointment where the doctor told him he was progressing as expected in his mental recovery.

His memory gradually returned, but he still had momentary lapses where he "spaced out" as the doctor explained, something that would likely stay with him forever. Dr. Lincoln suggested he do mental exercises to counter the forgetfulness, so Sonya bought him a stack of crossword puzzles, word searches, and new books to read for the summer.

"No TV until you've spent two hours in one of those books," she had told him.

Martin was never one for reading or any "mindless" activities, as he believed crossword puzzles were, but he also knew if he didn't take his rehabilitation seriously, he'd punch a quick ticket to the senior home with Alzheimer's in a few years.

I wonder if I'll still be affected when I return to 2018. Like when you die in a dream, it doesn't mean you die in real life. Time heals everything, right?

Time did heal Sonya's libido; she tried to jump his bones nearly every night. Martin typically agreed, but other nights he was too fatigued. Migraines struck some days, leaving him curled up on the couch with his hands grasping his head, trying to pull the pain out of his skull.

The only headaches he had previously were after nights of heavy drinking. Those held no comparison to the railroad stake drilled into his brain from the migraines. The doctor prescribed painkillers in anticipation of this, but they only dulled the pain to an uncomfortable throb.

These days were the worst. He couldn't go outside until nighttime, couldn't watch TV, couldn't *focus* on anything. Sonya cared for him, making sure he stayed hydrated and took as many naps as possible to get through the day.

In sickness and in health, Martin thought as Sonya felt more like his wife every passing day. Even on the worst of days, her grace sent a fluttering throughout his body, and he knew everything would work out for the best.

Since they had missed their planned trip, Sonya proposed a getaway to the mountains. She had a friend with a cabin willing to give them the place for a week. Martin gratefully accepted the invitation, needing a change of scenery after so much time trapped in the living room.

The day they left was a bad migraine day for Martin, so Sonya forced him to take a sleeping pill while she drove the two and a half hours to Snowmass Village. Martin resisted at first, but the urge to bang his head against the wall was the deciding factor in his agreement.

"I drove us across town with our lives on the line. I think I can handle a simple trip to the mountains," Sonya said as he swallowed the pills.

"I know. I'm sorry. I just hate feeling so helpless. You've done so much – everything for me. I just want to return the favor."

"It's only because I love you," she said with a grin. "And don't worry, you'll be returning the favor when you're back to your complete self. You're gonna cook me dinner and rub my feet every night for a month."

"I look forward to it."

Martin reclined his seat and dozed as Sonya drove out of the city.

* * *

Martin woke to the sound of crunching gravel beneath the tires as they pulled into a steep, uphill driveway. Rocks bigger than him lined the driveway, and tall trees swayed gently in the breeze. The cabin waited at the top of the hill, its faded exterior revealing that it had gone through plenty of seasons in the Rocky Mountains. The white garage door slid open, revealing two open spaces and a collection of cleaning supplies on a lone shelf.

"I've never had a garage in my life," Sonya commented. "Not growing up, not now. Let's see what the big fuss is." She parked the car with a childish grin.

"You're funny," Martin said, rubbing the sleep out of his eyes. His migraine had reduced to a minor throb, much more manageable to get through the day. "The only garage I ever had was used for storage when I was a kid, so I've never really parked in one either."

They parked and Sonya jumped out of the car, stretching after the long drive. Martin felt refreshed and ready to explore his new home for the next week.

"Leave the bags, let's go look around," Sonya said, her voice echoing in the garage.

Martin shuffled to the door he presumed led inside, and watched as Sonya jiggled the key before pushing it open. The exterior may have looked rundown, but the interior was immaculate and likely remodeled within the last few years. Hardwood floors gleamed, Southwestern art decorated the walls as they walked down a short hallway into the kitchen where granite counter tops and sparkling appliances awaited. The kitchen sink overlooked the mountains with a breathtaking view. The kitchen connected to the living room where an L-shaped couch was tucked into the corner, a throw rug in the center of the floor, and a TV above an idle fireplace.

"This is much bigger than it looks from the outside," Martin commented, noticing Sonya's bulging eyes as she studied every nook and cranny of the cabin.

"Yeah," she said thoughtlessly. "It has a basement. That's where the master bedroom is."

Martin remained in the kitchen while Sonya studied a rack of VHS movies in the living room. He looked out the window to the green mountains, admiring nature's beauty. The sight brought back that tug, tempting him to stay in 1996 and continue living his life without a concern of returning to 2018. He could even earn enough money to buy a place like this, and they could live happily ever after, watching the sun rise over the horizon every morning.

"I'm gonna go check out the basement," he said as Sonya

made her way to the kitchen.

"Okay, I'll be right down. I wanna see what all's in this kitchen. We may need to run into town and get some groceries, but she told me there should be enough in the pantry for us."

Martin crossed into the living room where a side door opened to a staircase. The wooden steps creaked and groaned underneath his feet as they led him to the first carpeted area of the house.

The entire basement was the master bedroom. A king-sized bed was centered between two nightstands, facing the wall where a TV stood on top of a shelving unit with more VHS movies. The master bathroom was separated by a curtain serving as a door. Martin hurried across the room in the opposite direction, though, noticing a door that led outside to a deck.

He stepped onto the deck to find another amazing mountain view, this one facing west where they could watch the sunset. A hot tub was covered, but he could hear the water bubbling beneath the cover's surface. *Who is this friend you have, Sonya?*

"A good friend to keep around," a voice said from behind, causing Martin to jump. He automatically knew the voice and goosebumps immediately covered his flesh.

He turned to find Chris standing in the doorway. The old man leaned against the door jam with his arms crossed and that familiar evil grin.

"Are we going for a dip, Marty?" he asked in a menacing voice.

"Why are you here, Chris? You said you weren't coming back. Is the future too boring?"

As much as the old man terrified Martin, he still felt the confidence to be stern with him.

"Yes, yes, I know I said I was never coming back, but it sounds like you're in more desperate need than I anticipated."

"If you can jump through time, shouldn't you have already known you were going to need to come back?"

"I knew it was possible, but you could've always changed your mind. It's like how God knows what you're going to do before you do it, but he still gives you the free will to decide for yourself."

"Is this about Columbine? Are you upset I'm trying to stop it?"

"No, that is something we can discuss later, when you return. I love your ambition. I'm here because you've decided to stay here in the past and live out life like 2018 doesn't exist."

Martin watched Chris cautiously, not sure if he should respond.

"You can't stay here, Martin." Chris spoke like a scolding parent. "If you stay, then I don't get my payment. Did you forget about our agreement?"

"Of course not; I owe you my emotions."

Chris grinned, his face softening. "Precisely. I can't take that from you if you stay here. You have to return to your present time to settle your debts. If you don't, well, let's just say it's in your best interest to pay up."

The old man's eyebrows elevated above his evil smirk, a maniac expression that would haunt Martin forever. Chris wasn't bluffing.

"I'll return to 2018 after I save my daughter," Martin said, defeated. "I want to bring Sonya with me. How does this all affect her?"

"Yes, of course," Chris said, clapping his hands together in celebration. "It works like anything else. As long as she's making contact with you when you take the pill, she'll come with you."

"But how is it for her? Does she fall asleep with me? Does she get the glowing skin?"

"Look at you with all of your knowledge. I'm very proud of you, Marty. I honestly expected you to drink for six months, but you've made an honest man out of yourself."

"Answer my questions," Martin demanded, not giving a shit what the old man thought about his life choices.

"She'll be travelling through time as property—that's just how it works for anything or anyone who doesn't take the pill.

"So her body doesn't stay asleep here?"

"Nope. She gets a free ride with you. Like a buddy pass." Chris giggled at Martin. "But why would you want to bring her with you when you're gonna become an emotional dud? Surely she'll want nothing to do with you once you can't even fake a laugh."

"Leave," Martin barked, ready to choke the bastard. "Get out of here. Go back to wherever you came from."

Chris smirked, still leaning on the doorway. "Marty, my friend. It's a good thing we're friends, isn't it? We can have these heated discussions without worrying about breaking our bond. We go together like a fly and a frog's tongue." Chris stood stiffly, and Martin mirrored the action, noticing he had slouched. "I'll leave you alone. I just wanted to stop by and make sure you were still coming home. It's your first time working with me, so I thought I'd give you a warning. Be back in 2018 by October 1, or else I'll come looking for you."

Chris pointed at Martin with a skeletal finger, swirling it in a circular slow motion.

"Ta-ta for now. Give Sonya my best."

Chris pivoted and disappeared into the master bedroom. By the time Martin rushed in, he was already gone.

"Everything okay down there?" Sonya shouted from the top of the stairs.

"Yes!" Martin yelled back, pushing his fear away. "Just admiring the basement. There's a hot tub!"

His voice sounded normal to himself, and he hoped it projected that way.

"I'll be right down. Didn't bring a swimsuit – guess we'll have to get in naked."

Martin hadn't been naked in a hot tub with a woman since college. The thought started to excite him, but his mind remained stuck on Chris. He hated how easily the old man could show up and find him in the most intimate of places. He stared into the vast woods of the mountains, wondering where the secret eyes were that followed his every move.

Martin crossed the room to the foot of the stairs. "Can you bring me a glass of whiskey when you come down, please?"

"Coming right up!" she responded, her voice echoing down the stairwell.

Just have a drink and relax. You're in a beautiful cabin with your girlfriend. Make love to her in the hot tub like you were 20 again. Don't worry about that old fuck.

Martin repeated these thoughts on a loop, but no matter how hard he tried, he couldn't shake the image of that maniacal grin, secretive voice, and frosty white hair. He just wanted to go home and forget he had ever traveled back in time. 22 years had already passed without Izzy, so he'd have 20 more miserable years left to live should he return now, and could trim a few off with more cigarettes and whiskey.

He could explain to Sonya his decision, apologize for dragging her this far into his mess, and pop the pill before she could realize what was happening. Tears streamed down his face as he listened to his own doubtful thoughts.

"Suck it up," he said to himself. "You've come this far."

He pictured Izzy walking home from school, her ponytail swinging side to side, her smile showing both flashes of her youth and her pending womanhood.

I promise I'll save you.

42

Chapter 42

The scorching heat of July gave way to an even hotter August. Martin continued his mental rehabilitation, and found a helpful recovery in reading, helping him regain vocabulary skills. He gave *The Notebook* a try after hearing Sonya rave about it so much, and found he enjoyed the story, although he'd never admit it to a group of strangers.

"I've been thinking about the future," Sonya said one night at dinner. "What happens here? If I go away, will there be people wondering where I am? Or does my life just vanish?"

"Time just sort of stops," he said, not having a clue how it actually worked traveling *forward* in time.

"What happens if I die in the future?" she asked.

"Of course you're gonna die in the future. We all do." Martin offered a smile, but Sonya was in no mood for jokes.

"I'm being serious, Martin. If my life is in danger like yours is here, I just want to know what happens."

"You won't be in any danger. I promise." He reached across the table and embraced her hand, rubbing slow circles around her palm with his thumb. "When we arrive, I'll fill you in on everything you'll have missed. I could go over the major events, but it'll be helpful to have Google."

"Google?"

"Sorry. It's a website where you look up anything you ever wanted. It's like Yahoo, but a million times better."

Sonya nodded, grasping the simplest idea of the future internet juggernaut.

"You know," Martin said. "I was considering staying in 1996 with you. Just leaving my life behind in the future and seeing where it goes from here. I wanted you to know that you aren't the only one who made a difficult decision. I thought long and hard about it, but decided it's not best for me to stay in a world where I already exist. That alone is a high risk. And then there's Izzy. If I stay in 1996 and save her, that leaves her with two fathers and a world of confusion. I'd still have to watch her life from afar, and that's not what I want to do. I want to be *in* her life."

Sonya nodded. "I love you," she said. "That's the only reason I'm going with you. I'm terrified. Don't you know how scary this is?"

"Of course I do. I had to do it by myself coming here. I'm just glad I have someone to share the experience with now."

"I just want you to be happy. What happened to your daughter is disgusting. I couldn't imagine living another day if something like that happened to me. You deserve to keep her safe and return to a normal life with her."

"You're an amazing woman," he said. "I've never known anyone with such a big heart. I only hope I can make it up to you, and make your life everything you want it to be in the future."

"I know you will. I wouldn't take this leap if I didn't believe so. I've been having some weird dreams."

"What about?"

"This old man. He never says his name when I ask; he only smiles. But it's not a friendly smile; it's pure evil."

Martin nodded. He wouldn't let her know the truth about the man she had visions of. If she knew he was waiting for them in the future, she might reconsider going.

Oh, that old man? He's only the keeper of time, and sure, he's probably from hell and has dinner with Hitler every night, but he's a nice guy, don't you think?

Hopefully Chris wouldn't take his emotions immediately upon arrival in 2018. He wanted to enjoy at least a day with Sonya before his soul turned numb.

How you gonna explain that one to her, big guy? Thank her for leaving her life behind to join an old, emotionless postal worker in 2018? That should go over beautifully.

Martin knew he should've been upfront about what lay ahead, but he couldn't afford to let her change her mind. *She'll be fine. Everything can be explained. Just get her to 2018 and take it from there.*

"I want to talk about next month," Martin said. "Saving Izzy. I want your help. I know I had told you I needed to do this alone, but I've thought it over and feel it would be best to have another set of eyes. It's a small house, but I can only be in one area at once. What if I'm covering the front and she slips out the back? Or vice versa? I just want to have all my bases covered."

Martin caught himself speaking abnormally fast. *Nervous much? Did it finally occur to you that the big day is only four weeks away now? Time sure flies when you're comatose and forgetful.*

"I'm happy to help however you need me," she responded

calmly. "What did you have in mind?"

"I haven't thought that far ahead, honestly, but perhaps I'll have you stakeout the area ahead of time. All we know is that Izzy goes missing at some point in the middle of night. Lela confirmed she checked on Izzy before going to sleep, and that was usually around ten; Izzy's bedtime was nine. So, I just want some eyes on the house in the hours leading up to then. It's too risky for me to hang out on the block, even from a distance. Maybe you can park a couple houses down and watch things. I really want to make sure no one is scoping the area ahead of time."

"And what will you be doing?"

"Probably pacing circles and trying to not puke my guts out. I'm going to show up when the sun goes down around eight. I need the darkness to blend in. I'll be dressed in all black and will hide in the shadows."

"Who knew you were such a ninja." Sonya made her attempt at humor, but now Martin was the one in no mood for jokes. "So what's your plan for Izzy? What will you do once she's safe?"

Martin nodded his head slowly, like a game show contestant who knew the answer for the big cash prize.

"Then we leave," he said flatly. He could tell Sonya was expecting a more elaborate response. "That's all there is to do. I can't risk her seeing me. All I can do is get back to 2018 as soon as possible and see how she is."

"And how will you go about finding her? Your life can completely change by her staying with you, and a lot can happen in 22 years."

"I'll be able to find her. You can find anyone in 2018 with the click of a mouse."

"I'll take your word. I just thought you'd have a better plan in place."

"I wish I did, too, but I just don't know how any of this works—travelling back into my present time, that is. Besides, I really do work at the post office in 2018 and can run an address search when I get back. I'm actually on my way to work when we return, so I'll probably go in and see what I can find before I quit my job."

"Why would you quit?" she asked like a disappointed mother. Martin waved two gentle hands at her to relax.

"I'm not going to need a job when we get back. I've done some investing and should have a small fortune waiting for me in 2018."

Martin had made a couple of trips to a small investment firm downtown and bought stocks he knew would grow by 2018. The stock broker had cautioned him against loading up on so much technology in his portfolio, but Martin insisted he knew what he was doing.

"We will be taken care of," Martin said. "Where do you want to live when we get back? Housing is through the roof, but we'll have enough money to live anywhere."

The words felt foreign leaving his lips. He never thought he'd get to say such a thing.

"I'd like to live in my same house," she said, distant as if her mind were already floating away to the future.

"I think we can manage that," Martin responded with a smirk.

He took joy in hearing Sonya speak about the future. While he knew she wouldn't back out this late, he wanted her to enter the journey with no hesitations. The more they spoke about the future, the more realistic it felt, even for Martin.

His life in 2018 really did feel like 22 years ago instead of five months—or ten minutes.

He knew how the world was in 2018, that wouldn't change. But *his* life could wind up completely different. If Izzy was okay, there was a chance him and Lela would still be married. How was he supposed to bring the new love of his life home to meet his wife and daughter? If he tried to explain what really happened, Lela would call the mental asylum.

A lot can happen in 22 years. I just hope it's all for the best.

43

Chapter 43

School was back in session during the final week of August, and Sonya had returned two weeks prior to prepare for the upcoming year.

"I guess I know how my students feel during that final week of school now," she had said in regards to her pending departure from 1996. "It's hard to focus on anything. How are you holding up? We're just a few days away from the moment of truth, can you believe it?"

Believe it he could. A lot more had happened than he had budgeted for on this journey: falling in love and a coma at the top of the list. More importantly, Martin discovered a life as a new man where drinking was only done in celebration, not as a major part of his daily diet. His coma recovery also led him to discover that he enjoyed reading books, something he had never taken the time to do in his past life. It was hard to focus on such a task while in a constant state of inebriation.

He also reaffirmed something he had long believed: *Fuck crossword puzzles.*

The blank white squares on those bastards teased Martin

every time he sat down to try and complete one. His mind simply didn't function in a way that could guess words from a vague clue.

Regardless of how things played out with Izzy in a couple of weeks, Martin knew life would be different when he returned to 2018. He'd have no need to work, he'd have Sonya by his side, and have actual hobbies that consisted of things besides passing out drunk in the living room while the TV flashed over his limp body all night.

No more hangovers. The feeling of waking up with a clear mind had been a big catalyst for Martin taking a new appreciation of his life.

All of these thoughts had flooded his mind, submerging from the depths of his psyche every time he glanced at the calendar and saw his date with destiny looming less than two weeks away. He fought to push them aside, dismiss them until they were needed.

This particular night was a Thursday, one more day until the school year's first weekend. Sonya had fallen into the groove of mindlessly telling stories about her students. She had made it clear that she wouldn't get too attached to them, considering she'd never see them again after another week and a half.

They had finished dinner and settled in to their new routine of Sonya doing the dishes while Martin picked up and swept the kitchen before sitting down together to watch the nightly news and sip glasses of tea.

See, this life won't be so bad in 2018. You basically have a wife again.

They would certainly need to pick up some new hobbies, seeing as neither of them would have to worry about going back to a job. He considered getting back into golf, something he hadn't done since before Izzy was born in 1984.

When they had finished their cleaning routine, Martin turned on the TV and adjusted the antennas for the clearest signal on Channel Nine before plopping down on the couch. Sonya joined him with the other part of their nightly routine: two glasses of steaming hot tea.

"I'm so tired," she said. "The first week of school is always the hardest." She swung her legs up on the couch and curled up on Martin's chest.

"It's only a couple weeks, then we're on to our new life together."

The news station played its familiar introductory jingle while graphics for channel nine danced across the screen. The channel's longtime anchorman, James Young, filled the screen with his typical stern expression to complement his strong jawbone and perfectly combed over gray hair.

"Good evening, Denver," he said in a booming voice. "We have tragic news out of Littleton that we want to cut right to."

The camera flashed to a school, and Sonya bolted upright on the couch, practically jumping off the edge.

"That's Columbine!" she shouted, pointing at the TV with a wagging finger. "That's Columbine!"

"A fire broke out today at Littleton's Columbine High School at 2:45, just a half hour before school was to let out for the day," James Young said. The screen showed different images of the high school they had just visited a few weeks earlier, charred and smoking like the bottom of a fire pit. There wasn't a trace of the building left. "Authorities are still looking for the cause of this enormous fire, but what we do know is that it started in the school's cafeteria and spread to the library. Since there was no one in the cafeteria at the time, it's unknown how long the fire had been burning before the alarms were set off, but by that time it was too late."

James Young choked up and fought for his next words.

"The flames completely engulfed the library, collapsing the second floor onto the first floor. So far, thirty six bodies have been discovered in the rubble in that section alone, with the count increasing by the hour. The fire spread from the library and took the rest of the school with it. Columbine High School is no more."

The words echoed as Martin felt a sharp pang in his stomach.

This is it. This is why you had no resistance that day. The past is toying with you now.

"Martin," Sonya said nervously. "Please tell me this was supposed to happen. Tell me this is part of history." She stood, gawking at the TV as she spoke to him, unable to break her stare from the gruesome images of charred skeletons and crying mothers. James Young's voice had all but drowned into background noise.

"It's not," Martin said through a clenched jaw. "This never happened."

"Well what are we supposed to do?" she demanded. "This is our fault, isn't it?"

She paced around the coffee table and sipped her tea with a trembling hand.

Martin raised his hand for her to calm down, feeling stuck to the couch.

"I know this looks bad."

"Looks bad?" Sonya snapped. "I've never even heard of Columbine High School until you got here with your story from the future. Then I'm thrust into the school to leave a letter for the principal, and now the school is gone. It's a pile of fucking ashes, Martin!"

"I didn't know this would happen," Martin said, remaining calm. He had to. If he showed his true emotions that were running frantically around in a panic, Sonya might actually lose her mind. "This must be how the past pushed back. I'll bet the principal read that letter today, finally. And this is what happened. I'd bet money that the principal didn't survive."

"How do you know this?" Sonya asked. She was clearly upset, but didn't seem to be angry–more of a mixture of terror and concern, infused with some guilt. "There have been a lot of questions I've refrained from asking, mainly because I'm not sure I *want* to know the answers. But now I need some answers. How do you know how this all works?"

Sonya crossed her arms while she stared at Martin. He still couldn't move from the couch, the feeling in his legs having vanished.

"You know the dream you had about the old man?" he asked.

She nodded her head in quick jerky motions.

"Well," Martin continued. "I know that old man."

Sonya stood frozen, the only movement coming from her lips, which furled in disgust.

"You mean I've been having nightmares about this guy and you knew about him the whole time?" she asked.

"I'm sorry," Martin said. "I didn't want you to be afraid."

"Tell me who he is and what he as to do with all of this."

"I'll tell you what I know. His name is Chris, and he's the reason I can travel through time. He calls himself the keeper of time, but I think he's a demon – or maybe an angel – I'm not really sure. He's never done or said anything evil, but I just get bad vibes. I met him right here in Larkwood in 2018 when he opened an antique store. I went in with my mom one day to look around and he lured me back to the store. When I went back a second time, alone, he took me into his back office where he has this lab of potions and powders, and that's where he makes these pills. He's visited me three times since coming to 1996, and he has all of the information. He's the one who warned me to never cross paths with my past self."

"But none of that explains about the past pushing back," Sonya barked. She had not calmed down one bit during his explanation.

"I'm pretty sure Chris led me to meet this other guy. Remember the liquor store that burned down a few months ago?"

Sonya nodded.

"The owner was also from the future. It's like Chris knew I would go into the liquor store and meet this owner. The owner was scared of me at first, but then explained many of the rules of living in the past."

"I used to go to that liquor store. You're telling me that sweet Asian man was from the future?" Sonya's words dripped with skepticism.

"Yes, and I watched him get murdered and the store get burned down. There are these people called Road Runners who travel through time and kill other time travelers. I'm still not clear what exactly their angle is, but they killed him and burned down the store."

Sonya shook her head, arms still crossed. "I don't know what to believe any more. I think I need a moment alone to think things over. This all sounded like a big joke and I've gone along with it. It's all become a bit more believable, and now this. All of these students dead and buried under the rubble of their own school. I can't even stomach the thought."

Martin pushed with all of his mental might and stood from the couch on wobbly legs. He jab stepped toward Sonya and extended his arms out for her, grabbing her around each arm.

"Sonya, please. I know this is crazy. I didn't want this any more than you, but this is what's happening now. All we can do is learn from it and be prepared for the next event."

"If you think I'm going anywhere near your past right now, you're out of your mind. I'd love to help you with your daughter, but I don't wanna see a worse outcome like this." She pointed at the TV as a lone tear streamed down her face.

"Sonya, let's relax and discuss this."

"I don't want to discuss anything!" she howled. "I don't want to risk my life. I don't want to risk others' lives. And I don't want to go to the future!"

Leave before you say anything that will permanently ruin your relationship.

Martin nodded and shuffled around Sonya, his legs stronger as he strode toward the front door.

"Where are you going?" she demanded.

"I think we both need a moment to cool off. I'm going on a walk."

"You shouldn't do that. You could forget your way home."

"I'll be fine. Just take a moment to calm down. I don't want to fight with you."

He left without another word and closed the door gently to not give any signal of anger. He wasn't angry, but rather anxious, and as he mindlessly walked through the neighborhood. One thought remained stuck to the front of his mind like a thumbtack on a corkboard: this is the past pushing back.

It had to be. He and Sonya had never fought. Not once. Now all the sudden she erupted into a ball of rage. Granted, she

301

had every right to be upset, but to the point of screaming and cursing at him?

He tried to play down the thought, listing plenty of reasons why she could have snapped: her upcoming trip to the future, leaving her life behind forever, not knowing how life would be in 2018, and the start of the school year. Combine all of these factors with a spark like the Columbine news and you get one distraught girlfriend.

But Martin knew better. Sonya had a knack for keeping her emotions in check, something he had fallen in love with. This behavior wasn't like her at all. While she may have been stressed out, she still wouldn't act out in such an outrageous manner.

Be cautious. You've thought this from the start. The past will throw anything your way to throw you off your plan. You have less than two weeks until the big day. Be ready for anything.

Martin reached the end of the neighborhood and turned around to return home. Sonya was right about there being a chance of him getting lost, and that's why he walked a straight line and didn't venture down any new side roads. The sun descended, splashing a fiery glow across the quiet homes and lawns.

Somewhere a couple miles away Martin was watching the news while Izzy brushed her teeth and changed into her pajamas, unaware that their lives would be flipped upside down within a few days.

44

Chapter 44

Sonya's tension had blown over by the morning. When Martin returned from his stroll through the neighborhood, he found Sonya in bed already and decided to leave her alone for the night.

She apologized in the morning and claimed to have no idea where the sudden burst of anger had come from.

"I have so much on my mind; seeing that news about Columbine just set me off. Then knowing you were keeping the secret of that old man from me pissed me off even more. But I understand why you did it. I don't think it's made anything better now that I know who he is. Might have even made it worse, but that's my own fault for making you tell me. I think the less I know the better. Sometimes it's best to just be left in the dark about certain things."

"You're still having dreams about Chris?" Martin asked.

Sonya grimaced. "Please don't call him that, it makes him seem human. And yes, I am. It's not much of a dream, though. He just sort of stands there in the darkness with that evil smile, and stares at me like he's studying me under a microscope."

"That's really strange."

"I know. Do you think it's actually him? Like could he really be in my head and not just part of a dream?"

Martin shrugged. "Anything's possible with that guy."

Sonya shivered at the thought.

"Well, I need to get ready for school. I hope we can put this behind us. I still want to go to 2018."

"I love you," Martin said, and kissed her on the forehead.

* * *

When the calendar flipped to September over the weekend, Martin felt a calm settle over him that he hadn't felt since arriving in 1996, nearly six months ago. The sense of doom he had felt turned numb after several weeks, but now he felt it starting to lift completely. He had grown over the last six months and was ready to save his long lost daughter.

Sonya had highlighted the big day on the calendar with a big red circle, and every time Martin looked in the calendar's direction he felt that circle staring at him like the Devil's eye from a pit of darkness.

He had one more full week and weekend to make it through before encountering the reason for his trip to the past. Martin spent that final week ensuring he had the few things together that he wanted to bring back to 2018. His conscience pleaded to follow Izzy for the week, insisting he would be able to prevent the crisis ahead of time, but he knew better. The past would never make this task that straightforward. Izzy would be right where she always was like any other day: walking home from school by herself, her ponytail swinging with each step she took.

As he had vowed from the onset, much to his disgust, he had kept away from Izzy and his past self for nearly the entirety of his time in 1996. His one close encounter had been plenty to reassure him that he had made the right decision. Next Monday would change everything, as he and Sonya would keep a close watch on his old house from the time school let out.

Considering Izzy went missing in the middle of the night, everyone assumed she had sneaked out of the house. While Martin could stop her as soon as she stepped foot outside, he also needed answers after all these years. There were holes to fill in the timeline of events. He'd follow Izzy until her situation turned dire. Where did she go? Who did she meet with? What was she up to? Martin had a hard time over the past two decades wrapping his head around the fact that his innocent angel of a daughter may have been living a double life. Was this the first time she left the house in the middle of the night?

Find out after this brief commercial break, he thought, and chuckled nervously to himself. Just six months ago—or ten minutes—Martin had a pistol in his mouth after a lifetime full of sorrow and desperation. Now he had hope and a clear mind, and a healthy body that no longer begged to be put out of its misery. He'd never been the type to pray, and often questioned the existence of God, but on this particular Sunday night he thanked God for everything, especially Sonya. *Maybe we sometimes get a second chance to right our wrongs, to love the right people.* Martin didn't know for sure, but knew he would never take life for granted again.

As he dozed off to sleep later that night, Sonya curled into a ball with her back to him and he felt something he never thought he'd feel again: a full heart.

* * *

Over the course of the week, Martin kept his mind distant from the upcoming task. He didn't want to overthink anything, and preferred to make quick reactions when the time came. Sonya agreed to follow Izzy home from a distance that week, every day after school, just to make sure she wasn't being followed by anyone else. Each day the reports came back negative.

Meanwhile, Martin focused on books and word searches. The book of crossword puzzles had been thrown into a drawer where he'd hopefully never have to see them again. Word searches felt more therapeutic, and reading different stories took his mind to another world altogether. While these helped occupy his mind, he felt a constant, subtle tug on his brain.

Excuse me, Mr. Briar, just a gentle reminder that you'll be changing your life on Monday, his inner voice said, like a doctor's office calling to remind him of an important appointment coming up.

He could no longer deny the growing uncertainty and anxiety forming. Every day closer felt like a pending date with doom.

What if I fail? What if I've gone through all this for nothing? What if there's nothing I can actually do to stop this?

It was a realistic possibility he had managed to ignore this whole time, but with his date with destiny looming around the corner, it seemed a flood of every imaginable possibility had come rushing into his mind. He fully expected a hard fight from the past next Monday night and knew he might come close to encountering death again. But there's always a price to pay for something you longed for, right?

When Friday night arrived and Sonya was home for the weekend, Martin couldn't eat, sit still, nor focus on reading. He felt as useless as ever, wishing he could jump forward to Monday night already and get down to business.

Sonya had done a good job at killing his doubts about the situation and put his mind at ease. He had wanted to hold off on drinking in the days leading up September 9th, but happily enjoyed a glass of whiskey. It was the most relaxed he had felt all week, and he fell into a deep, dreamless sleep.

* * *

On Sunday, September 8th, Martin and Sonya spent the morning cooking a grand breakfast. Sonya had been quiet on Saturday as they wasted the day on the couch watching TV, even ordering pizza for dinner to avoid having to do anything.

This morning, though, Sonya had an extra wave of energy as she stood at the stove, dancing to the radio as she prepared bacon, eggs, and pancakes.

"If this is my last full day in my house. I'm gonna enjoy every second of it," she had told Martin when he entered the kitchen groggy-eyed and confused at the scene of her swaying hips at 7:30 in the morning.

He was glad that she seemed relaxed. Even Martin felt

nervous about returning to 2018. Life really was simple in 1996. He could spend the days at work and come home to enjoy dinner and watch the news to see what happened in the world during the day.

Fuck you, Chris, he thought. *I could've had a great life here if you just left me alone.*

The thought of Chris forcing him back to 2018 triggered a tingle of hate for the old man. No one liked being told what to do, and Martin Briar was no exception.

After they devoured breakfast—Martin ate everything he could get his hands on thanks to his appetite returning—Sonya retreated into the bedroom to pack as many valuables as she could into an oversized gym bag.

"I've gotta pack my entire life into this one bag," she said, shaking her head as she stared around her bedroom.

"Don't worry about anything like clothes or stuff like that. We can replenish your wardrobe when we arrive—we'll need to, in fact, unless you want to look like you just arrived from the 90's."

"Oh, yeah? What do they wear in 2018, some sort of spacesuit?" she teased.

"Fashion doesn't change too much, I suppose. Although the young women seem to wear a lot less and show more skin. I wouldn't be opposed to you trying out that style if you really wanted."

He shot promiscuous eyebrows at her with a lewd wink.

"I'm sure you would like that. Tell me, are you the old man who always gets caught looking at the college girls?"

Martin cackled. "Of course not! I never get caught!"

Sonya burst into a cheery laughter and shook her head as she returned to her bag. "I'm not even sure what I should bring with me. I have some family heirlooms, but those would take up maybe ten percent of this bag."

"Then just take that. You don't need anything else. I came here with the clothes on my back and my cell phone in my pocket."

"Your alien phone that doesn't even work," Sonya teased. "I'm still convinced it's just a fancy Gameboy until you can prove otherwise."

They had plenty of discussions about the future's technology, most of which Sonya called "impossible." No, there couldn't be one device that made phone calls, took pictures, kept your schedule, *and* had games to play...and fit in the palm of your hand. She was in for quite the wake-up call in 2018.

"Just take what's important to you. Things can be replaced, but memories can't. So take any pictures, heirlooms, anything like that." Martin returned to a more serious tone. "No need to overthink it."

"Are you ready for tomorrow?" Sonya asked.

"Yeah, I feel good about it."

"No, Martin. I mean it. Are you *ready*?" She stared at him with crossed arms. "Our lives are going to change forever within the next 36 hours. I've come to terms with it; I feel like you haven't."

Martin didn't respond immediately and met her stare. Behind those eyes he had fallen in love with was a scared woman. Not scared in the sense of raw fear that made you want to hide in your room, but scared like a kid leaving for college for the first time. The fear of the unknown could cause even the most mentally strong person to crumble.

"I'm ready. All I've envisioned since I arrived here is bringing Izzy back home. It still doesn't feel real. I keep waiting to be woken up by my alarm, likely in a heavy sweat from all the booze I drank the night before, and realize this was all a dream. But I don't think that's going to happen."

Martin paused to gather more thoughts.

"I know I might die tomorrow. I've never thought about death before, not really, but now I can't help but wonder what it feels like to stop living. I know that's a realistic outcome, just like it was at Columbine. I know I might lose you. What if the past doesn't let you come with me? This could be our last night together, and if it is, I promise I'll come find you in 2018. You'll be in your 70's, but I don't care. I want to be with you."

Tears welled in Sonya's eyes, and Martin figured she had never considered these possibilities.

"Don't cry. Remember we're in this together," Martin said, wiping the tears from her face. "I love you, and if you want to wait 22 years for me, I'll be there in 2018 looking for you."

He pulled her in and kissed her on the lips.

Sonya sobbed into his embrace, her body shuddering against his as they would spend the rest of the day together in minimal conversation, wanting nothing more than to enjoy each other's presence.

The reality had finally sunk in for both of them. Tomorrow would change them both. Forever.

45

Chapter 45

"Martin, get out of bed!" Lela Briar shouted, her voice brimming with fear. "Hurry!"

Having worked a swing shift the night before, Martin hadn't arrived home until two in the morning, and hadn't joined Lela in bed until just before three.

He shot upright in bed, cloudy-eyed and dazed, and swung his legs mindlessly over the edge. His eyes felt swollen and bloodshot as he swayed to catch his balance.

"MARTIN!" Lela shouted again, and this time he was cognizant to know she was calling from Izzy's room.

Martin always poked his head into his daughter's room when he arrived home in the middle of the night. This particular night he had checked on her and saw a lump in the middle of her bed. The fall nights were starting to get cold, so he figured she was just extra bundled up.

He stepped around his pile of clothes and shuffled around the foot of the bed. Izzy's room was across the hallway where he met Lela, pacing frantically around the bedroom. The sheets were tossed into a mess, the closet door open and appearing to have vomited all of their daughter's clothes.

"What happened in here?" Martin asked.

"Izzy's gone!" Lela shouted, her brown hair in a frazzled mess, sweat glistening on her forehead. "I've been looking for her for the last half hour. I checked the basement, the bathrooms, everything. Even outside, she's gone!"

"I'm sure there's a perfectly good explanation," Martin said. "She wouldn't just up and leave without a word."

"Martin! She's gone. She's not here. It's 6:30 A.M. and she doesn't need to leave for school for another hour." She stared at him with bulging blue eyes, fear swimming behind them like a terrified fish. Her slender body trembled in panic.

"I'm sure she headed over early. She loves school, remember?" Martin tried to stay calm, but hearing his own words made the situation seem less likely. Even students who enjoyed school didn't show up an hour early. Hell, the school wasn't even open yet. "Was her room like this when you got here? Or did you do this?"

"I did this. I thought she was under the blankets—that's how it looked—then I kept pulling them back and she wasn't here. Martin, what do we do?"

Lela's voice transformed from fear into hysterics in a matter of seconds. "This can't be happening to us. These things don't really happen, do they?"

Martin's heart tumbled through his chest and stomach. You always heard about kids going missing on the news, but never consider it a reality – your reality.

"Was she here when you got home?" Lela asked in between sobs.

Martin scrunched his face. "I don't know," he said reluctantly. "I checked, and saw the lump under the blankets, but I didn't come all the way in to know for sure. I never do in the middle of the night."

Lela's body heaved as she buried her face into her shaking hands.

"Relax. We still have places to check, and we can't jump to any conclusions yet." *More lies, keep it up, Marty.* "Call my mom, see if maybe she went there. If not, then call the police. I'm gonna drive down to the school and to some her friends' houses. She's gotta be at one of those places. She doesn't know anyone else."

"Then go, I'll call your mom."

Martin's mother lived two blocks away, and Izzy would often walk there to visit, although never so early in the morning. He hopped into his car and drove slowly through the neighborhood, checking both sides of the street for any sign of Izzy. A light fog settled in, limiting visibility. Martin arrived to Larkwood Middle School to find it abandoned, drove around the grounds for ten minutes in search of any clue, and then stopped by each of Izzy's friend's houses in the neighborhood. With each passing house and no sign of Izzy, Martin felt the pillars that held up his sanity dissolve one by one.

The school pulled at him like a magnetic force, so he returned for one more look.

The green mass that was the school's lawn grew bigger with each house passing in a blur. When Martin reached the school's block, he turned left and drove toward the main entrance, again feeling pulled to it, as if he were watching himself drive the car in an out-of-body experience. As he turned into the school's parking lot he saw Izzy standing at the school's main entrance, only the school wasn't Larkwood Middle School.

It was Columbine High School.

Martin parked and jumped out of the car in a swift motion, sprinting for his daughter. She stood still, facing his direction, with her head down. Izzy wore pajamas, a matching set with Ariel and Flounder from *Little Mermaid* spotted all around.

"Hi, Daddy," she said, looking up. "It's okay, Daddy. I'm okay."

Tears rolled down her soft face as Martin embraced her. She remained stiff in his grip. Martin squeezed, but felt no life in the girl. She had no scent, no warmth, but it was her; there was no denying her green eyes or her sweet voice.

"Daddy, go home. You can't save me. Even if you did, they will still take me. Here." She looked back to Columbine.

Martin took a step back. Was Izzy implying that if she lived she would've been killed in the Columbine attacks? How would Izzy have gone to Columbine? They were nowhere near the level of income to even consider moving to Littleton. A lot could change in a three-year span, and maybe the Briar family continued in an alternate universe where Izzy never went missing and they moved across town to where she would meet her eventual doom at her new school. But Martin thought it to be a long shot.

"Izzy," he said through a swollen throat. "What happened?"

"It was an accident, Daddy."

"What accident?" Martin squatted to meet Izzy's eyes.

Izzy sobbed, yet remained motionless as she stood in her pajamas.

"It was an accident. Please don't be mad, Daddy. I love you."

Izzy turned and started to walk toward the school.

"Izzy!" Martin shouted, his legs frozen. "IZZY!"

When she reached the entrance, she turned and looked over her shoulder, locking eyes with Martin. "I love you, Daddy." She pulled the door open and stepped into the school, letting the door glide shut behind her.

The force that kept Martin's feet stuck in the ground like concrete had lifted, and he tumbled forward, lunging for the door handles and clawing at them like a rabid cat.

"Izzy, come back!" he screamed, his face moist with sweat and tears. He pulled on the door handles, but none of them budged. Through the window was darkness. No hallways, no office, just a pit of blackness. He knew the doors wouldn't open, but kept yanking at them to the point he thought his shoulder might pop out of its socket.

"Izzy, please!"

* * *

Martin sprung awake, crying, sweating, and panting. He was in his bedroom, Sonya by his side, stirring from his jerky motions. The sheets were soaked with sweat and clung to his lower back like leeches.

"It's just a dream," he whispered. "Just a bad dream. It doesn't mean anything."

Like hell it doesn't mean anything. Why do you keep lying to yourself? You haven't once had a dream about Izzy since she went missing, and now this happens on the eve of your supposed rescuing her?

Martin brushed his thoughts aside. Dreams are nothing but a collection of subconscious thoughts. He knew this, as his mother was big into analyzing dreams, but she always reminded him of this simple fact.

There was no Izzy, no Larkwood Middle School posing as Columbine High School, no locked doors that led into darkness. Izzy was always on his mind, and being so close to the actual events that followed her disappearance, the details came back vividly from wherever they had lain dormant after all these years.

"Just a dream."

He looked over and was relieved to see he hadn't woken Sonya as she continued her light snoring. Today would be the longest day of her life and she needed to be as rested as a cat on a Sunday afternoon.

Was it a sign? he wondered. *What if Chris put that dream in my head?* Considering everything that had happened so far, it wouldn't be a stretch of the imagination for the old man to do such a thing. But why would he have given Martin this opportunity to come back in time only to be told to go back home when the time came? *Just a dream.*

Martin lay back down, the damp sheets now cold on his flesh as he stared into the darkness of the bedroom. *Today is the day your life changed forever. It's not the anniversary of the day where you drink a little more to bury the pain. It's the* actual *day and you're living in it. Save her life, save your life, and go back home.*

Martin would toss and turn for another two hours before falling into a light sleep. Shortly after, the sun rose from the eastern plains, cracking dawn on the morning of September 9th, 1996.

46

Chapter 46

Martin woke several hours later to find it was almost noon, sleeping while Sonya would have dressed and gotten ready for her final day at school. He panicked at first, worried that he had slept through something important, but relaxed once he remembered that he had nothing to do until that night.

One last day of waiting around.

He expected the suspense to kill him. What could he possibly do to make the day pass, knowing what awaited when the sun went down? The game plan was set: Sonya would follow Izzy home one final time to make sure she didn't venture off, come straight home to meet Martin for a dinner that would surely go untouched, then return to watch the Briar house until the sun went down and Martin would show up in his all-black camouflage for a front row seat to the big show.

Martin warned Sonya of a boring stakeout. Every report Lela had filed in those following days mentioned that Izzy had to have gone out in the middle of the night—she had kissed her goodnight just after nine before turning in for bed herself. All he could rely on now was Lela's word from 22 years earlier.

The one good thing about suffering such a tragedy was the ability to remember every single detail. He could practically recite Lela's police statements after all of these years and hundreds of bottles of whiskey.

When he finally got out of bed, a lump filled his body from his intestines up to his throat, and would stay there all day, thanks to the nerves that refused to settle down. This caused a lost appetite and a constant urge to sit on the toilet and pray for it all to end.

He didn't bother with breakfast or lunch, instead stepping outside with hopes of passing the time and taking his mind off the night ahead. Some flowers in Sonya's garden needed final tending before they would close up shop for the upcoming winter, so he poked around with some lilies to find that a whole twenty minutes had passed.

Is there anything left that I need to get done? Martin ran through a mental checklist of things he needed to have done before returning to 2018, and for the first time he welcomed the thought of returning home, not knowing if he could bear the stress of another day in the past.

Everything was in order. He had invested money to cover his life in 2018, and had his return pill ready in his pocket, buried deep in the bottom where it had no chance of wiggling out. He had decided it would be best to keep the pill on his body rather than leaving it at the house. There was a chance he would need to make a quick decision and take the pill, having no time to return home, but the original plan was to convene at home after saving Izzy and decide when they would want to make the trip into the future.

Martin returned inside to find his body randomly trembling and his teeth chattering. He couldn't recall ever being so nervous. He shuffled into the living room and threw himself on the couch.

Relax. This is what you came here for. Did you think the day wouldn't actually come?

The way his life was going before he had swallowed that pill, he thought he'd have a few weeks to live before dying from alcohol poisoning or a self-inflicted gunshot. He never expected the past to provide a cure for his escalating alcoholism.

What if I relapse in 2018?

He had considered this possibility before, but didn't know how much stock to put into it. Did the past really cure him? Or did he take advantage of a fresh start in a familiar era? He believed the latter. Besides, whatever happened tonight would change the course of his life in 2018. He could wake up and no longer have to go to the post office. Maybe he really did catch a break and would live in Littleton if his daughter had never disappeared. His own life could look unrecognizable, and the thought didn't help settle his nerves.

If everything went smoothly and he saved Izzy, returned to 2018 with Sonya, and no longer had an itch to drink every bottle of booze in sight, there was still Chris. What exactly did he mean by taking away Martin's ability to feel emotions?

If someone tells a joke, will I no longer laugh? If someone dies, will I no longer cry? What precisely does it mean and how severe will it be?

He feared becoming a zombie, a shell of his current self, for Sonya. He had an obligation to keep her happy and safe in 2018, and anything less than that would result in a lifetime of regret for her.

I'm gonna marry that woman when we get to 2018. And we'll have the most luxurious honeymoon.

While wedding bells would have to wait, Martin at least had something positive to look forward to, should everything go horribly wrong tonight. He still couldn't rid his mind of Izzy telling him to go home, and deep down felt it was a sign that he'd be right back at square one after tonight: clueless as to what had happened and left with another two decades of heartache that would tear apart his soul like a vulture on a dead animal's carcass.

Snap out of it. You'll only fail tonight if you keep having these negative thoughts. Get your shit together and be confident.

"Easier said than done." He never had soaring confidence, even before his life had taken a turn for the worst. His only confidence in 2018 came in knowing that a hangover awaited him in the morning if he dared drink another bottle of whiskey.

The thought of pouring what remained in Sonya's alcohol stash had crossed his mind—the nerves had taken full control, after all—but he couldn't push himself to put his entire mission at risk. What if he passed out on the couch while Sonya went on her stakeout, and he missed the whole thing?

Go one more night without it, and you can drink all you want tomorrow. A new life begins soon. One with money, and no job to go to. Just a full bank account and a woman who loves you, and hopefully, a daughter who thinks the world of you.

Martin pushed the negativity aside and tried to imagine a universe where he, Sonya, and Izzy all lived in 2018. A world where they could laugh over dinner for having pulled off the impossible and reflect back to this specific day as the moment that shaped all of their good fortune.

These thoughts settled his nerves a bit, although not completely. He had passed a good amount of time and didn't realize the clock on the wall read 2:45. Sonya would be off work within the next hour to follow Izzy home for the final time.

The time was finally here, and he just needed to hang on to his last shred of sanity for a few more hours.

47

Chapter 47

Sonya wished her students a great rest of their evenings. The 3:15 bell had struck within the last minute, and Ms. Griffiths had her class ready to head out immediately.

"Bye, kids," she said while they herded out of the room and into the traffic jam in the hallway. She loved her eighth graders and felt a pull in her chest at the thought of never seeing them again with their big glasses, pimply faces, and squeaky voices.

Time for vacation? she thought. While the workday certainly had that final-day-before-vacation feel, she had to fight off the thought of what was actually happening within the next handful of hours. At home, Martin was probably a nervous wreck. She'd noticed how much more distant he seemed as this day had grown closer, and she was partially glad to be at work instead of home with him all day.

If he's this nervous, is it really best to be going with him?

Her mind had refused to fully accept that she was leaving her life in 1996 behind to run off with a man she had recently met, but wasn't taking a chance sometimes all you could do? She didn't have any serious intent on staying behind, but the thought wouldn't quite leave her alone.

She glanced at the clock with studious eyes. *3:20. It's time.*

Her classroom had actually emptied in five minutes, a new record. Normally a couple students would hang back to ask for help, or maybe a parent or two would drop in for a quick word. But today was her lucky day, despite a longing for something to stall her from leaving and officially starting the next chapter of life.

She had parked on the rear side of the school this morning so she could easily slip out of her classroom's back door and remain uninterrupted en route to her car. She grabbed her purse and paused, looking over her classroom that she had called home for the last twelve years. The vacant desks looked back at her sadly, begging her not to leave. The chalkboard had been freshly cleaned by her students and showed her the blank canvass that awaited on the other side of the door. Her students' artwork hung on the walls, giving the room a homey feel.

In two short weeks she had already formed a bond with her students that only a teacher would understand. Her students loved her, and she loved them.

Please don't be hurt when I'm gone.

Martin hadn't given her a clear answer on what would happen after she arrived in 2018. The thought of her students showing up tomorrow morning to an empty classroom with no word from their teacher tugged on every moral string in her body. Martin had promised she could get a teaching job in the future, but how similar would it be? Schools had already changed drastically since the time she was a student, and now with all the technology on the rise, would her job mainly consist of how to use computers?

She realized that she was getting ahead of herself, and blew a kiss to her abandoned classroom. "I promise it'll be okay," she said to the desks, and turned out the back door.

Some students ran around like uncaged animals on the open grass field between the school and the parking lot and she maneuvered her way through them like a native New Yorker pushing their way through Times Square.

She pulled her car around the building and found Izzy approaching the schoolyard's outer gate like clockwork. Izzy had apparently been a child of strict routine, going through the same exact motions every day in the way she packed her backpack and re-tied her shoes for her walk home.

Sonya crept down the road at a snail's pace as she waited for Izzy to cross the street. *Keep a safe distance.*

Martin had assured her that she had a much longer leash than he. Sonya actually existed in Izzy's current life, so if she accidentally drew attention to herself it wouldn't have a negative effect like it would if Izzy saw her father from the future.

Sonya kept close to the sidewalk and watched Izzy finally cross the street in her familiar pose with her hands crossed over her books and, this time, two pigtails bouncing behind her head with every step.

Sonya had gone through this same routine for the past week, but felt an extra flood of adrenaline today. What if something did happen right now? What if a creep in a van pulled in front of her and followed Izzy all the way home? It was only a two-block route and it would be impossible for an innocent child to be aware of a stalker. Sonya had done it every day, after all, with not so much as a glance over the shoulder from Izzy.

What exactly would you do if someone else got involved at this point?

Sonya had played out the scenario in her mind, and vowed to intervene should danger present itself. She kept a crow bar in her trunk and wouldn't hesitate to use it. Part of her hoped this would happen. If she could save Izzy before Martin had to get involved, they could return to a hopefully normal evening while they figured out their next steps.

Sonya turned onto Cherry Street and kept a distance of five car lengths behind Izzy as she trudged down the sidewalk. Her eyes bounced from the rear view to the left and right sides of the road in search of anything out of the ordinary. There was nothing but cars parked on the street and lawns covered with the first layer of browning leaves.

Izzy strolled along at the same pace as any other day, minding her business, oblivious to the teacher trailing behind. Sonya had never actually spoken to Izzy, but had seen her around the hallways in between classes. She kept to herself for the most part, occasionally giggling with two other girls during lunch and recess. Sonya had considered asking Izzy's teacher, Mrs. Weller, her opinion on Izzy, but decided it best to keep quiet should anything go awry.

By the time Izzy arrived home, Sonya's mind had drifted so far that she had to speed up to see the young girl step inside her house. She drove two houses down and waited for five minutes to see if anything would happen.

Sonya's heart raced at the thought that she might have just been the last person to see Izzy (aside from Martin's ex-wife) before she went missing. "Well, I guess that's that," she said into her empty car. So far, the day had gone according to plan. Izzy was home safe, undisturbed, and likely diving into her piles of homework. Sonya drove to the end of the block and took the long route home where she and Martin would sit down for a brief dinner before she'd return to watch the Briar house until nightfall.

Martin had insisted that she leave once he arrived—he'd be walking over—but she was starting to think she might want to stick around and see what happened. Besides, it would be beneficial for Martin to have a car handy in case he needed to chase someone down in another vehicle, or possibly flee the scene. This was one thing he had refused, claiming he would stop anything from even reaching that point. But she liked to prepare for any situation that might arise. If they didn't need the car, then no harm done. But if Martin found himself in a bind in the middle of the night while someone drove away with his daughter, what would he do? Chase them on foot?

She pulled into her driveway and took a deep breath, knowing a long night was ahead.

* * *

When Sonya entered the house, tension mixed in the air with deafening silence.

"Martin?" she called. The smells of baked bread rushed to her nose, sweet and tempting, despite her lack of appetite.

From the doorway she could see the kitchen, living room, and a glimpse into their bedroom. He wasn't in any of them.

He wouldn't have made me dinner and left. Dear Sonya, I changed my mind and am going back to 2018 without you, she thought, then giggled nervously. He hadn't been himself over the weekend, so she gave the thought heavy consideration.

"Martin, I'm home!" She shouted with more energy.

She dragged herself into the kitchen, where the bread scent was strongest, and felt an instant relief when she saw Martin's figure through the back window. He appeared to be rocking on one of the patio chairs, staring over the lawn that would be covered in blankets of snow in the coming months.

Sonya went outside and sat in the rocker next to Martin. He looked up to her and offered a warm smile.

"How was your day?" he asked, flat and distant.

"It was okay. Tough saying goodbye. How was yours?"

He rocked more before replying, and Sonya noticed how much of a shell he was of himself from just two weeks ago. He had lost a notable amount of weight, dark circles covered the spaces beneath his eyes, and thick streaks of gray had filled in across his scalp.

He traveled back 20 years only to age another 20 years.

She thought she wanted this all to be over, but Martin clearly *needed* it to be finished. Hopefully he'd have what he wanted in a few hours and could sleep easily.

"I've been losing my mind today," he said. "I've done so much thinking and I feel like I can't form another viable thought. I've never been so nervous for anything in my life."

She heard a tremble in his voice, but there was no visible sign of a pending cry, just the ragged expression of a man who has reached his breaking point.

"When I first got here I thought September 9th was so far away. It got here fast, and I know it'll pass just as quickly. Tomorrow will be here before I even realize it, and by then I'll know if my life stays the same or becomes what it was meant to be before all this shit happened."

Sonya wanted to suggest that maybe his life *had* become

327

how it was meant to be. Martin stared at the ground as he spoke and was clearly riding his final train of thought.

"It's so hard going into this and not knowing what to expect. I need to be ready to react to anything. I don't know how many times I've imagined my own death today. I know that shouldn't be at the front of my mind, but it is. I have to acknowledge it as a real possibility."

He stopped talking and stared to the ground where a roly-poly crawled slowly along the concrete. Sonya didn't know what to say to address his fears of death, but knew she needed to give him some comfort.

"I can't imagine what you've gone through today, but just know that I'll be here every step of the way. You're not alone."

She reached over and rubbed his arm, and felt a slight tremble coming from it.

"Thank you," he said. "You have no idea how incredible you are, and that makes you even more incredible."

"Izzy made it home okay," Sonya said, wanting to redirect the conversation. "No one followed her but me, and I saw her go inside and close the door."

Martin nodded as if he expected this information. "Perfect."

He stood from the rocker and put his hands on his hips as he stared into the distance.

"Let's go eat," he said. "I made your favorite meal."

By this he meant lasagna with baked bread, and she grinned at him.

"You know, you're pretty incredible yourself," she said.

Martin mustered a smile in return, through the thick layers of distraction that had taken control of his face.

"I sure hope I can be incredible tonight, for Isabel. I only get one chance to make this right."

"You'll be perfect, I have no doubt about it. Let's go eat so you can clear your mind. Maybe you can tell me more about the future?"

Martin nodded and followed her inside, where they would sit down for their final dinner of 1996.

48

Chapter 48

Martin changed his tune over dinner, and insisted that Sonya stay for an hour after he would arrive at his old house.

"I already know nothing significant happens until the middle of the night," he said. "The party doesn't start until after I show up, possibly well after I show up."

"What time do you think you'll get there?"

"The news said the sun will set at 7:18. I'll be there around 7:45, once it's officially dark." Martin spoke in between bites of lasagna. He ate like a starved stray dog hitting the jackpot with a tipped over dumpster full of food. After Sonya arrived home, his confidence skyrocketed. His senses were overloaded while he ate. He could hear every sound outside the house as if microphones were set up around the yard. Even the seasonings buried in the marinara sauce jumped onto his tongue.

I'm ready, he thought. *I'm not dying tonight, and Izzy will stay at that house if it's the last goddamned thing I do.*

After he did everything but lick the sauce remnants from his plate, Martin sat back in his chair, noting the clock that read 4:23, and grinned at Sonya.

"Are you ready?" he asked.

"I think so. I'm nervous, but kind of excited. I can't believe the time is finally here."

"I'm feeling good, too," Martin said. "I'm still incredibly nervous. Surprised I ate all of that, to tell you the truth, but I also feel focused."

"That's good," Sonya said as she finished her plate. She hadn't struggled with eating or sleeping as much as Martin had, having an ability to shove stressful thoughts aside and keep moving forward with her life. "I think I'm gonna head over there now. There's really no point in waiting around here. Even if nothing happens while I'm there, it'll still help pass the time. If I stay here I think I might go crazy."

If she wanted to go, Martin had no reason to stop her.

Sonya joined him at the head of the table and slung her arms around his waist. "I'll see you back here when it's all done."

Martin stood and nodded, pulling her into his embrace.

"Thank you for doing this. All of this. You could've said no. I can't wait to start our life together after tonight. It's going to be perfect."

Martin pulled her in tighter and inhaled the sweet scent of her shampoo.

"Don't do anything to put your life at risk," she said.

"Of course not. You either." Martin knew very well that if he saw an opportunity to save Izzy that would require his own life, he'd take it in a heartbeat. *Hopefully it doesn't come to that.*

"I love you," she said, planting a kiss on his lips. "I'll see you later."

Martin released Sonya from his arms and watched as she glided across the room, grabbed her keys and purse, and disappeared through the door with a quick glance over her shoulder.

Sonya was gone, leaving him three hours until he would start his walk through town. Even with a cloudy memory, he'd never forget the way "home" after all these years.

His past self would have just left for work a few minutes ago, giving Izzy a kiss on the head on his way out the door.

"I'll see you later," he had said, now wishing he could go back and never leave that night. *Why do bad things have to happen to good people?*

He could still taste the fruity smell from Izzy's hair on his lips after all these years, could see his final words to her hanging in the air, wishing he could grab them and have a second chance.

"Your second chance is tonight. Don't waste it," he said to the empty kitchen.

* * *

While Sonya watched the Briar residence from three houses down, Martin waited in their bedroom, dressed in black sweatpants and a black long-sleeve shirt, staring obsessively into the standing mirror that leaned against the wall. A black beanie and gloves rested on the bed to complete his stealthy attire. *I can't go out until it's dark; I look like a burglar.*

Martin studied the lines starting to fill his face and the streaks of silver in his hair.

When did I get so old? he wondered. *I've never felt better, and this is how my body thanks me?*

The damage was already done to his body, thanks to the

past decade of drinking anything he could get his hands on. However, the man he saw in the mirror was a different one than he had known. The man in the mirror had gained hope, wisdom, and a refined willpower that would help him achieve what he set out to do. It was a man in love, both with his child and the woman he had met on this journey. True love can carry a man through any situation in life.

Remember, no matter what happens tonight, you still have Sonya and a future.

He longed for a life in 2018 with Sonya by his side and Izzy alive and well, but knew dreams didn't always come true. Sometimes reality wins.

Through the windows, the sting of brightness softened to an orange glow as dusk approached. The digital clock on the nightstand read 6:08, giving him less than an hour before he'd leave the house. Somewhere in 2018 he was snoring in a back office and would soon wake up to realize this whole thing was a horrible hallucination, or a reality he still struggled to grasp.

"This is real," he said to himself. "Dreams don't carry on this long, and they certainly don't stay in chronological order."

No days had been skipped aside from the coma. He had to wake up every day like anyone else and drag himself through the summer weeks as September loomed.

Well it's here now, my friend.

Martin patted the pill in his pocket, knowing home was just a swallow away. He stuffed the beanie and gloves into his back pockets and moved to the living room for his final few minutes.

* * *

At 6:58, Martin Briar walked out of the house. The sun glowed above the mountains and would begin its quick descent within the next few minutes.

Martin had planned his route and calculated the walk to his old house would take around 30 minutes. As he strolled through the neighborhood, he saw families at the dinner table, others doing the dishes, and some huddled around the TV as Monday Night Football started.

He remembered occasional nights when Izzy would sit on his lap and watch the games with him, asking a laundry list of questions. She had always been curious, even with matters she didn't actually care about, like football.

I'm coming for you, Izzy. And you can ask me all the questions you want.

The first hint of darkness took control of the sky and would swallow up the city by the time he arrived to his destination.

Martin reached the end of his neighborhood within twelve minutes, right on schedule, and crossed 80th Avenue to his old neighborhood where the houses were newer, maintained with well-manicured lawns and modern designs that gave every home a view of the mountains.

He remembered when he and Lela had moved into the neighborhood. It was the peak of their relationship. Both had steadily paying jobs, and she was pregnant with the same child whose disappearance would destroy his life in the matter of one night.

The past could easily have placed Martin's mother on the front porch, smoking a cigarette and thereby throwing his entire night down the shitter, so he walked down the block one over from her house. He sensed the past wouldn't give him too much trouble and wasn't sure why – perhaps it was a hunch, or the eerie stillness in the air.

He passed Larkwood Middle School and found himself on the same route that Izzy took home every day, and imagined her walking by his side, head down, books in her embrace.

Dusk was officially upon Larkwood and the houses were no more than silhouettes against the sliver of orange that remained in the sky. Blackness filled in from the east, clawing its way to the Rocky Mountains on the west side of town. A few crickets chirped as Martin reached the corner of his old block.

He approached the stop sign where Cherry Street and 78th Avenue intersected and looked down the dark block. The night lacked moonlight as the street lights flickered on and wouldn't provide reliable light for the next half hour while they warmed up.

Martin kept to the west side of Cherry Street, where his house waited halfway down the block. He saw Sonya's car parked on the opposite side of the road, roughly three houses down from his, facing him.

Everything's in place and ready to go. Now, we wait.

Judging from the sky, total darkness was less than five minutes away. He'd wait until then before proceeding down the block, but prepared by slipping the black beanie over his head and making sure the gloves were snug over his hands.

He peered around to make sure no one was watching, and relaxed when realizing he was alone.

Down the block waited a new destiny and a second chance at life.

Who actually gets second chances in life? He trembled at the thought.

He started walking, taking the quietest steps he could manage, and headed toward whatever fate awaited him.

49

Chapter 49

Now that he stood in front of it, Martin remembered his house exactly as it was. It had an open front yard, half covered with leaves from the neighbor's massive oak tree that connected with a cement porch. Three windows spanned the front of the ranch-style home, with the front door centered between the first and second. Daylight would show the house's light green exterior, but the darkness made everything colorless.

Martin hid behind the scraggly bushes that separated his yard from the neighbor's driveway, peering around the lamp-post that splashed a soft, yellow glow in the middle of the street. From the sidewalk he waved his arms in Sonya's direction, the car lights remaining off.

He turned his attention back to the house. From his initial assessment, hiding on the side of the house provided the best view of the front yard and driveway, *and* the flexibility to run to the backyard should he need to. An intruder would have a hard time sneaking in through the back where chain link fences would create noise and attention.

Martin cut across the front yard to the side of the house,

scattered leaves crunching beneath his feet. The window above him belonged to Izzy's bedroom, allowing him to hear any encounter inside should it be loud enough. He crouched and felt devoured by the darkness.

I need to get comfortable; it's gonna be a few hours.

He wished he had his cell phone, but the battery had finally run out, even after remaining off for so long. The watch on his wrist had no glow; those were still a couple years away. If he really needed to know the time, he'd have to run into the middle of the street and check below the lamppost.

Rely on your instincts.

By his calculation it should only be 7:40, leaving him over an hour until Izzy would actually go to sleep. A thick curtain covered her window, blocking any potential for him to know if her light was turned on.

Martin peered back toward the street to see the car still parked. A car would drive by every few minutes, headlights filling Cherry Street, but not revealing the crouched man on the side of the Briar house. Each time one passed, Martin's heart raced with an extra boost of adrenaline.

It's not even eight yet, relax. Nothing happens until at least nine. Sit back, grab your popcorn, and wait for the show to start.

Martin did exactly this and sat on the ground, legs pulled to his chest as he curled into a ball like a roly-poly. And he waited.

* * *

Sonya watched from her car as the darkness fell over the city.

The sense that he would need an escape car swelled, and her instincts told her she needed to stay. What would she do at home, anyway? Sit on the couch and watch TV while Martin engaged in the fight of his life?

Absolutely not.

She watched him reach the lamppost, study the exterior, and disappear into the shadows along the side. He had waved at her, and she waved back, but the darkness concealed her gesture.

Don't worry about me – I'll be right here when you need me.

The neighborhood felt still after the kids had returned inside from playing at sunset. She tuned out the deafening silence in the car by whistling softly, knowing she also had a long, challenging night ahead before her new life could begin.

* * *

Sitting outside his old house had opened a floodgate of memories that Martin had to keep pushing aside to remain focused. He reminisced about the times he played with Izzy in the front yard, chasing her and pretending to be a dinosaur. Or other times they had played hide-and-seek on warm summer nights, and he had hidden in this same exact spot, watching his only child look around for him until she spotted him and called out, "I got you, Daddy!"

Life couldn't have been any more perfect.

Not knowing for sure how much time had passed, Martin figured it was at least close to 9 P.M. His ass felt like 1,000 ants were nibbling on it, so he stood up and stretched to get the blood flowing again. Any minute something could happen. He checked the backyard, found nothing out of the ordinary, and returned to his post when a car turned onto Cherry Street and crept at a snail's pace toward the house.

The headlights blinded Martin, leaving him no way to make out the car until it turned into the driveway. His heart tried to leap out of his throat, stomach churning, arms trembling as he realized this must be the person who ruined his life forever.

The car looked familiar, and it didn't register with Martin until the man parked and stepped out. He wore athletic pants and a zip-up windbreaker—another familiar look Martin recognized. A gold chain swung from his neck and illuminated the slightest gleam in the darkness.

Daniel?

His younger brother.

A world of confusion rained on Martin as he peeked around the corner.

What the hell is he doing here?

Daniel loved Izzy, and she reciprocated his adoration. He was the fun uncle, taking her to amusement parks, museums, and random stops for ice cream during summer break.

How is Daniel involved in this night?

Martin couldn't recall a single police statement that mentioned his brother. Daniel walked up the front steps and rapped lightly on the door. It only took seconds for the screen door to fly open from Lela's skinny arm, and Daniel disappeared into the house.

Dear God, please don't tell me this is what I think it is.

Martin kept his neck craned to look around the corner.

Any minute Daniel is going to walk back out and drive home. He just stopped by for something, right?

After five minutes passed with no sign of the door opening, Martin leaned back against the house, panting like a thirsty dog in the middle of summer. Tension had built up that he hadn't realized until he released his clenched fist and his tight jaw. *Think, Martin. There could be one hundred other reasons that he's here.*

He thought back and tried to remember what was going on in Daniel's life. Was there something troubling him where he felt he could confide in Lela?

As best he could remember, life was pretty simple for Daniel in 1996. He would've been recently graduated from college, and had jumped right into a job. He had no romantic relationship from what Martin could recall.

He didn't need a relationship because he was fucking your wife.

Martin couldn't bring himself to accept the possibility of what might be going on inside the house while Izzy slept in her bedroom.

He had no choice but to confront it. His and Lela's bedroom was on the same side of the house he currently stood, only closer to the backyard. He dragged his feet to the spot below their bedroom window, his gut feeling like a wrung out rag. The nerves fled as his mind focused on the new task ahead.

Did this even really happen the first time around, or is the past just fucking with me to throw me off right now?

He gave the thought a whole second of consideration before dismissing it. The past had never done anything to psychologically mess with his plans, but rather did things like run him over with a semi-truck, or set liquor stores and high schools on fire. Whatever was going on between his brother and ex-wife inside the house was all part of the original story.

Martin looked up to the bedroom window. Lela hadn't put

up a thick curtain as Izzy had, leaving flimsy blinds to fill the space. The room was black, not even the glow of a TV, but he could hear the faintest sound of a woman giggling. They were in the bedroom, not in the kitchen or living room having a discussion. In the fucking *bedroom.*

The soft laughter fell silent for a couple minutes before the sounds of moaning and groaning replaced it, followed by a pleasurable scream.

Jesus Christ, they didn't even try being quiet!

Martin felt his face flushing bright red, his temples pulsing with rage. His hands returned to white knuckled fists, shaking at his sides, as he fought off every urge to barge into the house and beat the living hell out of his brother.

How could they?

Martin stepped away, returning to his post below Izzy's window, thoughts from his past flooding his now distracted mind.

How long were they doing this? When did this start? Why did this start?

His and Lela's sex life was by no means lackluster. They had enjoyed each other at least three times a week, even when he started working the inconsistent hours. So why the hell did this come about?

Martin knew he should push these thoughts out of his mind—he tried, but failed—remembering he had come here to save his daughter, not learn about a lifetime of secrets that had remained buried underneath her disappearance.

Is this why Daniel moved away after the funeral? Did his guilt get the best of him and he couldn't bear to see us anymore?

Daniel had moved across the country to Delaware, citing a new job opportunity. At the time, it was positive news for a devastated family, but his phone calls became rare, and after two years, he simply stopped reaching out to the family. Their mother said Daniel would call her on occasion, but it was always out of the blue. Martin wondered if this was the real reason he left and broke off all communication. Even in 2018, with social media, Daniel Briar was nowhere to be found.

Just worry about Izzy.

The thought was easier said than done. He couldn't help but imagine the 1996 version of himself on his way home in a few hours, oblivious that his daughter was missing and his wife and brother had a quickie in his own bed.

He wanted to cry and scream at the same time.

Just worry about Izzy.

Martin peered back around the corner of the house, saw Sonya parked in her same spot, and wished he could go tell her the new developments.

Over the next twenty minutes Martin struggled to control his breathing and clear his mind. The night no longer felt still, but rather chaotic on Cherry Street. The crickets had silenced, leaving the only audible sounds to be his breathing and pounding heart. The temperature remained cool.

When the front door swung open, Martin almost missed it, too busy staring into the night sky, trying to piece his life together. Daniel stepped onto the porch, Lela joining him in her robe and slippers. She giggled as she ran a hand down his chest and stomach. Martin could hear their voices whispering to each other, but couldn't make out the actual words.

Lela planted a kiss on Daniel's lips before he hurried down the steps, jumped into his car, and left as abruptly as he had arrived. Still no sign of Izzy.

Lela returned inside as Martin watched the screen door glide shut.

He slid back to ground, relieved the adultery had passed, and allowed his mind to refocus on the task at hand. Just as his thoughts started to settle, Martin heard muffled shouting coming from inside the house—from Izzy's room specifically. He pressed his ear against the house, knowing he'd never be able to make out the words clearly, wishing more than ever to be a fly on the wall.

What he could hear was a back and forth between Lela and Izzy. Izzy's voice, though young and not fully developed, still projected. Lela responded with the same tone, only louder and approaching the level of a scream.

Is this what prompts this? Does Izzy run away after catching her mom in the act with her uncle? Why wouldn't she have just come to me and told me? Why run away from it all?

It pained Martin to think that his daughter might have carried this burden with her all of these years, feeling as if she had to leave her life behind because of the mistakes her mother made. *Why would she leave without saying goodbye? Was I that unavailable that she couldn't confide in me?*

Martin kept his ear pressed against the house like a burglar listening to a safe, patiently waiting for the click of the lock. As the doubts of his effectiveness as a parent continued to pour into his mind, he knew the next few minutes were the key to everything. The voices continued to rise but seemed more distant, likely having gone from Izzy's bedroom to the living room further down the hallway. He debated moving to the other side of the house, but decided to wait. He couldn't risk being caught in his own front yard at such a crucial time.

The sounds from Izzy's room had completely stopped, so he ran to the backside of the house and crept along the edge to see if the drama inside was continuing in a different part of the house.

For a moment he thought the shouting had ceased, but it picked up again, this time from the kitchen. The kitchen window overlooked the backyard, so Martin would need to stay put on the side of the house, especially with the backyard porch light turned on for when he would be arriving home later that morning.

Martin craned his neck and saw the kitchen light splashing across the backyard's grass. The voices remained muffled, covered further by a clatter of pots and pans.

Is Lela putting away the dishes while having this conversation with Izzy?

It wouldn't be the first time his ex-wife resorted to cleaning while in a rage. She used to claim that it helped clear her head.

The shouting reached another peak before abruptly stopping. It sounded as if Lela were screaming and was cut off mid-sentence.

Martin studied the window for any movement of shadows that would suggest the activity inside. There were none, and he pressed his head against the house to catch any sounds.

The bedrooms and kitchen had fallen into complete silence, as if no one were home, and Martin could only hear the sound of his own heart, pounding in his head like a distant drum.

This is it. The fight is over. Izzy must be in her bedroom packing up her things and getting ready to storm out of the house.

He knew it could take another hour or two before anything happened. Lela would need to go to sleep before Izzy made a run for it. She must have let herself out well after Lela fell asleep, but before Martin arrived home from work.

Martin squinted at his watch, but had no chance at reading

the time as it remained consumed in the darkness. He calculated it to be around ten o'clock, but couldn't pin down a precise time. Daniel had come over just after nine, had his romp in the sheets with Lela, and was out before she could even brew the coffee. Then the shouting had started and lasted between ten to fifteen minutes.

If the timeline held true, it was certainly no earlier than ten, leaving him a four-hour window until his past self arrived home for the night.

Martin returned to the backyard and found the kitchen light turned off.

Strange, he thought, remembering Lela had always left an inside light on for Martin on the nights he worked late, but pitch-blackness came from the back of the house. Away from the street light, Martin could barely see his own hand in front of his face.

She wouldn't have gone to bed already, would she?

Lela had always needed time to cool off after an argument.

It doesn't matter. This speeds up the timeline, if anything. Stay here and wait for her to come out.

Martin knew Izzy would come out of the back door. They rarely used the front door since the driveway stretched to the backyard where Lela's car currently sat in the darkness. Besides, the front door creaked and groaned when opened, making a silent escape impossible.

He crouched, ready to pounce on Izzy the second she stepped outside, waiting like a vulture circling its prey, anticipating the perfect moment to swoop in and change destiny.

When five minutes passed, Martin remained frozen, both from shock and disbelief at what his eyes witnessed.

Lela swung open the screen door and ran down the porch

steps to her car, unlocking the trunk, and flinging the door open.

With the house door and trunk wide open, Martin tried to piece it all together in a frantic attempt to make sense of what he didn't want to believe.

Don't you fucking do it, he thought as Lela returned into the dark pit of the house. *Please, God, don't let her fucking do this.*

He braced himself for what would come out of the door next, and when he saw it, his body fell into an instant state of numbness.

Lela appeared in the doorway, arms in front of her body as they held a white cloth draped over a limp body. Martin heard the faintest sob from his ex-wife as she dumped the body into the trunk and slammed the door shut. Lela returned to close the house door before dashing to the equipment shed in the back corner of the yard. She grabbed a shovel and sprinted back to the car.

She tossed the shovel into the backseat and fired up the engine and headlights, backing out of the driveway and leaving Martin alone in the darkness, still unable to process the horror of what he had just witnessed.

Lela killed her, he thought, lips quivering in unison with his now shaking body. *Two decades of wondering. And she fucking killed her.*

Martin turned back to the side of the house and vomited before making a run for Sonya, who was hopefully still waiting close by.

50

Chapter 50

Sonya already had the car running when Martin reached it. The adrenaline provided him a boost in speed he hadn't experienced since his high school days. He dove into the car just as Lela reached the end of the street, and turned right at the stop sign.

"Go!" he barked. "Follow her, and keep your lights off!"

Sonya obliged and swung the car around in a U-turn, tires screeching in the quiet night. Martin knew she had seen everything by the obvious shock in her bulging eyes and hanging jaw.

"Don't lose her!" he shouted as they reached the stop sign. Lela drove at a surprisingly normal pace as she crept away from the neighborhood, giving Sonya the perfect window of opportunity to catch up as a red light stopped her three blocks ahead.

"Stay 200 feet back, keep the lights off, and match her every move and pace from here on out." Martin felt like a movie director barking out his orders, knowing he had this one chance to follow Lela and see where she hid their daughter's body that would never be found.

Where would she go? he wondered as Sonya steadied the car two hundred feet behind Lela. They were the only two cars on the road, and it would likely stay that way for a while. Martin saw the clock on the dashboard reading 11:02, much later than he had mentally calculated.

I guess time flies when you're watching yourself get cheated on before your ex-wife kills your only kid.

The light turned green and Lela wasted no time crossing the intersection of Highway 85. Sonya kept her distance and followed as they drove through a dark service road with no street lights.

She only has four hours until I get home. She can't go too far. And if she's digging a hole, she needs to start right now.

The thought of the shovel sent a spark of rage through Martin. This meant Lela never thought twice about owning up to her crime, and had her mind set on taking care of the matter herself.

Sonya remained silent beside Martin, her eyes focused on the car ahead and waiting for Martin's next instruction.

Lela's brake lights filled the darkness, and they reminded Martin again of peering red eyes, much like the circle on the calendar in Sonya's kitchen.

Is that you, Chris? he thought, questioning his own sanity for a brief moment.

Lela turned right onto Dahlia Street, a quiet and scenic road that separated two lakes, but also connected Larkwood to the neighboring town of Grant. A thick fog blanketed the road and killed all visibility as Lela disappeared into the clouds. *The past can kiss my ass and take a seat in the back if it wants to try anything right now.*

349

Lela slowed down and flicked on her high beams, which actually made it harder to see as the light reflected off the fog, creating a virtual gray sheet of obstruction.

"Keep your lights off," Martin said calmly. "We can see her and that's all that matters. Get closer so we can follow her every move. This road is narrow and we could drive into a ditch."

Sonya nodded and closed the gap between her car and Lela. The fog provided them with coverage as they drove deeper in toward the lakes. She could pull up right behind the old Chevrolet and Lela would never know it.

Lela suddenly swerved to the right and slammed on her brakes. Sonya pulled up cautiously, stopping 100 feet behind as the fog lightened up just enough to see that distance.

"No, not here, Lela," Martin said absent-mindedly. "Not here dammit!"

"What is this place?" Sonya asked, speaking for the first time since they left the house.

"It's a lake we used to come to in the summers as a family," Martin said in a distant voice. "We'd have picnics and splash around in the water with Izzy. She always looked forward to it."

He fell into a deadly silence; Sonya nudged him to make sure he was okay.

"Now she's being buried here by her own mother."

Martin's bottom lip trembled as he spoke, and he sniffled to keep the tears and emotions inside.

"There's not even anything I can do to stop this," Martin said, slouching into the passenger seat as if it were swallowing him piece by piece. "She's already dead." The words came off his lips cold and surreal.

The amount of reality that had been dumped on Martin in the last two hours was the emotional equivalent of being buried alive, and he felt the suffocation of it just the same.

They watched as Lela jumped out of the car and popped the trunk open. Martin sat still, staring as if it weren't really happening. He shook his head as Lela struggled to lift Izzy's body out of the vehicle, a limp white arm falling below the sheet's coverage.

"Aren't you going to do something?" Sonya demanded, a stream of tears running down her face.

"There's nothing I can do," he said in a depressed voice. "Nothing at all. I just wasted the last six months thinking I had a chance at saving her. And she was going to end up dead before I even got the chance." He paused and looked down to his shaking hands. "I should've knocked on the door when I saw Daniel go inside. I should've done something then. This wouldn't have happened."

Sonya sat up stiffly in her seat and tossed her arms in the air. "You're telling me you're going to sit here and watch her throw your daughter in the lake? Are you fucking crazy? After all this, it ends with you sitting here in defeat?"

"What can I do?" he responded calmly. "I played out this scenario already. What do you think I've been doing for six months? I've thought every possibility all the way through to the end. I never gave this scenario much thought, but I did consider it."

Sonya stared at him with her mouth agape. Lela had carried the body and disappeared into the thick fog where the lake waited.

"What happens next is we go back to 2018, I tell the police that Izzy's body is in this lake, and then I confront Lela about it."

"Why? We could go find a payphone real quick and call the police. She can go to jail tonight. Why give her the chance to walk free like this?"

"Why wouldn't I give her two decades to sulk in her guilt? I'm sure she even reached a point where she thought she actually got away with it, that she would make it to her grave without having to confront anyone about it. I'm fine letting her live the next 22 years with that hope. I'll be there when it all comes crashing down, too. That's what I really want to see."

Martin spoke like a man possessed, keeping all emotion out of his voice, and even showed a hint of lunacy in his planning. He knew exactly how he wanted it to all play out when he returned to 2018, and he'd waste no time. It would be the early morning still, and he'd call in to work, letting them know he'd never come back, and then off to Lela's house where he would confront her and make her wish she had never tried to cover up her dirty actions.

For now, Martin only wanted to cry. And that's exactly what he did while Sonya begrudgingly turned the car around and drove back to her house. She didn't speak to him, and he didn't care why. He had an invisible dagger digging deep into his heart, twisting forcefully every time he closed his eyes and imagined Lela carrying their dead daughter through the house and dropping her in the trunk like groceries.

"Don't kill her, it's not worth it." Martin thought he had kept this in his mind, but had spoken it. Sonya looked at him, lips pursed while she drove.

Martin slouched further down in his chair, wanting to melt into a puddle of depression, and thought over the last six months.

I could've stopped this at any time. I could've picked her up after school today and told her I took the night off work to hang out with her. We could've gone to dinner and a movie, or fed the ducks at the park. I never imagined Lela doing this; she never acted guilty. Maybe all of the tears were the guilt. The guilt of knowing I would suffer forever because of what she did. The guilt of knowing I'd go my entire life without knowing the truth while she had to carry the burden.

Sonya pulled into her driveway five minutes later. "So what now?" she asked.

"Now we go to 2018."

51

Chapter 51

"I can't believe this is what happened," Martin said after they parked. "This wasn't supposed to happen. Izzy should be alive right now, sitting in the backseat."

Sonya pushed open her door with her shoulder and jumped out of the car. "Let's go," she demanded. "I know this is hard, but you're not done. I'm not letting you come all this way to stop here."

Martin watched her with puzzlement before following her into the house.

"I know this is fucked up," she continued, throwing her keys on the kitchen table and pacing around the living room. "I just watched it all happen, too. Let's get back to your time and make this right. Your ex-wife deserves to be locked in prison for the rest of her life, and you deserve closure."

Her determination radiated, providing Martin a temporary boost in confidence. "Are you sure you want to come with me? There's no ticket back."

"Martin Briar, for the hundredth time, I've made up my mind and I'm going. Please stop asking."

Martin nodded, and reached into his pockets to retrieve the small pill buried at the bottom. He held it an open palm like a wizard showing off an orb.

"Ten minutes and we'll go," Martin said. "I want you to make sure you have everything you want to take."

"Martin, my bag has been ready for the past week," she said, gesturing to the duffel bag that waited beside the living room couch. "I'm ready. Quit stalling and let's go."

There was no hesitation in her voice, no doubts or reservations. Just the sound of a woman ready to take the next adventure in life.

"Alright, let's go lay down in bed. Bring your bag." Martin found himself with an outbreak of nerves. He had his own reservations about going back to 2018. The world would be the same as he knew it, but how was he supposed to carry on after turning in Lela to the police. There would be news coverage of the cracked case after so many years. They would retrieve the body from the lake, and Martin would have to see the footage of it on a constant loop for weeks.

Reporters would hound him and throw him into the spotlight as the ex-husband of a monster. Sonya would need to remain under the radar for the beginning of the media circus. She didn't deserve such a chaotic welcoming to her new life.

These uncertainties came and went like a brief rainstorm when Sonya called out for him. "Martin, I'm ready." Her voice carried from the bedroom, and he realized he hadn't moved one step since they entered the house.

The pill rested in his sweaty palm, so Martin switched it to his other hand, worried it would disintegrate into its original powder form.

He shuffled into the bedroom to find Sonya lying down, her

hands crossed above her belly, and her bag strap wrapped around her arm while the bag rested on the floor below. She looked as beautiful as ever, even through all the drama of the past few hours.

I wish we met when we were both younger, he thought. *Our life together would have been so perfect.*

"Are you ready?" Martin asked.

Sonya nodded, keeping her gaze to the ceiling fan that spun in silent rotations.

He lay down next to her as he had every night for the past few months. He rolled to his side to face her and held her hands in his. "I love you," he said. "Remember, we're going to wake up in a dark room, but I'll be there. Don't be afraid."

A tear trickled down her cheek and Martin brushed it away with a quick swipe.

He rolled to his back, keeping her hand in his, closed his eyes, and popped the pill into his mouth.

As he fell into a daze, he imagined Izzy, beautiful and young, running through the park with the serene laughter only a little girl could make.

It'll all be okay.

* * *

The trip back to 2018 lacked the falling sensation, and even though he had Sonya's hand squeezed in a death grip, it disappeared as soon at the darkness took over. He heard voices blurring by in a rush. *Is this the next 22 years of my life being fast-forwarded back to present time?* he wondered.

Instead of waking up in a deserted lot, Martin jolted awake in a chair, eyes shooting open to the familiar sight of Chris's back office. He panted for breath, a drizzle of sweat dripping down his back.

Where's Sonya?

He peered around the room, heart thudding against his ribs as he jumped from the chair on to wobbly legs.

"Sonya!" he shouted. "Sonya!"

"Relax, old friend," Chris said from the darkness before flicking on a light. "She's here, just in a bit of a daze from the trip. Give her a minute to wake up."

Chris stood in the laboratory section of his office and smirked while he spoke, crossing the room to meet Martin.

"How was your trip?" Chris asked how a casual friend might.

"Where's Sonya?" Martin demanded.

"She's asleep on the ground behind my lab. I took her over to make sure she was okay."

Martin thought he was dreaming. He could see Chris in front of him, grinning and talking, but had the hazy effect that often accompanied a deep sleep. He tried to move his legs forward but they remained frozen in place.

"Easy, my friend," Chris said. "I know you're excited, but we have a debt to settle, remember?"

"Bullshit!" Martin barked. "You set me up knowing what would happen. I never had a chance at saving Izzy."

"I never said you would," Chris said, getting right in front of Martin's face.

Martin observed the evil lurking behind the old man's eyes, and desired nothing more than to leave. "All I ever offered was the opportunity to go back in time. You picked the time and location. I made it happen. We had an agreement."

"You played me," Martin said, shaking his head as he sat back down. He had caught a glimpse of Sonya's legs splayed out on the ground behind the laboratory counter and had no choice but to accept that as satisfactory.

Chris cracked an evil smile and put an open hand to his chest. "I would never."

"So what now?" Martin asked. "You suck the soul out of me and I go around the rest of my life unable to feel anything?"

"That's an option yes. But I always like to make a counteroffer."

Chris sat down in the chair across the table, his joints cracking in symphony.

"The reason I tell you the parameters of our arrangement is because that is the minimum I will take in exchange for your trip through time. You see, I'm not quite human, as you've probably figured out."

"What are you?" Martin demanded.

Chris raised his finger. "Don't interrupt me. I ask the questions around here. What I am is irrelevant. What feeds me—what feeds my soul, rather—are human souls. Sometimes all of the soul, sometimes just a small piece. I'm no glutton."

"So taking emotions is some sick way you feed off people?"

"Perhaps *feed* was the wrong word. It's more like *fuel.*"

Martin shook his head in disgust. *Same difference, asshole.*

"That's not very nice, Marty, and I'm not an asshole. You see, I help people. I send people to times they never thought possible. I've sent people to the future and the past, all of them with good intent. All of them with plans on making their lives better. You met Calvin, right?"

Martin nodded slowly, remembering his tortured friend

from the liquor store.

"I don't know how much he told you, but he was in 1996 from the future. He was researching how an impeachment process was carried out. Because where he's from, the history books have been erased and the good old United States is on the verge of a collapse from an authoritarian leader. Calvin worked for this future president undercover, and had high hopes in bringing him down."

"What happened to his body when he died? The one that was in his present time?"

"He died. What happened is what always happens when you die. You stop existing. I'm sure you've heard of people who go randomly missing. This is what happens."

"What does this have to do with *fueling* you?"

"It doesn't. You call me an asshole. I just want you to know whose side I'm on, and also understand that there's a price to pay for the gift I offer. Are you done with your questions, or can I proceed?"

Martin leaned back and crossed his arms, feeling more like himself, the jet-lagged sensation of traveling through two decades finally wearing off. "Go ahead," he said.

"You showed me something, Marty," Chris said, the smirk falling from his face. "You stretched your limits to try and stop Columbine. You showed a tremendous amount of courage. I don't know how you felt about it, but I believe there's a lot you can get accomplished if you had the opportunity to go wherever you wanted as you pleased."

The hairs stood at attention on Martin's arms.

"I can offer you that chance," Chris continued. "The chance to come and go as you please to different periods in time. You can use this for pleasure, research, or to make the world a better place. It doesn't matter to me."

Chris paused and Martin remained with his arms crossed over his chest.

"And what's in it for you?" Martin asked, skepticism nearly through the roof.

Chris smiled. "That, my friend, is the hard part for you. You'll get to keep your emotions, but I'll still need a payment in return, and it'll be something that keeps you up at night, wondering if you made the right choice."

Chris paused again, and Martin didn't sense that his old friend would elaborate.

"What the hell does that mean exactly?"

"I can't tell you. Think of it as a mystery box, a surprise."

"This doesn't sound like a fair trade."

"A fair trade? Marty, think of how long you can extend your life. You can go to any era in time and live there as long as you want, and it will still only be a whole ten minutes that passes here in your current life. You can virtually live forever."

Martin stared at the ground in deep thought.

Live forever? Just last week—in 2018—he would have laughed at the thought of living another day. But now with a fresh perspective and renewed energy, it seemed more like a second chance at life. The last 22 years had been a wash and passed by in one long, drunken blur. He thought back to 1996, watching Lela carry their dead daughter out of the house, and felt no urge to go through a similar disappointment again.

Martin shook his head, tears rolling down his face.

"You set me up. You made this bullshit offer to use it as leverage for a worse offer?"

"Not at all. Your original offer is still on the table. Why don't you take the rest of the day to think it over and let me know?

I know you want to get out there and confront your ex-wife. Maybe that will give you some clarity. You know where to find me."

Chris appeared calm as always, despite having a snarling Martin in his face, and stuck out a hand to shake.

"Fuck you," Martin said and turned for the back of the room where Sonya was finally stirring.

"Make sure you come back tonight. You'd hate to see what happens if you ignore me. I'll be here all night."

Martin looked over his shoulder as he walked away and caught the devilish wink Chris shot his way.

"Sonya!" he shouted. "We need to go!" Martin knelt beside her and brushed a hand down her arm. She slow blinked as her eyes fought to stay closed, clearly enjoying the sleep.

"What happened?" she murmured. "Are we here?"

"Yes, we're both here and we're okay. But we need to go. I can explain." Martin pulled her arms and propped her up from the ground. She looked around the dim room and studied the counter where piles of different colored powders formed small mounds.

"What is this place?" she asked.

"I'll explain, but we need to go. We have a lot to get done."

He led her by the arm and toward the door that led out of the office and into the store where they found Chris sitting behind the checkout counter.

"Sonya, meet Chris. I'm sure you'll have a chance to catch up later." Martin spoke as they sped by Chris, who kept his smirk focused on them.

"Pleasure meeting you, Sonya," he called out before they reached the exit.

Martin expected the world to be completely different when

they stepped outside the store, but felt an instant relief when he saw his car parked where he had left it.

"So this is 2018?" Sonya asked. "It doesn't look too different."

"You have no idea," Martin said, desperate to get off the property. "Let me charge my phone and I'll show you what the world is like. But first, I gotta pay a visit to Lela."

52

Chapter 52

Martin tried to organize his thoughts as he drove wildly through Larkwood, remaining silent as Sonya gawked out the window to the same city she had just left 22 years in the past.

"We have so much to do," Martin said, speaking more to himself. "*I* have so much to do. We have to go to Lela's, pick up the money I invested, and get you settled."

Don't forget your date with Chris so he can kill you from the inside.

Martin decided to not tell Sonya about the ultimatum Chris had given him. She needed to settle in before having such a bomb dropped on her.

What am I going to say to Lela? Do I just barge in and tell her I know she did it, and she better tell me everything? I could record our conversation if my phone's battery will hold up, and take it to the police.

He never thought he'd play a mental game of chess on how to get Lela to jail. They had remained cordial after the divorce. The divorce occurred more out of necessity than a desire. The pain cut too deep and neither of them had the energy to uplift each other, eventually fading away by seeking comfort through other means: Martin with alcohol, and Lela with food.

Their physical attraction had vanished. Martin supposed they both saw a piece of Izzy in each other, whether it was her eyes and smile from Lela, or her round nose and flat laugh from Martin. But now Martin knew the truth, maybe the attraction was gone because Lela had found it from someone else in his family.

Fucking bitch, he thought, and decided to lead in with that topic.

Martin turned on to Cherry Street and chills sprung up his back. He looked to Sonya who stiffened up once she realized where they were.

"Lela never moved out of the house?" she asked.

Martin shook his head.

"That's disgusting."

Martin snickered. "I never thought anything of it. But now, yes, it's very disgusting."

He pulled into the driveway, parking where his kid brother had all those years ago when he came over for a night cap.

"What do you want me to do? I'm not going in there with you," Sonya said, fidgeting in her seat in clear discomfort.

"Of course not. I want you to wait ten minutes and then call the cops. Tell them the address of this house, and that Lela Briar murdered Isabel Briar in 1996. Tell them to not cause a disturbance, that everything is under control inside the house. There's no need to barge in, Lela will hand herself over."

"How can you be so sure?"

"We were married for fifteen years; I know her."

Martin powered on his cell phone that had been plugged in to the center console. It had only reached a five percent charge, but would suffice for what he needed. He held it up for Sonya to see, and she studied it like a curious scientist.

"All you do is swipe your thumb across the screen like this to unlock it," he explained, brushing a quick stroke across the lock screen that showed a picture of a smiling Izzy. "Then just tap the green icon on the bottom left to open the dialer. The number is still 911—that much hasn't changed. Don't touch anything else for now. I'll show you what these things can do once this is all done."

He handed the phone over, and Sonya accepted it in two hands like it was the key to the city.

"Okay, I think I can do that," she said giddily.

"Perfect. Ten minutes. Don't worry if I come back out here or not before then, just make the call. There's a clock on the top right corner of the phone, go off that."

Sonya nodded before Martin leaned and kissed her cheek, causing a momentary blush.

"I'll see you in a bit."

Martin stepped out of his car and took a moment to stare at his old house, replaying that fateful night he had just witnessed a "few hours" ago.

He climbed up the steps and knocked on the door, expecting Lela to be awake by now. She didn't have to be at work until nine, and it wasn't quite eight o'clock yet.

The front door creaked open and Lela's face appeared, scrunched into a look of confusion. Her brown hair hung to her shoulders, and makeup attempted to cover the wrinkles starting to form on her forehead and chin. Familiar blue eyes bulged at the sight of her slim ex-husband. "Marty? What are you doing here?"

"Good morning, Lela, I hope I'm not catching you at a bad

time," he said as she unlocked and pushed open the screen door for him.

"Not at all, come in."

Lela glanced at his car and saw Sonya, looking away quickly as if she wasn't supposed to have looked. "Is everything okay?"

Martin stepped inside the house for the first time in at least ten years. Everything was rearranged. The furniture had been updated with an L-shaped couch that spanned the entire wall, facing a massive flat screen TV mounted to the wall. *It's good to see these TVs again,* Martin noted.

"Actually, no, everything is not okay. I received a phone call from Daniel last night."

Martin paused to let the words sink into Lela's receptors, and he watched as her mind searched for the light switch. Lela was dressed for work in a matching purple blouse and dress slacks wrapped snugly around what was once a tight body that had filled in with rolls in recent years.

"Daniel," she said in amazement. "How long has it been? I didn't think any of us would hear from him ever again."

"That's what I thought. He's doing well, apparently still on the east coast and loving life."

"Well that's great to hear. Is everything okay, though? Why did you come here to tell me that?"

"I think we should sit down."

"Okay?" Lela said hesitantly, and crossed the room into the kitchen that had also been updated with stainless steel appliances and granite counter tops. A square dinner table stood in the center of the room and Lela pulled out a seat as Martin followed, taking the seat across from her. The morning light struggled to claw its way into the west facing kitchen, leaving them in a dim setting. "What's going on?" she asked, a slight trace of fear in her voice.

Does a guilty conscience last all these years? Probably never thought you'd hear Daniel's name again, did you?

"Lela, we have a major problem. Daniel told me everything."

She stared at him, eyebrows scrunched, and he wasn't sure if she was playing dumb or truly confused.

"Told you everything about what?"

Her voice cracked on the word *what,* and he knew she was playing dumb.

"He told me about the night of September 9th, 1996. He told me about him coming over here. Fucking you and leaving. All before Izzy went missing."

Lela's face turned ghastly pale as she wiggled in her seat. She remained silent and looked down to the table.

"There's no point in denying it. I should congratulate you. I never knew. You would have gotten away with it, had he never told me. Do you have anything to say?"

Lela looked up to him with tear-filled eyes. Hearing the date of September 9th, 1996 spoken out loud always made Martin cry as well, regardless of the situation. Lela was no different.

"I'm sorry," she mustered through a clenched throat. "I'm sorry I did it, and that you had to find out this way."

"Did you know that's why he moved away? He felt so much guilt once Izzy went missing, that he felt partially responsible. Can you believe that? He didn't even do anything but slide in between your slutty legs."

"Martin, please," Lela said, now sobbing. "I didn't want to hurt you. I was just home alone every night. I couldn't take the loneliness any more. Daniel was in the same boat. We never planned on this happening. He came over one night to see Izzy, and after she went to bed things escalated."

She looked down to the table, shame taking hold of her face as tears and mucus dripped from her nose.

Let's go get her, Martin thought, and placed his hand on top of hers.

"Lela, I can forgive you. This was so far in the past. I'll admit when I first found out I was ready to kill both of you. But so much has happened since then, there's no point. You haven't had any contact with Daniel since then?"

She shook her head.

At least there's that. Maybe he really did leave because of the guilt.

Lela looked up and stared at him with watery eyes. Somewhere behind her deceiving and murderous eyes was the girl he fell in love with in high school. Lela Morgan, one of the coolest girls in school who had a line of guys around the building, begging to go on dates with her. The girl he used to watch dance in the car to the radio, using his hand as a microphone as she belted out lyrics at the top of her lungs.

He couldn't believe that same girl would end up as a child murderer. And not just any murderer, but one who thought she could actually get away with it.

"What happened after he left that night?" Martin asked once Lela's sobs had finally ceased.

"What do you mean?" she asked.

"I mean what happened when he left? What did you do? Watch TV? Go to bed? Surely something happened, time didn't just stop."

Time felt like it had stopped when he watched from the backyard as Lela carried their dead daughter to the trunk, and he knew she would have felt the same during that moment.

Tragedy has a way of freezing time for those involved, leaving the rest of the world irrelevant.

"Well, I went to bed, I don't know. That was a long time ago."

"You don't know what you did after you *fucked* my brother?"

"No."

"Are you sure there wasn't anyone in the house that night who caught you and was upset by it?" Martin slammed a fist on the table that caused Lela to jolt in her seat. "Are you sure, Lela?"

He fought every urge to call her a murdering cunt, knowing it would be best to lead her into her confession.

"Martin, what's this about?" she asked, sitting upright, clearly trying to hide how nervous she was being put under the spotlight. "How do you expect me to remember such a detail from over twenty years ago?"

"A detail? So carrying our dead daughter's body out to your trunk in the middle of the night is a small detail now?"

Her eyes nearly exploded from their sockets in a look that said *how the fuck do you know that?*

"What?" she asked.

"Stop playing stupid. I know what happened that night. I know everything. So you might as well tell me the truth."

He paused and studied her face, watching her try to calculate a way out of the accusations and running into road blocks at every turn. The more she realized she was caught, the more her face drooped in despair.

At least two minutes passed with them staring at each other, silently arguing over who would say the next word.

It was Lela. "I don't know what you want me to say."

"I just want to know what happened, and why it happened."

369

Lela sniffled and rubbed her face in frustration.

"It was an accident."

There's the confession.

"I never meant to do it, Marty, you have to believe me. I would never kill our little girl."

"But you did." Gone was the urge to cry or scream. Composure took over his emotions as he sat across from Lela like an interrogating detective.

Lela, on the other hand, had melted into a puddle of tears and repeatedly wiped the moisture off her face every few seconds.

"She caught me and your brother that night," Lela continued through sobs. "She caught us, and that's when everything came crumbling down."

Martin wanted to question the timing of events, remembering neither of them had appeared in any rush when Daniel left the house, but didn't want to tip his hand quite yet.

"It turned into a huge argument. Izzy insisted she was going to wait up all night for you to get home and tell you what happened. I begged her not to, promised that I would tell you myself—and I was going to."

Lela paused and ran through the events in her mind. The sobs were slowing, but had formed a thick layer of mucus between her nose and lips.

"We were arguing in her room after your brother left, and that's when I left for the kitchen. I wanted to take my mind off everything, so started doing the dishes from dinner. I thought she would have dropped the argument, but she ran into the kitchen and kept yelling at me."

Lela's lips quivered uncontrollably as the mucus dripped to the kitchen table in a neat puddle.

"She called me the worst mom on the planet. She told me to

burn in hell." Lela paused, mustering the courage to say the next thing. "She told me that you and her would live a happy life together without me. That neither of you needed me."

The heavy flow of tears returned, only this time silently.

"I couldn't handle her saying those things to me. I know what I did was wrong, but she wouldn't stop, so I threw the pan I was washing at her and it hit her square in the head, on her temple."

Lela stared to the spot in the kitchen where Martin presumed Izzy had stood that night.

"She collapsed right away and I rushed over to help her, but she wasn't breathing. I tried CPR, I punched at her chest, but nothing was working. I felt her skin turning cold, and I knew it was too late. Whatever I did killed her immediately." Lela looked into Martin's eyes for the first time since her confession had begun. "I didn't want to kill her. I didn't even want to hurt her. It was a freak accident."

Martin cleared his throat before speaking. "We have to get her body out of the lake. She deserves to be buried properly."

Lela shook her head. "No, Marty, please. If we do that, they're going to send me away forever."

Martin nodded. "I know." The police would be close by now. "Don't you think you've gone long enough living out this lie? I mean, had you come clean about it at the time, you'd probably be out of prison by now. You could've cleaned up the rest of your life and lived out the rest of your days with a somewhat clear conscience. Now you'll have to think about this every day until you die."

"Marty, please. Please don't do this." Her words dripped with desperation, but her voice showed the defeat of a woman who knew she was going to prison.

"I've already done it. The police are outside."

New tears streamed down her face. "Marty, I'm so sorry. I loved our family and I fucked it all up. There hasn't been a day that's gone by where I haven't thought about the three of us together again. I'm so sorry."

Martin stood and shuffled around the table to Lela who buried her face into her hands. "I love you, Lela. That never stopped. I even forgive you for cheating on me with my brother. But you've ruined my life. I lost every motivation to live since Izzy died. I've been a zombie for the last 22 years all thanks to you. I've almost killed myself, and I will *never* forgive you for killing Izzy."

He leaned over and kissed her on the back of her head. The once love of his life, who had turned into an accidental murderer, fell silent when a thundering knock came from the front door.

Martin glanced over his shoulder and saw two police officers. "It's time, Lela," he said. "Should I let them in?"

With her head still down, she nodded in a quick, jerky motion.

Martin smiled. When he set out to save Izzy six months ago, he never imagined this adventure would end with Lela confessing to murder and being taken into custody. Then again, he didn't have any idea what to expect.

"Just think of this as payback for getting away with this for so long," Martin said as he walked toward the front door.

He opened the door to find the officers waiting patiently, nodded at them, and stepped aside. "She's right in there," he said, pointing to the kitchen where she still sat with her face buried.

Martin returned to his car where Sonya gawked out of the

window. Even though a sick feeling continued to gnaw at his insides, he felt relief knowing justice would finally be served to Izzy's killer. She'd never be back, and he had accepted this fact over ten years ago, but the closure felt as perfect as a frozen drink on the beach. He no longer had to wonder what happened to his daughter, wonder if she was still alive somewhere, or worry about her killer or kidnapper causing her any further harm.

With one final matter to settle, Martin was ready to move on with his life for the first time since 1996.

53

Chapter 53

Martin couldn't keep the smirk off his face as they drove back to the Wealth of Time.

"She's going away for a very long time," he said. "A very long time."

"Are you okay?" Sonya asked. "I mean this all happened so fast. Last night you found out about all of this, and this morning you confronted your wife who confessed to it all."

"I feel great. Don't get me wrong, this is not the outcome I wanted. I thought I was going to save Izzy and bring her back home. It's going to take some time for this all to really sink in. Hell, I'm still trying to process the fact that I actually traveled through time *and* was able to bring you back with me. Nothing about these last six months feels real yet, and who knows if it ever will."

"I definitely understand that."

"I have to go see Chris right now. I have a matter to settle with him, and I think it's best if you stay in the car again. Then I promise I'll show you all that 2018 has to offer."

Sonya kept quiet as she stared out the window and Martin

left her to soak in the surroundings, hoping she would open up to him again at some point. There was a definite adjustment period to accept the fact that you traveled to another era in time, and Martin understood this. Sonya might be distant for a few days, possibly weeks, but he'd be there when she was ready to immerse herself in the times.

How bad could it even be? he thought ahead to his meeting with Chris. *I've already lost my daughter, and lived through it twice.*

He knew better than to doubt Chris's ability to destroy him, whether emotionally or mentally, but Martin felt on top of the world and ready to take on whatever the old man threw his way.

"I don't like the vibes I get from this old man," Sonya said when they pulled up to the store. "I told you he was in my nightmares."

"Well, I can't say anything about him being in your dreams, but Chris is a pleasant man. I wouldn't worry about anything."

The words felt fake coming out of Martin's mouth and he hoped Sonya didn't notice.

"If he's so pleasant why can't I come in with you?"

She got you there.

"I just need to speak with him in private. Remember, it's not everyone who gets offered this opportunity to time travel. There are sensitivities to consider."

Sonya stared into the store, ignoring him, and Martin assumed she didn't find that answer acceptable.

"You know what. Come in with me. Look around his store for something you might like. He and I can talk in the back."

She perked up at this. "Okay. Deal."

"Let's head in."

Martin stood from the car and couldn't believe that only an hour had passed since they arrived back in 2018. That one hour was all it took to bring Izzy justice and put his mind at ease from all the sick doubts and thoughts that had plagued it for more than two decades.

They faced the storefront together, hands held. Thick gray clouds filled the entire sky to create an unsettling gloom over the city, and the air came to a standstill.

"Everything will be fine," Martin said, both to reassure Sonya, but also himself.

Sonya led by taking the first step up the small three stairs to the entrance, and Martin reluctantly followed, realizing he wasn't as ready as he had believed to encounter Chris with his new proposal.

Sonya wasted no time and pulled them both into the store, the bell chiming from the entrance.

The store was deserted, as it seemed to be more often than not, and Chris sat behind the cash register reading a copy of *Dracula.*

"Ah! Martin and Sonya, please come in."

Martin's blood froze at the sound of his voice, and he assumed Sonya's did, too, as she stopped halfway between steps.

"Good morning, Chris," Martin mustered through a tense jaw, receiving back that smirk that could haunt a grown man's dreams for months.

"A great morning it is. I take it everything went well where you just came from?"

Martin started to walk again, and now he pulled Sonya along. "Yes, I would say things went as best they could, considering the circumstances."

"That's what I love hearing. Happy endings!"

Chris clutched his gut and cackled like a loon.

"Let's cut the bullshit, Chris. Can we talk in your office?" Martin asked.

"It would be my pleasure." Chris hopped down from the stool he sat on and extended an arm toward his back office, the door already open and inviting anyone who dared enter its darkness.

"Stay here, look around," Martin said, turning to Sonya. She nodded in return, but he could practically smell the fear oozing from her. *Bet you wish you would've stayed in the car now, right?*

He released her hand and turned to Chris who stood like a statue with his arm out, patiently waiting for Martin to enter his office so he could feast on his soul.

"Everything's on sale today," Chris said to Sonya. "Pick anything you like and I'll give you a great deal." He winked before disappearing into the office and closing the door behind them.

"That's quite the lovely lady you have there, Marty," Chris said as he worked his way around to his desk. "Have a seat."

Martin sat down across from where he had just slept over an hour ago during his journey back in time.

"What's the deal you want to offer me? I need details." Martin sat back and crossed his arms, ready to enter negotiations, despite knowing Chris could get whatever he wanted at this point.

Chris leaned back in his creaky chair and propped his feet up on the desk. "Do you know what the strongest human emotion is, Marty?"

Martin shook his head quickly.

377

"It's pain," Chris said flatly. "Pain drives you humans. If you think about it, you carry out your life to avoid pain. Pain is scary and no one wants to confront it on any given day. When a human experiences pain, they release so much negative energy into world. So much that I can practically grab it with my hand like it was a floating piece of paper in the wind."

"What are you getting at?" Martin asked, arms staying crossed to show he wasn't interested in the sentimental speech.

"Relax, old friend. It's all part of the offer. You see, my original offer is still on the table. You can agree to hand over your ability to feel emotion. It won't affect you quite as badly as you think, but you can forget about things like joy, pleasure, and happiness. But at the same time, you'll also never feel pain, sadness, or grief again. I think it's a fair trade."

Martin gestured at the old man to get on with it, growing impatient as the seconds passed.

Chris ignored Martin in a clear reminder of who was in charge.

"The alternative offer I want to make you has two main components. One being a Juice that you can take to travel through time as you wish. No questions asked. Think of it as a permanent round-trip ticket. In exchange, you will experience pain that I can feast on. Not a physical pain, but an emotional and mental pain, and it will come when you least expect it. I can't tell you what the experience will be, as I don't even know. It's one of those matters I carry out when the time feels right. So, if you think you can handle it, if you can live through terrible pain once more, then you'll be able to continue life with your emotions intact, and the ability to travel anywhere in time."

Chris stopped and crossed his hands behind his head as he stared at Martin.

"So what'll it be, my old friend?" he asked.

Martin uncrossed his arms and sat forward in his seat.

"I need you to answer my questions about time travel before I can consider this," Martin said. "I want to know the rules. I want to know who the Road Runners are and what they're trying to do. I want to know why you decide to randomly show up."

For the first time Chris had no deceiving grin to offer, but rather a flat expression of thought.

"Well, Marty, there are hundreds of little rules that you will experience for yourself. I'm not going to cover those with you. I gave you the golden rule to live by, and perhaps I can share more if you accept. As far as the Road Runners, those are a group of people trying to take control of the world. They're dangerous and shouldn't be trusted."

"Then how did they get access to travel through time?"

"They weren't always bad, Martin. They received access just like you are now, and made decisions for the worst. This ability comes with great responsibility, and some people just can't handle it. Perhaps it's my own fault for bad judgement, but that's what they say about hindsight, right?"

"What's your angle with all of this?" Martin asked. "Why not hold on to this ability for yourself? Why do you share it, and what do you want out of it?"

Chris leaned forward in his chair, the smirk returning.

"I've told you already what I want out of it. I need to feed myself, and I feed off human emotions. I've always had this ability. I've been around throughout the existence of time, you see. It's like I live in the same world as you all, but not really. I've lived in all of the worlds, and it gets lonely. That's why I started to share this gift with others, so there could be other people in my world."

Martin locked eyes with the old man and thought for a moment that he could see the thousands of years of history brimming behind those gentle, blue eyes. Maybe he was telling truth. He'd never know, but he was sold on the opportunity.

I've lived through time-travelling, and how sweet it was.

He thought of the bank account waiting for him, loaded with money from his investments made in the past, thought of meeting Sonya and having his life changed forever. A lot of good had come from time travel.

"If I agree to this, what happens next?" he asked, prompting a slow nod from Chris.

"It's quite simple," Chris said. "You go home today with your Juice, and continue living life. There's really no strings attached aside from the pain I'll bring to your soul."

"What about Sonya? Can she have the Juice?"

"She can drink it but nothing will happen. It's created specially for you. She can always travel with you the same way. So, tell me, Marty, do we have a deal?"

Martin sat in silence. *How bad can the pain be? I've been to hell and back. Me and Sonya can see the world.*

He wouldn't have given two shits about having life experiences before his journey into the past, but now it felt as if a thousand doors of possibilities opened in unison.

"Deal," Martin said, and stuck out his hand instinctively. Chris grabbed it quickly, and Martin felt the coldness of the old man's flesh.

"I'm happy to hear that. Please, let me grab your Juice so you can get out of here. I'm sure you have lots planned with your beautiful lady."

Chris skipped across the office and disappeared into the dark corner where his laboratory waited. The sounds of glass bottles clanging against each other echoed around the room before Chris let out a grunt followed by, "I found you!"

He appeared in front of Martin in chilling quickness with a glass canteen filled with purple liquid held out in front of him.

"Here you go, old friend. 128 ounces of the finest time-traveling Juice your soul can buy. All you need is a single drop on your tongue and it works the same way as the pills."

"How do I choose where to go?" Martin asked as he grabbed the heavy bottle of purple liquid.

"Simply think about it. You'll be transported to the same location of your current body, though. So if you want to visit, say, ancient Rome, you'll need to first travel to Rome and then take the Juice. When you fall asleep and wake up, you'll be rubbing elbows with Julius Caesar himself!"

Martin studied the bottle that felt no different than an over-size bottle of wine.

"So this is it? I'm free to go and wait for some tragic thing to happen to me?"

"Don't bother waiting. It will happen when you least expect it."

"Will I still see you around?" Martin asked, knowing he never planned to come back to this godawful store again.

"I'll drop by from time to time. But don't worry about me, get out of here. The world is yours!"

Martin nodded toward Chris and gripped the bottle tightly in both hands. Outside the office door waited the world in 2018 as he knew it, with a woman he loved, and a life that had finally moved on after his daughter's tragic murder by his ex-wife.

More adventures waited outside the walls of the Wealth of Time, along with a lurking shadow in his soul that waited for life-altering pain.

Martin left the back office for the final time and didn't look back. He grabbed Sonya from a nearby aisle and they departed the store as quickly as they had arrived. A long future waited ahead for them, and he had never been so eager to start the rest of forever, with her by his side.

Acknowledgements

This book came to light thanks to my kids. Raising two little ones isn't easy, but memories are constantly being created with each passing day. I've found myself in the middle of these moments, wishing I could stop time, so we could just keep playing without worries of bed time, or having to go to work in the morning. This sparked the idea to start a story about a man who could freeze time, but I found there wasn't much to do with that quite yet, so it evolved into this time-travel thriller. The freezing of time is an element that appears later in the series, though, so stay tuned for more on that! Long story short, I want to thank Arielle and Felix for inadvertently sparking this story idea.

Big thank you to Dane Low for creating another masterpiece of a cover. I look forward to plenty more to come.

Behind every book is an editor working just as hard as the author. Thank you to Stephanie Cohen for making this the best finished product it can be, I can't wait to see how the rest of the series goes!

For all of my Advance Readers, your enthusiasm gives me the drive to keep going, so thank you for being every book's first audience.

Lastly, and never least, thank you to my wife Natasha for being the first reader and giving the honest criticism up front. Hopefully this series is the launching pad we're looking for to take our life to the next level.

Andre Gonzalez
Jan 15, 2018–Feb 4, 2019

Enjoy this book?

You can make a difference!

Reviews are the most helpful tools in getting new readers for any books. I don't have the financial backing of a New York publishing house and can't afford to blast my book on billboards or bus stops.

(Not yet!)

That said, your honest review can go a long way in helping me reach new readers. If you've enjoyed this book, I'd be forever grateful if you could spend a couple minutes leaving it a review (it can be as short as you like) on the Amazon page. You can jump right to the page by clicking below.

US

UK

Thank you so much!

Also by Andre Gonzalez

Books are listed on order of most recent publication:

Wealth of Time (Wealth of Time Series, Book #1)

Erased (Insanity Series, Prequel) (Short Story)

The Insanity Series (Books 1-3)

Replicate (Insanity Series, Book #3)

The Burden (Insanity Series, Book #2)

Insanity (Insanity Series, Book #1)

A Poisoned Mind (Short Story)

Followed Home

About the Author

Born in Denver, CO, Andre Gonzalez has always had a fascination with horror and the supernatural starting at a young age. He spent many nights wide-eyed and awake, his mind racing with the many images of terror he witnessed in books and movies. Ideas of his own morphed out of movies like *Halloween* and books such as *Pet Sematary* by Stephen King. These thoughts eventually made their way to paper, as he always wrote dark stories for school assignments or just for fun. Followed Home is his debut novel based off of a terrifying dream he had many years ago at the age of 12. His reading and writing of horror stories evolved into a pursuit of a career as an author, where Andre hopes to keep others awake at night with his frightening tales. The world we live in today is filled with horror stories, and he looks forward to capturing the raw emotion of these events, twisting them into new tales, and preserving a legacy in between the crisp bindings of novels.

Andre graduated from Metropolitan State University of Denver with a degree in business in 2011. During his free time, he enjoys baseball, poker, golf, and traveling the world with his family. He believes that seeing the world is the only true way to stretch the imagination by experiencing new cultures and meeting new people.

Andre still lives in Denver with his wife, Natasha, and their two kids.

You can connect with me on:

◉ http://andregonzalez.net

🐦 http://www.twitter.com/monito0408

🅵 https://www.facebook.com/AndreGonzalezAuthor

🖉 http://www.instagram.com/monito0408

Subscribe to my newsletter:

✉ http://andregonzalez.net

Made in the USA
Columbia, SC
29 April 2019